I0760401

To Believe in the Demon King

Book Two

Monica Shantel

To Believe in the Demon King

To Believe Book Two

Monica Shantel

This is a work of fiction. Names, characters, and incidents either are the product of the author's imagination or are used fictitiously. Any resemblance to actual persons, living or dead, or events is entirely coincidental.

To Believe in the Demon King

Book Cover by Monica Shantel

Illustrations by Monica Shantel

ISBN 978-1-960696-95-3 (Paperback) ISBN 978-1-960696-07-6 (Hardcover)

Second Edition

For those who were told their emotions made them too weak.

Fee
Zeeslang Waters

Neverland

S

mooie duisternis patch

Skull Rock

Training Area

Camp

sman's ree

Mermaid Lagoon

ve

"Lia Stone" 7/28/19

"Kace Pérez" 9/10/23

Spotify To Believe Playlist

Monica Shantel

Neverland needs a savior.

00: Libertad

The sun beat down on me as people lined the streets, hurrying in and out of the buildings. I glanced back as a mother broke down, kneeling and praying for her missing son. He'd been missing for a month now. Maybe she had hope, or maybe it was beginning to fizzle out.

Taking a walk to the beach, a memory flashed across my mind. My parents had always been so strict, so keen on making sure that I didn't act like a boy. From the time I'd been born it had been this way. They focused so much of their attention on trying to make me dress as a little girl, but they couldn't pretend forever. As I grew, I began asking questions. Why did I want to do boy things? Why did I have a penis? Their fantasy had been shattered.

And so I spent the entirety of my young years telling everyone I was a boy, making sure the community shamed my parents. There had even been such an incident when they attempted to set up an appointment with the doctor to get my parts mutilated for their benefit. The doctor refused, and rightfully so.

They had to dress me the right way eventually.

They did, making it known that they hated the idea. They tried to scold me for playing in the dirt, building sandcastles. They scolded me when I stood as I pissed. No matter what I did, it wasn't feminine enough.

Because I wasn't born female.

"Un día seré libre," I mumbled.

One day.

As sand seeped between my toes, I shoved my hands into my pockets and walked along the edge of the water. The tide was low this afternoon.

Someone bumped me from behind and long brown hair flung into my view as a girl hurried past me, glancing back. "Lo siento."

I tried to give her an apologetic smile but the last time I'd even looked at a girl that way, my parents nearly beat it out of me. It wasn't enough for them to believe I was a girl. They reminded me that I was too masculine. Being romantically interested in a girl further crushed their twisted hopes and dreams into dust. It proved to them I was truly a boy, a boy who had an interest in girls.

Part of me screamed to go after the girl and strike up a conversation. However, I could never escape the hatred that was my parents. I could not escape the darkened eyes, the scowls as I smiled at a girl passing by.

Maybe today was that day.

Facing the ocean, I stepped into the shallow waters that rushed at my ankles. "Whoever is out there, listening, I am begging someone to take me away. I despise such a cruel place. I want to be free. I wish to be able to be the fullest extent of myself and run wild like a boy should." I stepped closer. "I hope for nothing more than to escape the fate they have for me so I can live again."

I'd been met with silence. Expected.

THE SUN HAD SET, disappearing beyond the horizon. The stars lined the sky. The moon lit up the water, almost as if it were glowing.

But something in the distance appeared to be off. Something...twinkled.

"It's warm here this time of year, is it now?" a boy asked from my left. He stood, staring at the ripples of waves. His accent wasn't American, nor was he from here. It was thick, however, much like my own. "I hear you're looking for a new home."

"I suppose." I got up from the beach, eyeing the boy. He was taller than me, but skinnier. Much skinnier.

"Take my hand." He reached out. "I can offer that."

Stepping back, I swung my left shoulder back. "I am not into that kind of relationship."

His laugh came out bitter, and humorless. He'd seen things for his age. He looked my age and yet his expressions appeared the wiser. "I have not come to offer my hand in marriage, nor to offer it in shagging." His eyes softened at my weariness. "It's friendship—loyalty that I ask."

"Loyalty for what?"

He glanced at the ocean, pointing out beyond the edge of it. "For a kingdom on an island. A place I have created by magic just for lost children, a place where a magnificent tree whispers to me. Somewhere that is safe to be truly yourself. *You called and I came.*"

Straightening my shoulders, I lifted my gaze from his ragged attire to meet the color of the rivers in his eyes. "Sounds like a plot for murder."

A shrug. "I assure you it's not. Take my offer or leave it," he paused, unsure of what name I went by.

"Kace." I stepped closer, giving him my hand. "I have not much left to lose."

The corner of his lips tilted upward to his right, his eyes lighting the shadows of the moonlight. "I promise you'll never ask to come home, Kace. If you do, I'll let you take a stab at me for good measure."

He tightened his fingers around mine, slipping a dagger from the sheath in his belt. The sound of waves grew, wind picking up in the trees.

Just as my body began to feel as light as the clouds, the boy leaned in and whispered, "They call me Peter Pan."

01: First Snowfall

The air grew colder as night fell, darkness surrounding my warmth. I pulled the cloak tighter, mentally thanking Kace for having lent it to me in the first place.

Neverland was not as it first was when I arrived. Lili was now Pan's equal partner in crime. She lost, and I only had *myself* to blame.

I walked back to my cabin but stopped as I saw a white snowflake pass before my eyes. There was no such thing as snow in Neverland. Until now, that was. Was it an annual season, or an anomaly?

I placed my palm flat out, catching another. "Where did you come from?"

As I peered up into the gray sky, millions of snowflakes began to fall freely. They almost looked like little delicate creatures trying to make a soft and happy arrival as if trying not to anger the island itself. They could have been.

"Snow on Neverland. That's new. I guess your sister was right," Kace said from behind me.

I turned to find him watching the fragile designs of winter itself. How utterly lovely to experience such beauty in a land where beauty existed in many different ways. A unique pattern had never been one. Neverland thrived on routine. At least it had before my sister let Pan claim her soul.

"Why is this happening?" I asked him.

"I would like to say it's because of the balance of Neverland being shifted. With two rulers and two shadows inhabiting Skull Rock—which is basically the heart of Neverland—the island must adjust somehow. Neverland was Pan's wish alone so it could only inhabit one in charge. I expect more changes to come." He stepped closer. "Let's get you back to your cabin. We will need to keep warm or die trying."

I followed him to my room just a few feet away. I opened the door but stopped and turned on my hell to face him. "I won't let this happen. I am going to have to find a way to get my sister back and change Pan along with her. But I can't do it alone. I'll need your help." I gave him my best hospitable look, hopeful that he would maybe work with me *again*.

He gave me a small nod in response. "Consider me your ally for this mission. We will restore Neverland if it's the last thing we do."

I closed my door and scanned the bed. After taking off the hood of my cloak, I set my dagger on the dresser. I still had memories every night of Lili and I sleeping in this room. Now she slept in Pan's. I hadn't been a good enough sister and that was on my part.

Climbing into bed, I tugged the cloak as close to my body as I could get it.

I still hated Pan with passion, and even more so as he had taken my own sister from me. Together, they were destroying our home.

A scowl escaped me at the thought of his existence, I wanting nothing more than to take him out completely. He was a scoundrel. He was the scum from the bottom of my shoe.

While gripping the handle of my dagger, I imagined slicing his head clean off. I wanted to watch the blood squirt from his neck, tainting the ground as a reminder to never allow anyone that much *power* again. I wanted to watch him suffer.

He deserved misery and pain, and I was destined to give it to him. I wanted him to feel the wrath of my fury for what he had done to Lili. Pan was going to fear me—for my hatred of him fueled my determination.

As I lay down on the mattress, it sank with my body.

I couldn't be too sure about how we were going to save the island from itself, but we would. I had to ensure Lili would come back to me.

Drifting into a peaceful sleep, I forgot all my troubles of today for just a little while.

WHEN I AWOKE, I was shivering, nearly freezing from the air that now surrounded me with its icy touch. I couldn't get myself warm enough, so I jumped out of my bed and ran to Pan's cabin. I pounded on the door, my own breath forming before me. The snow was colder than I'd ever experienced back home. And now it came up to my ankles. How long had I been out?

Pan opened the door with an unpleasant look just waiting to be slapped off. "Why the bloody hell are you bothering me at this hour?"

"It's freezing. You must do something. Please," I begged.

He studied my shaking limbs and chattering teeth, lifting his eyebrows. He glanced back into his room and faced me again. "We're finding ways to warm up. I suggest you do the same." He closed the door in my face.

I contorted my expression into disgust, unable to comprehend that he was sleeping with Lili. I was not going to go do that. He had to know I wasn't anything like her.

Turning away, I released a small sigh. I ended up back at my cabin and tightened the cloak around my body. As I sat on the bed and closed my eyes, I thought of ways I could stay warm.

Train.

Jumping up from the bed, I briskly walked to the area and pulled my dagger from my belt. I began to swing and jab at the air, pretending it was

Pan I was fighting.

"What are you doing?" I heard the familiar voice behind me.

I turned to give Kace my attention, still swinging my dagger at nothing to keep my body warm. "I'm trying to practice *and* keep warm. I'm killing two birds with one stone."

"What does that mean?" Kace questioned.

I held back a laugh. "It means I'm killing two birds, warming up and becoming a better fighter, with one stone by doing them at once. It's a figure of speech."

He rolled his eyes as he stepped closer. "I know what that means and what a figure of speech is. I was asking what does it mean to practice when you're by yourself? You don't have the skills." He smirked a little.

I allowed my laugh to slip this time. "Shut up. I have skills, okay?"

Kace laughed inwardly in return and came over to me. "I have to warm up, too, so let me help you practice." He pulled his silver dagger from his belt, wrapping his fingers around the embossed, bronze metal. "Ready? You are just as bad as Lili when I first trained her."

I faked a gasp. "I am not that bad." I pouted and jabbed his side.

He waved his blade around. "That was too easy."

We both began to train, sharpening our skills. *Pun was intended.*

Kace swung around, slicing my cheek. He straightened himself and stepped back. "Lia, I am so sorry. I did not mean to do that."

I gently touched the blood. I brushed it off as nothing by swinging my blade at him, across his hand. I gave him an artful smile. "Never let your guard down." I looped my fingers under the string that formed a bow where the cloak came together around his neck. "Keep your friends close." I yanked him towards me. "And keep your enemies closer," I whispered.

I took notice of how close we had gotten, letting go and clearing my throat while he fixed his cloak, saying, "Let's continue, yeah?"

"Yes. The snow isn't stopping anytime soon, so neither are we," I replied.

We continued to train all day, keeping our body temperature up against the cold. We finished and went back once it got too dark for either of us to see.

I turned back and told Kace goodbye before I retreated into my cabin. However, some commotion was going on in the middle of the camp. It could be heard throughout the whole island if I knew any better.

I stood and tightened my belt around my hips as I went outside to solve the problem. I moved the boys out of my way as I walked into their circle, stopping just inside.

Looking down upon the new boy that sat in the middle of all this, his eyes met mine, a piercing stare the only welcome I'd receive. There was a reason why, but I couldn't let anyone else *know* that.

I shook my head and cleared my throat, not giving him any leverage to threaten me. "What's your name?"

"It doesn't matter to *any* of you." That was the wrong move. I was the easy one to deal with. I couldn't say the same for the two who ruled this dreadful island.

Lili emerged from the circle with Pan, eyeing the guy. She snickered and shot a look at Pan. "You brought another lost boy? What about girls? Haven't I proven we can be just as strong?" She knew who this new member was. *We both did.*

Pan ignored her with the cross of his arms. "State your name."

"I said no." He had guts but then again, he didn't know the things Pan was capable of.

Pan slowly squeezed his fingers, cutting off his air supply.

The guy began to struggle for air, scratching his throat as if he could tear it open and inhale. Pan closed in on him and let go, the guy coughing endlessly. Before he could speak, Pan conjured up the clouds of black smoke in his eyes. "When I ask your name, you listen to me. What is your name?" he asked louder this time.

The teenage boy finally stopped choking, his lungs most likely irritated and in need of hot tea. "Asa. My damn name is Asa."

Lili looked over at Pan with a smirk. "Asa? What an interesting name. Never heard of it before."

Lies.

Asa rolled his eyes, but she still caught sight of it. She looked at him and tilted her head a bit, admiring his ability to rebel against the authority. "I used to be just like you, Asa. Now I'm ruling with Pan himself. The dark side is much more intoxicating." She looked toward Kace. "Show our new lost boy around the island. Don't forget to inform him of our rules." She spun around and walked back in the direction of their cabin. Pan followed behind like her new puppy.

Kace waved Asa over and led him off into the woods. Asa knew he had to comply or else. I just hoped he wasn't stupid enough to go exploring the *or else* option.

With careful consideration, I trailed behind my sister and her lover.

Lili pulled Pan down to her level and kissed him, whispering something I didn't quite catch. She gave a long sigh and frowned a bit. "Could you imagine if I never came here? I would still be stuck at home with my parents. All I want is the chance to love and be loved. I deserve that."

Her words cut my throat like a knife. I couldn't help but assume that she had only done all of this for love. The broken girl had craved what she never felt. Did I not love her enough?

I thought I had.

Pan cupped her face, rubbing his thumb over her cheek. "I can't imagine it because I don't want to. You're here now. Forget about your parents." He paused, "although, you could tone it down on the power trip."

Her fingers reached up and grabbed his that still held her cheek. "You like it." Before he could respond, she closed the gap and locked their lips together once again.

I wish I could say it disgusted me, but it didn't. It sunk its teeth into my heart more than anything. The kiss between them wasn't filled with hostility or poison. What passed between them was desperation and a craving that only two halves of a whole could produce.

I left the two of them in their privacy as I disappeared back to the cabin. I turned to watch all the lost boys as they danced while they waited for their breakfast. I couldn't focus on much, but I could try to form a plan to save my sister and her new boyfriend. It surely wasn't any easy task. Nothing was going to be the same as it once was.

Snow now blanketed the island. Two beings ruled over everything that took residency here. Worst of all, the new lost boy—*Asa*—would never know what once had been.

02: Sight of Blood

As I knocked on the door, I puffed my chest out and reeled back my shoulders.

Demand to see her and refuse to take no for an answer—at least that's what I repeated to myself.

The door swung open, revealing a devious Pan. "What is so important?"

"I need to see Lili." I folded my hands together in front of me. Despite how I'd been feeling during all of this chaos and the inexplicable change that seemingly happened over night, she remained my sister. By blood, and by water.

With an immature roll of his eyes, he said, "Yeah, of course you do. Do you not know she doesn't want to see *you*?" He raised his eyebrow in question.

I ignored the insult and pushed past him, not really thinking twice about the consequences. She used to be the kind of girl who defended good guys like me. If she still existed in there somewhere, I'd receive no punishment for my behavior.

I halted at the sight of Lili who slept soundly in his bed. I supposed it was their bed now that she'd taken full residency in his massive cabin. The moment I took notice of their clothed bodies, I thanked the heavens.

Pan came into my view, arms crossed and veins in his neck bulging.

"Can't you see she's busy? She has a lot of responsibilities. It's only fair to let the girl sleep." He pressed his lips into a thin line to keep his serpent tongue from snapping at me.

I took another glance, observing her peaceful form. She looked so innocent while the monster stayed tucked inside her bones. One would never have guessed she had killed Hook.

Sighing, I scratched my arm underneath my cloak. "I'll let her have her beauty sleep but send her over when she wakes up." I left the cabin and walked to the training area. I needed to train while I could. My skills were inadequate at best.

The snow crunched beneath my brown boots. I wondered for a moment if we were even on earth in this realm, but I knew we had to be. Time may not have existed but everything else fell into line with earth's rules. Weather, gravity, and mother nature.

I wrapped my fingers around the icy metal hilt that hung in my belt. I had to ignore the coolness seeping into my body if I wanted to stay focused. I practiced different moves in different positions based on the many fights I'd seen before.

Glancing to my right, Kace and Asa entered the training area. Kace pointed to some targets as if he was teaching Asa to practice his archery.

Asa rolled his eyes and caught me looking his way. He grabbed some arrows and a bow, marching over to some targets to shape his skills.

Kace approached me with a small smile. "It turns out that abused boys are closed off," he joked.

I laughed a bit. "Right." I put my dagger back into my belt and cleared my throat. "Well, he knows the rules and tricks?"

"Of course. Are you worried about Pan coming down on him?" Kace teased me.

I gave him a nervous laugh and twirled a strand of my hair. "Of course."

Kace didn't believe my excuse but dropped it anyway. He focused on something or *someone* behind me and straightened his posture out of respect.

I turned to see who it was, coming face to face with my other half. "Lili, I see you're awake now."

"I was told you wanted to speak to me." She crossed her arms, barely acknowledging that I meant business when I wanted to discuss this.

When I told her we'd talk in private, we headed to my cabin. She sat down on the bed as I tapped my chin. "Interesting new lost boy. Asa, correct?" I questioned her.

She shifted uncomfortably, almost as if she still had *Lili* inside her. "What about him?"

I came closer, cupping her face. I wasn't afraid of her, and I couldn't let her intimidate me. We'd once shared a womb. We would always be equals. "You know damn well what I'm talking about. Asa. Asa Stone. I seem to remember that last name somewhere else, or am I wrong, Liliana Stone?"

She slapped my arms away from her face. "What is your point? Are you going to tell Pan? Do you really think that he's going to go easy on him just because he knows us?"

"He is going to figure it out eventually. Playing dumb gets both of us into huge trouble. You know how he is." I narrowed my eyes at her, threatening her silence.

If Pan knew Asa was related to us, there was a small chance he might go easier on the kid.

She scooted her butt across my mattress and leaned her back against the wall. "Listen, I don't want to cause problems, but I will if I have to." I nearly scoffed at that bullshit statement.

Her eyes darted to the windowsill as a sigh of relief washed over her. "What Pan doesn't know can't hurt him."

"He will know. He's *Pan*. He knows everything. I hate it just as much as you do but he always finds out. He has ways of knowing, whatever those are. If we don't tell him soon, we are going to be in just as much trouble. Asa will most likely be killed," I warned her.

She sighed. “Oh, Celia... It is quite sad that you worry so much. Just go with the flow.” She slipped off the bed.

“Go with the flow? You mean like when you killed Hook? When you let Pan inside your head? Having a plan is how we win.”

She came closer, matching my height. “You barely understand what I’m capable of. We haven’t even scratched the surface. Sharing blood does not matter to me. And if I do find out you’ve told Pan, I’ll make sure you pay.” She left the cabin, a thick layer of hostility her new signature.

I groaned, refusing to believe this was what I was up against. “So much for sisterly bonding.” I turned around and froze, only able to get out a single word. “Pan.”

He peeked at Lili who now walked near the fire. He turned his head back to me, leaning against the doorframe. “What was that about? Seems like you two got into quite the quarrel.”

“Nothing. It was nothing.” I reached for my dagger as a reflex, but he noticed.

“That is not going to help you.” He vanished from the doorframe. “I’m magical, don’t you remember?” His question echoed from behind.

I faced Pan, swallowing my fear. “I still stand by my answer.”

“Answer? Or an excuse?” He chuckled and grabbed my arm, exposing my skin. He flipped out a little pocketknife. Since when did Peter Pan carry around a pocketknife? “I would hate to see such determination go to waste.” He pressed the tip into the soft underside of my forearm. “You may want to tell me before this gets ugly.”

I’d be damned if I caved to Pan. “No.” Lili still came first, and if she forbade me from telling, I’d keep my lips locked.

His eyes searched mine for any hint of submission before falling on my arm. He started to cut into my flesh. “What about now?”

I chewed on my lip, trying to keep my mouth shut. If I could just prove myself strong...

He cut deeper, going up. “I won’t stop. You will eventually bleed out.”

A small howl spilled from my lips.

Pan was right. He had no remorse when he killed, and he would gladly do so. That was Wendy's demise. If I bled out, I would die. If I did, Lili would forever be stuck like this. I'd either never save Neverland, or I would risk saving Neverland to put up with my sister's punishment.

"Okay! Please, stop!" I cried out.

He stood back and gave me his attention.

I sat on the mattress, feeling woozy. "Lili and I know Asa."

This piqued his interest. "Asa? How so?"

I held a piece of cloth against my arm to keep the bleeding to a minimum. "Asa is our cousin."

"Pardon?" Pan came closer. "How did your cousin end up on my island?"

"Well, let's just say our family is really something special. I've now told you so if you don't mind, I would like to take care of this wound." I stood from the mattress, teetering.

Pan snickered. "I have business to deal with." He left me alone once again.

I walked out of the cabin and looked around for some means of first aid. I was no expert with medicine, but I assumed that I would need stitches. I walked through camp as someone yelled out my name. I turned, Kace approaching quickly. "Lia, what happened?" His eyes displayed worry that Pan himself could never replicate.

"Pan cut my arm to get information from me." I sighed as if it was no big deal. This wasn't an everyday occurrence, but it could've been. Too easily.

Kace led me to his cabin, and I stopped. "Uh, how are you—"

He answered my question before I could finish it, "I'm second-in-command. We live on a dangerous island and sometimes boys need aid. I happen to be the person who gives it, if you remember when you fell off that mountain." He waved me inside and I complied.

I took quick notes of everything inside his room. There was the usual bed and dresser, but also another desk in the corner that had drawers filled with things.

Kace strode over to it and opened the second drawer. He pulled out a little kit with some supplies that could help patch me up. He grabbed a cot that was folded between the desk and the wall, setting it up for my convenience. "Take a seat."

I did as I was told and showed him my arm, watching the blood slow down just a bit without my help. I knew this would sting like a mother, and I was just going to have to suffer through it.

Kace eyed the cut and lifted both eyebrows in surprise. "You may want to lie down for this." His gaze shifted up to me.

I shook my head, refusing to look like a wimp. "No, I can handle this." I glanced at the cut, and things started to feel fuzzy. My head didn't feel like it belonged to me. It wasn't long after he pulled out a needle and thread that lightheadedness engulfed me. The needle was curved, and thicker than a sewing needle.

"I..." I couldn't get any more words out. I began to lean back, forgetting that the cot was to the *side* of me.

Kace looked over, quickly grabbing my arms, turning my body in the right direction until I lay on the cot. "I tried to warn you." He let out a low chuckle and grabbed a small stool, dropping onto it with his knees at least two feet apart while he leaned into my bubble. Resting one elbow on his thigh and the other near my shoulder, he held my arm and gave me one last look. "This is going to hurt."

I focused on the ceiling. Just from the sight of blood, my head decided to let go of steadiness. I'd seen the muscle inside my body. The last thing I ever wanted to catch a glimpse of. The poke was small, but I didn't look over as he began pulling the thread through, tying it.

Kace cleared his throat. "You don't seem to be in much pain."

"Pan cut past the nerves. I can't feel anything." I could manage some words now, and that was good enough for me. I was regaining stability.

Kace nodded. "I am not the best first aid, but with your help, I learn something new." He focused on the stitches. "All done." He wrapped gauze around my arm and put his supplies back.

I stayed put, allowing my body to recuperate before I jumped back into action.

Kace poured some liquid on the needle. "Are you feeling okay?"

I nodded a bit in response and gently touched the bandage that now covered my arm. I couldn't move any muscles near the injury, and I assumed that had to do with having my nerves damaged. They would fuse back together, right? Would I regain feeling in my arm?

Oh no, I was going to be numb forever.

And I couldn't tell Kace. He'd just make fun of me for my emotions, too. Just like they all did. "I feel fine. I guess if I have to get cut and get stitches, at least it's past the nerves. Saves me some pain." *Nice lie.*

"I do think it would've bothered the rest of the camp if you were screaming." Kace grabbed a blanket from his bed and laid it over me. "While you heal, you can sleep here for the night. I'll let Pan know where you are."

As much as I wanted to protest, I couldn't. Pan had control of Neverland. I had to play by his rules even if that meant letting Kace tell him I was at my most vulnerable.

"Okay, just be quick. I don't want to be alone." I reached out and wrapped my fingers around his.

Our eyes dropped to our hands, and I pulled mine back swiftly. "Sorry."

Silence billowed into the room like smoke from a fire.

The door swung open, hitting the wall with a thwack. Lili stopped just in the frame, shock written over her entire expression. "Lia, our brother is here."

03: Family Reunion

The look Kace gave me said more than I wanted it to. "You should worry about this later. Stay here."

"No. Kace, this is my brother. I can't just stay here. I have to see him." I sat up, twisting my body until my legs hung over the edge and feet touched the floorboards.

Kace rubbed his face with a groan. "You guys are so damn stubborn." He put his arm around my waist to help as I got up from the cot. "You just lost quite a bit of blood." He walked with me out to the camp.

We came to an abrupt stop when the familiar face came into view. It was true. *He* was actually here.

Lili circled him to show she held power over our older brother. "How did you get here? We all know you're not underage." She paused in front of him.

He laughed at her futile attempt to intimidate him. "I saw you run around naked when you were a toddler." With a shrug, he said, "The shadow creature already questioned me. Asa was my ticket here." He pointed to our cousin.

Kace gave me a puzzled look. I cowered, knowing this was going to be a lot to explain.

Pan shook his head in disappointment. "Bloody hell, it's become a family reunion."

Lili eyed him suspiciously, then shot a glare my way. I swallowed, laying my hand over Kace's.

She approached her boyfriend. "We didn't plan this. We most certainly didn't ask for this." She gestured to Asa and Jaren.

Asa scoffed, waving his hand around. "It was more selfish than anything. It got me out of that hellhole."

Pan looked at me, and I shrugged my shoulders in response. "I told you. Our family is screwed up on all sides. Uncle Joe is just as terrifying as his brother." His brother—our *father*.

Jaren closed the last couple of feet between the three of us. Lili, our brother, and I. "All right, let's go. I'm taking you back home."

Before Pan could toss some threats into the ring, Lili stepped in. "I like it here. I have more friends here than I did there. Besides, I'm a queen! I'm *never* leaving," she spat.

Jaren met my gaze. I used my hand to pull the cloak closed. "She's right. We like it here, believe it or not. I've made friends. I've learned so much." I peered up at Kace. I couldn't just leave him alone with Pan. I had business to finish.

Jaren yelled out, "Fuck me!"

I winced. Pan even seemed taken back by the outburst. I was becoming a stubborn one, but our brother had always been that way. He came to take us, but he'd never stood up for us back home. Why now?

He ran his fingers through his black curls. "I didn't come here for no damn reason. I won't waste my trip. You'll come with me eventually."

Lili choked on a laugh. "Whatever you say." She blocked Pan's view of Jaren. "I think we should talk in private for a moment."

Pan glanced at our brother before nodding. "All right, Little Flower." The two of them headed to a more private area.

Jaren pointed to them. "What's that about?"

"How long have we been gone? I mean, how much time has passed since we went missing?" I tried to take some of my own support by shifting my weight and not depend on Kace so much.

Jaren rubbed his face and sat down on a log. "It's been over a year since you both left home."

I gasped.

No, it couldn't have been. It couldn't... But it *could*. No time had passed since we got here.

Kace gently squeezed my side in reassurance. It helped only a sliver.

My brother came over to us, and within seconds glared daggers at Kace. I cleared my throat to capture all four eyes. "Excuse me, but if it's been a year, I'm eighteen now. I get to decide where I live and who I live with," I said firmly.

Jaren's eyes narrowed. "What are you trying to say, Celia?"

"I'm trying to say back the hell off. Kace is my friend and he's been helping me deal with stuff. I am not the same Celia who left you behind. I have to fend for myself. You'd be surprised to hear that people change, Jaren." I returned the *pleasant* stare.

I exposed my arm, showing off my bandage. "Kace fixed it. Where have you been? Catching a ride with Asa and hiding in the bushes. I need you to know that I'm not here on vacation. I live here now. This is my *home*."

After a roll of his eyes, he decided against saying anything else and walked off—and I didn't dare stop him.

Waiting for a minute of silence to pass, I took a deep breath.

I turned to Kace. "I apologize for that." My eyes fell on my bandage, and I released a sigh. "I should probably get inside and sleep." My eyelids grew heavy and so I let them close.

Kace took me back to his cabin and let me lay in his bed. He used that thin blanket to cover me while he stayed on the cot, and then I was out like a light.

THE POUNDING WOKE ME, causing me to put too much pressure on my injured arm. I groaned in pain and sat up, rubbing the sleep away.

Kace opened the door. "What? Do you have to bang on my door?"

Lili replied, "Yes. It's important. We need to welcome the new lost boys and set *new* rules." New rules? Sounded a lot like a cat pissing out of spite.

Kace brushed her off. "Okay, all right. I have to help Lia out first." He closed the door and looked back at me.

I squeezed my heavy eyes shut. "I'll get up..." I slowly got off his bed, not too ecstatic about the idea.

Kace came over and helped, and I didn't decline. I was still half asleep. He guided me out of the cabin and sat me on a log near the blazing fire in the middle of the camp. The warmth of the flames felt amazing against my clammy skin.

Pan and Lili stood in the middle, power gracing us like a storm amidst a flood.

He spoke first. "We shall introduce you to our new members, Asa and Jaren. They may be related to Lili but do not treat them any differently than you would new lost boys."

My eyes moved to Asa as he scoffed. I smiled a little.

Lili cleared her throat and stepped forward. "It has come to my attention that there are some boundaries here on this island and age is one of them. As you all know, everyone here is under eighteen. Unfortunately, Jaren is not." She gestured to him. "Because of this, he has thirty days to leave from the time he arrived. Adults cannot physically survive here for very long. If Jaren is here at the end of thirty days, he'll decompose. Magic comes with a price, and only *we* are immortal here."

Jaren straightened his posture. He didn't seem too pleased with the idea given the uncomfortable shift in his body. He only had roughly twenty-something days here until he would die, and the time would sneak up on us like a cat to a mouse.

Coughing, I looked at Kace with worry etched on my face. Would Pan let our brother go back home? Of course he wouldn't. That would risk the exposure of Neverland, and everyone would be trying to get in. Corpses would litter the beaches.

Kace closed his fingers around mine. I didn't want to think about it, but I couldn't get my brain to stop whirling around the terrible thoughts. I was going to lose my brother forever. What was I supposed to do? I could find a way back home with him and I could give up on Lili, or I could stay here and watch him slowly die in the several weeks.

Everyone's voices tuned out. I had to choose. My sister *or* my brother.

A shadow fell over me, blocking me from the warmth of the fire. Jaren, of course. It couldn't have belonged to Lili or Pan. They didn't *have* shadows.

He bent down. "I made my decision. I came here to take you both home, so you can choose to come with me, or I will stay until you do. If it means I end up dying here, so be it. I made a commitment. I won't give up on either of my sisters." His stare never wavered, his expression soft.

There was no way he could possibly give his own life for us. Part of me began to wonder if this island could change people quickly. It seemed to make all of us lost children want to fight for those we loved. Could it be? No. He had to be lying. He couldn't possibly sacrifice himself for us and he knew it deep down. He would bail before thirty days was up, and we wouldn't be going with him.

I glanced over at my sister talking to Pan about something else, then my eyes locked on my brother. There wasn't anything else to be said.

I stood up from the log, assuming this meeting was over.

"I'm not done. Sit," Lili demanded.

I sat back down as I was told. Jaren was already on his deathbed. What else was there to add to the meeting?

She cleared her throat while folding her arms. "We need to implement a new rule. I will not tolerate disobedience. Pan and I discussed this, and we both agreed it will whip you into shape." She stepped over a log. "I know that some of you are very rebellious children. That's not how this island keeps order." Her eyes landed on me.

Furrowing my brows, I placed my hand over my heart. Me? I wasn't a very rebellious child. Hardly a child at all. I wasn't proud to admit it, but I did have a tiny crush on Pan when I'd first arrived. However, that didn't make me defiant. She was projecting onto me.

After all, it was I who suggested telling Pan about our relation to Asa.

Lili looked at the other lost boys and smiled, but it lacked all sweetness. Sin laced the promises like salt to the rim of a margarita.

"We are now putting in place a three-strike policy." She pointed to every one of us, confirming we were paying attention. "We give you no food for twenty-four hours for the first warning. The second warning will come as a night in the cage. The third warning is but a final example to everyone else as to what happens to those who disobey. You will be killed and strung up for everyone to see. Strike three and you're *out*."

04: Forgive and Forget

I sat on my own bed, messing with the string of the gauze around my pale arm. No blood seeped through. Enough of it was lost when I had been sliced. Sitting here wasn't helping my arm or my body temperature. Standing, I pinched the cloak around my chest as I left toward the camp. Asa was sitting by himself.

I walked over and gently kicked his foot. "Hey, cousin."

He didn't say a word. With a sigh, I dropped next to him. I knew it wasn't personal. Asa did this to everyone. He was an only child, and he was used to keeping his problems to himself.

He stretched.

"Maybe you can teach me how to grow longer legs," I joked. My attempt to make him laugh failed. He focused on the ground instead.

I exhaled and said, "You came here for a reason. You were hoping for more than what your parents gave you. We all were." I glanced at the snow, a memory flashing before my eyes of when I used to eat snow in our backyard. Didn't all little kids do that?

As I shivered, I moved snow with the toe of my boot to reveal the damp earth beneath it.

Asa looked at me. "Don't do that." When I tilted my head—brows knitted—and pointed to the snow, he added, "don't pretend you give a shit.

We were never friends. We never will be."

"We're family." I faced him.

"That's all we are. Family means we're related by blood. It doesn't mean I have to like you." He got up and disappeared, leaving me to wallow in self-pity.

I turned my head in the opposite direction of the person who plopped beside me. Kace grabbed my cheeks, making me look at him as he wiped away my tears. "What's wrong?"

I didn't want to cry. Hardly did I ever want to weep in front of anyone, or in private. I hated it just as much as anyone else did. But being too emotional wasn't a choice I was given. My tears always had control of me.

"It's not fair. I have family here and I can't even talk to a single one of them," my voice sounded small—and weak like I was.

Kace tugged my head against his shoulder. "A family is supposed to be there for you, but they can't even get that right. *They're* the problem."

I wiped the rest of the waterworks when enough of them had humiliated me. I scooted to give Kace his space, then groaned. "I just wish that he would stop being so pertinacious. If he wants to survive, he needs to make friends."

"Your sister didn't make many friends aside from me," Kace commented.

"And how did that turn out?" I gave him a look.

"Point taken." He nodded a bit, focusing on the fresh powder falling before our eyes.

I tossed my foot. "Do you think Asa will ever open up?" I gazed up at the gray sky.

Kace followed my eyesight. "Most people hate Pan. He's difficult and he's got his issues, but he isn't all bad. He *wasn't* always bad. He has his reasons." He shrugged and met my eyes.

I chewed on my bottom lip. "I guess I just have hope that he can change. Lili had that hope, too, but now I can only dream that I don't end up like her, too."

Kace stood. "Do you want to come with me to check on your wound?" He held his hand out for me.

"I think you may need me there," I said with a laugh. I grabbed his hand, following his lead. "I guess it doesn't hurt to check." I sat down on his bed as we entered his cabin.

He grabbed some new gauze and put it aside while he removed the strip around my arm. He cursed, rubbing his eyes before cursing under his breath again. As if he needed to ensure that his eyes weren't deceiving him. "What did I do wrong?" He began to search his desk, trying to solve the mystery.

I peeked at my stitches. The area was red and inflamed, and I think one area had some pus. It appeared infected just by the shade of the site alone.

Kace shook his head. "We're going to have to call Pan. I don't know what else to do." He left the cabin for a minute or two.

Why did it get infected? He cleaned the blood and tied close the wound. Grabbing my gauze, I inspected it, but it looked fine to me. Microscopic bacteria wouldn't wave its arms and shout hello at me, though.

The door slammed against the wall. Pan came over and grasped my arm, giving it a once-over. "Yes, her arm is definitely infected. The blade I used wasn't clean." He looked at Kace.

Kace narrowed his eyes. "You cut her using a dirty blade? Pan, we don't have modern medicine here. Do you want her to die?" His nostrils flared a bit, the brown in his eyes nearly vanishing behind the anger creeping up.

Pan's eyes moved from Kace to me. "I don't really care, but it sounds like you do."

"Oh, God forbid I care about someone," Kace said with sarcasm seeping heavily from his lips.

The monster that called himself our leader laughed in his face. "There is no God here, just me." He twisted himself my way.

With a sigh, I asked, "Can't you just fix me? I told you about our relation to Asa. Is it really necessary that I die from an infection?" I gave him my arm, demanding to be healed.

"People in your world cure infections, don't they?"

"Are you serious? They use antibiotics. You don't have that." I crossed one arm over my chest, then put it down as I realized how stupid it looked.

"What are antibiotics?" Pan asked, his tone laced with annoyance.

I got up and walked over to Kace's supplies. "Tell me why you won't heal me. It takes two seconds and no effort." I spun on my heel.

He shrugged. "Because in your world, things don't get cured with magic."

"We're not in my world. The rules have changed. Magic is the norm." I pulled my dagger from my belt. "This is my home now, Pan, and I intend it to stay that way. I don't *use* antibiotics. I use magic." I showed him my arm.

He strode over to me. "I don't take orders from you."

"You sleep with my sister, right? She may be your demon queen but if you let me die, she will always hold some form of hatred for you, and you can't reverse death." I shoved my arm in his face once again, knowing I'd won.

He scowled and touched the cut, fusing the skin back together and forcing away the disease. My skin returned to its healthy shade, and Pan hurried out the door.

I sat. "We can cut these stitches out now."

Kace brought over his knife and began removing the stitches. "Does that twin thing work? Lili told me no but I wanna hear your perspective. How deep does that bond go?"

I twirled the string of my cloak around my forefinger. "We can get a sense of how each other feels. The only difference is we're now used to it. You learn how to tune it out and become your own person. I have emotions, too." I watched him take out the last stitch. I smoothed my fingers over the scar, my skin no longer a sickly hue. Regardless, this area was forever damaged.

Kace double-checked my arm before leaving it be. "Now we can focus our priorities on other important things, like getting your brother home."

I looked at him with a subtle smile from the thought of Kace caring enough to help me. "Yes, that is crucial. I refuse to let him give up his life for us. He deserves better." When the last words left my lips, a sorrowful smile replaced my once genuine one.

As mad as I had been at him for choosing now to care about us, I couldn't imagine losing him altogether. I wouldn't picture his body decomposing. I wouldn't let it become a reality.

We walked back out to the camp while the boys ate their lunch.

I grabbed a bowl of salad and berries, sitting down to eat. With Wendy dead, who was gardening?

Dixon—the guy I met the night Lili slept with Pan—had disappeared from the island, and maybe that little pirate was now the secret gardener. Would Pan put him to work, or kill him outright for taking refuge here?

No question. He'd outright rip his heart from his chest with great pleasure after what Dixon's captain had done to Pan.

I looked over at Asa who sat by himself per usual. He didn't touch his meal. Why refuse food from people you didn't want to take orders from?

After finishing, I walked over to him and took a seat. "I don't give up that easily. I know you hate it here, but we are your family whether you like it or not. If you want to survive, you better buckle up."

He looked at me, asking, "Who said I wanted to survive?"

I rested my hands on my thighs, forcing my back to straighten up. "You did. You came here for a reason. If you weren't looking to survive, you would've let your abusive parents beat you to death. Deny it all you want, but the truth doesn't become a lie just because you refuse to believe it."

He scoffed at my argument. "Shut up. You don't know me."

I threw my head back with a laugh. "For crying out loud..." I didn't finish my sentence. Shaking my head, I got back to my feet. "You are crying because nobody loved you, yet now that someone wants to, you push them away. You need to grow up, pun intended. Nobody will hand you happiness. You have to achieve that yourself." I left him with those words to think about.

Kace's eyebrow arched. "What was that about?"

I sighed after taking a moment to realize the power of my tone. "Was I too harsh?"

"It wasn't too harsh. We're in Neverland so you aren't required to go soft on the boy. He'll have to eventually get the hang of it."

I nodded, taking a deep breath to calm my nerves. "I came here, expecting everything. For a while, I got just that, until the pieces began to fall as the rose-colored lenses came off. I get challenges thrown in my face. I have to work to save my sister. Nobody here is handed the silver platter." I glanced back at my cousin who glared at the ground as if that was what did him wrong. "Asa is no exception."

05: Clone

DAGGER IN HAND, I traced its silver blade before placing it back in my belt. If I could avoid my sister and Pan today, everything would be just all right. I wasn't in that great of a mood.

I despised being ignored. I despised it when someone didn't acknowledge my effort. Was it so hard to do at least that?

Tears threatened to spill over the rims of my eyelids *again*. Growing up, I heard things like, "You're too emotional," and, "I'll give you something to cry about". I'd always had my sensitive side invalidated by everyone around me, but no matter how many times those words stung, the tears never stopped.

So it became habitual to only let my emotions out in private.

In one swift movement, I pulled my dagger out and stabbed it into the wall. I shouted in frustration. I didn't need to let it get the best of me the way it had Lili. She held in her feelings, and it led her down the wrong path.

I finally allowed the tears to fall. There was no promise of tomorrow. Hardly friends, no family left. I didn't even have music to make everything better.

I just wanted to be recognized as a person.

I screamed into the ceiling. I didn't care who heard me at this point. If it saved me from becoming Lili, I would take it. When no sound came out, my throat was left sore and scratchy.

I needed to train.

I yanked my dagger from the wall and left my cabin. I stomped through camp and toward the training center. The moment I arrived, I practiced throwing knives into the trunk of a tree. The stares wore into my soul, threatening my existence. I turned to the lost boys and straightened my posture, giving them no part of weakness. "Take a damn picture, it lasts longer."

Then I grabbed a bow and set of arrows.

I jumped at the English accent behind me. "Anger is not going to help your training."

Whipping around so fast, I almost lost my balance, but I held my own. "Stay out of this. It has nothing to do with you."

"Does it not?" Pan questioned.

"It does not," I spat. I was not going to let him intimidate me. I was not in the mood for his bullshit today.

He brushed me aside like a crumb on his table. "If you're looking for a way to remove your anger, might I suggest murder? It works for your sister." He leaned down a bit.

"My name is *Lia*. Believe it or not but we all have different ways of releasing anger. I tend to avoid hurting people." I narrowed my eyes on him.

"Whatever you say," he hissed.

He exited the area. The last time I saw Pan, I'd also felt a feeling never felt before, after he left my cabin, but I hadn't been able to place it. Still, I was left clueless—wishing on a star.

I faced the targets again, watching them as if they'd grow legs and walk away. I grabbed an arrow and shot it at the target. It flew past the board, straight into the trees behind it. I dropped my head in shame, utterly useless.

Instead, I went to search for Asa. It was no surprise when I found him by the camp. I walked right up to him and kicked his foot.

He gave me a look. "What?"

I planted myself right beside him. "You can't just ignore me forever. Unfortunately, for you, I'm your family." He grumbled and looked away. I went the extra mile and put my head on his shoulder. "Asa... You can't pretend I don't exist. We have to stick together. Whether you like it or not, I'm all you have now. Lili is dark. Jaren is leaving."

"I can ignore you as long as I need to." He stood without warning, leaving me scrambling in the snow as I looked up at him. He left without another word, not bothering to apologize.

I let out a sigh before getting up. "Fine. Whatever." I went in search of my brother, to get him back home somehow.

As I walked through the forest, I yelled, "Jaren!" I crossed my arms when I got no response. Everyone I wanted to talk to was ignoring me, and the one person I wanted to avoid was bothering me.

"Fine, freeze out here. I'm going somewhere a bit warmer," I mumbled with a shiver. I walked back to camp and entered my cabin, the silence blanketing me the way I wish summer would. I approached my dresser and pulled out a small ribbon and tied my hair back into a low ponytail.

I needed to go somewhere peaceful. My anger was still boiling and I refused to let anyone send me over the edge.

I pulled my hood on and yanked the cloak tighter before exiting the cabin. My boots left footprints as I came upon the beach and tilted my head. I had never seen snow on a beach. I halted at the sight of a fin disappearing beneath the water, then narrowed my eyes.

Whales were possible, but I doubted they were going to be way out here. With what little knowledge I had about them, I knew their fins were thicker than a fish. These fins were thin, almost guaranteed to rip to shreds if they came across rocks. They belonged to another species entirely, one common around these parts.

Mermaids.

A head popped up and beautiful eyes bore into my soul. She came as close as she could. "Did you bring food? We are *starving*. It's been at least a week."

I tilted my head in confusion. I had never fed them, had I? No, I would never feed someone else to a mermaid.

Another head popped up above the ocean's surface. They waited for a response, but I gave none. I didn't know what to say. The mermaids stared at me, their gazes never leaving my own.

"What do you mean it's been a week?" I finally asked.

The redhead spoke up, "You always feed us." Her purple tail swayed behind her head.

Dismissing them, I replied, "I didn't come for that. You must be talking about my sister." My body froze. They were talking about Lili the entire time. Had she really been killing people for them? Of course she had. Everyone here kept confirming that my sister was now a murderer. She didn't have plans on stopping.

"You have a sister? But you look the same," the brunette mermaid spoke softly, her voice never faltering.

"We're twins—identical," I replied. I didn't want to be Lili's twin anymore. We were polar opposites. I north, her south.

I shook my head to throw away the thoughts. I left the beach, unsure of how I was supposed to feel around man-eating mermaids. They seemed so sweet. They looked so beautiful. They sounded like angels. They were anything but sweet, beautiful angels. Instead, they reeked of cruel, ugly demons. They were the spawns of the Demon King himself.

I got back to my cabin and walked inside, stopping when I noticed my brother. "What are you doing here?"

"I thought we could talk," he answered.

I paused for a moment, then nodded. I sat next to him. "I guess we have to talk about a few things." I folded my hand in between my thighs for warmth.

Jaren put his hands in his jean pockets. "I want to know everything that has happened before my arrival. I need to know why Lili is so cold now."

I laughed at his unintended pun. "Sorry..." I cleared my throat. "I guess I'll start upon my arrival then." I scratched my ear while anxiety took over. Lying to my brother wasn't an option.

He took a seat next to me and waited for my answer. It was more than an answer. It was a life story. It was *our* life story, or more likely hers. It was not something I would wish on anyone. Lili was stuck deep in Pan's clutches, and I was struggling to free her.

I started at the beginning of their bickering and eventually led to his pretty lies. She wanted him, but she played him, and him her. Then Lili gave into Pan suddenly, no reasoning.

Jaren managed to understand. "Lili, our sister, is dating Pan. She's killed. Are you sure this is Lili? Maybe Pan put a spell on her or maybe he switched her for an evil clone, and she's locked somewhere."

"It could be a possibility. I'm not sure what he did to her. She isn't going to stop unless I bring back who she once was. That's not why you came here, though." I glanced at my legs. "You need to leave. We have to find someone who will get you out of here."

He refused. "Not without either of you."

I wanted to ask why now, why he was just now choosing us, but I wasn't in any mood for an argument with the one person who wanted to see me. "I won't leave without saving Lili."

"Then let's save Lili. We have a short time to do it, but that's our goal, right?"

"I suppose..."

"Then I can bring you both home." He flashed a smile. It wasn't exactly a promise. I never wanted to go back there, and Lili would never leave. "You're twins. You must know how to save her."

As he called us twins, something inside me ignited. A spark grew into a blazing fire that even the firefighters could never douse. "I'm tired of being compared to Lili. I don't want to be the girl who looks like the Demon Queen of Neverland. I want to be known as Lia." I pulled out my dagger. "Cut my hair. To my shoulders." I turned my back towards him.

He grabbed my hair, removing the ribbon. "Uh, sure, I guess." He grabbed a bit and started slicing through.

"The mermaids thought I was Lili. I don't want to be compared to her if I can help it. I know that's asking for a lot." I closed my eyes, hoping he could chop it off at least decently.

Hair was thrown to the floor.

"We should also find someone who can get you off this island. You don't have much longer, Jaren. I won't watch you die. What if we can't save Lili in time?" I swallowed the lump forming in my throat.

"I can't leave without you guys. I came here for a reason, and I won't waste it." He finished, handing me my dagger.

I shoved it into my belt and looked at the locks that scattered the floor. I reached up and touched my curls. It felt so much lighter than before.

But I was going to get him home whether he liked it or not. I didn't want to sit back and watch him die and I sure as hell wasn't going to.

"All right," I lied.

We both got up and I walked him to the door, saying my goodbye. Before I could close it, a hand stopped me. I opened the door to reveal the culprit, my expression showing obvious irritation. "What do you want, Pan?"

"Is that any way to talk to your leader?" He let out a displeased sigh. "I'm a little disappointed. Heartbroken, even. You didn't tell your brother about our kiss." He patted his chest where his heart should have been. "Did that kiss not mean anything to you?"

06: Tit for Tat

I reeled my shoulders back a bit to loosen the stiffness. "I haven't even told Kace. It's been over a year now, and you're with my sister. It bears no importance."

Pan overstepped his boundaries, grabbing hold of my hair. "Why did you cut your hair?" A frown fell over his features. How lovely to have the great Pan himself disappointed that I cut my own hair..

I pushed his arm away with the back of my hand. "It's my business, and I don't want to be Lili's clone anymore. I've got no more to explain to you, and I didn't even owe you that one. Consider yourself lucky." I closed the door on him.

I didn't bother to clean up the locks on the floor before I let the darkness take me away for the night.

I woke to a gentle knock. I dragged myself out of my bed and to the door of my cabin. I opened it. "What are you doing here?" I rubbed my tired eyes.

Kace lifted his eyes from under his hood. "If we're going to save

Neverland, we might want to start making progress."

I nodded. "Right... I guess let's go."

Kace chuckled amongst the two of us so that he wouldn't be heard by anyone else. Who else would be up at this hour to be able to hear us? "I meant we can work from here. It would be too risky to work anywhere else. We'd be on his map and the crows would be more likely to watch." He pointed to my room.

Crows? Why did he care so much if they had eyes on us?

I glanced back, studying the only two pieces of furniture I owned. My own hair still littered the floor. I turned to Kace again and let him in. When he noticed, his eyes met mine. "You cut your hair?"

"Yep." I pushed some hair behind my ear.

Kace nodded a bit. "I like it."

My eyebrows shot up my forehead.. I wasn't used to men saying they liked my haircut. Then again, no woman was ever used to that. If they did acknowledge it, it usually wasn't a compliment.

"Thanks," I sputtered.

We both took a seat on the bed.

Kace leaned back. "Okay, so I'm not sure how we can bring them back exactly. I'm the right-hand man but know the know-it-all. They're entirely different." He laughed.

I'd never noticed it before, but around me, his smile seemed so genuine. Here, in these conditions, one would never have imagined Pan's best friend had a real smile like Kace's. It was refreshing after all the stress.

"That's why we have two brains working together as one." I laughed a little and scooted until my back hit the wall. "I want to assume that whatever turned Pan evil also turned Lili evil. How much do you know about Pan, Neverland, and his abilities?" I looked at him.

He cleared his throat. "Well, we think Pan is evil—"

I gasped. "Wait, really? I didn't notice. It's a good thing someone here has a brain."

Kace gave me a side eye. "You didn't let me finish." He took a deep breath to regather his thoughts. "I know that he's evil but it's not what fuels his power. Pan was always magical whether the darkness had control or not. He just uses his abilities differently. Deep down he has his true self trapped. Getting him out is where things will get tricky.

"This island is run by Pan and his magic. The three are connected, but the darkness is what you'd call a conflict. A defining plot point. It's not needed, but it does hold importance. With two wicked rulers, the island is off balance. It will continue to get worse until we figure out how to balance it. Lili is not magical; therefore, she cannot help Pan rule the island. Only *Pan* can do that himself," he explained.

In other words, we had to restore the balance while also shutting the darkness into a dark chest in the attic. It seemed easy enough.

Kace waved his hand in front of my face, bringing me back. "Hey, you still there?"

"Yes." I shifted, straightening my torso. "I was just processing what we need to do." I coughed a bit.

Kace focused on the wood across from us. Grain ran down in one ultimate direction, but not all lines followed the same path, forever changing the way it looked. No two pieces of wood looked the same because no two trees grew the same.

And even if Lili and Pan had both succumbed to the demons, their means of getting to that point differed. To figure out how to bring them back, we first needed to figure out what led them there in the first place.

I coughed again before a shiver racked my body. I pulled my cloak closed. "Well, anything else to add?"

His head turned towards me. "I know that this island is younger than Pan, but it still needs him, nonetheless. We're old. We can't leave this island because if we do, our true age will show, and we will return to the dust that formed us. There's only one way off this island, if we want to avoid decomposing that is. That's through Pan. There's also Tinker Bell, but the two hate each other. She won't help anyone. I've never considered her a valid means of escape."

Escape. He called it escape. Why would Kace use that word if not to imply he was trapped? Did he wish to return home?

"Tinker Bell is here? Who else? Are there any other girls I should know about? That would be ironic." I choked on a laugh.

"Who?" asked Kace.

I dismissed my joke. If he didn't know, she probably didn't exist.

My own breath formed before me. "We need to hurry with a plan. A concrete plan. It's getting colder. We won't be able to survive soon enough." I shifted my eyes to Kace's.

He released a sigh. "I don't know how to save Neverland. I've never had to worry about it. I'd just go with Pan's rules anytime."

"It seemed so simple, huh? Well, it's not anymore. That day is long gone now. Is there anything specific you remember about Pan going dark?"

One brow dipped while the other jumped. "Yes. Pan went dark right after Hook used us."

I furrowed my brows. "Wait, what?"

"Hook and Pan used to date, a long time ago. Pan is a lot older than he looks. Hook used to be younger before she left the island, and after, his demon side emerged."

I picked at my fingers. Could it be? Hook and Pan dated? "How did she make him go dark?"

"Hook was always a rotten person. Everything she did with him meant nothing to her. It was for her own pleasure. She did the same to me, too. Only I didn't know at the time. Pan isn't the kind of guy to kiss and tell. His heart still beat red then. However, Hook used both of us at once and that snapped him. From that moment forward, Pan was never himself. Not the Pan I'd originally met. He turned to the darkness and let it consume his soul in its entirety."

I curled my fingers. "Is that why he didn't allow lost girls? Hook ruined every thought for him. He's got this joy for killing."

"I like to think that maybe he imagines every person he kills is him killing Hook. Although now he has Lili and *she* killed Hook, so I assume that he's content. That doesn't change the fact that the balance of Neverland is falling but it is what it is. Pan's emotions are tied to the island, but the balance of magic along with rulership is another story."

I nodded as a thought popped into my head. "We'll continue this tomorrow. I have to do something." I jumped from my bed and left him behind in my cabin before he could stop me.

I knocked on Jaren's cabin—which he shared with the other boys—and gave up on patience, so I walked in to find him out of bed. "What are you doing here?" he asked me.

"Jaren, I have found a way for you to go home. I think I can send you home!" I shouted a little too loudly.

He groaned and lay back. "I'm not going anywhere. We agreed that I would stay and help you save Lili."

"You don't understand the seriousness of the situation like I do." There was no use arguing at this hour. I needed to force him home.

I huffed and left his cabin, venturing off into the hills. I stopped when I heard familiar voices. Lili and Pan. What were they doing up at this hour?

I followed them, but they echoed off in the distance, making it a bit harder to locate the source. I didn't know why I was searching.

When they came into view, I slid behind a trunk. Lili was pacing back and forth in front of a woman I'd never seen before. Why were they with her?

My sister stopped in front of her. She mocked the girl, using a high-pitched voice, "Pan is just so hot!" Her face returned to its stone-cold state. "He's *mine*. And you deserve to die for not listening to me in the first place. Don't you think so?" she asked her boyfriend.

Pan nearly blended right in with the trees in his dark green attire. Had this new girl tried to get with Pan, or was Lili out of line?

"She tried to stir the pot." He crossed his arms.

Lili glanced at him. "Shall I do the honors?"

"Why not, Darling?"

She scowled. "Don't call me that. I'm not Wendy."

The corner of his mouth twitched. "I know, Little Flower."

She dropped the scowl. "I need you to hold her while I do the job."

The girl attempted to flee but Pan snapped his fingers and a rope wrapped around her ankles, sending her to the ground. He walked over and grabbed her by the arms, pulling her upright, holding her in front of Lili. "Go ahead." Pan nodded toward her.

She slipped her dagger from her belt as the helpless girl begged, fighting against the restraints. "Please, I didn't mean it! I'm sorry! I'll do anything!" I had never seen someone so helpless—so desperate.

She thrashed as she pleaded for her life. Her eyes watered, her voice shattering like glass.

Lili shrugged a bit. "Tempting but no." She plunged the blade into her abdomen. "You're the enemy. This is what happens to my enemies." She ripped it out, examining the blood.

Nausea swirled inside my stomach.

Blood. It made me queasy, but that much made my lunch want to come back up.

The girl slumped in Pan's arms, and he dropped her to the ground. She choked as blood spilled from her lips, slowly inching towards death.

A death that seemed to come too slow yet too fast all at once.

Life poured from her body, and with it, her soul. Everything this girl once was had been snuffed out.

And Pan just watched in awe. "Little Flower, I never thought I would find love after Hook, and yet you amaze me every day."

My hands shook against my control. Unable to comprehend what my own sister had just done to someone else, I begged for the memory to bury itself inside my head where I could never find it.

But it didn't do that at all—and Lili had so ruthlessly torn a human from this world. No mercy. Just pure chaos. A monster let out of its *cage*.

07: Shadows at Dusk

There'd once been a time when I was surrounded by males and females—girls and boys if you will. I went to school every morning and rarely missed a day. I covered up my bruises with makeup, made up excuses, and tried to keep a good distance between me and my friends. If they knew too much, questions would arise, and I would never see the light of day again.

Now, I was surrounded by boys and one girl. If you could call a murdered a girl at all, that was. She ran the island with Pan, and together they wreaked havoc on all the poor souls who'd experienced nothing but abuse, neglect, and the feeling of being unwanted.

Was this any better than the life we lived before? At what cost?

Back when I'd been in school, I had a few friends. We weren't tight-knit but I kept them by my side to help me survive the day. When they tried to pry into my life, I let off the gas. I almost shut down until they got off my ass about it. I wondered if those friends even missed me. Did they still remember my name?

"Lia, you in here?" Kace asked, poking his head inside and knocking in the frame of the open doorway.

"I'm here."

He smiled and stepped inside, but the minute his eyes landed on my face, the light was sucked from his brown eyes. Concern was all that had been left behind. "What happened?"

As much as I didn't want to bother him with my issues, I knew I couldn't keep it in. I wanted to tell someone, and Kace was my best ally.

Twirling the string of the cloak around my finger, I said, "Lili killed someone. She just...murdered an innocent girl in cold blood."

Kace released a deep breath and sat beside me. "I apologize that you had to see her in that state. It can't be easy."

I shook my head, glancing at him. "It's not. I stood there when our dad hit her. I did nothing but stand there and let him hurt the one person who understood my pain. She never did anything wrong, Kace. She was your average teenager. She snuck out to go do things. She had to be reminded to do chores. She talked back when she shouldn't have. She was punished not as a daughter, but as a criminal in prison. It pains me that she's taken this path but at the same time, I understand. She had nobody to protect her and now she's unleashing the same hatred our father did. She's a product of her environment." The result of utter destruction.

Something inside me fluttered as his warm fingers brushed the top of mine.

That was nothing. It meant nothing.

He took a moment of silence to gather his thoughts and when he did, he cleared his throat. "She's a victim who's turned into the perpetrator. It's a vicious cycle. Are you afraid you'll end up that way?"

Another shake of my head. "Not at all. There isn't any urge in my body that wants to shed blood or cause harm. I just wonder how she ended up with that darkness and yet I have no ounce of it. Doesn't quite make sense." Yet if I didn't succeed in my plan, something worse was going to come. I'd become a failure of my own doing.

With a nod, he said, "I suppose that's another mystery to solve." Kace nudged me a bit. "What else is there?"

I rubbed away the headache. "She killed an innocent girl, and I didn't stop it. I'm a coward, and I need to fix that. I can't let her kill anyone else." Cowards didn't belong on Neverland. They certainly didn't deserve to *rule* it, either. I stood from the bed and began pacing. "I'd once had friends my own age. Not that you aren't my own age, but in a way, you aren't entirely my age." Getting back on track, I cleared my throat. "We all went to school together. We laughed. We shared notes. It was wonderful, and I miss that. Wendy is dead and my sister is cruel, and I'm the only girl left. I *miss* the feeling of talking to another woman."

Kace tapped his chin. "I see. What about Tinker Bell? Although I'm not so certain that she...is around anymore."

I dropped onto my knees on the mattress, leaning in. "Where can I find her?"

He flashed me an apologetic smile. "I'm sorry, I don't know. She used to come around here when she and Wendy were dating but Pan squashed that fast. Haven't seen her since."

Furrowing my brows, I sat. "She dated Wendy? That's not in the fairytale."

"What is in the fairytale?"

"Wendy and Pan have a small thing. Nothing serious or...real. It's like a childhood crush."

"That's not what happened in this version." He crossed his arms. No. This version was very real and here, everyone could die at the hands of Pan himself.

I swallowed my questions. "Well, they dated but now Wendy's gone. I don't want to swoop in and tell her I need a friend if she's struggling. It wouldn't be okay."

"Maybe you could just be there for her. Friendships have to start somehow, and she may need someone to lean on." He leaped from the bed. "Trust me when I say she's not going to hate you. There's a lot you could learn about Tinker Bell. She's a wonderful person when you get to know her." He exited the room.

The search for Tinker Bell would have to wait until the blizzard let up. I couldn't risk my life with too many promises on my shoulders. The last thing I wanted was to prove my stupidity.

I peeked out the window and all I could see for miles was a sheet of white covering the island. I'd always hated winter. It was too icy—too deadly. It reminded me of all the horror movies of people getting stuck and *freezing* to death.

I took a few buckets from Pan's porch and boiled lots of water. When I set them into the snow, they cooled fairly quickly. Then I took them back to my cabin and poured them into the tub.

With nothing else to keep myself warm, I locked the bathroom door for privacy using a ribbon and knotting it to a built-in towel rack.. Glancing at the tub, a sigh passed my lips. I needed the hot water to keep me alive until this was over.

I untied my cloak and dropped it to the floor. I pulled off my boots and socks first before removing my shirt. The ice from the weather threatened to bring me to my knees, but I wouldn't give in.

I discarded the last of my clothing before stepping into the tub. I sat back. Chills ran up my spine, and in just minutes I was warm again.

When the muscles around my bones relaxed, I lay back and put my head under the surface. The water rippled, distorting my view of the ceiling. A dark figure appeared, and I immediately sat up, searching my bathroom but he'd gone. What the hell was that?

I pushed my hair away from my face and took a deep breath. "Pan, I swear if you're spying on me, I will make sure you don't make it out of this life." Threatening him probably wasn't the best idea but I did not need him to invade my privacy. It was a violation of my safety *and* my rights.

I got out and grabbed a towel, drying myself off. I dressed in a hurry and pulled my hood on, exiting my cabin. I found myself at Pan's, and when he answered the door, he didn't seem pleased.

"Are you spying on me?" I asked.

He snickered. "You're not that special, Lia."

"Who was in my cabin just now?" I pointed to it.

"Probably your boyfriend. You two hang out a lot." Pan shrugged.

I almost scoffed at that. Kace would never stand over me when I was naked. He was a respectable man.

"They disappeared the second I looked at them. Kace doesn't have that ability." I narrowed my eyes. "But you and your shadow do."

Pan rolled his eyes. "Nobody is spying on you." He slammed the door in my face.

I turned around, facing the storm. Someone had been inside my cabin and the thought of not knowing who scared me. If Pan wasn't the only one here with a shadow, who else had one? I knew Lili didn't have one anymore, but I doubted she would be in my cabin. She had no interest in me these days.

Hands landed on my shoulders, and I glanced at the owner—Kace. He guided me to his cabin and closed the door. "What are you doing in the storm?"

"Kace...someone was in my cabin."

"What? Who?"

"I don't know. They were watching me, and I can't...shake this feeling of dread." I pulled my hood down. The strands of hair surrounding my face had frozen in place. "Whoever they are, they're a *threat*. I'm terrified." Glued to him, my wide eyes had Kace worried more than I'd been.

He closed the gap between us and grabbed my hands, warming them in his palms. He lifted one, cupped between his, blowing hot air into it. "Whoever this asshole is, we will find them and kill them." He switched and breathed life into my other fingers. "You are much stronger than when you arrived. They're hardly a match against you."

"If I can't take a bath in peace, what can I do? I didn't have my dagger. I had nothing. They could have killed me right there and I would have been defenseless. He could have held me under the water and drowned me."

Ripping myself from his bubble, I gasped for air, sitting down on the bed. "I'm not invincible. I almost died after falling off that mountain." I looked at Kace.

"And I won't forget that. Lili was terrified of losing you, and even if she is a monster now, she still cares about you somewhere in there. If someone is after you, she will protect you even if it's under bad intentions."

Those words somehow comforted me. They reminded me that I had Lili to back me up. She could never let me die, even if she was someone else now. I would do the same for her. Unconditional love was all I had as my saving grace.

"Who could it be?" I whispered.

"I wish I had an answer but for now, we have to speculate. We'll figure it out. We'll catch this asshole and you'll be able to bathe peacefully again."

Who here hated me? Asa did, but I knew he had no energy to even bother. He wanted to stay to himself. Lili wouldn't want to kill me. Pan couldn't have done it because despite our differences, not a single lie slipped from his tongue. Was it someone outside of the camp?

"I have to go." I rushed out the door and got back to my cabin, locking the door. I furrowed my brows. "No... I had locked the door." I looked back at the knob on the bathroom door. I slowly approached it and inspected the handle, but nothing stood out.

Somehow, they got through the door and disappeared before I could catch them. There was only one person who could do that, and unless someone else had his powers, I couldn't suspect anyone else. Pan may have told me he didn't do it, and I had no reason to believe he did. Not this time.

Gripping the handle of my dagger, I walked into the bathroom and turned around until I faced the door again. Someone was screwing with me.

I was going to train harder. I would team up with his enemies. I would do everything needed to make sure that whoever he was, he paid the price for violating my privacy. He believed he owned me because he could break in and out of my cabin, but he was so far from the truth. He didn't even own himself. He was merely a puppet like everyone else.

I glanced into the mirror and swallowed my fear. I couldn't show any weakness. I couldn't give him anything to celebrate. I wanted to see him cry and scream.

This island controlled everything and yet they had no idea. Well, I knew. I knew the truth and I was going to take them down and save Neverland. It was up to me now, because if I failed, I'd lose my life as the price.

I'd be damned if I buckled under the threat of the unknown.

08: Anna Bell

Once the blizzard passed, I headed out to the lagoon. It was the one place where I'd be able to think. My thoughts were too vulnerable in my cabin.

I stopped at the edge of the water that had iced over, admiring my reflection for a moment. A figure appeared next to me, and I whipped around, pointing my dagger at their throat. "Try me again." Except it wasn't him.

She swallowed, putting her hands up. "Sorry. I didn't mean to sneak up on you. It's just been a while since you've visited me. How's it going with Pan?"

What? "I'm not Lili." I put my dagger away.

"Oh." Her cheeks reddened. "I... You looked just like her."

"Who are you?"

She hugged herself and scanned the sky. "Tinker Bell. The cold makes it hard for me to fly. I get around on foot these days."

"Aren't you supposed to be short and blonde?" I lifted an eyebrow.

She pressed her lips together. "What's your name?"

"Lia. So, were you always a fairy or were you human once?"

Tinker Bell sat on a rock. "I'm guessing Lili is your sister then, and you're twins? First I've ever heard of twins coming to the island, much less of them being women."

I pulled my cloak tighter around my shoulders. "We are. Are you going to answer my question now?"

"Why do you think she's his lover?"

"Take that as a no," I mumbled. "She caved to the only love she thought she could find."

She nodded a bit. The only thing green about her were her emerald eyes. The rest of her life was showered in darkness. Her hair, her clothes, and her wings. She was hurting inside, the whole world was aware.

Looking out at the ice, I cleared my throat. "Were you human once?" I would try this one last time.

"We all were."

"What?" I tilted my head to my right.

With a shrug, she said, "I was born in New York. Wendy and Pan were born in England. None of us were born with magic. Pan got his magic from this island, and Wendy got hers from getting high with Pan."

"Where did yours come from?"

"From Wendy..." She took a deep breath. "She would show me her abilities as she discovered them. She wasn't the greatest at control, but she did her best. She was so happy when she showed them to me, like she had a bigger purpose."

I almost started crying at the thought. Wendy was such a nice girl and she never deserved what she got dealt. Pan was *inhumane.*

Tinker Bell quickly changed the subject. "I was born in 1922, in New York, New York. My name is Anna Bell. They named me Tinker because I've always traveled around the island and used metal to make things to survive."

"Anna Bell," I whispered. "It's a pretty name. I prefer Anna over Tinker."

"Wendy did, too. She hated that I go by Tinker."

I laughed a little. "Tinker Bell reminds me of someone else and you are not her."

Silence fell over us both as the crisp air slapped our faces. As much as I wanted to retreat into my cabin until this was over, it wasn't logical. Someone had been watching me and I needed to somehow form a plan before Jaren died here.

"Did Pan ever spy on you? You or Wendy?" I faced Anna.

She shrugged, her eyes drifting to the sky. "I mean, of course. He was nosy and he wanted to know what was going on at all times. That's how he found out about us and once he did..." She cleared her throat. "Let's just say that back in the era we all come from, our relationship wasn't exactly...acceptable."

"No relationship was acceptable in those days. Not unless you were white and straight." I released a sigh.

Anna turned red. "I'm sorry, I didn't mean it like that. I'm so used to the different races on this island that I forget where I come from. In 1922, I had it easy in certain aspects."

With a shake of my head, I approached her. "I'm not here to compare tragedies. You're gay and I'm black—well, half black. Let's not dance around that. What do we both share, though? We're women." I sat beside her. "And as women, we must stick together. You've struggled with your sexuality, and I'm not here to overshadow any of that. We've both dealt with awful people." I gave her my pinky. "I promise."

Nodding, she linked hers around mine. "Tell me, what is the world like now? What year is it?"

I smiled a little. "Well, very different from 1922. Every marriage is legal now. However, that doesn't mean the hate has disappeared. Wherever good exists, evil follows. But there isn't segregation anymore. The black kids get to go to school with the white kids now. There're definitely things that we have to work on, but we've made some progress. A little. Not as much as we should have made by now, but humanity judges those who are different, and it takes a lifetime to change their minds. As for the technology..."

Anna leaned in. "What about cars? Have they improved?"

My laugh bounced off the rink in front of us. "Have they? They've changed from your little black cars to actual machines that have many features. Cars are everywhere now. Everyone uses them, and they're not hard to come by. In fact, we get cars from every country now. Germany, Japan, Korea. But I didn't come to talk about cars today." My grin fell. "I need your help."

"With what?"

"With Neverland. It needs saving. Pan and Lili need rescuing, and I think someone is spying on me when I'm at my most vulnerable. My brother is also here and if he doesn't leave within the next week or two, he'll die. And to top it all off, I have to save Neverland before then so he can leave without any worries about us."

Anna jumped to her feet. "No, I couldn't. I'm sorry, but I am in no state to get involved. Pan despises me, and I've vowed to stop messing with anything that might piss him off. Especially now that I've got nothing else to lose."

"Then do it for Lili. Please. I need my sister back."

She shook her head as she turned and began walking away. She paused. "It was nice to meet you, Lia." Within seconds, she disappeared into the winter wonderland, fog encasing her.

I knew it was too much to spring on her, but I was running out of time. I didn't have the option of taking things slow.

Part of me feared that maybe saving Pan was out of the question. Was he too far gone? Anna was gay, and it made sense that when she got a chance to come here and escape the judgment, she didn't hate herself. She never had.

But Pan was straight. He was raised to believe people like Anna and Wendy deserved to be miserable. Was it worth it to save someone who might have believed such horrid things?

No, Pan was with my sister. In his day, their relationship was illegal. In his day, white people treated black people as if we were nothing but vermin. Yet, he didn't seem to judge her, so how could he have a right to judge Anna and Wendy? But Wendy was dead and as far as I knew, it was because of his anger. His hatred led to the permanent loss for Anna. She no longer had someone to hold, and Pan was to blame.

Pan was to blame.

Was he the one watching me? I didn't want to believe he would lie to me, but he was the only one who had any abilities to spy on someone. He had more control than anyone else here.

"That was quite the bonding. Lili and Tinker used to bond like that, too, before she became my equal." Pan leaned against a tree, admiring the colorless sky.

"I have nothing to say to you " I faced the lagoon.

Hands landed on my shoulders. "Why is that? Let me guess, she told you about her and Wendy and now I'm the bad guy."

"You have always been the bad guy, Pan. Now you're just a villain with no redeeming qualities." I shook his hands off me.

He walked beside me, halting. "That's not true."

I glared at him. "It is, and you know it. You kill innocent people. You're not a vigilante."

Pan sat down. "What I did was wrong, but I will not apologize for killing Wendy. She was anything but innocent."

I scoffed.

"Lili never told you about the rumors, or what Jacob did." He swallowed. "Jacob had started these filthy *lies* that Lili and I were sleeping together so she could get what she wanted from me, like a nicer cabin. There may have been rumors about blowjobs, too." He folded his arms across his chest. "But because of them, Jacob thought he could get a piece of her. And surely he tried. That's when she broke her hand. She'd fought back."

Whatever heat I had left was gone now. I couldn't begin to imagine the fear that Lil had been put through. That boy tried to steal her dignity. He tried to take away her right to her body. He was dead now, and for that, I was thankful.

Otherwise, I'd have killed him myself. I was not above self-defense.

"I killed him." Pan glanced in my direction. "I wasn't going to allow rapists on my island. Those were the people my lost boys were trying to forget, and I'd be no better if I didn't do something about it. So, I took his life. I fed him to the mermaids. I thought that was all behind Lili, but then I found out who started the rumors. It wasn't Jacob. It's not usually boys who shame other women, but *other* women."

I furrowed my brows and looked at Pan. "What?"

"Wendy started the rumors. She encouraged Jacob to force himself on Lili. She wasn't all innocent, Lia. I'd created a monster when I yanked her from Tinker Bell. I took her away from her love, so she tried to destroy the one person I cared about."

I didn't want to believe him, but he had blamed himself, and knowing Pan would never do that, it had to be true. Wendy changed when she no longer had Anna by her side.

Feeling sick, I stood up. "So, Anna lost Wendy because she wanted revenge for what you did to her. I'm not excusing what she did, but you are just as guilty. You admitted yourself that you created her."

He nodded with a shrug. "Yes, I did. That's why I don't want Tinker to get too close to anyone else. She's lost too much."

"She lost Lili because of you. She lost Wendy because of you. If you are so worried about her, stop taking the only comfort she has on this island. She has a right to be here as much as the rest of us and she deserves to feel wanted." I pulled my hood over my hair. "She deserves to know that she isn't alone." I began walking away. "And the next time I find you in my bathroom when I'm at my most vulnerable, you will never get to enjoy being *inside* my sister again." I made it back to my cabin and locked the door.

The wind outside picked up, whistling a tune for the camp to fall asleep to. If it were that easy, I'd be asleep now. I'd be lost in a wonderful dream where nothing could harm me, and everything went right.

But the cold made it impossible to fall asleep. *Pan* made it impossible to rest. Everything here kept me awake and eventually, it'd all catch up to me. I just hoped I could be the hero before that happened. I simply needed to get Jaren home and then maybe I could focus on rest.

As I stood at my window, a figure waited in the distance, watching. The black shadow amongst the white backdrop. When the wind picked up, he disappeared. I took a step back and caught the reflection of that same silhouette in my window, behind me. I spun around with my dagger in hand, but fingers wrapped around my throat and squeezed the breath from my lungs. My weapon did nothing—for he was made of billowing smoke.

Tightening its fingers, it said, "Be careful what you wish for, Celia. Every wish is twisted here in Neverland."

09: Breathtaking

I paced back and forth in my cabin, replaying the incident—what the shadow said. He warned me, threatened me, as if he knew my plans. Nobody knew my plans except Anna and Kace. I'd almost shit myself. I didn't know what to do about the shadow.

I stopped at the sound of a knock on my door. I turned towards it and swallowed my fear. "Come in," I told whoever was on the other side.

Kace walked in and knew right away that something was off. "What happened?"

"The shadow came back. It threatened me this time and I couldn't fight back. I was helpless, and I think Pan's trying to warn me. I almost died!" I yelled.

He gave me a pitiful look that I didn't want. "I'm sorry."

"Yeah, it's easy to be sorry when you're protected by him." I scoffed, before mumbling an apology. "Lili's gone, and I'm afraid that we can't get her back. If we do, how is she going to even begin to understand what she's done? I haven't even scratched the surface about the aftermath of it all. Be careful of what you wish for." I glanced at the bathroom door.

He didn't say anything. The room filled with a deadly stifle that pierced through what hope we had left. I could try to save Neverland, but I had to face the reality that if I did, sacrifices would have to be made.

As I glanced back at Kace, he'd already gone. The ache in my chest was a strong indicator that I'd wanted his shoulder. I sat on my bed, resting my head in my hands.

The tears started flowing on their own, soon too uncontrollable. The sobs got louder and my whole body swelled with the sorrow that I couldn't hide in a bottle. I fell onto my bed and let them relinquish my dreams until the darkness took me away. I *wished* to be someone else.

THE LIGHT SLIPPED THROUGH my eyelids as I opened them. As soon as I saw a figure sitting on the floor beside my bed, I shot up with a gasp and scooted back. When his gaze met mine, his brown eyes washed me in relief. It was just Kace.

He cleared his throat immediately. "Hey, I didn't mean to scare you. I'm not really sure what cheers you up, but these might help?" He lifted the flowers from the floor. He handed them to me.

I leaned forward and grabbed them by the stems, holding them together like a bouquet. I memorized every shade of pink from the baby to the bright. "Why did you run?"

"What do you mean?"

"Why did you leave when I was confiding in you?" I looked into his eyes.

He scratched the back of his neck. "I didn't mean to leave you alone. I was trying to find a way to cheer you up. I'm not very good at this thing. It's been a long time since I've dealt with girls in this situation." Guilt settled in his face, his gaze never fully locking on mine.

"The gesture is thoughtful; I'll give you that. But for future reference, people don't like to be left alone when they're going through something. It's better to comfort someone and be there for them. Even if you're not good at it, it's the thought that counts."

He nodded and sat down on my bed. "Okay. I will remember that." He finally *looked* at me.

I put the flowers on the other side, the opposite side of which Kace was sitting on. I leaned my head against the wooden wall. "I just don't understand how this happened I want to but I can't. This island will be the death of me."

Kace sat back with me. "I won't let that happen."

"I'm losing my own family. Pan's shadow is threatening me. What else do I have to live for?"

He frowned. "Other people who do care about you."

"Like who? Nobody really cares. That's just a false hope we give ourselves." My eyes fluttered shut for a moment. "I guess I was so used to being liked by everyone but now I can't handle not being liked at all. I know I'm being a big baby about it, but the people I love most don't love me back."

"No, you're not being a baby. I'm still human and one thing we all share is love. We want to be loved. It's natural." As I peered at him, he shrugged and turned his head my way.

I studied the details of his face, such as his full lashes and dark brows. The curls that sprung from his head like they had somewhere else to be. His sharp jawline. "I guess you're right. I just..." I couldn't finish my sentence. Goosebumps covered my arms. "Lili always felt like this. She was never actually accepted by anybody here. And...I was never there for her. She felt so alone and it's no wonder she's become a killer. She didn't have anyone to love her except for Pan. People do crazy things for love. Humans need it to survive." I gazed up at the ceiling.

Silence ensued.

She did what she needed to survive. It wasn't the best choice, but it was *a* choice. If we could get her and Pan both back to normal, they could keep each other stable. I'd promise to be a better sister. I'd never brush her off again.

I dropped my head a bit. "I can't give up on her. She needs me. She needs true love, from me and everyone else. She at least deserves that even if she's done wrong. Without it, she'll get worse. She's done awful things but she's still my sister. She deserves a second chance."

"Of course she does." Kace smiled a bit. "Just like Pan does. He was just a boy who wanted to be remembered, but he went about it the wrong way."

We both understood them—Pan and Lili. They were just kids who didn't know how to deal with being unwanted. They only had each other. We'd prove to them that they were worth more to us. Even if we had been so careless for so long.

I was brought out of my thoughts when something—no, someone—pressed their lips to mine. As hard as I tried to remember what we had just been talking about, I couldn't.

I couldn't think straight.

I started to kiss him back, afraid that if I stopped now, we'd make the mistake of going our separate ways. The kiss was warm and inviting, unlike the rest of this island. He reminded me that even through all this destruction, I wasn't alone. He'd always have my back.

His kiss was firm. Driving for forgiveness. And he received every ounce, too, as I melded to him. My fingers itched to tangle themselves in his hair, but I forced them under my thighs.

But his hand slid under my jaw and urged for more. Not the kind where I'd be reluctant to give. Our clothes clung to our bodies, and rightfully so. His teeth grazed my bottom lip, and he muttered his sorry.

When we both pulled away, I took a minute to steady my breathing.

Then I asked, "What was that for?"

Kace choked on his words. "I... I don't know why I did that. I just kept thinking '*wow, she looks so cute and I want to kiss her*,' and then I did."

I didn't know what else to say. I enjoyed kissing Kace. I *really* enjoyed kissing Kace. And based upon the length, he must have liked it, too. Was I supposed to just ask him what he thought?

"You okay?" he asked me.

"I don't understand kissing or feelings or any of that stuff—not with you anyway." I nodded a bit, still reeling from the dizzy spell.

He chuckled. "Nobody here does."

"What was that? I mean, did you like it?" Why did I ask that?

Kace gave me a funny look. "Yes, why?"

My cheeks heated up. "I've never kissed a boy before."

"Well, now you know I liked it." He grinned.

I wondered what it meant for us. I was too shy to ask that question though. "We should probably do something else to keep warm." I was thankful when Kace didn't suggest sex as a joke. Pan was that type of guy, but Kace was not.

Kace instead suggested, "Let's go figure out how to get your brother home."

I had almost forgotten about Jaren. "How much longer does he have?"

"Nobody knows. It's impossible to tell."

"Not impossible if you keep track of how many days go by. The fact that Neverland has night and day is the only real way to tell time here." I wished I had thought of it before. I would know how long Jaren had, but there was no way of going back in time to track the days all over again.

We both got up from the bed and left my cabin. I went to Jaren's and knocked. I didn't hear anything, and I thought maybe he was busy sleeping, or mad at me. "Jaren, listen to me. I know that you don't want to leave without us, but you have to. It's the only way to live." I got quiet as a response.

When he didn't answer after another few minutes, I walked inside, stopping dead in my tracks. "Jaren. No!" I ran over to him, grabbing his hands. They were so wrinkled and fragile now. "You're going to be okay. I promise." But I *couldn't* promise that.

My rims began to water, tears falling shortly after. "Help! Someone help me!" I screamed to the rest of the camp.

Jaren tried to speak but it barely came out. His whole body displayed a lifetime of regrets. Wrinkles covered every crevice, and he'd aged like a dried plum. His hair had fallen out. He had nothing left on his head but skin.

Kace came running in and skidded to a halt. "Lia," he breathed so quietly that I could barely hear his voice.

I couldn't make the huge ache in my chest go away. Not this time. My brother was wasting away before my very eyes. "Do something! Please, get Lili! Get Pan! I can't let him die." I shook my head profusely, refusing to accept his fate. I sniffled, cradling his cold hands in my own. "Jaren, I promise we will save you. Please, trust me."

Kace brought back Pan and Lili, but they didn't seem bothered like I was. "Please, save him. Send him home. I just want him to live. I want to have hope that his life gets better than this."

Pan was about to say something, but my sister had cut him off. "Yeah, we can't do that. Rules are rules. If we make an exception for him, we have to bend the rules for everyone. You can't enforce rules if you don't abide by them."

I swallowed and got up, clenching my fists. "How can you stand there and watch our brother die? He never did anything to you!"

"Exactly. He never did *anything*. He stood by as our parents abused us. He was never a good big brother." Lili shrugged it off like no big deal.

Tears continued to cloud my vision and soak my cheeks. "What if that was me?" I pointed to our brother.

She fixed her gaze on him. Something in her eye flashed but it had disappeared before I could pick up on it. "I'm not picking favorites, and my family doesn't get a free pass."

"That is such a piss poor excuse. You're just a coward. You can't stand up to Pan to tell him to save our brother, so you play it off as something else. You're pathetic, Liliana Stone. You are a *disgrace* to our family."

"Don't talk to me that way."

"Jaren was the one who fought hard with me when you went missing!"

I closed the gap between us. "Our parents told police you ran away, but he made sure people searched for you. He was my ally—*our* ally. He's here for both of us." Bones rattled from within. I wanted to slap the sense into her, but I didn't move.

"I never would have left if he'd cared about me in the first place. Remorse doesn't work on me," she whispered, threats lacing her words.

I turned away from her and sat by Jaren, promising to stay with him until he passed.

I held his hands once more and tried not to think about it. "I love you. I know we didn't talk very much but I love you regardless. You're my older brother, and it means so much that you came here looking for us. I believe everyone can change and this was yours. You don't have to worry. I forgive you. You can go in peace." I kissed his drooping cheek.

He barely squeezed my fingers.

We sat there for what felt like hours. I listened as his breathing faded and his soul exited his body. I could barely process that my brother was gone. Just yesterday he was a young man who'd barely hit twenty. Now, he'd been skin and bones with his spirit long gone from this plane.

Cries seeped endlessly. Arms wrapped around me. Kace was comforting me like I had told him earlier.

Nothing could erase this pain. I'd lost nearly everyone by now and every day that went by, more hopeless continued to coat the tragedy that I called my life. Every moment I stayed on this damned island, I was one step closer to losing myself.

10: Grief

With Jaren gone, I had no reason to get out of bed. I spent all my time wrapped in blankets, forgetting the world needed me. Did it? Pan and Lili seemed to be doing just fine as monsters. They weren't even fazed about Jaren's death.

Kace tried to visit but every time he walked through my door, I sent him away. It was easy to stay here. The hard part was getting up when I had to use the bathroom.

Every muscle in my body ached. Every bone weighed a ton, but my skull weighed nearly three. A lump sat in my throat from all the endless sobbing I'd done before I was left dehydrated. Why was there a point to any of this?

Kace entered with a glass of water. "You should drink this."

"Please leave," I whispered in a hoarse voice.

Unlike the other times, he didn't. He approached my bed and sat near my stomach. "I can't leave you. You told me to comfort you and right now, you need it now more than ever. I've never had a sibling so I don't understand this pain, but I'm here for you. Your world is crumbling, cariño."

I squeezed the pillow in my arms. "I wish to be left alone."

"And I left you alone for at least a week. It didn't do you any good because you're in the same spot I left you. Now I'm going to stay. Jaren wouldn't want you to give up on your sister."

"What the hell do you know about Jaren and what he wanted?" I sat up in a hurry to look him dead in the eye. "You don't know shit." I choked on another sob, but it didn't make it out this time.

He brought the cup of water to my lips, and I drank some. "I didn't know Jaren very well. You're right. But I was there when he arrived. I was there when he died. I learned from those encounters that he cared about you two. He wouldn't want you to give up on Lili for her sake."

I covered my mouth and hurried off the bed, but I tripped over the blankets. I puked up the little food I had in me all over the floor. After sitting back with my legs tucked under me, I wiped my mouth. The only image left of my brother was his decomposed body. I couldn't stomach it.

Kace came over and squatted beside me. "I'll get something to clean this up." He left the cabin, returning with some rags. He cleaned up my puke and helped me to the bathroom, in case I needed to throw up some more.

"Where are you from?" I asked in a quiet voice as I sat on the toilet with the lid down.

He grabbed another rag and got it wet before pressing it to my face. It was warm, and I enjoyed that. "Segovia."

"Where is that?"

"Spain."

I tilted my head just a little as I looked at his brown eyes. It did explain his mesmerizing features. No American boy ever looked this attractive.

He cleared his throat. "It was a long time ago."

"How long?"

"Do you really want to know?"

"Are you older than Anna?" Then I remembered she went by a different name to everyone else. "Tinker Bell. I know that she was born in 1922."

He shook his head. "Try twenty years younger."

I attempted to do the math in my mess of a brain, but I forgot what numbers were.

"1943." He smiled a bit. "I haven't spoken Spanish in quite a long time. I've been around Pan for so long that I've been practicing perfecting my English. Nobody here speaks Spanish." Sorrow laced his smile. "But Hook did."

I knew she had to have come from somewhere, but I never knew where. "Was she also from Spain?"

"El Salvador. Spanish differs based on countries, but we understood each other for the most part. As awful as she was, I enjoyed being able to talk to her in my native language."

"El Salvador..." I furrowed my brows. "That's down south, right? Central America."

"Correct. Lili never would have known her geography."

Shifting on the toilet, I balled my fists. "I'm not Lili."

Kace's eyes widened a bit as he reached for my hands. "Oh, no, I apologize for the way it came out, but I meant that when I was still friends with Lili, she was the worst when it came to history and geography. You know your stuff. You're smart. It's a wonderful little surprise. Where is Spain?" He sent another smile my way.

"It's in Europe." I wrapped my arm around my stomach. "It's beside...what is it beside?" I wrinkled my forehead. "Ah, yes! It's by Portugal and below France. I remember because Spain is like another one of those romantic countries. It makes sense for it to be near France and Italy."

His sugary-sweet laugh tickled my ears. "Romantic? We've established that I'm hardly romantic."

I shrugged. "Compared to who? Pan? Pan kissed me when I arrived just to make my sister mad. That's hardly romantic. You kissed me for a good reason, and not a selfish one." Part of me was angry with myself for bringing up the kiss. Now was the worst time, and I didn't want to talk about it. It was done.

His demeanor shifted as he faced the sink and set the rag down.

"Pan kissed you?" The kiss from Pan had been quick, and meaningless. Therefore, I never considered it to be my first kiss. I'd rather picture Kace as my first. He more than earned the title.

Nobody but Lili had known, and I never wanted anyone else to know. It was humiliating to be the butt of Pan's joke.

He shook his head. "You think I'm romantic then?" He changed the subject but based on the color draining from his knuckles, he couldn't just let this go. My only options were to talk about the kiss with Pan, or how romantic Kace was. Both were less than pleasant.

"Romantic in your own way, sure. How many guys will clean up my vomit? You've stayed by my side. You've helped me train. You come back even when I push you away. You don't do these things with bad intentions or selfish desires. You do them because..."

"Because why?"

"Because you care about me," I whispered. My eyelids grew heavy, and I let them close. The first thing that popped into my head was our shared kiss. It hadn't been the type most people asked for—which was one filled with passion and desperation. They craved the honeymoon phase. But no. It was *our* kiss. It was perfect the way it played out, one that sent my mind spinning. It'd been slow yet inviting. It was exactly the kind of moment I wanted my whole life.

Arms looped around me and helped me up. I opened my eyes as Kace took me back to bed. "You're tired. Get rest tonight, but tomorrow, we are going to be training. No excuses. No arguing." He tucked me into my blankets.

I grabbed onto his cloak as he turned away. He paused, waiting for me to speak. I wanted to ask him to stay. I begged myself to say something. But my tongue had become too used to the quiet. Dry. Swollen in my throat. Nothing came out. Instead, I released his cloak, and he left my cabin.

Despite what he said about me being tired, I wasn't. I was wide awake now that my stomach was empty and begging for food. Yet, I would give it none.

Before I could focus on the ceiling and roll back into a hole of pity, someone walked in. I thought maybe Kace had come back to stay with me like I wanted, but I was wrong. It was the one person I didn't want to see right now.

"Get out," I said.

Lili shook her head. "You can't ignore me forever. I do rule this island."

"I don't care what you want right now. I don't care about you at all. You let our brother die. I want nothing to do with you."

She approached my bed, attempting to intimidate me. In this state, nothing scared me. Even Pan's shadow couldn't scare me. "That's not your choice."

"It is *my* choice. It's my choice because I'm still alive and you can't take that away from me. Don't be like Jacob and force me to do what you want." As soon as the words left my tongue, I regretted them. I hadn't intended to compare her to Jacob. It was a bad move.

I expected her to threaten me. Maybe she'd hit me and call it even. I wouldn't blame her. However, she stayed silent. Without another word, Lili left me to mull over my thoughts.

I knew I'd hurt her deeply this time. If she had just reacted, I would be out of timeout by tomorrow. That wasn't so much the case with silence. This was a pain that would fester inside her. She would bottle it in and constantly think about it.

There was no energy left in me to run after her. For a split second, I didn't feel guilty. She had killed our brother, and many others. She deserved to wallow in that shame for some time, even if I compared her to Jacob.

But no. She wasn't Jacob. She was still my sister. She'd been a victim of her surroundings for so long that eventually it took hold of her, and now she was doing what she knew best—being the villain. She'd been raised to be one, so how could she be anything but?

Kace said so himself. Jaren would want me to help Lili. That was his goal, to get us home safe and sound. If I was going to do right by him, I needed to get out of bed and continue to my original plan. As his last dying wish, I would save Lili no matter how hard it got, or what the cost might have been. She was raised to be a monster, but she deserved her happy ending. She deserved her second chance.

Sitting upright, my eyes closed. "I'm going to save her for us both, Jaren. I promise."

I threw my blankets off and left the cabin. The icy wind threatened my warmth, but I only sped up my pace until I arrived at the training area.

With my dagger in hand, I practiced moves that would help me win any battle against my sister. She was my twin, and I could easily picture her fighting tactics to make my own better.

I had also worked on my archery skills in case I ever needed it.

The temperature was no match for my determination on a night like tonight. No, not with a million thoughts running through my head, keeping me active all night long. I may have even been sweating.

I'd be prepared and better than ever when I trained with Kace. He'd be shocked by my improvement. I wanted to show him that as grateful as I was for his help, I wasn't only good when he was around. No, I was my own person and I had to be able to stand on my own two feet in Neverland. I came here for a better life. I came here to better *myself*.

The Celia Stone that I knew a year ago would cry over the smallest things. She was weak—unable to defend herself. That wasn't who I wanted to die as. I wanted people to remember me as a fighter and someone who stood her ground. I wanted them to see me as the girl who stood up for what she believed in. I was a strong woman, and I refused to be seen as anything but. Everyone I loved was hurting and I was the one person who was able to help them. I could never live with myself if I didn't do what I was supposed to. I'd never be able to die in peace.

11: Not a Monster

As I spun around, the blade sliced the trunk of the tree. I paused, breathing heavily as I glanced at Kace. "How was that?"

"Better. I see you've been practicing on your own." His smile lit up the whole area.

With a nod, I slipped my dagger back into the sheath. "If I don't, nothing will ever get better." I wanted to see the light at the end, as hard as it was right now.

Kace lessened the size of the gap between us. "Have you been doing okay? You vomited last time I saw you, and you're dealing with a lot right now."

Was I doing okay? That was a question left unanswered. Maybe I was for someone who just experienced what I did, or maybe I was trying to push away the pain. I couldn't be too sure of what was happening in my head. I couldn't pinpoint my emotions

"Lia."

I forced a smile. "I'm doing fine. Let's get back to training."

Kace cleared his throat. "Maybe later. I have to talk to Pan right now, before he's too busy."

"Right," I said with a sweep of my arm, allowing him to go first.

The longer we avoided talking about the kiss, the more I wanted to talk about it. I still couldn't manage to get the questions out. Whatever the kiss meant for us would be a secret for a while.

Kace left the training area and I stayed to practice more of my skills. I had to do anything that kept my mind off Jaren's death. I had to stay sane.

When I finished my training session, I headed to camp. However, I didn't stop there. I kept walking past it and eventually ended up at the beach. I walked along the water not getting too close. If I got wet, I'd freeze to death. I walked along until the edge of the sand turned into a cliff, and I knew I was passing Cannibal Cove. I followed along the edge of the cliff and stopped when a large snake-like creature emerged from the sea. What was that?

I took a step to get a closer look, but my foot caught the edge, and I lost my balance. I gasped as I fell over the edge. It hadn't been too high up, but when I hit the water, it was painful, nonetheless.

I fell back first, limbs furling upward toward the surface. When I straightened my legs out and swam to the top, I gasped for air.

A monstrous sound echoed, and I whipped around in the waves, attempting to see the creature. Was this monster what I thought it was?

When a large head with two black eyes rose above the surface, ripples moved towards me, and I struggled to stay afloat while avoiding the water that crashed against the cliffside.

I couldn't get any screams out. I swam towards Cannibal Cove as fast as I could, but this monster was faster. It disappeared under the water, and I stopped, spinning in every direction.

A scream left my throat as the creature lifted its head from under me. I grabbed onto the sides as best I could to keep from falling off it. It halted, and as soon as I looked to my left, the screams stopped. I glanced down at the eyes of the monster, swallowing. I climbed off its head and onto the edge of the cliff, scooting back in the grass. "You...saved me."

The creature made a noise before diving back under the ocean—disappearing.

I stood, wincing at the pain in my ass. I glanced back at the vast deep, searching for him one more time, but he was gone. I headed back to the camp and as I arrived, I avoided eye contact with the lost boys.

Rushing to the fire, I threw my entire body inches from it as shivers slithered down my spine, teeth chattering. I let out a sigh of relief.

"What happened to you?" Pan asked from behind me.

It was humiliating to tell him I fell off a cliff, but he'd find out eventually. He always did.

"I fell into the ocean. This...creature saved me. It was like the Loch Ness monster." I shook my head, teeth chattering.

"What is that?"

I looked back at him. "It's like a...water dinosaur. It has a long neck. It's a legend."

Pan sat beside me. "You claim the sea serpent saved you."

Scowling, I said, "I don't claim anything. He did save me. I fell in and he lifted me back up to the cliff. How else did I survive?" I narrowed my eyes. "Unless you want to admit I saved myself from being eaten by a monster."

He rubbed the bridge of his nose. "He's dangerous. He doesn't save people, Lia."

"So, what's your version of my story?"

He sat back. "Simple. You fell in the water when the tide was high, but you want a cool story to go with it."

"You have magic and yet you find it hard to believe a creature saved my life." I moved closer. "Get inside my head. However you do that, look at my memories and you will see it."

Pan's laugh coaxed my fears to rest. "You really think I can do that?"

"You can't?"

He shook his head. "No. Even if I could, I wouldn't. I don't wish to see whatever you and Kace do when nobody's around."

I made a face. "You are disgusting. I know it's hard to believe not everyone is giving sexual favors, but that's not us. Kace and I are friends."

Friends. I hated that word to describe us. Why couldn't I just ask him about our kiss?

Pan laughed again, this time more rudely. "I doubt that, but whatever helps you sleep at night."

"I have no reason to lie. It's not like Kace is a bad guy, or that I'm secretly crushing on you. I'm not. If Kace and I were together, I'd want you to know to piss you off. We aren't. We're friends and it's nice to have someone on this island who doesn't look at me as a sex object." I shrugged. At least I hoped Kace didn't look at me that way.

He got up. "Whichever story you want to believe, fine, but don't go telling my lost boys about your adventures. I don't need them jumping off cliffs, too."

I faced Pan. "Do you need my proof? I can get your proof. You asked *me* what happened. I didn't tell you without you asking first, so I have no reason to tell tall tales."

He scoffed with a roll of his dark eyes. "No."

"Have you ever interacted with him?" I folded my arms across my chest.

He shrugged. "Not particularly."

"Thought so. You haven't met him, so you don't get to decide if he's good or bad. I have, and he saved my life. Whatever made-up story you have of him, it's a lie. He *is* friendly. He doesn't want to hurt people. Most of the time, creatures never do." I turned back to the campfire and left Pan to his own stories. He went to his cabin.

I was simply thankful I didn't have to go back into the ocean to prove him wrong.

After I warmed myself up with the flames, I headed to my cabin and grabbed leggings from the drawer. I tied them around my butt to lessen the blow when I went to sit down. I needed padding, and I was certain I had bruised it from the impact.

As I sat, I winced and pulled my hood over my head. I wrapped the blankets around my shoulders and pulled them tight. I despised winter.

Who wanted to live in places where winter made up eighty percent of the calendar year?

I didn't even enjoy when winter made up twenty-five percent.

I lay back on the bed, relaxed. I was in the perfect position to fall asleep, and yet my eyelids didn't grow heavy. After the worst scare of my life, I had too much energy. Too much adrenaline. Kace had plans of his own, so I wasn't about to bother him. Pan refused to believe that a creature could be harmless. Lili was probably too busy comparing herself to Jacob after what I said, and I didn't blame her. What I said to her was wrong, and yet I couldn't seem to leave my comfy bed to apologize.

I had nobody else, aside from Anna. But the reality was that I wasn't leaving this room. Grief weighed me down just enough that when I lay in my own bed, I couldn't gather strength to get back up. I became Velcro.

There wasn't anything to do but replay how things would have gone differently. Maybe I could have forced Lili home with Jaren, and they'd both be okay.

Instead, I was stuck as my sister killed innocent kids, and my brother was no longer alive to help. After all these events, I wondered how Asa felt about it. Could he possibly feel guilt, or sadness? No. He was probably in his own cabin just staring at the ceiling. He was about to fall asleep and dream of good things while I was glued to my nightmares.

It was impossible to tell how long the nightmares would last. They were always the same. They involved Jaren and I, and in these terrors, I would be about ready to hug Jaren until I realized he wasn't there. He was never going to be there again. It reminded me that every time I closed my eyes, he was permanently gone no matter which world I lived in.

It was horrifying to think they'd never go away. There was a piece of me that knew he was never coming back and I had to be the one who lived with that. I now carried the burden that Jaren and Lili refused to.

The first thought that popped into my head each morning I woke up was the fact that my brother was gone. Vanished. He was nothing.

Nonexistent.

It let me hollowed out. It was hard to motivate myself to leave the bed once I was in it. I didn't want to move. I wished to just stay here forever, and never see someone die again. I was afraid of losing everyone else. What if Kace or Lili died? I'd have no reason to keep going. I'd rather end my own life than bear to live without them. I needed to hold onto hope, but it was difficult to grasp the concept when I didn't see a light at the end of Jaren's death. There was nothing good that could come out of such a tragedy.

How did anyone cope with loss? How did they find the motivation to move forward? I had never lost anyone before him and this pain weighed heavy on my chest. It sent flashes of awful images. It reminded me of how puny I was in this world, and just how effortlessly I could be taken out of it.

I could have died today. The sea serpent could have killed me, but it didn't. There had to be some sort of reason as to why I was spared, but what could it be?

Then I had to ask myself—was I okay with dying? Would I accept the inevitable or would I fight for my life? Maybe I couldn't accept my fate. I wanted to change it. I wanted things to be different for me. With a tragic beginning defining my life, I strived for a happy ending to leave in my memory.

Chapter 13
12: Confessions

A day once existed—one where Lili and Pan used to have fun at the beach. It had proven to be such a beautiful place filled with memories and hope. It blossomed from redemption.

Now, the shore was empty, hopeless, and rotting away as memories sunk down to the abyss. Nothing was left but the thought of what could have been.

"I thought I might find you here," Anna said as she came down the sand.

I glanced back at her, arms around my knees. "What's up?"

She dropped beside me. "I heard about what happened. I'm so sorry."

My tears had all been used at this point so no more left me. Every day that I lived, I was reminded that my brother no longer did.

Anna buried her hands in the sand and looked out upon the water. "I know it's hard, losing someone you love. But it's harder when you don't have anyone who is there to comfort you. It's difficult to get by when you think you're alone and that you can't make it through."

I rested my cheek on my knee. "You know what I regret the most? All those days I spent mad at him for not being a better brother. I never once tried to bond with him like I've done with Lili. I gave up on him. I can never go back and fix my mistake. I forever have to live with this shame."

Her hand landed on my back. She rubbed in small motions to tell me I wasn't the only one who felt this way. Anna hadn't tried hard enough to be with Wendy when Pan stepped in, and now Wendy was dead.

She let out a musical sigh. "It feels awful. I know that much. However, you can't spend your whole life blaming yourself. If you blame yourself, you'll never be able to get through the grief. You must accept what you cannot control. You can't be expected to be the perfect person for everyone, and there's no shame in being a human. You are just a human, Lia, and that's okay."

I punched the sand beside me. "That's what they all say."

"Because it's true."

Closing my eyes, I took a deep breath. I was riddled with guilt because of how weak I was. I wanted to be a better person, be a stronger woman, and yet I was still as vulnerable as I'd always been. I didn't want to move an inch, and maybe I never would.

Anna cleared her throat and pulled her hand away. "A little birdy told me you kissed Kace."

"Who?"

"A birdie." She laughed a bit. "An actual bird. Crow, more precisely. I can communicate with animals, having green magic and all. It's like earth magic. Anyway, do you want to talk about it?"

I shrugged. I knew deep down I wanted to, and with Anna, maybe I'd feel comfortable. I missed having another girl to talk to about this stuff.

"Or we can watch the waves."

"No, I just..." I shook my head, eyes falling to the seafoam. "Kace kissed me, and I kissed back. But that was like two weeks ago. We haven't talked about it since then."

"Have you seen him?"

"Of course I've seen him. He's been helping me train and he kept visiting after Jaren died. He does that. He makes sure I'm taken care of, even if we are just friends. He probably thinks he's in the friendzone."

A small smile crept up her face. "That's special. He cares about you."

"But that's the thing... I want to talk about the kiss so badly and ask him what it means but I can't get myself to do it. I see his face and I want to tell him that I want to kiss him again. But I'm always so scared. I don't have the kind of guts needed to talk about that kind of stuff." I focused on each grain of sand in front of my boots.

"That kind of stuff is scary, yes, but what's the worst that can happen? He says that the kiss was to see what it felt like and he realized he didn't like you that way? It would hurt to hear, but at least you would know the truth. You could never blame yourself and ask what if."

I touched my thumb to my bottom lip. "That's the problem, though. If he says that he doesn't have feelings for me, I don't think I can just be friends anymore. It would be difficult."

"And it's not difficult right now?" She nudged me. "Life is full of these things, but you have to be willing to take the risk. Trust me. You'd never get to be content if you didn't try." She pursed her lips for a moment. "It was a longshot when I asked Wendy if I could kiss her. She hesitated at first, but eventually she let me and what happened then? We had a chance to be together and experience love. Life is about taking risks that could lead to your happiness."

I laughed, waving my hand up. "So, I should ask Kace if I can kiss him again?"

"You should ask him what it meant to him, then tell him what it means to you." Anna nodded, crossing her arms.

I chewed my lower lip. How'd he react? If I was going to make such a big leap, I had to prepare myself for the worst now, so I didn't come apart at the seams. He could say he didn't have romantic feelings for me, and I would have to accept that. Then, I'd have to accept that we couldn't work together because it would be too difficult for me to see his eyes and be reminded of my unrequited love. Because if I never told him how I felt, I would have to see him every day and suffer due to my own doubts. I couldn't be my own downfall. This was something I *could* control.

"Okay, I'll tell him." Chills slid down my body. "I'll tell Kace how I feel." I furrowed my brows. "How do I feel? I mean, I can't stop thinking about the way he kissed me and now I get these images of us cuddling to keep warm, and there's laughter." The pit of my stomach dropped. "Anna, I'm scared."

"Don't you worry. That's normal. You like Kace more than a friend. There's no shame in that. He may feel the same way and if you get the guts to ask him, you could finally be together. Picture how happy you would get to be. You'd know that someone cares about you, a lot more than you originally thought."

We'd be together, as if we'd been trying this the whole time. That was silly. I knew that I liked him, but I also didn't want to lose the friendship we had. It meant so much to me. If he felt the same, then just maybe I could have both.

However, if he didn't return my feelings, what did that mean for me? We'd go our separate ways and I'd have to fight this battle alone.

I prayed that Kace savored the kiss as much as I did.

I cleared my throat and looked at Anna. "Let's not talk about me for a while. What about you? How have you been?"

She folded her hands together in her lap. "I've been...okay. I'm coping."

"Do you want to talk about it?"

She shook her head. "No, don't let me burden you with my problems. You have enough of your own."

I frowned. "Anna, that's not how this works. I don't want to unload on you and then be told you'd be a burden to me. We're friends now." Friends—what a strange word.

With a sigh, Anna did as I asked. She unloaded her problems so she no longer had to carry them alone. Like me, she'd been grieving her loss and she struggled every morning. She rarely ate and she'd been losing weight because of it.

Based on the odor coming from her, she'd also lost the will to bathe. But even in this weather, did anyone want to wash themselves in the sea salt? All she wanted to do was sulk around. She had nobody to remind her she'd get through this. She was the only one in her life who could get her out of bed.

A part of me felt better now that she trusted me enough to confide in me. I wanted to be there for her as much as she was for me.

The rest of our day on the beach was spent in small laughter about the stupid things of the world.

The wind picked up and she went back home while I went back to mine. I stopped before I closed the door, peeking over at Kace's cabin. His door was closed, and curtains were drawn. I wanted to ask him now, but I just couldn't muster up the courage. Not tonight. All I wanted was to curl up in my blankets.

I shut my door and sat down on my bed, blowing hot air into my hands as I rubbed them together.

I hated not being able to get over the grief to fix my sister already. I needed energy. I needed to forget about the trauma and move on. I wanted it all to be over with. My brain, as hard as it worked, couldn't just pretend we hadn't watched our own brother wither away in our arms.

What worried me the most was how Lili would handle the news when this was all over. Once she was back to normal, would she be sad at all for what she did? Maybe. Maybe not. I couldn't tell how much remorse she had in her body.

She confessed to killing Hook when Wendy and I were hanging out with her. She said she felt guilty for it, but I'd seen the lack of shame plastered to her face, and I wondered if she had any remorse in her at all. I prayed she did. It wasn't like I wanted the guilt to overcome her, but I wanted her to be more human than monster and the only way to make sure she was, was to feel the shame of taking innocent lives.

Had she been born this way or was this the way she was raised? They said those who didn't feel remorse were born that way, but I didn't want to believe anyone was beyond redemption. Especially my own sister. The human mind was a force to be reckoned with. It was complex in so many ways.

If it was just a result of how she was raised, we could reverse it. I could teach her how to feel remorse. Was that possible? Was teaching an emotion a thing?

However, if she had been born this way, I could never teach her anything. She would never feel guilty, but maybe it was possible to at least teach her that murder was wrong. There were many sociopaths in this world who lived very normal lives, and if they could do it, my sister could, too.

Was it possible for one twin to be born without emotions? No, it wasn't. Or maybe it was, but not for Lili.

I thought back to all the times I saw emotion in her eyes. She had experienced pain. She experienced joy. There was no way my sister lacked emotions and if that was true, I had hoped that remorse was buried somewhere in there and she was just hiding it to feel better. I would get Lili back to normal and we would be sisters again—real sisters. That was all I could ever ask for.

She tried so hard to push me away, but I never gave up on her. That wasn't in my nature. You didn't give up on those you loved, and Lili could rest assured, knowing that I would never let her slip through my fingers. I was her only hope of being whole again. Inside the monster she was, was a version of her that was begging for me to save her.

13: Pink Flowers

I WIPED THE BLOOD from my cheek before swiping my dagger off the ground. I tightened my fingers around the cold metal and straightened my back, eyeing him.

His worried expression was everything I needed. He feared me, enough to throw him off track.

I backed him up against the tree, pressing the blade against his neck. "Don't. Move."

Kace swallowed, the blade nicking his skin. "Don't do this, cariño. I didn't mean it."

As I tilted my head slightly, I narrowed my eyes. "Kace, I'm not going to kill you. I'm testing my skills." I pulled back, relief washing over him. I sighed. "I just need to train to distract myself from everything. It's been rough." I slipped my dagger back into my belt and hugged myself.

Kace peeled his backside from the trunk and stepped forward. "I wish there was something I could say to help."

My gaze landed on him and I placed my palm towards him, stopping him. "I'm trying to be polite but if you come any closer with your weapon, I will tear you apart."

He put his hands up in defense, taking a step back. "Point taken."

Rubbing my hands against my face, I let out a deep, shaky breath.

"How dangerous"—I paused—"to finally have something worth losing." I dropped my arms at my side.

Kace didn't say a word or move an inch, and respectfully so.

"I feel so betrayed. She did this to me. Lili did nothing while our brother died. She's an absolute demon forged by the fiery pits of hell. How can I save her after this? She's going to know what she's done." I admired the sparkling sheet of snow for daring to give us beauty when we needed compassion.

Kace said, "You lost your sister to darkness. You lost your brother to death. It's a tough thing to handle and nobody deserves that. I'll be here if you do decide you need me." His footsteps faded into the distance behind me.

I looked up at the gray sky, thankful the snow had given up on snowing us in. It had been snowing a bit less lately, which was a good thing since it wasn't melting anytime soon. I didn't want to get stuck inside my cabin.

When I made it back to my room, my bed mocked me. If I lay in it, I would most likely never leave. I knew what would happen if I allowed my energy to reside within depression. I couldn't do that to myself again.

I grabbed my dagger, studying every embossing and last detail. What did we even need to train for? What was that purpose? Who was after us? Nobody was against us besides Pan. He warned of pirates once, but how would they become a threat where their captain had given her life?

After leaving the desolate space, I decided to go on a walk.

One foot in front of the other. Cloak tightly tied. Hood up. Dagger at the ready.

Whispers drifted from the bushes. I ripped my dagger from my sheath and whipped around. This must've been why we had weapons.

Peering behind the bushes with my dagger against my side, my jaw dropped. "What the hell are you doing back here?"

Hunter and Trevor looked at me, shushing me. "Be quiet! We're trying to find her." Harsh.

"Who? Lili?" She was the only other *her* on this island. I crouched down a bit, keeping my voice low.

"No. A new girl arrived but she ran off. Lili and Pan sent us to find her," Trevor said.

With a nod, I straightened my cloak. "I'll help you find her. She'll trust me more. I am a girl after all. I've never hurt even a fly." I pushed myself to my feet and scanned the woods.

A new girl, huh? Interesting. I wondered what her name was.

My footsteps were quiet, carefully placed as I kept alert for any movement. I heard a scream, but I didn't recognize it. It was definitely female, but it wasn't the Demon Queen herself.

I took off running towards the sound, hoping that they hadn't found her. If Pan or Lili found her first, she'd become dead meat. Growls filled the air, mixing with the screams. I pushed harder until something came into my view. I immediately skidded, almost toppling over.

My eyes grew as the monster turned his attention to me. I backed away, dagger pointed. "Come after me. I'm the one who has a chance against you." Did I really believe that?

The furry giant took a step towards me. He bared his sharp teeth, threatening me. He growled and took a few more steps. I jumped back as someone came from my left, plunging their weapon into the beast.

Kace brushed himself off as it collapsed to the ground. Blood stained its white fur, coating it in a sickly goodbye. He faced me.

Before he could speak, I yelled, "So giant killer bunnies are a thing now?"

Kace pulled his dagger from the flesh and shoved the bloody weapon back into his belt. "Of course. Anything is possible on Neverland." He helped the other girl up on her feet. "I'm Kace and that is Lia. You might want to stick with us." He waved to her to follow him as we all began our walk back to camp.

"I didn't know there were blood-thirsty animals. How have I never come across a murderous bunny?" I looked at Kace while we kept walking.

He glanced at me. "Rabbit. Bunnies are babies and that was an adult."

"That's not my point," I said with sharpness.

A light chuckle climbed his throat. "You've never really gone far off the trail. The killer rabbits live in the forest, but they don't live near the trails we usually follow. And before you ask, no, we can't eat their meat. It's tainted. The rabbits have a mutation that happened as a result of Pan going dark long ago. He fuels this island and when he uses his magic for immorality, it has side effects. Therefore, we train. We must always be able to defend ourselves. Killer rabbits aren't the only beasts we have to steer clear of."

We stopped when we entered the camp. Pan and Lili spotted us with the new girl.

Kace put his hand up, his eyes meeting the new girl's. "There's nothing to fear. What's your name?"

She looked at us and hesitated before she spoke, "Faith."

"How old are you?" I asked.

"Sixteen."

Before we could ask her more questions, Lili pushed us both away from her. "Ah, so our new girl decides to run. Breaking the rules is a big offense. It deserves punishment. No food for twenty-four hours." She turned and walked away.

Faith gave both Kace and I fearful eyes.

Kace coughed to clear his throat. "You'll learn pretty quickly things are not what they seem here. Pan is our leader, but his morals may seem a little off balance. That girl was Lia's twin. She is Pan's partner. You've just received your first strike, so two more and Lili *will* kill you. I highly suggest you listen."

I smacked my hand against his chest. "Be nice about it."

"Was warning her not nice enough?" He shot me a look, both eyebrows raised.

"It's in the tone. Your tone sucks." I shook her hand. "Kace is a bit of an airhead at times. Rogue, really. It's good to have another girl here." I decided against informing her about anything that had happened already. I didn't want to scare her off. "We'll show you around."

She followed us to the training area. "This is where we train. What you just saw is *why* we train," Kace told her.

Faith slowly walked over to the bows and arrows. She picked up a bow and arrow, studying the weapon. Her brows knitted together, eyes mixed with bewilderment and curiosity.

Kace's eyes fell on me. "Has she ever seen an arrow before?" He redirected his attention and approached her. "Arrows exist because long ago, some guys realized they wanted to stab their enemies, but their enemies were too far away."

Faith didn't say a word as she pulled the arrow back against the bowstring. She let go, and it hit the center of the target. Kace and I dropped our jaws.

Her eyes pierced Kace. "I wanted to stab that target from here. I guess I mastered the purpose of the arrow." She walked over to the little knives and picked one up. She threw it at another target, hitting the bullseye again. "I should've mentioned I had practice back home. We all have that in common I assume?"

Kace displayed confusion. Her newfound confidence was a little surprising but not entirely out of line.

Faith stalked up to him. "I pretended to be the helpless girl because you can't trust everyone. I had to see what kind of people I was living with. If I ran away on purpose, that should tell you a little about me." Where had I seen someone like her before? Who did she remind me of?

Aha.

Lili. She was the *good* version of Lili.

Faith wiped her hands on her pants. "I will need a cabin, and some clothes would be nice."

Kace scoffed at her. "Good luck. Nobody else got that from Pan. You have to earn what you want."

"Then I will make him give it to me." She shrugged, unaware of what Pan was capable of. She exited the area before we could show her where else to go—and not to go.

Kace slowly made his way over to me. "She's a catch." A catch? What did that mean exactly?

"She's Lili 2.0. Fearless. A tad cocky. A show-off. That's both a good and a bad thing. Faith is going to be in danger when she meets Lili for more than a few seconds. It's like we try to get closer to saving Neverland and something else pops up. Everyone needs saving now." Including Kace and I. I needed to salvage our friendship.

Anna told me that I had to go for it, or I'd forever regret my own decisions. Now was a better time than ever. "Can I ask you something?"

"What do you want to ask me?"

"I need to ask you if we could be something more than friends."

He choked a bit. "Whoa, where did that come from?"

"We've kissed. You brought me flowers. I'm not the best with this stuff, but you've unlocked these feelings that I now can't seem to get rid of." My cheeks heated up. "I don't want anyone knowing about us."

"Why?"

"Because I'm sure Pan wouldn't like it." I gestured between us.

His gaze darted around the area, his voice low. "I see your point. Then we can keep it subtle. Life is short, even in Neverland. Why not take the opportunity now?"

I pushed some hair behind my ear, looking down at the snow at my feet. He had a point. I couldn't use the excuse that I didn't want to get attached and lose him since we were already best friends. I never realized the feelings I had for Kace until now because I was too focused on everything else all the time. They'd always been bubbles sitting on the top of a glass of milk. There, but you wouldn't notice unless you tried. What was there to argue against his offer?

Kace was pure, in the rawest form a man like him could come. No red flags waved in the distance or even in his presence. Kace was even becoming more defiant in his relationship with Pan.

How could I say no?

"No."

Kace was taken back by my response. I was, too. "Why not?"

I shivered and tugged the cloak against my arms. "How could we keep it a secret from Pan? He knows everything. He will kill one of us if he finds out, and he *will*."

An exhausted yet disappointed sigh escaped him. "I know it's scary, but we are getting closer to saving Neverland. Once we do, Pan won't care. He doesn't even like you. He likes Lili, and truly likes her. His feelings for her have been simmering for a long while, whether anyone here wants to acknowledge it or not. We deserve to make our own choices." He gestured between us. "We are technically adults. It wouldn't affect him. I just need to hear you say yes."

I studied Kace, taking a moment to observe the yearning in his hazelnut eyes. I noted the line at the side of his lips as his lips curved upward into a smile.

Then I said, "Yes."

14: Flying

Kace fixed my cloak, tying the knot tight so it wouldn't loosen. We both heard a persistent, authoritative knock.

I answered the door, surprised to find Pan. "Pan just knocked? Absurd." I formed an O shape with my mouth as a joke.

He noticed Kace behind me and crossed his arms. "What's going on here?"

"You stole my sister, so I stole your best friend. That's what's going on." I realized how that sounded. He'd stolen her and started dating her. He probably assumed I did the exact same to Kace, which wasn't entirely a lie. "Listen, Pan, I'm just making friends. Kace is nice enough to be my friend. He was teaching me how to tie a good knot, so my cloak won't slip off. In case you haven't noticed, it's freezing here. I gotta stay warm."

"There's a new girl. Make friends with her."

He wasn't wrong. I could make friends with the new girl. Why wasn't I befriending Faith? Oh, because she reminded me of Lili. I couldn't handle befriending a girl who was a better version of my sister. The guilt would be too much.

Pan tapped his foot impatiently.

"Turns out she doesn't like me. Girls fight, too." Girls did fight, but I was just being petty and not putting in an effort to befriend someone like

Faith.

Pan rolled his shoulders "I guess I'll have to note this to Lili. We can't have the new girl disliking our VIP member of Neverland, now can we?"

I choked on my laugh. "Excuse me?"

"I'm in love with your sister. That makes you a VIP member. You're welcome." He flashed me a sly smile and the smallest nod I'd ever witnessed.

I rolled my eyes in response. "This member doesn't care what you decide to call me." I pointed to myself using my thumb.

Pan got a bit too close for my liking. "I think you care, Lia. You and your sister might be so different, but I see you both the same." He disappeared before I could respond. What on earth did that mean?

Kace hurried over, furious as he searched for Pan. "You? No. I will not let that happen."

"What are you going on about?" I squinted my eyes.

"Pan is flirting with you. It's disgusting. Wait till Lili hears about this." He went for the door, but I grabbed his shoulder.

"No. No. Pan wouldn't flirt. He tried that at first but gave up. He loves my sister. They might be evil but it's genuine."

He snickered and crossed his arms. "I know Pan. He wouldn't tease just any girl about being a VIP member. He was flirting. I'm a guy and I can recognize another guy flirting with someone. It's a guy thing."

"It's not a guy thing. It's a people thing." I turned my nose up at him.

"Okay, fine. Pan is still people. I know how men flirt. That was flirting. He just flirts differently with you than he does Lili because you and Lili are *different* people and different things charm you," he argued.

I coughed. "I am not charmed by him. I never will be. Don't worry. I do not find Pan attractive. His personality is disgusting."

He kept his mouth shut this time.

"I don't believe Pan actually wants me. He just wants what he can't have. He wanted Lili, and now he has her. He doesn't have me, and he knows he can't have me. That is all."

He tried to hide the twitching on his lips, but he failed miserably. "If you say so."

I dropped the subject because it was no use trying to argue with him. Kace's mind was set in stone. If he believed Pan truly liked me, he believed such a thing, but I didn't. Pan was a complicated boy, but simply just like the rest. Lili would flip if she knew Pan's motives towards me. Lili went dark for him, and he was choosing to abandon her.

He could try all he pleased to win me to the dark side as well, but I was going to win this war. He didn't know the one thing that he needed to know. Lili was easy because Lili had troubles. Lili was attracted to bad boys. I was nothing like that, and Pan would fail for the first time in his insufferable existence.

We barely left my cabin when I heard yelling, "How could you? You liar!" Faith was kicking and screaming at me as the lost boys dragged her over to the cage.

Pan locked it. "You know the rules." He walked away. If looks could kill, Pan would've been dead from the intensity of hatred within her glare.

Kace shot me look that made nausea swirl inside me. "He is flirting with you. You lied about Faith not liking you and he's punishing her for hurting you."

I just brushed it off and faced the roaring campfire. Embers floated into the air until they faded into nothing.

"I need to go check something out. I'll be back." I left Kace, venturing into the woods. I stayed on the paths, saving my curiosity about the wild animals for later. I needed more information and skill before I did that again.

Now, I needed to clear my head, to figure everything out.

Lili burned with a darkness so profound that even Pan could never douse her flame. Pan supposedly wanted me for some unknown reason. My brother had wilted like a flower in my very embrace. Kace was my boyfriend or something. My cousin refused to talk to me.

How did I even begin to sort this out? Where did I start? It was so overwhelming at this point. I was Celia Stone. I was in no position to fix *anything*.

Footsteps sounded behind me and I grabbed my dagger from my belt. "Who's there?"

A figure emerged from the trees. "It's just me. Put that away."

I put my weapon back, taking my time. "What are you doing here? You hate my guts, remember?"

Asa looked at a tree. "Yeah, that's true. I was just out here to get away from the people. It turns out that we have a new lost girl who is already disobeying from what I hear."

"Yeah, so?"

He sighed, disappointed in my response. "Nevermind. We clearly don't like each other."

"Correction, you don't like me. I have no problem with you. I've even been trying to befriend you since you got here. Strange, huh?" I shrugged.

He chuckled. "Point taken." Did he just laugh at me?

I squinted a bit. "Why are you still here?"

"I'll be leaving then." Asa turned and began walking away. I wanted to say something—to stop him. I wanted to mend everything, but I couldn't be bothered. I had other priorities.

So, I let Asa disappear into the woods and leave me. I didn't have time to worry about his unresolved feelings. My focus was going to be on my sister and Pan. I had to save them. Everyone else was going to have to let me do that first because time was running out.

I walked on, ignoring the cold air that wanted to steal all my warmth. I looked at the ground and kept walking. This somehow soothed all my worries and all the bad thoughts. Everything was beginning to fade away like it was never a problem to begin with.

I closed my eyes for a few seconds, getting lost in my steps. My balance faltered and I immediately opened my eyes and screamed as my body leaned. The snow had been slick, and unforgiving. Relentless. Vengeful, even.

It allowed me to slip and plunge from the cliff. I didn't have a chance to grab anything to stop my fall. My scream ripped through the air as the water swallowed me, waves rushing and throwing me against the rocks. They didn't stop when I went under. They continued to toss me like a rag doll.

My body temperature dropped drastically, and the muscles in my body shut down. Darkness took over and the icy grip slipped away from me.

I became numb.

THE VOICES SURROUNDING ME had been muffled, barely audible. I could hardly hear my own heartbeat. It beat as fast as a snail could run.

The voices became clearer, and it was then I realized the voice had been right next to me the whole time. "She's going to be okay. She has to be okay." *Kace.* The worry in his words riddled me with guilt. I'd been so careless. I had never heard such intense terror lace his tongue.

I tended to forget that lost boys could fear anything at all.

"Kace, I need you to keep your mouth shut if you want me to fix her. I need to focus," Pan explained.

The world stilled. I thought I had stopped breathing due to the quietness of my own breath. It couldn't be true. I had to be breathing, or how else would I be able to hear their voices?

A tingling spread throughout my whole body that gradually grew into more. The weight had been lifted, and I felt free. I felt light, almost as if I was floating.

"Quickly, I need something to warm her up until we get back to camp," Pan commanded for everyone on the island to hear.

My wet body was wrapped up with a thick piece of cloth like a newborn baby. I was lifted from the ground as two arms held onto my frame on the journey back to the camp.

They set me down near the fire when we approached. The crackling sounds blended with the voices of boys who would never go through puberty and other boys who'd forever be stuck *in* puberty. My body warmed quicker this way and my heartbeat grew louder with every passing minute.

"What happened?" a female asked in desperation. The female voice could only be from my sister since the only other female was still locked in a cage.

Kace answered, "She's freezing. My best guess is she fell into the water."

"She's blue! Oh my gosh, she's dead." I had never heard Lili so petrified, but maybe she hadn't been a lost cause.

"She's not dead. She's going to need to be kept warm if she wants to live. She just happens to look dead. That's all. Bluish color, the faintest heartbeat. Not dead." I'd never heard Pan respond so calmly. What did he have to be alarmed about? Nothing.

A small laugh escaped my lips, alerting everyone that I was conscious. "I just wanted to fly."

"What do you mean? What is she talking about?" Lili questioned Pan.

I opened my eyes and peered up at the face hovering over me. Pan mumbled, "Bloody hell, I feared this would happen."

"What's wrong?" Lili's raised her tone.

Kace's face appeared in my view, and my eyes met his. I reached up to caress his face. "So soft and so warm."

Lili shouted, "I'm still waiting for an answer, damnit!"

Kace replied before Pan could. "She's high."

"What?" She crossed her arms.

Pan looked at Lili, then Kace, then me. "It's a bit hard to explain to humans who don't understand magic very well. This is why I don't use my magic on anyone unless I absolutely must. The results can be a bit maddening to people, including the person I'm using it on."

"I don't understand," Lili stated.

Pan reeled his shoulders back. "Lia is high off of my magic."

15: High

KACE HELPED ME TO my cabin where he kept me warm in his cloak, wrapping it around my shoulders. "Maybe you should change into dry clothes? It may help."

I smirked a bit. "You'd like that, wouldn't you?"

"Excuse me?" He furrowed his brows. "No, I mean you just warm up faster."

"Kace, I know you're a guy. You want to see all this." I gestured to my body. "You can't help it." I grinned.

He released a sharp sigh, pinching the bridge of his nose. "Cariño, I'm being serious. I don't want you to die."

I rolled my eyes. "Fineeeee. I'll change to make you happy. Dixon would have liked this, though," I muttered.

Before I could say something, Kace hurried from my cabin to give me privacy. I stumbled over to my dresser and grabbed new clothes. I took off the damp ones and started to pull my new clothes on. I was about to put my shirt on when my feet started to lift off the ground.

My laugh lit up the whole room. I moved my arms as if I was underwater, swimming. "I'm flying!"

Kace ran in at the sound of my words and widened his eyes as I continued my slow ascent to the ceiling. He reached up and grabbed my arms, pulling me back towards the ground. "Cariño!" He pulled my shirt from my fingers, putting it on me before leading me to the bed. He wrapped me in his cloak again and held me down.

I pouted, mentally crossing my arms. I had no strength to fight his chest and forcibly cross them just to prove a point. "I want to fly. Let me fly."

He shook his head vigorously. "This is just you being high off the magic. I can't let it control you. It's not good for you."

"But you can fly with me!" I exclaimed. My excitement took us off guard, his grip loosening, and then I'd jumped forward onto my knees just a little to close to his face. His lips were moist, as if he'd licked them. I wanted just a tiny taste of that.

But his refusal turned me off quick. "I need to keep you grounded."

I giggled and hugged him, clinging to him. I smushed my cheek against his. "We look so beautiful together."

"Let go of me. I don't want to play with you right now." Kace tried to pry me off, but I was fiercer than he took me for.

"No," I whispered. I kept my voice too quiet for him to hear my words. "I love you." I patted his other cheek and sighed in contentment. I gasped. "Kace, we need a ship name!"

"A what? We need boat names?"

I laughed again, bopping his nose. "No, a ship name is a name where we mash our names together because we're a couple. Kace... Lia. Kala! Oh, it's so cute. Our ship name is going to be kala. Like, our kala ID?" I joked.

Kace let loose a chuckle. "Okay, I have no idea what that means, but kala it is."

With the tilt of my head, my eyes drifted down his expression. "Hm."

Kace pulled his face back to look at me more. "You're judging me, aren't you?"

"I am. It's what I do; it's a hobby of mine." I shrugged with a smile. "You won't let me fly so I can only judge." My pleasantries vanished. "Wait, we need to find a name for Pan and Lili. Pili. No. Panli? Ew, gross, absolutely not." I stroked my chin.

He suggested, "Pali?"

I squeaked, covering my mouth. "Yes! That is cute! See, you're getting the hang of this ship name."

"Why are they called ship names?" he questioned.

My eyes lowered to the mattress. "Beats me. It's interesting to think about how my sister and Pan got together. They genuinely are happy with each other."

"They got together so fast."

"Well, technically it had been almost a year, so they took their time. We just didn't know it." I wrapped my arms around his neck. "Can you please let me fly?"

His lips grazed my ear. "I don't want you to fly away from me."

"Aw... Don't leave me!" I squeezed.

"I won't," he whispered so even the crow at the window couldn't hear.

"I feel so sleepy."

"Go to sleep."

"But I want to be with you."

"You are with me, Lia. I won't be going anywhere. Just go to sleep." He planted a small kiss on my forehead.

I did as I was told.

"SHE'S NOT HIGH ANYMORE. She's no longer floating," Kace said through the thick fog surrounding my brain.

"Good. The high is over. Will you leave for a moment while I talk to her? She's awake," Pan said in his usual tone. Casual. Subtly hiding danger.

A set of footsteps walked away, and a door closed behind them.

"You can open your eyes."

I opened my eyes and slowly sat up, rubbing away the grogginess. "What happened?"

Pan came closer. "I saved your life and you got high because of it."

"What?"

He bent to my level. "It's none of your concern now. Most people don't remember it anyway. It's a side effect of the magic wearing off."

I didn't say another word because I didn't know what to say. I'd actually had magic in my system.

Pan stood. "You seem fine now, so I'll leave you. Just remember to follow the rules so you don't end up like Faith." He spun on his boot and headed out. Kace came in shortly after.

I got off my bed, giving him a questioning look. "What happened to me?"

Kace scratched his head. "You got high off Pan's magic. Can we talk about something?"

"What is that?" What had I done? What exactly had I said?

"Us. I wanted to ask if we could tell Pan yet. I can't keep this a secret from him. He can't exactly kill either of us. I'm his best friend. You're his lover's sister. We're safe," he argued.

I shook my head. "We can't. He can still try to keep us apart. I don't want him to know until it's *safe* and I can confirm that one hundred percent. I don't want to lose my first boyfriend already. I want to do more things with you. Is that fair?"

He groaned, running a hand down his face. "Fine, but we have to eventually tell him. It will only hurt us if we wait so long. Trust me. I know him."

I couldn't argue against that. He knew Pan better than I did. I was just afraid of the repercussions of our relationship being public with Pan around.

Some commotion picked up outside in the center of camp, so we dropped out of the current conversation to go check on everyone else. Faith was free from the cage, only now to be restrained in Pan's grip.

Lili came out from behind him and observed Faith's narrowed eyes. "Don't worry. It'll be over soon." She looked at the lost boys and me. "Our new lost girl here has just struck three punishments. We caught her sneaking into Hangman's Tree, and we all know that's against the rules." Lili pulled out her dagger. "This is how it works, *boys*. You don't follow the rules and you face the consequences." She grabbed Faith's dark hair, yanking her head back. She sliced the blade across her throat. Blood gurgled as choking sounds echoed into the sky.

I clung to Kace, holding back the tremors. This was not my sister. I couldn't keep watching her do this. She'd killed too many people and it wasn't going to stop. Not until so much crimson stained her hands that even her bones ran red.

Kace tightened his fingers around my hand, gaze fixed on my sister.

Pan dropped her lifeless body. Lili wiped the blood from her dagger onto her shirt, glancing at us. "I warned her, but she didn't want to listen."

Pan cooly said, "We should take her body down to Cannibal Cove."

"Why Cannibal Cove?" I whispered to Kace.

"It's where they take all the dead bodies, to feed them to the mermaids."

"Why not Mermaid Lagoon?" I looked at Lili, my stare piercing her soul as if I could reverse all the wrongs.

He shrugged a bit. "Mermaid Lagoon is different."

"Kace, she just murdered someone exactly like her. For doing what she did. How are we supposed to save Lili?" The rims of my eyes brimmed with tears that soon began to spill, their clear coat painting my cheeks red.

He pulled me into his arms, forgetting that we were supposed to stay a secret. "I'm sorry. I don't know how to fix this."

My shoulder slumped. "It's too late. Lili is gone, isn't she?" I gazed up at him.

Kace shook his head. "I like to believe everyone is redeemable."

"Why? How can you believe that when your best friend has been so cruel for as long as we've known him?"

"Because I *know* him. I knew him when he was just, and he still can be. I just haven't figured out how to help him yet." He brushed my hair from my face.

I shook my head and looked down. "I can't do this anymore. Kace, I watch my sister slowly die every day. That isn't Lili. Lili is gone, and she isn't coming back. I'm so sorry but I have to give up before I lose myself in the process." I'd once told her if saving Pan destroyed her, was it worth it? I now had to face the same reality. "Neverland is hopeless. It's all futile."

Kace cupped my face. "Do not say that. Don't you dare talk like that."

"Admit it, Kace. It's too late. You know it's too late for them. She's killed too many people and she isn't coming back from that. I've tried so hard, but I can't do this anymore. She let our brother die. I've spent so much time trying to understand and love her because she's my sister, but I can't do that any longer. I can't love Lili." My love turned out to be conditional. What a twist. "I can't save her. It's time to let it go." I lowered his hands from my face, my fingers wrapped around his wrists.

Kace gave me a pitiful look before I abandoned him for my cabin. I couldn't bear to see him see me like this. I just couldn't continue the way I was. It was killing me inside to see my own sister rip apart souls. My mental state was taking a hit. It was hurting *me* to hold onto hope when there was none.

My sister killed all my *faith*.

I lay back against the mattress and looked up at the ceiling, counting every line.

Where did I go from here? The mission was over. I could focus on my training and maybe Kace if he let me still be his girlfriend—if we could skate past this crack.

I didn't know how we could make it work if we had two different goals. He was set on fixing everything and I had given up. He had been here for so many years and yet he didn't lose sight at the drop of a hat. How did he believe in happy endings?

If he could give me some of his, I'd be grateful. But alas...

Neverland was forever going to be chaos. The real Lili had died the day she begged Pan to take her from *our* home.

16: Charm Bracelet

Lifting my index finger to inspect the cut, I let out a sigh as I looked towards the sky. When my eyes landed back on the ocean, I focused on one tiny strand of water that strayed from the body, up towards the clouds. How was that possible?

I dropped my hand and it fell back into the waves. I looked down at my own fingers and shook my head. No, was it possible?

Pan got his magic from this island, and Wendy got hers from getting high with Pan.

No, that was absurd. It had to be.

And yet, when I lifted my finger again, a strand of the waves lifted along with it. I had just a little bit of magic and all because Pan had used loads of gold magic to save me from an impending death.

I stood and headed back to camp. The camp had been empty more times than not since the balance had shifted and snow began to coat the island. Nobody wanted to leave their cabins unless there was a fire or training going on—anything to keep warm.

Voices echoed in distress. I followed the direction in which they came and when I approached a few figures in the distance, my breath caught in my throat. It was happening all over again.

Lili was going to murder *another* innocent person.

She held him against her chest as she shoved the blade into his abdomen. Blood poured onto her shirt, staining the fabric for eternity.

She dropped the fresh corpse, and he became one with the snow while the breeze gently said goodbye to his body. She faced. "It's done. Anyone else?"

"I mean, aside from who we've gotten already, yes. I need you to kill one of the lost boys, your pick. There are too many mouths to feed, and my supply is running low. With Wendy gone and nobody to make food or grow a garden, we must make sacrifices. This weather makes crops harder to grow and my magic doesn't quite work with what Wendy would do. Are you up for the challenge?" He crossed his arms, his gaze darkening.

"I'm always up for it. Now, tell me, what is it that I will get if I do this? Don't get me wrong, Pan, but I do like an extra reward. I don't do your dirty work for free." She puffed out her chest. It was anything but confidence that she had. She was a coward. She had succumbed to the darkness that once raised her from birth.

A smile laced with sinful intentions sat on Pan's lips as he tapped his chin. "Is there something you have always wanted?"

She furrowed her brows, going deep into thought. Whatever could she want now? From the look in her eyes, she was ready to admit defeat but then they lit up as an idea popped into her head. "A charm bracelet."

"What?" By the confusion in his tone, I guessed he'd never seen one before..

"A charm bracelet is a metal bracelet that goes around the wrist. It has links to add new charms. Charms are little 3D metal objects that represent something, like a shoe, for example. You add onto it as you go. I could get a new charm for every new kill." She smiled with pride. Lili always asked for one every Christmas, but her wish was never fulfilled. Big surprise in my family.

"All right. Let me go back and get you one. In the meantime, pick your next victim." He vanished into thin air. I wondered how much magic I had from the one-time high.

I followed her to the training area where the boys practiced their skills.

Kace sidled up beside her, but she didn't turn to look at him as she said, "If you're about to ask my intentions, they're not good as usual. Pan needs me to off one of you guys. Food is getting low."

"I hope that doesn't mean me. The second-in-command should be out of the question," he said. He pulled his hood down and locked his eyes on hers. "If it includes all lost boys, Pan would include himself. He is the first lost boy, which is what makes him our leader."

Something sparkled in her eye, but only I seemed to catch it. I couldn't quite pick up on it, but it had been deadly. Dark. Grotesque to even the point that Pan would question Lili's sanity.

It disappeared as quickly as it'd come. "Kace, you don't need to worry. You're not included in this." She looked at him, lifting her eyebrows in surprise.

"Good. I wish it didn't have to be anyone at all." He appeared scarily calm considering what was about to happen to one of his friends.

"It has to be. Wendy is gone now, and with nobody to tend to the garden, we have to lessen the stomachs." Lili crossed her arms, searching for the weakest link. Nausea reared its ugly head once again in the depths of my stomach.

"Pan can't just put someone else in the garden?" he asked. I'd gladly offer to tend to the garden if it kept everyone alive. Why did Pan need someone to grow food anyway? He could make anything appear.

"I get to kill someone else and that's all I need to hear. If you don't like it, you can kiss my ass. You're not in charge here." She fixed on one young boy, tilting her head. He was struggling to pull the arrow back.

Kace noticed who she was watching. "You aren't going to kill him. You may be wicked, but you remember Eric. The little boys make us feel like we have real friends here. You wouldn't dare hurt a little kid."

She turned towards him. "Don't tell me what I will and won't do. I may just kill him to prove you wrong."

"Am I supposed to be impressed?" His expression fell flat.

Lili narrowed her eyes. "I have authority over you."

"And? I liked you more when you didn't. You've let the power get to your head." He shrugged.

"Pan does the same damn thing!" she yelled.

I couldn't believe he was defying my sister so well. Maybe he was sick of her, too, and he was doing something about it because I'd given up. Was this his attempt to prove me wrong?

He let out a bored sigh. "I follow his rules. It doesn't mean he impresses me with them. I follow your rules, but you don't impress me either." He left her to wallow in her own frustration.

With a groan, she faced the boys again, studying them. The one boy jumped up with excitement. "I got it! I got it!" His arrow stuck in the outer ring of the target. Another boy patted his shoulder, smiling at him.

I tilted my head as the boy celebrated his first achievement. With practice, he could make a good weapon. Enemies wouldn't expect a child to have any tactics. He would be useful.

Lili picked out a boy who was just off on his own, who seemed to hate the world. Knowing her logic, she thought he would only slow us down with his problems, so he would have to go.

We both went to Pan's cabin and waited for him. Lili sat inside on the bed, while I stood outside by the window.

He walked in a few minutes later, holding up a chain bracelet. "I got this for you. I hope it fits. It already has charms of the ones you killed. Hook, Faith, that one girl, and some other lost boys." He helped her put it on her wrist.

"I think it's perfect. This will definitely be perfect." She held his hands while looking at the bracelet.

He grabbed her chin and pulled her face up to look at him. "As long as you're happy, I'm happy." He kissed her. I wanted to puke at the sight. It was sad and disgusting all at the same time. They smooched over skeletons.

"It'll be so fun. I found my target, so I'll have to test out this bracelet." She left him and went to the camp where the boys now circled the fire.

Lili found the boy she picked, tapping his shoulder. "I would like to talk to you in private."

He looked at her, scowling. "I don't think so."

"Get your ass off the log and come with me, or it's going to be much worse for you," she spat.

"Everyone knows what you do to boys who go with you. I ain't about to get myself killed that easily." He turned back toward the fire.

The poor boy had dug his own grave. Why was she so addicted to murder? What did she get out of it? Lili didn't play games and she certainly didn't give up on her kill.

"Stop!" I yelled as I ran between them. "Please, don't do this, Lili. Please. I will tend to the garden. I'll make sure everyone has food. Just please don't do this." My begging came off as pathetic, but it didn't matter to me. I wanted to stop the bloodshed somehow, and this was the only way I could.

"Of all people to be against me, my own sister hurts the most." She gestured to me as she spoke to the boys. Lili closed the distance between us and paused for a moment. Her palm met my cheek and a stinging sensation coursed throughout my nerves. "You don't get to speak to me that way either. You're nothing special."

I swallowed. "I'm your sister. Do you remember when I fell off the mountain? I almost died and you saved me. You carried me back home and made sure I was taken care of. You were so worried. What happened to *that* Lili?"

"She was ripped away from me. She no longer exists." She grabbed a strand of hair from my head, twirling it in her fingers. "Your haircut is hideous."

"That's because it's not for you," I said.

Another palm to the cheek. Something warm yet cold dripped from my nose. Blood. Something she seemed to crave now, even from me.

Kace took long strides over, stopping at my side. I didn't know why; it wasn't like he was about to talk back to her.

Lili glanced at him. "How cute, your boyfriend is here to protect you now. You always were the weakest of us both."

I begged to differ. Weakness was giving in to the darkness and choosing the easy path. It was easy to use what abuse she had taken and inflict it on others. It took strength to fight the demonic voice.

She walked around the circle, eyeing the boys. "You may not want to admit it, but I am your leader now, too. You do have to listen to me." She stopped behind the hateful boy. In a swift motion, she pulled back his head by his hair, using her dagger to slice his neck open. Like clockwork, the crimson stained the front, making a mess of his body.

The boys watched in horror as she dropped his head and lifted her arm, admiring the new bracelet as a new charm formed on it. "I would be very careful of how you treat me. I have a reason to hate you guys. With me in charge, Pan supporting me, and my strength, you guys stand no chance. In one second, you could be gone."

She put her arm down. "I love to kill, and I will find any reason to take a life." She circled them as the boy's lifeless body collapsed. She put her arms behind her back and stilled. Her gaze zoomed in on Kace and I—a piercing glare. "I don't make friends anymore. I only pick out victims."

17: Message in a Bottle

My reflection stared back at me as we studied the red mark Lili left behind. I'd cleaned up my bloody nose with the help of Kace, but it was clear to me now that Lili wasn't afraid to kill me or Kace if it came to it. I wasn't so sure Pan would allow that—not Kace anyway.

And now it became apparent what I'd seen in her eyes. She was out for blood, but most specifically, Pan's. He genuinely loved her and she wanted to rip him apart. Why? If she could have killed him as the lost boy he promised her and gotten away with it, she wouldn't have hesitated.

Part of me hoped Kace was right about Pan's little crush on me, because if he did feel that way, he would at least make sure Lili didn't kill me. Still, I wasn't depending on him to keep me alive.

Whoever Lili once was, she was gone now. Nothing but a heartless monster was left behind. If she could let Jaren die, she'd easily snuff out my life. She was addicted to the thrill of taking what wasn't hers.

I left the cabin and headed towards the garden. When I arrived, I kneeled in the snow and frowned. I had promised to help with the garden, but it was impossible to grow food where winter was growing thicker. It was no wonder why the food was getting scarcer. All we could find was meat, and it wasn't even enough to survive off. The animals here were dying. They weren't built for the intense winters.

I rushed over to the well to see how the water source was doing. It was hard to see, but from the small glare, it was iced over. Something else caught my eye, and immediately, I wanted to get it out.

Climbing down wasn't a viable option if I wanted to keep my life.

I bent down and grabbed some rocks, throwing them down onto the ice. It cracked a bit but didn't make much of a dent. I found a bigger stone and threw it down, and then a hole formed in the ice. I quickly grabbed the bucket and threw it down. I moved it around in the water until the object had been scooped up. I pulled the rope down through the pulley as the bucket started to come back up.

Once it reached the ledge, I reached for the item. I furrowed my brows at the sight, feeling like maybe I was in some sort of pirate movie. It was a message in a bottle.

I stuffed it into my cloak and raced back to my cabin. After I locked the door, I opened it up and dumped out the piece of rolled paper. I unraveled it, swallowing as I began reading.

To Whoever Finds This (hoping it's one of my sisters),

When Lili went missing, we all thought she ran away. That was just the type of girl she was. She would sneak out, go to the river when she wasn't allowed, and she'd get away for a little while. But she'd always come back. This time, she didn't. Days passed. We hoped and waited for her. Lia was the one taking it the hardest. It wasn't as if they were close. None of us were.

Eventually a week passed, and we started to wonder if maybe she wasn't ever coming back. Then a month passed. Our parents didn't bother to report her as missing. Lia tried her hardest, but they wouldn't budge. Once that first month hit, Lia went to the police and reported her as missing. When our parents found out, it became chaotic. Violent. They beat Lia until she was almost in a coma.

For some odd reason, they didn't want Lili to be a missing person. They didn't want people to look at them and think they were bad parents for raising a girl who got kidnapped. No, they wanted Lili to look bad and the only way to ensure she did, was to say she was a runaway.

There were rumors that Lili ran off with a boyfriend to do drugs. When I asked Lia, she denied all of it. Lili was not the type of girl to turn to boys, and she had tried drugs before, but they didn't help her. Our parents were making up lies to make Lili look like this terrible person. She wasn't.

Three months passed. No sign of Lili. Nothing in her room had been taken with her. It was all there. If she ran away, why leave behind everything? If she was kidnapped, why wasn't there any signs of it? None of it made any sense. She just vanished without a trace, and nobody could find her. We tried so hard to get Lili to come home but wherever she went, she couldn't hear us anymore. Lia would get pestered about it at school and I'd get pestered at work. We were sick of it. We were tired of the useless questions about our missing sister. Nobody took it seriously, or if they did, they had no idea what it was like to be constantly worried.

One night, Lia vanished. Just like Lili, she was gone. I went to the police immediately, ignoring my parents. The police suspected maybe there was a neighbor or someone we had trusted who wanted to take both Lili and Lia for horrible reasons. What could anyone want with twins? So many awful ideas ran through my head.

What if they were experiments? What if someone was doing unspeakable acts?

See, I'd always been a shitty brother. I'd never tried to help my sisters before. I did as I was told until I could save up money to leave that awful house. Once Lili went missing, I was ridden with guilt. All I could think about was how I'd never once protected Lili and I was the worst brother to exist. I tried to protect Lia from that point on as we tried to search for Lili. I learned things about Lia and Lili that way. We were siblings. We were supposed to protect each other. The police couldn't find a single suspect, and there was no way to track the girls. After five more months passed, their birthday passed, and they were legally adults at that point. Everyone gave up.

Our parents forgot about them. The police assumed they were dead with no evidence. The whole city just stopped caring.

I never stopped looking. I couldn't. It didn't make sense. I searched Lili's room all over again, but I still found not a single drop of evidence. By now, it'd been over a year since Lili and Lia went missing.

When I finished with Lili's room, I searched Lia's. Maybe whoever took them got sloppy and left behind evidence. Maybe. That was the only hope I had to hold onto.

It worked.

Both windows were wide open when my sisters were taken. That was where they'd left the room.

So I searched around Lia's windowsill and the carpet beneath. What I found was...magical. I found gold dust.

I thought maybe it was glitter, but Lia didn't have any glitter. I licked my finger and picked up the smallest pieces I could. Darkness fell over me, and when I looked up, he was right in the window. The shadow. His eyes glowed red and I thought maybe he was some monster that took my sisters. But he spoke to me. He told me that he was Pan's shadow and

HE CAME FROM NEVERLAND. MY SISTERS WERE THERE, SO I TRUSTED HIM. SURE ENOUGH, HE WAS RIGHT. WHEN I ARRIVED, MY SISTERS WERE IN NEVERLAND.

AS I WRITE THIS NOW, I'M IN NEVERLAND AND I'M DYING. MY BODY IS AGING AND I CAN'T MAKE THE PROMISE LIA WANTS ME TO, TO LEAVE HERE WITHOUT HER AND LILI. NO. LILI IS IN TROUBLE. SHE'S LOST WHO SHE IS. LIA NEEDS MY HELP. I REFUSE TO LET MY SISTERS THINK I DON'T CARE ABOUT THEM. I'M NOT THAT BROTHER ANYMORE. WHO I AM, IS THE BROTHER THEY NEEDED ALL ALONG. I WON'T DIE ALLOWING THEM TO THINK I NEVER LOVED THEM. I WILL DIE KNOWING I HAVE DIED FOR A GOOD REASON. THEY DESERVE TO KNOW THAT SOMEONE LOVES THEM, EVEN IF IT'S NOT OUR PARENTS.

I JUST HOPE THEY CAN FORGIVE ME FOR ALL THE PAIN I'VE CAUSED. I KNOW I DON'T DESERVE IT, BUT MY LOVE FOR MY SISTERS IS REAL. I WRITE THIS FOR THEM.

SIGNED, JAREN STONE

Tears rolled down my cheeks as I laid the letter on my dresser. I wanted him to know I did forgive him. I wanted him to have his second chance, but that was taken away.

When Lili went missing, we spent more time together than we ever had before. We bonded over our missing sister, but it was still a bond, nonetheless. It was the one time in my life that I felt like I truly mattered to someone, and I didn't have to hide the truth. Jaren experienced the same abuse. We could talk about it and understand one another.

He refused to leave because he wanted to prove that he was sorry for never being there for us. He refused to leave Lili as a monster, and what was I doing? I was letting him die with a stain on his heart.

If he was still here, he'd tell me to get my ass out of my cabin so we could save Lili. He'd make sure I didn't give up on her, and yet I had.

I was the worst sister. Lili may have killed people, but I was doing Jaren a disservice. His death meant nothing if Lili never got a chance to be herself.

I couldn't do that to either of them. I couldn't break a promise to my brother. I couldn't let my sister suffer because of what our parents taught her to do. Even if it ended in my own bloodshed, I would be the exact sister Lili needed. I would save her from this fate, or I'd die trying. Because if I gave my life for a good cause like this, it'd never be in vain. I'd never regret my decisions. Not for *her*.

Jaren deserved to be proud of us. He deserved to die knowing that everything turned out better than he'd ever hoped. What purpose did his tragic death serve if the family cycle continued? Lili, the abuser. Lia, the coward. We were exactly like our parents, and I could never live with myself if I didn't change that.

"I promise you I will not give up. I will never give up again. Lili needs me and I can't let her fight this alone or sit in the dark forever. You and I both know that our parents are the real villains and if we allow ourselves to end up like them, we are no better," I whispered to Jaren's grave. To Lili's shadow.

Except our parents never killed anyone. Lili had.

Pan had been a morally gray man. He'd neglected the lost children's needs, but he never abused them like our father did us. Lili turned into our father and with a neglectful partner at her side, it could lead to nothing else but destruction and the downfall of Neverland.

I turned into our mother. I was the coward who stood by and watched as children suffered the abuse. I was no better than my own mother. Jaren would never wish that on any of us.

No—I couldn't allow myself to be my mother. I wouldn't continue to be a coward. I would rise; I would be better than that. I would make sure Lili didn't stay like our father. If Neverland was supposed to be a better place where children could come to be free, then I'd help return it back to that dream. Pan would be the promise, and Lili would finally get a chance to be happy. She would be treated like she mattered, because she did.

We would have the opportunity to get our happy ending, and all I had to do was step up to fight for us both.

18: Transmitted Magic

A lift of the finger and the water rose. That was all I could do. I had tried other gestures and focused on lifting more than a single strand, but nothing worked. I had gotten high once, *maybe* twice. I barely had any blue magic.

"What was that I saw?" Kace emerged from the trees.

I glanced over my shoulder and shrugged. "That was me trying to see how far my magic goes. Not very far, I guess."

He plopped down next to me. "You have magic now?"

With a nod, I showed him the limited ability I had. He was amazed, but I was bored. I wanted to do more. I craved to learn more.

"How does that work?"

"When Pan used his magic on me, it gave me a form of magic—blue magic. But the problem is I only have so much to use, given that he's used magic on me twice. I can't do more than what you see." I wrapped my arms around my knees. "Is there a way to get more blue magic without getting high?"

"You mean without Pan using magic on you? No." He shook his head.

I yelled out in frustration and threw my fists in the sand. "I can't do anything useful! Why do I have any magic at all if it's so useless?"

Kace leaned back on his hands. "I'm sure there's a reason. You'll get more, right? Maybe. Maybe we could ask Pan."

"Ask Pan? Ask Pan to use magic on me to give me more so I can defeat him and my sister? Yeah, I'm sure he'll be jumping at the opportunity to make that happen," I said with sarcasm lacing my tongue. "If you're right about his crush on me, maybe he'll just...give it to me without question. But there lies one problem. I don't want anyone else to know I have magic."

Kace glanced at the ocean and tried to come up with a plan, but we both knew Pan would eventually find out. It wasn't even him I was worried about. If Lili knew, this could cause a war. She would not be keen on the idea that I had blue magic just like Wendy did.

Anna had magic, too, green magic I think she called it. However one attained that, I couldn't be sure. Maybe I could ask her, or maybe I could ask Pan. I was counting on *his* feelings to keep me alive.

I stood from the sand, and Kace hurried to his feet to follow. "Are we going to see Pan?" he asked.

"We?" I turned to face him. "I think it's best if I go alone. We've already gotten on Lili's kill list, and I don't want people to see us together more than they have to. The last thing I need is for her to find out we're dating. She already makes comments about you being my boyfriend. And what do we both have in common? I'm just as terrible a liar as she is. One twitch and she'll realize that you truly are my boyfriend."

He rolled on the balls of his feet, nodding as he glanced at the ground. "All right." He lifted his head. "I'll leave you alone then."

It pained me to hear those words, knowing who said them. I knew deep down that Kace didn't want to leave me alone, but it was for our safety. Corpses couldn't save Neverland.

I thanked him and began walking up the shore. His footsteps sounded behind me, and I turned to face him. "Kace, I thought I told you to stay. You're not safe with me."

He nodded, but he didn't say anything. The second I started towards the trees again, Kace gripped my wrist and pulled me back, bringing our chests together. Before I could even get a word out, he grabbed my face and crashed his lips onto mine.

Two seconds was all it took before I kissed back. There was a certain feeling that lingered. I couldn't quite place it, but I knew it was one only we shared on this island.

His lips tasted of berries fresh from my slow-growing garden. They led the dance, his thumbs brushing across my cheeks. My fingers tangled themselves in his cloak. Our bodies radiated the heat needed on such a chilly winter day.

Kace pulled away, but his lips were still just centimeters from mine. The kiss had taken both of our breaths away, leaving us fighting to catch them again. For the first time, this close, I took notice of the light brown specks in his right eye. Charming. Unique. Forever engrained in my memory.

"I just thought about how we've hardly kissed, and I didn't want to make any mistakes by letting you go," he whispered.

I nodded a bit, blinking a few times to break my spell. "I should go now, before anyone sees us down here." I gave him one more assertive kiss before he let go of me, and before I turned around, I caught sight of something far more intimate than I'd ever witnessed. I'd pretend I didn't see it for his sake.

Kace got a boner, and he yanked his cloak closed to hide it from me.

I walked up the shore, swallowing and trying to cool the red in my cheeks. He was a respectable man, even if he was turned on by the kiss. It wasn't as if I hadn't enjoyed it, because I did. I just enjoyed the kiss in a different way than he did.

I was the one who needed an emotional connection before the sexual attraction came. I was the one out of my element. It was me who was strange, who was supposed to kiss Kace and want to rip his clothes off right there.

But I didn't. No matter how hard I tried to tap into my hormones, I didn't want that yet. When we kissed, I enjoyed his warmth, and the security he brought. I just loved being in his arms. I didn't ask for more, at least not now. I simply craved his support, and I was afraid he might not understand that.

As I approached Pan's cabin, I lifted my knuckles to knock on the door, but it swung open before I could. "You're here because you want more magic. I was afraid this would happen," Pan said, waving me inside.

I hesitated at first but stepped in, scanning the room. Lili wasn't here. Not now, at least.

I faced Pan. "Well, can you give me some?"

He closed the door and walked to his dresser. "No, I'm not going to create another Wendy situation."

I frowned. "Pan, I'm not going to create nasty rumors about Lili. That's not who I am."

"That wasn't Wendy, either, but the power eventually gets to you." He cleared his throat, betrayal befalling him. "I was sucked in. She wasn't always this innocent girl. She appeared that way, but she got a taste of my magic and got her first high. She kept coming back for more. I refused, the same way I'm refusing you. But she was...persistent." A sly smile crossed his lips. "She promised me things, and I didn't say no. So, we started a routine. She would do things and I'd get her high, and she got more magic. The power grew."

Bile rose in my throat at the thought of what she did. I didn't need *that* image damaging my mind. "And?"

"And she ended up being the villain, Lia. I don't want you to be the villain." His features softened.

I crossed my arms. "So Kace was right. You do have a crush on me."

A sudden laugh filled the room. "Crush? No, I don't have crushes. It's fun to tease you because you're Lili's sister, but it's not because I want to sleep with you or anything. You're too easy for my liking."

I grinded my teeth, gripping my arms. "I am not easy."

"Sure you are. When you came here, you let me kiss you. You trusted me right away. Now you're dating Kace. It's not always a bad thing, Lia. If you were difficult like Lili, you'd be in her place right now. You've kissed two men in Neverland, and Lili has only kissed just me." He leaned against the dresser, folding his arms. "I still remember that day. I pushed her off the cliff for a thrill, and when I swooped down and saved her, she wasn't thankful. She was angry that I scared her. She never was appreciative. I always thought flying was fun, but I guess she doesn't think the same." A frown troubled his expression. "She's a cracked soul. Tough, but with enough pestering, I can slip my way in and make her whole. My other half. Even with Hook, I'd never felt this vulnerable—like she could tear me apart at any moment and I'd allow her to. With Lili, I'd beg for her forgiveness. I'd do anything she asked of me if it meant she'd run her fingers through my hair one more time, promising to stay." Utterly exposed. His heart had been entirely hers, and she had no idea the damage she could inflict.

I could reveal to him that she wanted his life. But I didn't have the heart. He was a man in love with a woman who craved his demise.

Dropping my arms, I huffed. He also knew about Kace and I. I should have known. "You won't help me, so why am I still here?"

"You tell me."

Why was I still here? "Anna said she got green magic from Wendy. How?" That's why I hadn't left yet.

He furrowed his brows. "Anna?" Then seconds later they shot up. "Ah, yes, her. Tinker Bell. Magic can be transmitted through saliva. Those two certainly shared a lot of it. But blue magic comes only from the source itself—me. And since Tinker Bell never got high with me, she got a different kind, the kind that is passed between making out. Green magic."

"Will Kace get magic?" He knew. There was no use in holding back the questions.

Pan smirked at me. "Hard to hold your tongue, isn't it?"

My cheeks heated, eyes growing wide. Of course. It could only be transmitted through lots of making out, and we had *only* kissed.

"Nevermind."

Pan pushed off his dresser and closed the gap between us. "You'll get there eventually." He chuckled, grabbing my chin. "But with how little magic you have, he won't hardly get anything at all." His brows creased as he focused. "But I do have to warn you, Lia, that you might be related to the woman I love but you are certainly not protected. If you dare hurt Kace, I will see to it that you are miserable the rest of your days here. Not an ounce of mercy. After all, we know what happened to the last woman who hurt him."

Hook. Hook was dead, but Lili killed her, not Pan. He knew that, and he knew that we knew. Either way, I agreed not to hurt Kace. I never had any intentions of doing that.

Pan let go, but he didn't put more space between us. Instead, he studied my eyes. What the hell was he doing? "You love him."

"What?" I choked. No, that didn't make sense. We'd barely started dating. Maybe kissed a few times. We'd been friends for almost a year.

He simply replied, "You love Kace." His eyes eased up at these words, no longer threatening my existence. "We can't help who we love, or when we fall."

I took a step back, but I stumbled over my own foot. I grabbed hold of the wall and fixed my posture. "You don't know what you're talking about." I left his cabin in a hurry, shaking my head. No, no. He was trying to trick me, to throw me off my game. That was it. I didn't *love* Kace. I hadn't known him long enough. Right?

Except I had. Time here was hard to follow, and it could have been eighteen months since I arrived. I couldn't remember. Jaren arrived a year after I had, but who knew exactly how much time had passed since his death.

I lost my balance and fell into the snow. Did I love Kace? Was that true?

I stayed there, on my knees, contemplating my entire relationship. We became friends shortly before Lili turned monstrous. She introduced us, and we never strived for a friendship, but when he found me at Cannibal Cove that day, something clicked. We worked well together. He was funny, and kind. He accepted me, and he didn't make me feel the way Lili and Pan did.

We teamed up when she went dark, and we'd spent more time together since. I knew the real Kace, and he was nothing like Pan. He respected me. He reminded me that I wasn't worthless, and I could be strong if I tried. He was there when Jaren died, and he was there when I got high. He was always there, even when he shouldn't have been.

From friends to more than friends, we stuck together. We'd kissed, and we always tried to protect each other from harm. There was something we shared that nobody else could understand about us, and I knew deep down that I'd die to save him if it ever came down to it. I wasn't sure if he felt the same, but it didn't matter right now. I couldn't deny it, and Pan was right.

I was deeply in love with Kace.

19: Magic in Neverland

I SWALLOWED MY FEAR as Anna circled me. "It's true. You love him."

"I do. Why does this even matter right now? It's not exactly a big deal. We *are* dating, and love isn't unheard of in Neverland. You loved Wendy. Pan loves Lili in some twisted way. I love Kace. Let's just drop the subject."

Anna sat down in front of me. "Let's look at the real picture here for a moment. If it wasn't a big deal, you wouldn't have told me. Love is always a big deal. It's one thing to just kiss someone, but another to love them and want to die for them. You want to spend your entire life together. Can you see Kace in your future?"

I shrugged. "All the time. But then again, that's because I have no plans on leaving this island and he's always going to be my best friend."

"Friend? Do you just see him as your friend?"

Chills ran up my spine. "No. I can see us training together, swimming, and cuddling." I smiled a little. "In my little world, we're training and I catch him off guard, and next thing you know, he's trapped against a tree. Then, I swoop in and steal a kiss." I cleared my throat.

Anna nodded. "That is love. You can't manage to rid your mind or heart of him."

"Why?" I stood from the ground. "I mean, why me? I'm here to be happy and save Neverland. I'm ruining everything by loving Kace. He's a distraction."

"He's *hope*."

After taking a deep breath, my eyes fell shut. What kind of woman was I for letting this happen? Strong women didn't kiss someone at the end of the night. Saviors didn't fall in love. I was destroying everything by such foolishness. My sister needed me most and I was here thinking about kissing my best friend. I was weak, and I'd never be able to measure up to anything worthwhile. Worthy people didn't allow love to distract them.

Anna interrupted my thoughts, "Are you okay?"

I nodded, sitting back down. Nothing but a liability now. "What about you? Pan told me that you got your magic from...making out with Wendy. Something about magic being transmitted through saliva. Anyway, is that how you became a fairy?"

Anna straightened her posture, her legs crisscrossed, and her hands dangling over her knees. "That's not the full story."

"What do you mean?"

She glanced at her lap. "I mean, yes, I got my green magic because of Wendy's blue magic, but it wasn't..." She coughed. "It wasn't from making out."

"But Pan said..."

"Pan was *wrong*. He's afraid to admit the real reason I got my magic. He knows if I admit it, you'll want to get it, too."

My eyes lit up. "How do you get green magic?"

Anna nodded to the well. "Wendy intentionally gave me magic when she worried about Pan finding out about us. She dropped some into the water. I drank magic, and it's that easy to attain. But you don't have enough blue magic to pour it into the water, if that's what you're wondering."

I furrowed my brows. "Then why would he lie if I can't give anyone else magic?"

Anna scanned the area, then leaned in. "Because you can attain more blue magic through one other way."

My eyes bulged. “How?”

She got up and helped me to my feet. “Follow me.”

So, I did. I followed Anna all the way to Hangman’s Tree. No, this was forbidden. He’d catch us. “I can’t go in there.”

“That’s where he stores extra magic. He’s got gold, blue, and green magic bottled. A few of the other forms have been harder to attain, such as red.”

Red? As in red magic? What the hell did that do?

“He stole your magic?”

“Not all of it. Magic is like blood. You take some, it replenishes itself to full capacity later. That’s why you can give magic. When he uses his magic on you, it goes into your body and when you get high, it basically transforms as a form of blue magic, and it coats your blood in a way. Like this extra protective barrier. When you put your magic into the water system, those who drink it end up with magic that transforms in our body as green magic. It can’t be transmitted through saliva, since that’s not where the magic resides. However, it can be...transmitted through sex. But it can only be through sex with penises. Since Wendy and I are women, we can’t exactly pass magic that way.” She swallowed. “Well, Wendy *was* a woman.”

“My sister is having sex with Pan, so why hasn’t she got magic?”

She shrugged. “He’s probably using condoms. It can’t pass through. He doesn’t want her to get magic.” Did I entirely blame him? No, she held too much power already.

I looked at the tree. I could go in and steal blue magic, and then what? Could I save Neverland with it?

“What does blue magic do?” I asked.

She pointed to the snow. “It’s connected to water sources. Think of magic as...elements. Green magic deals with the earth, while blue magic deals with water.”

“If that’s true, then what about air and fire?”

“That’s what gold magic does. Flying. Pan deals with the air, but it’s stronger because he’s the one tethered to the island. His magic is like the ocean, and our magic is like small rivers that lead to it. As for fire, that's tied to red magic. But nobody is quite sure how to attain that yet," she said as matter-of-factly.

I nodded a bit and looked at the ground. "So you're a fairy because you have green magic? That's strange because you can fly, and flying is part of the air."

"I'm a fairy because the earth needs wings. I can't get to the tallest trees on my own. Pan doesn't use wings, and he can transport through the air. Become one with it. I cannot quite do that."

Yet I couldn't seem to tell myself to steal from Pan. What good would it do? He'd punish me and I'd never be able to serve for the good of the island.

"Let's go back," I said, and I turned on my heel.

Anna gestured to the tree. "What about the magic?"

I glanced at her. "If Pan knows I took it, I'll never defeat him, and he'll surely find out before I have a chance to master it. I can't risk that. Besides, water doesn't defeat air. He can do just about anything. I can lift a strand of water."

Anna nodded a bit. "I won't force you."

"Thank you." I kept walking, and she followed behind.

The truth was out. Pan had magic and I could take it when I needed to.

"What now?" Anna asked.

What did we do now? I feared maybe Pan would find out that I was befriending Anna. What if he suspected that I was dating her, too? No, that was silly. He knew I was dating Kace. I doubt he knew throuples existed, and I was glad. I didn't want Anna to pay the price for our friendship.

I faced her. "We train. We train as if our life depends on it, because it does."

"Me? Train?"

I cocked my head up. "Pan lied to me. He told me that magic turns people evil. Power goes to their head. Look at you. You're still a good person. He used that as his excuse for why Wendy became the way she did, and I don't know why she did, but I know he lied about it. It's up to us to save Neverland and I need your help. Are you willing to help me?"

Her eyes darted around the trees before landing back on me. "I suppose. What else do I have to lose?"

Those words sent an arrow to my heart. She'd already lost Wendy, and she didn't love anyone else. It wasn't fair. Why couldn't Pan just punish Wendy with the cage? Was killing her worth it?

"I'm sorry," I whispered.

Anna lifted her shoulders. "Don't be. It's time that we act. I'm going to do this for Wendy."

"Action, yes." I led her to the training area.

It was empty during this time of day, and since winter had begun. Hook was dead, and nobody was about to go swimming. With how much snow was coming down, nobody was about to dock at the island, either. We had no real threats, and training was lowered to a minimum.

I grabbed my dagger. "Okay, so you have to always be prepared, and that means predicting every possible move your opponent makes."

Anna bent down and grabbed a rock. "I'm prepared."

I jabbed my blade at her side, but she sidestepped it. I spun around and swung it at her abdomen, but she bent her torso back. When she came back up, she knocked her hand against my wrist, throwing my dagger to the ground.

She dropped to the ground and rolled over, grabbing it by the handle and jumping to her feet.

"What the hell?" I swallowed.

"Did I forget to mention I used to train here? Lili likes to believe she's the first lost girl, but there was a time when I was part of the camp. I left when Pan tore Wendy and I apart." She swiped her foot behind my leg and tripped me. She dropped on top of me, my own blade to my throat. "I think I could teach you some tricks."

I swallowed the lump, nodding. "Certainly."

"Cariño!" Kace yelled as he ran towards us.

Anna stood down and gave me my dagger back. "Hello, Kace."

His forehead creased as he studied her. "Tinker Bell?"

She gave a shrug paired with a small smile. "'Tis I—don't wear it out."

I got up from the ground, shivering as snow seeped into my cloak from my neck. "We were training." Only I hadn't realized that she was a master at it.

Anna shot me a prideful look. "I've decided to join this little club you have. I suppose Lia could use some training."

I dropped my jaw. How insulting.

Kace nodded, grinning. "It's been a long time."

"It has been. I never thought I'd come back here." Her eyes danced between the trees.

Without saying any words, Kace pulled Anna in for a hug. "I'm glad you did."

Anna slowly wrapped her arms around him. "Thank you," she choked. It must have been hard to reconnect with everyone after losing Wendy. None of this was fair in any way.

I patted my hair down as I said, "I should leave you guys to catch up. I need more training anyway." I pulled my hood up and smiled a bit as I walked past them. I found my way back to my cabin and locked the door behind me. It wouldn't exactly keep out the one person I wanted it to, but it was worth a shot.

Something passed by in the corner of my eye, and I froze. "Who's there?" I asked. Such a stupid question.

When nobody responded, I whipped around and straightened my posture at the sight. The shadow had grown in height. How was that even possible?

He reached out and grabbed hold of my cloak, pulling me closer. "You're making a mistake. This war can only end in bloodshed."

"Avoiding it ends in more bloodshed. I'm willing to take my chances." I couldn't let it scare me this time. If I did that, I'd lose all credibility.

He wrapped his cold fingers around my neck. "Are you willing to pay the price for victory? Will you sacrifice who you love?"

Kace. He was talking about Kace. Was Kace going to die? No, this shadow couldn't predict the future. Nobody here could.

"Who are you?" I forced out.

He chuckled darkly. "Not Pan's shadow. No, *cariño*, I'm much worse." He closed the distance between us. "I'm the nightmare that lives in the darkness." He squeezed his fingers. "I'm the darkest part of him, the one you claim to love."

I widened my eyes as fear began to burrow into every crevice of my soul. He was *Kace's* shadow.

20: The Woods

I TOOK ANOTHER BITE of my soup, stopping when a presence drifted behind me. I peered up at Pan. "What do you want?" He was probably pissed that I had been told to steal magic from him. Anna usually got the worst end of these things, so I'd take the blame for this one.

He bent down to my level. "I need to talk to you in private. Finish your soup and meet me at Hangman's Tree." He stood and disappeared.

Eyes falling on my bowl, I ate slower, taking my sweet time. Was I in trouble? Possibly. Would he kill me knowing I was in love with his best friend? Unlikely.

When I finished, I put my dish in the bucket by the campfire and went into the woods. I found Hangman's Tree fairly quickly, facing Pan with whatever confidence I could muster up. "Why are we here?" I carefully eyed the place to make sure he had no tricks up his sleeve. Branches reached out with purpose. Leaves hung down like those of a willow tree, hoping for a taste of the magic this island offered.

He leaned back against the wide trunk. "Relax, Lia. I'm not going to try anything. I just want to talk. I want to talk about you and Kace."

I froze, eyes slowly drifting over to his. "What about us?" I was going to play dumb. It would most definitely be a bad idea, but I wasn't making very good choices right now. The last thing I wanted was to put Kace in harm's way.

"You know exactly what I'm talking about. Don't try to play dumb." He pushed himself upright and began stalking the area. I kept my gaze on him the whole time, head to toe. Ensuring he wasn't going to try anything with me. "You and my second-in-command have something going on between you, which you know I know. I've already discovered that it's nothing harmful," he paused, "yet."

"What do you mean?"

He released a sigh. "You poor girl. You have no clue." He stopped just a few feet away. "You and Kace are dating, correct?" His eyebrows shot up for a second.

I swallowed and slowly nodded. "Correct."

"Ah, so you've decided to cooperate. Smart girl." He waved his hand, looking up toward the gray skies. "I have no problem with you two being together. I only have to make sure that we are on the same page when I say this." His face darkened, his iris' withholding all the power from Neverland. "You've fallen in love with Kace and if you *dare* hurt him, I will not hesitate to kill you. I don't care if you are her sister. He always comes first. Am I clear?" Hadn't he already told me this?

I replied, "Crystal."

His demon retreated back to the corner of his mind, replaced by a lovely smile. "Good. I'm glad we had this talk, Lia." The air whisked him away the same way it always did—like a ghost.

I glanced back at the spot where Pan had vanished. Huffing and puffing, I started a journey farther into the woods. I didn't stop to think twice about my stupid decision. My curiosity peaked, and I yearned to explore more wild animals. Nobody could really stop me at this point.

I followed the trail only for so long before I took a sharp left and ditched the rules altogether. All that surrounded me now were tree trunks and pine needles—and of course the ever-so-lovely snow.

I scanned the area, my senses on high alert. I hummed to keep my fear at a minimum.

A twig snapped to my right and I spun. I slipped my dagger free, knuckles white as I held it out in front of me. I'd almost frozen to death in the river. Now I was going to be mauled by a killer bunny or worse.

Rabbit. Bunnies are babies and these are adults.

Damn Kace was already getting inside my head. I guess our relationship was affecting me in more ways than one.

Another twig snapped behind me. I turned around and found a panda leaning against a tree. Adorable was an understatement. Who didn't want to hug a loveable bear?

Killer rabbits aren't the only beasts we have to steer clear of.

This panda couldn't be vicious. Nothing that cute beared—pun intended—monstrosities.

I barely stepped back when the panda's eyes zipped through the trees and landed on me. Menacingly, he got onto all fours.

I swallowed. "I'm not here to hurt you. I can let you live in peace." I put my hand out to defend myself. Pointing the dagger at this wild animal wouldn't be the brightest idea.

The panda watched me like a predator observing its prey. I attempted to take a few more steps back but the panda charged.

A scream escaped, and I began to run in the opposite direction. I tripped over a root sticking up. As I flipped onto my backside, the panda jumped, using all its weight to hold me down, snapping at my face.

I yelled, "You're supposed to eat bamboo—not people!" I grabbed my dagger and wiggled my arm free from its paw. I stabbed the blade into its neck. It cried out before falling next to me. As I stood, I yanked the weapon free.

The blood was hard to see against the black fur, but it was there, sticky and warm between my fingers. I pushed my hair back and breathed heavily as I searched the woods. The trail was gone, and I was all alone. I didn't know where I was. I was completely vulnerable in these woods with wild, man-eating animals.

I whipped in every direction, trying to see which way I came from. "Shit!" I slapped the trunk of a tree and turned my back to it, falling against the bark. I didn't even know if I had enough skills to survive these woods, but I had to try. I couldn't go down without a fight.

After pushing myself off the tree, I started off in a random direction. I wasn't someone who could tell her north from her south. I couldn't use the sun, either, seeing as it had hardly been around these days. Even if it was out, I would've been super uneducated about which directions the sun would rise and set in. I knew it rose and set in the east and west, but I didn't know which was which. I looked up at the sky, but following the stars was a no go because the clouds had covered every inch. I was truly screwed.

I kept walking, careful about my steps this time. I didn't want to be heard by any other animals. I had made it without any mishaps throughout the day, but the darkness fell upon the island, and I was finding it harder to keep going. I could barely see. The cold was growing heavy, and crisper as it nipped at my face.

A tree a few feet away seemed homey. I stopped, glancing up at the branches. Could I sleep there? No, I wasn't a lion. I could barely sleep on a bunk bed without falling off the top.

My breath came out in a puff of chilly air. I had to keep moving. I couldn't let the darkness or the icy wind stop me. I wanted to see Kace again. As a *friend*, right?

I kept my feet moving for another few hours, but eventually they started to ache. The heels of my feet were causing me pain in every step, and I just wanted to sit down. Giving up would be so easy.

But if I didn't keep moving, I'd freeze. I couldn't stop. I'd be eaten in my sleep if I was lucky.

My toes numbed by now. The snow has seeped through my boots, socks soaked. Knee deep, I trudged on, fighting against the powder.

Needles and snow continued to fall on top of the fresh blanket I walked through.

I pulled my hood on tighter, trying to keep my ears warm. They were becoming useless to the point that the sounds of crickets were beginning to fade.

My stomach grumbled and ached, reminding me of the dinner I never got to eat. I couldn't eat the animals. Kace had warned me that they were poisoned.

It all felt so hopeless. I had every reason to stop and give up on life. I could just give into the elements without a second thought. I only had to stop moving. But I kept my feet in motion. One foot in front of the other. I couldn't give up on Kace. Nobody else would care if I died out here but he would. It would crush him. I didn't want him to give up the hope he had left. My relationship with him was the only reason he had any and I couldn't take it with me to the grave.

Every step became icier—more numb. All my senses were losing touch with reality, shutting down one by one. Touch had gone first, and taste slipped slowly after. Smell was going quickly, and my hearing wouldn't be long to follow.

I wondered if anyone at the camp was wondering where I was. What were they thinking? Did they even know I was gone?

They had to know. *Kace* had to know. He'd be scared to death. Was Pan trying to calm him down? Was Pan trying to find me? No. He would've found me by now. He knew exactly where I was, but he didn't give a shit. I knew that to be true. The sooner he rid himself of me, the better for him.

Everyone was probably sleeping while Kace worried endlessly about whether I was alive or not.

I couldn't tell what time it was or how long I had left in the night. The clouds had cleared about an hour or so ago, which was all the hope I clung to.

A guttural growl emerged from the trees, and I halted. No, please no. I was not in any state to fight anything off. I was a goner. I couldn't defend myself. "Please, go away," I whispered.

The growl stalked closer against my wishes. The large beast circled around until I could see what I was up against. "You've got to be kidding me."

Its red fur popped against the white scenery and black skies. Foxes were normally much smaller, but these mutations were a force to be reckoned with. They were the side effects of Pan losing himself to the monster.

I whimpered. "I can't fight you... Please, let me go."

Before I had a chance to pull out my dagger, the large animal lunged at me. I fell over as it pinned me, the fox baring its teeth.

The fox ripped into my shoulder. My scream traveled through the trees and into the sky, but I didn't know if anyone had heard me.

The gaping wound was exposed to the frigid air and the fox turned its head away as if something else caught its attention. It ran into the woods, disappearing in the darkness as quickly as it came.

I grabbed onto my shoulder and sat up with whatever strength I had left. I began to cry. I wanted to survive but it was getting harder every second I stayed out here. I had everything against me. I was certain I wouldn't make it out alive.

Screaming once more, it echoed, bouncing between trees and shooting into the sky at last. I got up and pushed forward, scowling. I wouldn't be a quitter. That's exactly what Pan expected and what Kace feared.

I had to prove that I was stronger than I looked. I didn't want Pan to take me for the weak girl he saw me as. I had to survive this no matter what it cost. I could lose my toes, but it wouldn't matter. I could lose my ears. I could lose everything but at least I could say I never lost my dignity. I was going to go down fighting for my life. Neverland couldn't steal my will to *live*.

21: Pillow

Stumbling was the easy part.

I dropped down to my knees before collapsing into the snow. Numb—that described my entire body. This was my end. My heartbeat slowed. My vision faded in and out. My hearing was beginning to go whack, too.

Something whispered in my ear, "Follow the needles..."

I looked up and locked my gaze with the pine needles. They hadn't fallen off the tree in a random order. Instead, they all pointed in one direction. A direction that must have led back to the camp.

Dragging my feet along, I scanned the area for that voice, but I didn't know where it had come from. Had Pan helped me? Had he helped me save myself? Would he so as dare to do that?

As I made it to the clearing of the camp, Kace spotted me in an instant. He rushed over and caught me just as I fell into his arms. "Cariño, what the hell happened?" He looked for culprits, but nobody stood out. Nobody had done this but the wild animals. "Let's get you inside." He helped me into his cabin and set me down on the cot.

What could I say?

After he grabbed supplies, he began working on fixing up my injuries. I needed to be thrown into a fire right about now.

Kace finished bandaging up my shoulder, then he looked at me and tied his dry cloak around my shoulders, being careful not to touch my wound. "I'm so grateful you made it back." He handed me a bowl of hot soup, helping me sit up.

I scarfed it down, not even giving time for the food to cool. I was far too hungry while glaciers iced my veins. I nodded a little. "I can't feel my toes." I dropped my gaze to my toes.

Kace followed my eyes. "Why did you go out there?"

"I don't know. I wanted to see the other animals." I took some more bites, burning the taste buds on my tongue.

So long little dudes. See you in a few weeks, when you get better. If I'm still alive...

He cleared his throat. "Was it worth it?"

"Don't. Please... Don't lecture me on my stupidity." I continued to stuff my mouth with pieces of carrot and potato. I finished the bowl with shivers as the food warmed my core. When it had warmed the rest of me, I almost cried out in relief.

I glanced at Kace, sighing. "I'm sorry. Can you please get me three pairs of socks to wear?" My eyelids started to grow heavy. I hadn't slept all day or night. Exhaustion was all I had left to ease.

He got three pairs of socks. I began to put them on my feet, sighing in contentment as my toes began to warm up. He helped me get the last of the socks on, then he moved me onto his bed. I wrapped myself in the cloak, keeping the warmth trapped inside. I closed my eyes, and within seconds, a dream flashed before me.

I OPENED MY EYES; I was sure of it. But I couldn't see. I couldn't breathe. Something soft covered my face. I reached out and grabbed at a pair of arms, gliding my hands up to find a face. They were smothering me with a *pillow.*

I could just give up and let my time end here. But what about Kace? He'd be alone. Pan would deem me a quitter. I hadn't worked so hard training just to lose.

Feeling for their face was impossible. Where were they? The pressure lifted, everything falling silent. I threw the pillow off and sat up, scanning the room. Nobody was here. I gasped for air and looked at the door. Someone tried to kill me. Someone had *actually* tried to kill me.

I jumped out of the bed to find Kace.

Attempting to catch my breath from the shock of the incident wasn't easy in this weather. I just stumbled around the camp like a crippled person—which I was. "Kace!" I didn't care if anyone saw me in this state. I had spent all night surviving the woods. I earned the right to act crazy after what happened. I was still alive and that's all I really cared about.

Arms wrapped around my torso from the back. "Whoa, what's wrong?"

Every part of me relaxed when I recognized the voice. "Kace..." I placed my hand over his, his hands firm against my abdomen as he took most of the weight from me.

He whispered against the top of my ear, "You are not in any state to be up and walking. It's only been two hours since you fell asleep. Come on." He helped me back to his cabin and lay me back down.

I grabbed his hand, refusing to let him go. "Someone tried to kill me."

"What do you mean?" He brought his face closer to allow me to speak softer.

I shifted my eyes to his, losing myself in those light brown flecks of his. What was wrong with me? "I couldn't breathe. I tried to fight it off and then he was just gone. He was trying to suffocate me."

Kace scanned the cabin for any signs of a break in. "Where did he go?"

"I'm not sure. I didn't hear him leave, and I didn't see him." Was I just losing my mind? "We can't tell anyone else. Please... I just wanted to find you. I'm too scared to be alone." I glance at our intertwined fingers.

He pressed a small kiss to my temple. "I'm here now. If he comes back, I'll kill him." He gave me a smirk as if bragging about his skills. Men and their egos—so interchangeable.

Taking a deep breath, I contemplated sleep. But I needed it to keep my sanity. "Okay... Please don't leave me. Please," I begged.

He pulled me into his arms, tightening his embrace until my muscles relaxed. "I won't. You got yourself a bodyguard."

I was out like a light.

Opening my eyes, I quickly sat up. "Kace!"

"Hey, I'm right here." He looked at me from his desk.

I lay back down and rubbed my hand against my face. "Sorry. I just assumed..."

"I left you?" he finished my sentence.

I turned my body in his direction and slipped my hands under my cheek. "That's not what I said."

"You were thinking it."

"Fine, whatever, you can believe what you want." I twisted onto my, facing the ceiling. "Don't you have to go be obnoxious somewhere else?"

"I have nowhere else to go until six," he replied.

"You can't even tell time here." As I sat up, I looked over at him.

"You don't know how far my skills extend to." He shot me a playful smile.

I dangled my feet over the side of his bed. "I need to find out what those skills are."

"Later." Kace got up from the chair and approached me. "We need to find the person who tried to kill you."

He looked so much taller now. Sure, I'd been sitting down, but was he always this tall? "Do we have to?"

His muscles flexed as he folded his arms across his chest. "Uh, yes, we do have to. He tried to *kill* you. We have to find the criminal."

"He? Lili is not exempt from this investigation. She let our brother die." I stood, no less having to peer up at him than I already was. I called them a *he*, too, but that was neither here nor there.

"Okay, so anyone and everyone is included. Am I also a suspect?"

"No. I trust you."

With a smile, he gave me a peck. "I'm glad you trust me enough to know it's not me."

"You also don't have a quiet walk. Although, you could've snuck out another way since it is your room. However, I would've heard something. It can't be you." I dismissed the idea with the wave of my hand.

He choked on some air. "Well, thanks for eliminating me from the list."

"I'm somewhat of a good detective."

He cocked an eyebrow. "I highly doubt that. If you were, you wouldn't have given up on your sister because it got too hard."

My jaw dropped. "Kace, why..." I didn't finish my question. I didn't know if I wanted to hear the answer to it.

"I understand that it's been difficult. I'd never refute that. I'm also not going to excuse her actions, but you must understand she had nobody to turn to. I was her only friend when she got here. She worked so hard to be accepted, but she barely got that. She wasn't taught how to love. She doesn't know what it even means. Lili needs to be saved from herself."

I played with the string from my cloak. "I need time to come up with a plan."

"How much time? How much time do you think is left until Neverland is nothing?" He tilted his head in question.

I dropped the strings. "I need time to fix my mental state. In case you haven't noticed, I just spent a whole night alone in the woods. I was freezing, scared, starving. I was dehydrated. I nearly died, attacked by two different animals. Now someone here in camp is trying to kill me. I have to focus on saving my own life first. I can't save my own sister if I can't even save myself. I can't help anyone from the grave."

Kace sighed, his eyes shifting to his boots before resting back on my face. He kept opening his mouth to say something but then decided against it.

I wanted to make it better, but I didn't know what I could tell him. Instead, I went back to playing with the strings.

He grasped my hands, pulling them from the bow at the front of my neck. "Let's go find the asshole that tried to kill you."

We left his cabin and went to the training area.

I started to scope out the area and everyone in it. "Well, see anyone with hatred towards me? Even someone who looks suspicious will do."

With a nod, he searched the area, pretending he was just observing the lost boys.

Pan came, and almost immediately, everyone turned their attention to him. "Even after the incidents over the past month, things are going to proceed as normal. I'm aware some of you want to rest, but we train every day. I also do not want to hear anyone asking for their wounds to be healed."

We all went back to our training when he finished, and I glanced at Kace. "What was that about?"

"Have you asked Pan to heal you?" His gaze never left Pan as he asked me that question.

I shook my head. "I haven't. There was one time but that was a while back, when he cut my arm. I haven't asked him to heal me since."

"Someone else has asked him to heal them. Maybe it's our suspect. Maybe he was trying to get away, but he hurt himself." He finally looked at me.

"Maybe, but that means that Pan knows he tried to kill me."

He shook his head, shrugging. "Not necessarily. He could've just told

Pan he lost in a fight. If Pan knew, he would've probably made a big spectacle out of it. And you said you were a good detective?" He gave me a teasing smile.

"Hey, I said *somewhat* good." I stuck my tongue out. "We can still spot him. Or her. Would Pan have healed Lili if she had tried to kill me?"

"Most likely." He picked up an arrow and bow, stretching it against the string. With one eye closed, he released it and it flew, then hit the bullseye. "He loves Lili. He would do anything for her."

"He does love her, doesn't he?" I'd seen it in his eyes.

Kace dropped his arms, bow still in hand. "You told me he does."

"I did? When?" I tilted my head.

"When you were high. You told me he loves her." He went back to practice his skills again.

"Oh." Turning away from him, I raked my gaze over the circle of boys. A blonde boy sat on the sidelines in a maroon-colored shirt. I squinted my eyes, noting the way he watched me. I gasped when my eyes met his. "Asa."

22: To Love or Not to Love

My eyes couldn't be playing games on me. "It was you!" I pointed right at Asa as he shot to his feet.

Kace's eyes darted to us before realizing what I was talking about. My own cousin tried to *murder* me.

Everyone stopped what they were doing, giving us an audience.

I stomped over to Asa as Kace grabbed my arms, holding me back. I fought against his restraint but it was no use. Weak, as usual.

"I can't believe you tried to kill me! I've tried to be nice to you and you push me away!" Anger boiled before spilling over the pot, sizzling as it hit heat and evaporated into steam.

Pan appeared. "What's going on?"

Breathing heavily, I tried to rip myself from Kace's grasp again. Useless. "He tried to suffocate me in my sleep. It's so obvious that it couldn't be anyone else." I could've just gotten Asa killed but I didn't care anymore. I just wanted to see him pay for his crimes.

Pan glanced at Asa and grabbed his shoulder. "We need to have a chat." Asa's eyes swirled with terror before both vanished into nothing.

Kace pulled my back against his chest. We both feared what I might do if he didn't hold me back.

He whispered into my ear, "Let's go on a date and distract you. Pan is going to handle this. We can come back to this when we are more level-headed."

The shaking in my limbs eased up as I focused on steadying my breathing. "You know what a date is?"

"I'm not too young to know what a date is. Dating was a thing even in my days." He smiled a bit, pushing some of my curls out of my face. The heat fled my face, only to return the minute Kace's knuckles brushed against my cheek.

We didn't have nice clothes to change into and I didn't have any way to do my hair or put on makeup. So Kace and I went to his cabin to stay out of the wintry jungle. After I'd spent a whole night in the woods, I'd rather spend my days inside.

"There's not much to do." I looked around as if I was searching for some secret passageway to escape. Asa had used it.

Kace chuckled, slipping his hand in mine. "Well, for starters, we can learn about each other. I'll tell you about where I come from, and you can tell me about where you come from."

We sat down on the bed.

I nodded a bit. "Sounds fun. I don't know a lot about you, so what should I know?" I asked.

He leaned back, hands behind his head. His shirt started to ride up his stomach, and something in me sparked. "I'm an only child. Mom and Dad wanted a girl, but they got me instead and tried to raise me as a girl."

"What?" How could parents do such a thing to their own child?

"They dressed me up in girl clothes. They tried to name me Dolores, but I kept changing it to Kace." I stifled a laugh, picturing Kace as Dorlores. "It caused a major rift. I wanted to play in the dirt and do boyish things. I loved the outdoors and rough-housing, as you call it. My parents couldn't accept that."

I pulled my legs up into a crisscross.

"Eventually my parents began to get physical about it. When I got a bit older, I kept telling them I was a male whether they liked it or not."

"You get what you get and you don't throw a fit... I guess even adults need to be taught that." I gestured.

"My parents wanted to go further. They wanted to mutilate the boys. The doctor didn't approve of that. He said my parents were crazy for wanting to do such a thing to me, and even as hard as he tried to report it, nothing ever happened. We went back home and that was the night that I had asked for help. I had opened my mind enough to believe maybe I could escape somehow before my parents forced that surgery on me. Pan appeared out of nowhere and promised a better life. I wound up here and have been grateful since."

I averted my eyes from his bare stomach. "I'm glad. I'm glad you got away from those awful people. So, when you ended up here, was Pan the nice guy?"

He chuckled a bit and shifted, his pants moving down his hips a tad. Goodness gracious, could he stop with that? I could hardly look his way. "He was. Pan was great. He was witty but also still a bit cocky. Genuinely, he was a good guy. I told him about my parents and he wanted to help any other boys like us both. I think the idea that Pan lived on this island and had the freedom to be himself ultimately lifted his spirits."

Pull up your pants.

"Why didn't he want to help girls back then?"

"I told you about Hook using both of us. She was the one who ultimately ruined who he was. After her, no lost girl could step foot here. But girls had come and went before then, most not making it long unfortunately."

Before Hook, he didn't have anything against us.

"He just wanted a place for boys to be boys. I wanted a place to be myself. We all did," Kace said.

Put down your damn shirt.

"When Wendy came here, was it before Hook or after? Was Pan nice when she first arrived? I just wonder if maybe..."

"If Pan and Wendy ever got together? No. But I do believe he had a small crush on her at one point. It never went anywhere because Wendy never returned the feelings. And she wasn't always the maid. Pan made her the maid when Hook screwed us over. Pan stopped trusting women and he blamed Wendy for why he ended up the way he did.

"Pan thought that when Wendy didn't return the feelings, it forced Pan to find love in someone like Hook which in turn got him torn to shreds, so his monster came out. When Wendy then had been sneaking around with Tinker, he punished Wendy by forcing her to hide away as just a maid and made her sleep in the cage. Wendy was his attempt at learning to trust girls, but she didn't do so well with that. Hook became the final straw and that's what led Pan to the extinction of lost girls in Neverland."

I picked at my nails. "What about Lili? How does she play into this? I mean, is Pan going to trust women again?"

Kace shrugged and sat forward, his shirt finally covering his abdomen. *Thank you. God. I can breathe again.* "Lili is certainly helping with the lost girl situation but hurting more than she's helping." Oh, he had *no* idea. "Faithfully, we can fix that."

He didn't know that I was fighting for Lili again. I wasn't giving up. I just feared my love for him was a distraction. I wasn't ready to lose Kace just because my sister wanted to slit throats for sport.

"Pan knows about us," I whispered.

He furrowed his brows. "He knows about us? I should've known. But it sounds like he isn't going to break us apart."

"For now. If I hurt you, he won't hesitate to kill me. You know how Pan feels about betrayal."

Kace scoffed. "Yeah, I know." He leaned back into the pillows, and I internally groaned. *More abs.* "Just don't hurt me."

That was easy for him to say. He was in this relationship all the way. I wanted to be, but I loved him and that made things harder. It was a distraction from the end goal. However, if I told him that, it would hurt him and I wouldn't live to defend myself.

"What about you? Tell me about your family. I know Lili told me some things, but I want to get both sides of the story." He rolled his hand for me to go on.

I looked up at the ceiling to focus my eyes somewhere other than his skin. I shrugged. "Where do I start? Mom and dad had their issues. They weren't the best parents, but I can't say they were the worst. Although, I never felt what Lili felt. Mom and dad didn't treat me as badly as they did her."

He gave a slight nod.

I continued, "I guess I remember most of what it was like when Pan came to me. I never asked for any of this."

The trees outside my window swayed gently in the wind, creating a rhythm as if they were dancing to the music of the night. The moonlight lit up half my room through my window. The other half had been left out, hiding from whatever tragedy was left in our family after my sister's disappearance.

Cop cars drove by, looking for her. She'd been missing for nearly three months now. Nobody was giving up yet and I hoped they never did.

I was so alone without her here, so lost without my other half. Had she run off to the river? Did she fall in and get swept away? No, she wasn't dead. I would know if she was. I just knew she was still alive.

She used to tell me that being lost didn't mean you were alone. Was she lost? Was she alone?

I was.

A light knock tapped on my window. A boy waited, so I opened the window. "Who are you?"

"I know where your sister is and I can take you to her," he replied, a thick English accent lacing his tongue.

"My sister doesn't like boys." He mumbled something about it being ironic that she ended up on his island. I went to close my window on him, but he

gripped my arm.

"Let me take you to her." He yanked me through the window and up into the sky. I'd fainted along the way from all of the impossibilities. Surely I was just dreaming.

"I remember all of this like it was yesterday. He pretended to care about her well-being. How can he act so nice but be so vicious?" I turned to Kace.

My eyes flickered down to his bare stomach one last time, and then I'd felt it. The switch. Or a spark. It had flipped—ignited. And I was the one left imagining peeling his shirt from his body in a fit of passion.

His smile appeared, but subtle. "He wasn't acting so much as he was rather reliving who he once had been."

23: Hallucinations

I YELLED AS I cut a branch in two with my blade. Everyone thought I was losing my mind. Why did nobody believe me?

I glanced back at the camp.

"Lia, we should talk," Pan said. He stood in the doorway of his cabin, arms folded across his chest.

He was asking me for a punishment. He wanted my opinion on punishing Asa. How did I answer?

I followed him into his cabin, stopping when Kace came into view. "What's going on? Did you kill Asa?" I swallowed the shame, eyebrows creased in fear. What had I done? I didn't actually want him to die.

Pan closed the door, shaking his head. "Asa never tried to kill you. As much as I enjoy punishing lost boys, I can't punish him for something he never did."

"But someone was there. They tried to kill me. They held a pillow over my face." I straightened my shoulders.

Kace gave me a look of pity. What the hell was that? "Is it possible you imagined it? Maybe you're having trouble with everything that's happened. You've been through a lot lately." He stood up and attempted to grab my hand, but I yanked it away.

"No. I did not imagine it. Someone was there. They tried to kill me. Why don't you believe me?" I had to hold back the tears that formed on the rims of

my lower lids.

Pan rubbed the bridge of his nose. "You said you didn't even hear them leave. No footsteps. You couldn't feel them at all. You imagined it, Lia. Your brain is trying to adjust to all the trauma."

"You're wrong. I didn't imagine any of it. I'm sane!" I turned on my heel and ran out of the cabin, ignoring their calls. I headed straight to the woods, and maybe it was a stupid decision, but I was not crazy. I'd prove it somehow.

I stopped beside a tree and narrowed my eyes at a creature in the distance. The last thing I would do is approach it. And if I let it spot me, I'd be a goner. It was me or him.

A few steps forward, then a few more before I sprinted towards it. I jumped on its back and fell into the snow. I flipped onto my back, eyes darting around the woods. It was gone. No, that wasn't possible.

Sitting up, I wiped the snow from my face.

The creature popped up again, and I leaped to my feet, taking slow strides. The only sound heard for miles was the soft crunch of my boot against the snow.

As I approached, I hopped onto its back, wrapping my arms around its neck, but again I hit the snow. On all fours, I searched the area. This wasn't right. This creature was like Pan. It had air magic, or gold magic, whatever they called it.

Magic. That was my ticket to proving I wasn't losing it. I had to steal the magic from Pan.

Finding my way home from the woods was a challenge, but I eventually came across the camp. Kace saw me, but I ignored him as he tried to get my attention. I ignored *everyone* and walked straight through, to Hangman's Tree.

I stopped in front of it, exhaling.

"Lia, what are you doing?" Kace asked from behind me.

He'd used my name. How clever of the boy.

I walked towards the tree and placed my palms flat against the trunk, feeling around. When a door opened up, I stepped inside.

"Lia!"

The room inside was a lot bigger than I had thought and finding this magic wouldn't be easy. I started looking, dropping objects all over the place.

"Lia, stop. You shouldn't even be here. Let's just go get some sleep." Kace approached, but I sidestepped him every time.

I found a shelf full of bottles. The blue one called my name and I reached for it. Kace grasped my arm and spun me to face him.

I opened the bottle. "I won't let you bring me down." I chugged it.

"No!" Kace ripped it from my hands but it was too late. "Why would you do that?"

"I know what I felt. I know what happened. You refuse to believe me. Asa is lying. He tried to kill me." I grabbed another bottle—green magic. "I need proof. I need strength."

He took it from me. "You need sleep. This is not like you."

I narrowed my eyes on him. "And your shadow threatening me is? Is that like you, Kace?"

"What?" He furrowed his brows.

"Everyone knows Pan's shadow is detached, but do you care to explain why yours is—why he wants to kill me?" I yanked the bottle from his hands, but before I could get it down my throat, it was thrown to the ground. The glass shattered and magic went everywhere. "What the hell?" I shouted.

Pan's nails dug into my wrist as he twirled me, pulling me into his face. "You are in no state to be drinking magic. You are never in any position to take magic from me."

"Pan, take it easy. She's not wholly there," Kace said.

Pan's jaw clenched, but he let go of me. "Think twice before stealing from me again."

Kace grabbed my hand, dragging me out of the tree. "I just saved your life."

"Am I supposed to be grateful?" I whispered. "Am I supposed to be happy that I've been accused of being a liar?"

He came to a halt and turned to face me, our chests bumping. "You know better. You know better than to piss off Pan. We were trying to help you. We took your word for it. He questioned Asa extensively. Asa has no reason to lie about killing you, but he didn't do it. You refuse to believe anyone else's truth but your own. Your sister tried to tell you her truth and you refused to believe it. You wanted to see the best in everyone but sometimes, it's not there."

"What are you saying?" I choked on a sob.

"I'm saying that you need to step into her shoes and quit being so damn selfish for once." He let go of me, stepping back. "Get some sleep." He disappeared in the direction of his cabin.

A few tears rolled down my cheeks as I dropped my gaze to the ground. I gasped for air before breaking. I fell to my knees, and the cries grew louder.

Something brushed against my hair, and I looked back to see Kace's shadow. He circled me until he stood in front. "You're always so weak."

"Go away."

He bent to my level. "And nobody believes you, do they? They think you're losing your mind."

"Leave me alone!"

He grabbed my jaw, making me face him. "But you got one part wrong, Lia. Asa didn't try to kill you."

I choked on yet another sob. "*You*. You tried to kill me. But why? Kace..." I had thought maybe Kace cared about me, but I was wrong. I'd fallen in love and put myself in harm's way. Pan warned me not to hurt him, but nobody ever warned Kace not to do the same to me. "Why?"

"Don't you get it?" He growled. "I'm trying to make you a fighter." His fingers tightened. "Kace is pathetic. He can't do what is needed to make you strong. Look at you. You're crying on the ground. You're woeful."

"Screw you!" I shouted.

He snickered. "Not me, but certainly my better half." He sounded nothing like Kace. "Get your ass off the ground. Stop crying. Kace said what you refused to admit to yourself. Lili didn't become a fighter by curling into a fetal position."

"And now she's different."

"And now you'll be dead if you don't get out of the winter storm. No amount of crying wins a battle." He stood, gesturing for me to follow.

I slowly pushed myself onto my feet, wiping away the tears. I cleared my throat. "Why are you helping me? Pan's shadow is cruel. Why aren't you?"

He barely looked my way. "Never thought you'd ask those questions. They're not important. Let's focus on getting you to fight."

"I know how to fight."

"You don't have the heart of a fighter. You survived the woods. But what happened when you were confronted with the truth that Asa didn't kill you? You ran. What happened when Kace told you the truth about yourself? You cried. You might fight for your life, but you're a coward in the face of true words. You're hardly a fighter." He led me to the training area, waving me over.

I followed him over to the targets. "I can almost hit those."

"Can you hit them when someone is telling you what you don't want to hear?"

"What?"

"Let's test it." He gave me a bow and arrow. "Aim for the bullseye."

I fixed my position and aimed.

"Why are you afraid to face the truth?"

Facing the shadow, I lowered my bow and arrow. "What are you talking about?"

He pointed to the target. "Focus on that."

I sighed and pointed at the target again.

"You're afraid to love Kace," he said.

The arrow hit the edge of the target once I'd let go. I'd gotten worse. "What are you talking about?"

He laughed, maniacally. "I'm *his* shadow. Why are you afraid to love him?"

"Like you said, he's terrible at preparing me for a battle. If I love him, I'll never save Lili." I grabbed another arrow and this time, it hit one of the inner rings.

He stood behind me, his chill breezing by me. "You're afraid to love, but isn't it your love that's going to save Lili?"

"This love is different. Loving Kace won't save Lili." I glanced at him.

He leaned down, whispering, "No, but it'll certainly save Kace. It'll save *you*. Saving you will save Lili, will it not?"

I swallowed. "What do you want from me?"

He pulled back with a humph. "I want you to admit the truth. I want you to face it—embrace it. That's the only way you will ever be stronger. If you refuse to believe, you'll never get far."

Grabbing another arrow, I aimed at the target and let go. It hit the outer rings again. "I love Kace." Arrow. "I'm in love with Kace." Aim. "I'm afraid he won't feel the same way." Shoot. "I'm afraid our friendship will be over, and it'll be my fault." I lowered the bow, staring at the arrow that had finally hit the bullseye. "I'm afraid of losing him," I breathed.

Silence engulfed me. Snowflakes started falling, landing everywhere they could. I turned my head to face his shadow, but he was gone. I'd done what he asked me to. I faced the truth.

If I was going to carry this out, I had to put my words into action. I had to tell Kace how I felt. I'd never be able to save Lili if I kept it buried inside me.

I left the training area and headed to Kace's cabin. I lifted my hand, ready to knock, but dropped it. Was I ready for this? Maybe not, but I'd never be.

After knocking, I waited for him to open the door. Nobody came, and I wondered if he was so tired, he wasn't going to wake up.

I turned the knob and stepped inside his room. It was empty. Kace was nowhere to be found, and now I worried something had happened to him. No, he was strong. He wouldn't do something stupid like I would after our fight. I had to believe he just went somewhere private to get space. Shaking the ice from his veins.

I sat in his bed, relaxing my shoulders, and releasing a sigh. He'd be back soon. He had to come back eventually, right?

Of course. He would never leave me for too long. Even if he didn't love me the way I loved him, he loved me somehow. He would never leave me to do all this alone. Wherever he went, he'd come back from—and I'd be here when he did.

24: Light

I scanned the area before approaching Hangman's Tree. "Let's see what you're really made of, Pan." I opened the door and stepped inside. I made sure everything was clear. I wasn't about to get caught this time.

The broken bottle of green magic had been cleaned up by now, so I decided to grab the bottle of gold magic and stuff it into my leggings. I needed to keep this as leverage.

I searched through his books and found a bit on his backstory, but that wasn't what intrigued me. No, what intrigued me was his connection to Neverland. His emotions were tethered to it.

Swallowing the lies, I discovered the very thing he kept dear. Neverland had never lost its balance. It had never been out of balance to begin with. Pan had gone frigid, and numb. He wasn't truly happy with my sister like this. He wasn't happy at all. Maybe a part of him knew what her end goal had been—to kill him all along.

When I looked to my right, I caught sight of his dagger on the table. I picked it up and twisted the blade between my fingers. Why didn't he carry this with him?

I set it down and picked up another book. What was Pan hiding? Why was he so protective of it?

"I thought I might find you here," someone said.

I jumped and pulled out my dagger. Wasn't sure why I kept trying to use it. Everyone here was better than I was. "Damn, Anna, you can't just sneak up like that."

"I didn't sneak up."

"I didn't hear you come in."

She leaned against the wall. "That might be because I have green magic. It's magic of the earth, remember? This tree is made of the earth, and I can mold through it. It was difficult to master."

Setting the book down, I pulled out the bottle. "I got it. Well, magic. I already drank the blue magic, but I have gold magic, too."

She pushed herself off, hurrying over. "Whoa. Do you realize what you could do with this? Lia, you could be more powerful than Pan."

"Hardly. He's the one connected to the island." I sighed.

"Because it's his wish, sure. But if you have blue and gold magic, that's..." She cleared her throat. "You have more abilities than he does."

"I don't want to rely on magic to save my sister."

She grabbed my arms, stepping forward. "It might be your only choice. This is an island that exists only on a wish, and if you have more magic than Pan... Think of everything we could do together!" She lifted a finger, closing her fist. A vine from behind me wrapped around my arm. "Where's the green magic?"

"Pan destroyed it. He caught me and he broke the bottle before I had a chance to drink it. I wasn't thinking straight. Now I am, Anna, and I don't want to have all this magic." I tightened my grip around the bottle. I could create more green magic, couldn't I? All I had to do was use my blue magic to enchant the water. Then it'd be all mine.

"Don't give up on the option just yet." She grabbed the bottle and admired it. "Keep it just in case."

Chills ran up my spine as her vine retreated. My eyes shifted to Anna. "All right."

She turned around and ran her fingers through her long hair. Some days

I envied how easy her hair was to maintain and brush through. Not a curl in sight. She'd changed into a more versatile outfit for combat.

Her shoulders slumped forward. "I apologize for being away. I was...recharging." I took a few steps towards her, but she turned around in a hurry, stopping me. "Some days I do okay and other days I don't. Wendy's death hits me."

"I'm sorry." I studied my fingers. I'd taken blue magic, the one thing Wendy had. Did it remind Anna of her? "I'm sorry that I took what was hers. I'm not trying to replace her."

She shoved the gold magic into my hands as a few tears fell. Her jaw clenched. "You could never replace her. Nobody can." She walked towards the door and paused. "I'm sorry, too." Like that, she became like the roots and molding through the trunk.

This time, I didn't waste more time standing around. I hurried around the room, skimming every book I could find, and just when I was about to give up, I found some that piqued my interest.

"Magic," I muttered. Each book was labeled for which magic belonged to which. I thought I had read wrong when I came across the types of magic, but I hadn't. There were *five* types, and I'd only ever heard of the four.

Gold magic—air. Blue magic—water. Green magic—earth. Red magic—fire. And yellow magic—light.

I grabbed the books on red and yellow magic and took them with me, as well as the bottle of gold magic. I returned to my cabin and locked the door, sitting on the bed. I opened the book. Nobody here had yellow magic. Was it hard to find? Useless? It made no sense.

Green magic was attained by drinking blue magic. Blue magic was from getting high off gold magic. Yellow magic was mixed in there somewhere, right?

Then it hit me. *Sex*.

Yellow magic came from sexual contact. Anna told me you could get magic that way, but since Pan had never had sex without a condom before, nobody knew what kind of magic came from that act. And it wasn't as if Anna or Wendy would have ever experienced magic from that kind of thing.

I wasn't about to sleep with Pan to get yellow magic, but I knew someone who would love the idea. I just needed to talk her into it.

Closing the book, I left my cabin and knocked on Pan's. When Lili answered, she riddled me with a nasty look. "What do you want?"

"I want to talk to you."

"I don't want to see you."

"Do you want to get magic?" I wasn't going to tell her what kind of magic. The last thing any villain wanted was *light* magic.

She straightened her posture. "I'm listening."

I pulled her outside, towards an area that was more private. "Pan can give you magic, and he knows it, but he's been keeping it from you." He didn't want her to have light magic, either, but I wouldn't mention that.

She narrowed her eyes. "How? What are you talking about?" If she could get yellow magic, we'd have a chance at winning.

After scanning the area, I whispered, "Through sex. You can get magic by having sex with him, but he can't know that you're trying to get magic. It's the condoms that stop magic from spreading. If you poke a hole in his condoms, he'll never know, and you'll get magic." Was I a terrible person to suggest it? Maybe.

But seeing as nobody aged, it was impossible for her to get pregnant. So the only logical explanation to why Pan used protection was to keep the yellow magic to himself.

She crossed her arms. "How do I know you're not lying?"

"What do I gain from you having unprotected sex with Pan? I'm not exactly interested in that part of your life, and quite frankly, you aren't going to get pregnant. You want magic, don't you?"

Lili scoffed. "What do you gain from this, is what I meant. You wouldn't be helping me get magic for no reason."

Shit, I hadn't even thought of that plan.

"Because Kace's shadow told me." Well, to an extent.

"Kace's shadow?"

"He's been...threatening me lately. He doesn't want you to have magic either and I figured if his shadow is evil, I should do the opposite of what his shadow wants." His shadow wasn't entirely wicked, if I could call it that. But it sure had an interesting way of showing its affection towards me.

More scoffing. "I'm evil, too. Lia. If he doesn't want me to have it, there's a good reason."

It was time to pull out the big guns. "What do you want more? Do you want Kace's shadow making all your decisions for you, or do you want to make your own? You will never be Pan's equal without magic, and everyone here knows that." I didn't mean those words the way they came out but I had to hit her where it hurt most to get her to listen to me.

Her hands balled up into fists, but she relaxed her shoulders. "Fine, I'll poke holes in the condoms. But if I end up pregnant, you're the one removing the fetus." She turned on her heel. I wasn't even sure how that'd be possible. Sperm didn't just fertilize the egg. It took at least half a day or longer, and by then it would die, forever lost and searching.

I grabbed her arm, stopping her. "Wait." I pulled her back to me, hugging her tight. "I miss you." I almost started crying, but I stopped myself this time. No more emotional Lia.

She didn't return the hug, but when I let go, something flashed in her eyes. Was it shame? Lili was in there somewhere, begging for me to rescue her.

I let her go back to her cabin with Pan while I returned to mine. The books were watching me, and I felt a tinge of hope. Later, I'd research more about red magic, but yellow magic gave us a fighting chance. What would happen if an evil being had light magic?

Someone chuckled behind me. "You lied to her."

Glancing back at Kace's shadow, I frowned. "I didn't lie. I just didn't tell her every detail. There's a difference." My eyes fell to his feet before I met his glowing red eyes. "What happened to her?" I plopped onto the bed. "Do you know?"

He released a sigh. "Her shadow was ripped away."

"Like Pan's?"

"Pan ripped away his own shadow. Lili...she wanted to save him. She tried to, but he ripped away her shadow. Once you go dark, you never go back on your own." He crossed his arms, leaning his bicep against the wall.

I furrowed my brows. "So, if your shadow is separated, you're evil? But...Kace..."

"That's not important right now. What is important is that Lili gets that magic." He gestured.

That had to have been why Kace was so harsh with me. Now, he didn't want to see me at all. Had I lost him for good?

"Cariño."

"What?" I looked at him.

"You did the right thing."

"By doing what?"

"By convincing Lili to get light magic. You told a few lies about me but that's all right." His laugh was lighthearted. "It'll be good for her."

I rubbed my palms along my thighs. "What happens if an evil being gets light magic?" I took a deep breath.

He shrugged. "I don't know. It's never been done before. Pan never had light magic." He never could sleep with himself, so I supposed light magic was impossible for him to ever attain.

"Is it more powerful than gold?"

Kace's shadow shook his head. "No, nothing is. But it's...it's enough power to combat the demon side. Lili has a fighting chance. Light can illuminate out the darkness, and vice versa. Let's hope this magic is powerful enough to save them both."

Save them both.

I hoped it was enough. If it could hold her off long enough from murdering innocent people, I could find a way to bring the two of them to their shadows. I just wasn't sure how yet.

Kace was possibly battling his demons, and I had nobody by my side but Anna. Except I didn't even have her because she had her own issues to sort out. So why was Kace's shadow helping me?

"Why are you not trying to kill me now?" I locked eyes with him.

He looked out my window, eyes dancing through the trees. "Oh, uh, I think I heard someone coming this way. See you around." He vanished.

I waited in silence, but nobody ever came through the door. He lied to me, and he was avoiding my questions. Something was up, but what?

With my plan of getting Lili light magic put into motion, I could focus on a few other things. I could focus on Kace's shadow for now. I could save him, too.

Tomorrow's journey would be all about his shadow and finding out where Kace was. I'd prepare for any outcome. Maybe he would try to kill me. Maybe I would lose, but at least I could find some answers before shit hit the fan.

Kace would want me to save him from the darkness, so I would give him exactly that. It was my turn to protect him from harm—my turn to tend to his injuries.

I had to be *Neverland's* savior and I'd be alone for the ride.

25: Diego

I'd spent my entire morning searching for Kace, and Pan. Neither of them were around. Even Lili was gone. If all of them were missing their shadows, they were a team of three now. I was left as a team of *one*.

It got lonely when I had nobody to talk to. The lost boys were afraid of talking to me, knowing that I had a target on my back for Lili's new policy. Nobody wanted to die, and I understood that. I couldn't blame them for putting their lives above my selfish needs for a friend.

As I ventured into the woods, I shot my hand out, palm facing away from me. "Damnit. It doesn't work." I dropped my arm.

"What are you trying to do?" he asked.

Kace's shadow was back. He was the only one around anymore. Did I have any other choice? Not right now.

I faced him. "Trying to use my magic. You know the blue magic I stole from Pan? Yeah, I drank it and I'm trying to use it, but I guess it doesn't work on snow." I frowned.

He glanced at the white powder around us. "It does, but water and snow are two different forms. Water is a liquid and blue magic has an easier time controlling liquid. Snow is a solid, which means it'll take a bit more work to get your magic to manipulate it." He gestured. "You have to really focus. Concentrate on the snow alone and imagine it as it is, not what it once was.

Picture yourself in control of it—its master."

Doing as he said, I focused on the snow and pictured the snowfall coming to a complete stop. I shoved my hands out, and it immediately froze in the air.

The shadow dropped his arms. "How did you do that?"

"I did what you said. I pictured myself just doing it." I turned in a circle as I stared at the sky.

He grabbed my shoulders and made me face him. "No, Lia, this...this is different. The most you should have been able to do is stop one snowflake, maybe two. But you stopped millions. That is *impossible*." He grabbed my hand and studied my palm. "This isn't right."

"What's wrong?" A frown crept onto my lips. "Maybe I'm just more powerful than we thought. Isn't that good? Isn't that what we wanted?"

He wrapped both of his cold hands around mine. "Magic is this powerful when..." He let go as if I'd burned him, backing away.

"Where are you going?"

He vanished without saying another word.

Anger stirred inside me, and the snowflakes started to grace the island.

He left me without any explanation of my own power. It was cruel, and unfair. *How dare he?*

I grabbed the edge of my cloak and squeezed as I whirled around on my heel and walked further into the woods. Kace's shadow was worse than he was. No, that wasn't true. Kace was ignoring me, and that stung worse than his shadow not telling me what my power was.

Something chirped to my right and I stopped, looking around the area. There couldn't be birds in this weather.

As soon as I gave up and began walking again, I heard it again. I searched the area, high and low, and found the source up above. It moved in a tree, and when I climbed up a few branches to see it, I gasped.

"You poor thing." I grabbed the lizard by the sides of his belly and put him on my cloak. "You must be freezing."

I hopped down and studied his little face. "You must be...Diego. You certainly look like a Diego."

I took him with me. He could help me search for everyone else and find a way to bring them back to the light side. Wherever they were, they were not going to suffer much longer.

Diego and I traveled through the woods in search of a living soul. Of course, a living soul that wasn't deadly, if that were possible.

I fought my way through, but the snowflakes made it hard to see anything. Then, an idea hit me.

I closed my eyes and shoved my hands out with the image engrained in my brain. When I looked at what I'd done, I patted Diego on the head. "We did it. We stopped the blizzard, Diego." I smiled at him and kept walking. It was easy to walk with all the flakes dangling in one spot.

I searched near the mountains, the cliffs, and beaches. Nobody was around. It was as if everyone vanished into thin air, like Pan did.

Diego stared straight on like nothing could bother him. I'm sure with his size, nothing could. He was able to hide from all the predators and live a peaceful life.

My toes were frozen once I returned to my cabin. Instead of curling up in a thin blanket, I grabbed extra wood and started up the fire in the middle of the camp.

Lost boys started exiting their cabins to warm up by the heat, and I did the same. Nobody said a word, at least not to me. They talked amongst themselves, and I pictured Kace coming over and taking me by the hand and asking me to dance. Except he never came.

He was nowhere to be found.

Instead, I had Diego. I twirled around in the snow, next to the fire.

Kace's shadow told me I needed to be a fighter. I did that by refusing to lose any parts of my body, especially my toes. If I lost my toes, it would only set me back on my progress and I'd have to learn to walk all over again. Now who wanted that to happen?

“Dinner!” Pan shouted as he appeared near the garden with bowls of soup.

Everyone rushed over and I watched, keeping out of their way. I was the last to get my bowl but when I did, I made sure to eat it slowly. If I scarfed it down, the warmth would only last a second, and I’d just gotten my tastebuds back.

I ignored the look Pan gave me. Whatever he wanted, he wasn’t about to get it. Lili was going to take magic from him like she rightfully deserved, since he’d been abusing his power. He ripped away her shadow and now he needed to pay the price.

The flames before me crackled, embers floating off into the sky as snowflakes came down. The snowflakes may have been a solid form of water, but there weren’t enough of them to put out the fire.

Pan sat across from it, but I avoided his looks. When he played his flute, the silence continued on as it always had. The other boys danced around in the snow, moving their limbs and bodies to the beat of the music.

It still hurt a little that I couldn’t hear the flute, but that just meant I never truly had been lost. Maybe I didn’t belong here at all.

No, I would avoid those thoughts like the plague. I was here for Lili. I had come for her, and I was going to stay for her. I wouldn’t lose sight of my mission.

When I finished my soup, I put the bowl back in the tub of the other dirty dishes. I turned around to return to the fire, but Pan was gone, and the boys were no longer dancing. Where had he gone? Wherever he went, it didn’t matter to me. I’d tried to find him all day and he didn’t want to be found. I wasn’t going to sprain an ankle over it.

“Who are you looking for?” someone asked.

When I faced her, I straightened my back. “Why do you care?”

Lili laughed, shaking snowflakes from her hair. “Why don’t I care? I’m still your sister. You helped me, and I’m helping you.”

“I was looking for everyone, but it’s no longer important.”

"I poked holes in all the condoms. Now it's just a matter of getting him in the mood. It's been harder, lately." She glanced off into the distance. "But that's none of your business."

I nodded a little and pulled my hood down. "Are you doing okay?"

Her eyes landed on me. "Okay? In what way? Am I still the bad guy? Yes."

Treat her like a person, then maybe she'll have a better chance.

"Bad guy or not, I want to make sure you're doing okay. You're still my sister. You saved me when I fell off the mountain. We've had good times together."

"Hardly. You only started to care when I went missing."

I didn't disagree. Instead, I nodded. "I did. I was a terrible sister and I'm sorry for that." No number of excuses would work. I had to show her that I'd changed.

She didn't know how to respond to that, so she decided to change the subject. "How's Kace?"

"I wouldn't know. I haven't seen him in about a week now." Had it been that long? I was sure it had been. So many nights, so many sleeps without him.

"Where is he?"

"Can't find him."

"Aren't you two dating?"

We were supposed to be, but I wasn't so sure now. Maybe he was rethinking everything about us. Maybe this was the end of us.

"Lia."

"I don't know anymore." I shrugged a bit and rubbed my wrist. I hoped I was wrong. I hoped I was so wrong, and Kace was okay. The last thing I wished for him was harm to come his way. The last thing I wanted was to be out of his life.

Lili searched my eyes and her expression softened. "You're serious."

Did she think I was lying? It was never a ploy to lie to her, and not about my own problems.

Her arm twitched, but seconds later she stepped forward and wrapped her arms around my torso. I hadn't expected it, but I didn't turn it down. I rested my head against her shoulder and closed my eyes. As awful as she smelled, it didn't scare me away. Nothing could ruin this moment. I needed this hug from her now more than ever and she knew it.

When she let go, the cold swooped in and made me promises. I wanted her to hug me again. I wanted her to never leave me again.

Lili was still in there somewhere. This hug had been the boost I needed to keep going. I was fighting for that—for us to be this close again.

She wasn't here to tell me I would lose or warn me to back off. She had come to talk and comfort me in my time of need. She was the family I had left. Without her love, I didn't want to keep going on. She'd been my rock from the start, but neither of us knew it until the day she begged Pan to save her from me.

26: Kace's Shadow

A MILLION TIMES I'D imagined how this would go down. Never once did it occur to me it would be as simple as this.

"I'm sorry," Kace whispered against my lips as he pulled away. "I know I can't make up for it, but I needed some time to process how I reacted, to make sure I didn't take it out on you. I was angry with you because that's what Lili did, and I don't want you to end up like her."

I thought maybe we would yell at each other. Maybe he would tell me that I was wrong, and we'd have to leave it at that and take a break.

"You called me selfish." I swallowed.

He nodded a bit. "I know. I'm sorry for that, too."

"But you meant it." *Face the truth. Don't be weak.*

With a sigh, he nodded again. "It was selfish of you to act like your sister. I wanted you to put yourself in her shoes and see that her same actions got her into trouble. I wanted you to realize the way she fought the battle didn't work."

Did I tell him about his shadow? No. Not yet. He made it clear he didn't believe me, and I wasn't about to dredge up more frustration.

"You called me a liar," I whispered. "I was wrong for how I went about it, but it hurt to hear that you thought that of me."

"I know."

I ran my hands up his chest, gripping the edges of his cloak. "There are a few things you don't know."

"Which are?" He placed his hands over mine, wrapping his fingers around them.

It was time to tell him how I felt. In one breath, I muttered, "I'm in love with you."

The earth stopped spinning. The silence around us became deafening. Was this the end of our friendship?

The gap between us disappeared as Kace's lips landed on mine. I knew almost immediately it was just the beginning. Fear was always just that—a means of holding you back.

No kiss had ever been this needed. Passionate. Yearning. Every word I'd whispered, he inhaled. He kissed me with every fiber of his being, as if we'd never been apart. The desperation grew, and his security enveloped me.

Lifting his hands, his fingers tangled in my curls. His tongue slipped along my bottom lip, but he apologized before I could respond.

When we both pulled away, relief washed over me, and all tension left my muscles. Everything was falling back into place again.

"I want to show you who I found in the woods."

His forehead creased. "Who?"

I let go of him and walked over to the bathroom grabbing Diego from the sink. I showed him to Kace. "He was just there, hanging out. He's not evil, which I suppose is good. Maybe only the furry animals turn sour."

"What were you doing in the woods?"

A small fire sparked in my amygdala. "I was trying to find you. I couldn't find anyone." Good answer, because it was partly true. If I could find all of them, maybe I could figure out how to save them and solve why his shadow wasn't wicked. Kace wasn't either. None of it made sense.

Glancing down at his feet, I furrowed my brows. "I have an odd question."

He nodded. "What is it?"

"I know Pan's shadow is detached, so does that mean he has no shadow?"

Kace confirmed it. "He doesn't have a shadow."

"And Lili doesn't, either, because Pan ripped it away. No shadow is what makes someone turn dark."

"How do you know that?"

"But you...you have a shadow."

Kace looked at his own feet. "Of course I have a shadow. Why wouldn't I?"

Kace's shadow wasn't *his* shadow at all. It was someone else's and they were lying to me. That was why he avoided my questions about Kace. He knew the truth yet told me a bold-faced lie.

Shaking my head, I backed away from him. "I have to go talk to someone." I wasn't sure who I was going to talk to, but it had to be someone who was connected to this shadow. They were going to tell me who they really were, and I wasn't going to take no for an answer.

I left him alone in my cabin, but I didn't go to the training area to find him. No, I went to the woods. That was where I seemed to hear from him the most.

"What are you doing back out here?" his *shadow* asked.

With a lift of my chin, I faced him and reeled my shoulders back. "You're not Kace's shadow. Kace has his shadow and Pan doesn't. If you were his shadow, it would be missing just like Pan and Lili's. Who are you?"

"I'm afraid that's not true."

"You told me to face my fears and face the truth, but you can't even take your own advice." I stepped closer. "Who the hell are you?"

"*Cariño*, it doesn't matter. What matters is that you're becoming strong enough to save everyone."

I narrowed my eyes. "Asa. Are you Asa's shadow?"

"Focus on saving them."

I tightened my fingers around the hilt of my blade. "I want to focus on finding out the truth so I can! Who are you?" I screamed.

The shadow vanished. I gritted my teeth. He just left me again because he wasn't who he pretended to be.

Someone cleared their throat from behind me. "He's me."

When my eyes followed the sound of his voice, proving that this was who stood in front of me, it didn't make an ounce of sense.

"Why...you? You're the one trying to help me? That's not right." Maybe I *was* losing my mind.

Pan took a step forward. "I'm afraid it is, Lia. When your sister arrived, she befriended a boy named Eric. He was just a piece of me, a figment of the imagination created when I was at my most vulnerable. Eventually I told her the truth. I created him, just like I created Kace's shadow."

"You played me." *Don't cry.*

Worry filled his eyes. "I didn't play you. I lied about who I was. Everything else was true."

"Why? Why did you lie to me? Why couldn't you just tell me the truth?" I swallowed a lump.

"Would you have trusted me if I had just come to you as myself? No. I wanted to help you become a fighter, but I couldn't risk getting rejected. I couldn't create another Kace because that would catch up to me quickly. Kace's shadow was the best bet. You'd trust him and fear him at the same time. You knew too little about the shadows in Neverland to even bother looking at his shadow. I figured I had time before you knew the truth."

I twirled the string of my cloak. "So, are you the good guy now? Helping me stop you and Lili?"

He scratched his neck. "I'm not sure how to answer that."

Squinting my eyes, I said, "You know about Lili's plan to poke holes through the condoms. You're avoiding sleeping with her, aren't you?"

This made Pan chuckle. "Well, yes and no. I do know about the plan, but I don't think I want to stop it. If I told Lili I wasn't using a condom anymore, she'd probably have too many questions, and then she'd know I want to save her. I keep my shadow detached to keep her from finding out the truth." Winter existed because he no longer wished to be the villain.

"Why not poke holes?"

He wiggled his finger at me. "That is something I didn't think of. You were clever to suggest it to her."

He was on our side, but would I tell Kace? No, he wouldn't believe me, and Pan would deny it. It would have to stay between us until Pan decided he wanted to tell Kace.

"Why now?" I asked.

"Why now what?"

"Why are you just now deciding to save Lili? You ripped her shadow from her and now you seem to regret that decision."

Something flashed in his eyes and this time I could grasp it. *Remorse.* Once could experience it even without a shadow—while the demon had hold of them. So why didn't Lili experience it? "She's my other half, in the best ways. I thought it needed to be in the worst.. Maybe I would like it if she wasn't always fighting me, but I enjoyed that side of her. That's what made her who she was. She was independent. Strong-willed. Even compassionate."

I opened my mouth to respond, but he cut me off, "I can't take her back and attach her shadow. She'll see right through the lies. That's why I need you to do it. You still have a shadow for her to want to rip away, so she'll have reason to take you to Skull Rock. You have to fight her, and I'll help you."

It was at that moment that I knew Pan was sincere in his words. Everything he did was not out of spite. He did it out of desperation. We both wanted to save her and if I didn't work with him, I'd be selfish all over again.

"I'll work with you," I forced out.

A smile blessed his features. Everything inside me warmed. Our biggest threat was on our side. Pan had been the most *powerful* of us all and he was helping us, even if Kace had no idea.

Whenever Kace and Anna found out, I hoped they wouldn't piss him off. The last thing we needed to do was piss him off. Anna hated Pan for what he did to Wendy, and she had every right. But at the same time, the enemy of my enemy was my friend. If I didn't team up with Pan, my sister would never get her shadow back and she'd forever be just a murderer. I needed her to be anything but.

"Goodnight, Pan," I said in a quiet voice. It had barely carried past the snowflakes I once stopped, but he heard it just as he needed to.

Lili would achieve some light magic to suppress the darkness. Pan wasn't going to stop her. I wanted to tell Kace and Anna so badly but if I did, Pan would possibly back out. I wasn't about to turn him against me after we just teamed up.

Part of me was still weary, but I knew better now. He was madly in love with her, and she wanted his heart so she could crush it herself.

I remembered when Pan came to my window, promising to take me to Lili. I never had a single idea of what was in store, but I agreed for Lili. Everything I was doing now was for her, and it always would be. Would I ever do anything for myself? I had so much to make up for, for never being the sister she needed all those years. I loved Lili with every ounce of my being, and I wasn't going to let that go. I was angry with myself for ever giving up on her. That was the part of Lia that needed to be obliterated.

"Goodnight, Lia," he said.

Pan turned to leave, but I caught him before he did. "I just need to ask, why are you afraid that my blue magic is so powerful? You left me without an answer."

He glanced over his shoulder, swallowing what seemed to be terror. "The only other person with magic that powerful is *me*."

27: Mermaid Lagoon

The snow began again, flakes the size of quarters. I wasn't sure if we would be able to leave our cabins soon.

Those words kept replaying in my mind like a movie. Pan said I was as powerful as him, but what did that mean? It meant I could take his place, and he was afraid of no longer being the leader. How did I feel about it, though? I had no idea.

I heard a firm knock on my door. Maybe it was Pan but he rarely knocked. My best guess landed on Kace.

"Come in," I told whoever was on the other side.

I looked up at them as they walked in, eyebrows shooting up. "Since when do you knock?"

Lili laughed a bit with the shake of her head. "Fine, I'll barge in like I own the place because I technically do."

I changed the question, "Why are you here?" My fingers fiddled with the strings.

"Are you not my twin sister?"

I'd avoided what bothered me most days but today my tongue slipped. "Does that really matter? You killed our brother." After she'd killed so many innocent souls, including our brother, I struggled to see her the same way, if at all. It sounded cruel, sure. I wanted to save her, but I had to know if she felt even a drop of shame.

"Oh come on, you mean the boy who always stood aside while our father beat us? The silent are just as guilty." She crossed her arms as if her argument held up. I was about to crush it.

"If the shoes fits. You killed our brother and therefore, I don't owe you a second chance by your logic. Two wrongs do not make a right." I twisted the knot between my thumb and forefinger.

She tried to hold up her confident act though. I knew that somewhere deep down, she was drowning in the bloodshed. "I'm the Demon Queen."

"Well, you're a demon. That part's accurate." I snickered.

"I heard about Asa trying to kill you," she said, changing the subject. Now I knew why she really came here.

"You killed him, huh?" I finally dropped the strings of my cloak.

"Well, I punished him. I starved him and put him in the cage. I skipped to strike two since his offense was pretty serious." She shrugged. "He tried to kill you." This claim was no longer accurate, but I wasn't about to expose Pan dressing up as Kace's shadow.

"He did. He tried to kill me, and he got punished with the cage. You killed our brother and got no punishment. Our brother was innocent. The system is backwards. You die if you don't kill anyone but fail trying—punishment. If you succeed—safe. That seems to be how it works around here. So, tell me, when is my death sentence to be announced?" She probably could kill me easily at this rate and I'd be damned if I believed she wouldn't.

Lili narrowed her eyes on me. With nothing more to say, Lili left *my* cabin.

I left it as well to go visit Asa in the cage. I needed answers and my blood was still boiling.

I squatted down in front of the cage. I had yet to spend a night here. "We need to talk."

Asa turned his head away from me. "I have nothing to say to you."

I grabbed the bamboo bars and brought my face closer. "Look at me, you coward."

He finally gave me his undivided attention. "What?"

My grip only tightened. "You refuse to talk to me, and I deserve to know why. You're my cousin so I will get answers one way or another. Do not forget that my sister is that one who will kill you with no mercy. Why do you hate me so much?"

"Why does your sister hate you?"

"So you hate me for the same reasons?" I laughed, no humor present.

"You have done nothing to earn anything you have here. Your existence spoils you and that's unfair to the rest of us. You're a lost girl without trying. You got special treatment from Pan even before your sister was with him. You have a cabin without earning it. How is any of this fair? Pan brought you back when you drowned. Even when you lie about me, someone believes you instead." So same reasons as Lili. And Pan, as well as Kace, refused to believe me.

Chills rushed down my spine.

He was right. Pan treated me differently from everyone else and I never knew why. I was dating his best friend and he was okay with it. If Lili had dated Kace, who knew what Pan would've done to her. He never gave her fair treatment.

Why was Pan nicer to the sister than the girl he claimed to love? In his sick and twisted mind, love was pain. And unfortunately, Lili believed the same.

"Pan didn't save me when I nearly died in the woods. Nobody saved me. I saved myself." I told it to myself more than anything, to make it less weird that Pan gave me privileges that nobody else had. Was Kace right? Did Pan really like me? Or did Pan only do all of this because he liked it when a girl challenged him? Lili no longer hated his guts, and this could be why he was messing with me. However, we were on better terms now.

I stood and pulled my hood on. "I hold all the power now." I turned from the cage and walked the other way. I wasn't sure where I was going to go.

As I circled Pan's cabin, I traveled down the beaches to Mermaid Lagoon. It was dangerous and the mermaids were carnivorous, but they wouldn't eat me. My sister still fed them as far as I knew. I even controlled the water they resided in.

Looking out at the waves, they shimmered beneath the gray sky. Mermaid Lagoon was different from the regular beach. The water here held more magic, so I didn't question more than that.

I'd never been here because I always feared the mermaids. I was taking my chances to explore the parts of Neverland that had originally been bad for business, now that I had the same amount of power as Pan.

It was truly stunning for the shoreline. The rocks had been made of caves filled with crystals, split open for display, outlining the sides of the beach.

To the left of Mermaid Lagoon was a cliff steadily getting higher. On the other side of the waters was flat land with grass that once gradually got greener and more prominent as it got farther from the sand. There was forest beyond that.

I hummed, the gentle waves rolling along. I was genuinely surprised this beach wasn't littered with mermaids.

I pushed some hair behind my hair as a light breeze brushed against my face.

Kace was loyal. He could still stick around me even after my sister, and his best friend had turned against me. Kace has defended me numerous times against Pan. Kace still had hope for Pan even when it wasn't warranted, but he'd always been right. I'd never seen anyone like him. He was truly a treasure to keep, and I wouldn't let anything ever come between us. Not ever again.

Mist began to roll in from the ocean, covering where the snow met the sand. I could take a wild guess as to what that meant.

Many colorful fins flipped up out of the water before disappearing in the depths. The light reflecting off the iridescent scales mesmerized me. Some tails had scales while others were smoother than glass. Vibrant colors, and glistening fins.

Ranging from purples, pinks, teals, blues, greens, and others, they shifted hues as they changed angles.

I started to walk along the beach, careful about each step. I nearly tripped over something, but fixed my balance and bent down, pushing the snow away from it. I pulled the object from the snow and sand, brushing it clean. A seashell. It was by far the most beautiful seashell I had ever seen—a small replica of a mermaid's tail.

"You shouldn't be messing with that," a voice from my right said. I put a face to this voice and caught a mermaid watching me intently.

A crown sat atop her head. She must have been the leader. It'd been made of white and orange seashells with different gems that reflected all colors of the rainbow. Gold chains hung from a few crevices.

I smoothed my thumb over the inside of the shell. "Why? It's just a shell."

"It's not yours."

"It's sitting on the beach." I gestured to the spot I pulled it from.

She eyed me carefully. "So you wouldn't mind if I went to your room and picked something up from it and told you it wasn't yours?"

I huffed. "Fine." I put the shell down. "You have a bunch of others on your head." I pointed to her crown.

She swam over to one of the rocks, grasping onto it as her eyes met mine. "Same reason someone would want every piece of clothing they own. I shouldn't have to justify why I want my stuff left alone. Why do you want a seashell so bad? Go to the other beach and find some yourself. This is our beach, and you are not welcome here. You should go before you regret it."

"Why?" I stepped forward, testing my boundaries. "What are you hiding?"

The mermaid smirked at me. "I'm not hiding anything. It's about what *you're* hiding."

"What does that mean?" I crossed my arms.

"This beach will take your deepest secrets and twist them around." She hummed a haunting lullaby. Like a nursery rhyme set in minor key. I couldn't quite place which one it was.

"Like a genie but with secrets instead of wishes, or something similar?"

She shrugged. "If that's what a genie is, sure."

"So, if I don't leave your beach, my secrets will be twisted? How is this going to work? I'm not exactly sure what my deepest secrets even are, so how does a magical beach know?" I gestured around me.

"I don't control how the island works but every location is different. Mermaid Lagoon has abilities to bring about your darkest secrets and I just wanted to warn you before it was too late. Of course, this beach is dangerous because we eat people. That's only one excuse, however. We don't tell most people the other reason. This beach is...enchanted. It simply seeps inside you and studies your every desire. It messes with your head. You will never be the same if you don't leave now," she warned.

Magic was still so fascinating yet so confusing. A tingly feeling I had felt twice before dabbled in my nerves. I could feel it wanting to *control* me.

Unable to fight it off, it clung to every muscle. Every bone. It wore me like a skinsuit. What were my darkest secrets? I feared the worst to protect whatever hope I had left.

It intensified, and the humming faded out. A light flashed before my eyes and my view of the beach disappeared.

Then the name of the lullaby hit me.

Hush Little Baby.

28: Kasey and Petra

I dropped on my hands and knees, grunting. I stood and brushed the dirt off my knees and squinted at my arms. My arms had never been this thick before. Where did I end up?

Looking around, this place looked exactly like Neverland, but it was barren of winter. I went to push my hair back, but it was short. *Really* short. Almost nonexistent. "Huh?"

I widened my eyes at the sound of my own voice. Deep. How could my voice be so low? I slowly pulled the cloak open and lifted my shirt. I almost fainted. I had abs. I had pecs. I didn't have boobs.

As I put my shirt down while walking along the soft ground still damp from a previous rain shower, some cheers echoed from the direction of the camp. I quickly made my way to ask what the hell was going on. The snow had gone, and I was not a female.

Coming to a halt, what I saw baffled my brain. There were so many *girls*. Pan would have a fit if he saw this.

She stopped when she saw me, narrowing her eyes. Did I know her? Did she know me? She came over, folding her arms over the green shirt. "Who are you and how did you end up on my island?"

"Where's Pan?" I asked, a gruff voice bellowing from my vocal cords.

She lifted an eyebrow in the exact same manner that he did. "My name is

Petra. There is no Pan here. State your name before I make you." She lifted her hand, ready to use magic.

Her green eyes stood out just like Pan's. Her hair was the same shade of dark chocolate brown, falling in short waves to her shoulders. Her height towered over my own.

A girl emerged from the crowd, curly black hair falling down her chest. She took off the hood of her cloak. "Where did you get my cloak?" She pointed at Kace's cloak still hanging around my neck.

I almost choked. "Kace?"

"Kasey," she corrected me.

Petra's lips curved into a smirk. "Welcome to Neverland. You are the first lost boy." I really was a guy.

A bunch of girls covered in dirt stood behind her. They wore the same handmade clothes as the lost boys from my universe. Their belts held weapons, too.

As I eyed them, Petra cleared her throat. "I'm waiting on a name."

"Lia...m," I finished. I would have to worry about telling them where I came from later. For now, I needed to make sense of all of this.

"Why are you here? You don't belong here." Petra was just as demanding as Pan was.

"I ended up here, from Mermaid Lagoon." It was more believable than, '*I came from a different universe where you guys are all boys*'. That was good enough of an excuse for her anyway.

But I didn't miss the curious glint in her eye.

I followed her into the camp, but I glanced back at Kasey. She watched me as if she expected I would do something out of line. She didn't know that she and I had a thing back in my world. Nobody knew I even came from that world.

Petra looked at the other lost girls. "I think we should inform our new visitor of our rules."

Visitor. She assumed I wouldn't be here for long. She knew something but I didn't know what she could already know. Pan knew everything so it came as no surprise that she would as well.

Petra went over the rules of this island, the same as what Pan implemented.

I took my time to study every detail about this island. I was searching for a difference in the structure.

Something sharp poked my side and I jumped back. "What the hell?" I looked to the source and saw a girl holding her dagger out. Did she just attempt to stab me?

Petra didn't seem too fond of me. I didn't think she would treat me with special privileges here. "You shouldn't be here. We don't take kindly to boys." Her eyes flashed with animosity.

"And why not?" I crossed my arms across my chest. It wasn't anything super magnificent, but I did train regularly, so that checked out.

"Boys are sexist pigs."

Damn. She just said that with no mercy.

"Maybe boys think the same about you," I commented.

She pointed her blade at my throat. "Watch it, *boy*. We own this island. You have no rights."

No matter where I went, I just happened to be overrun by the opposite sex. Lovely.

I rubbed my head. "Even though I did nothing wrong to you guys personally. That sounds so fair."

She gave me a smile that mocked me in the wrong way. "Sounds like a personal problem."

I wanted to slap that smug look from her face and watch her cower. Being a male certainly ruined everything.

I walked past her for both of our benefits. It angered her but I didn't care. I put my hands on my hips as I approached Kasey. "You're cold, yet curious. I'd picture you to be more...forgiving." I gestured.

She gave me a strange look. "Why would I be forgiving?"

"Because you don't always agree with Pan." I realized my mistake and corrected myself, "I mean Petra."

When she raised an eyebrow in question, I continued, "You may think I'm the bad guy. But you haven't always been this way. I don't know a lot about this place, but Petra was nicer once upon a time. You guys were mistreated and abused by those you trusted. You have no reason to trust me but I was abused, too. My sister killed our brother, and my cousin tried to kill me, in a sense. We're similar. A wise guy once told me and my sister that we have a lot more in common than just our sex."

She didn't know what to say.

"Your parents were wrong in trying to raise you like something you're not. They didn't accept you as you are and they will pay for it." I walked to the training area to continue my training. I might've been in another universe, but training was still important. I had to keep up on my defense, especially on an island of girls who wanted my head on a stake.

The girls observed as I picked up an arrow and pulled it back against the bowstring. I let go of the arrow and hit the edge of the target. "Even after a year I still suck." I laughed to myself and approached the bows.

"Impressive but our lost girls can do better," Petra said.

"I'm much better with a dagger." My eyes shifted to her. "You'd be surprised at what I've survived. I've fought off wild animals. I've survived a night lost in the woods while it was below freezing. I watched my brother die in my arms. I watched my sister turn to her demon for consolation. I've seen much more than you can imagine."

"You're better with a dagger you say? I'll challenge that bold claim." She stepped forward as the lost girls began to circle around us.

Despite our switched genders, I was not going to question the strength she had compared to me. "I'll take that challenge. Wait till I tell Pan that I beat him as a woman."

I pulled my dagger out, wrapping my fingers around the bronze handle. It was the weapon I was familiar with. I had a fighting chance.

Petra slid out hers—better looking than mine. Her handle was made of gold, the silver blade had been pristine and freshly sharpened.

She swung her arm around, but I blocked her weapon with mine. She moved her head a bit. "Not bad." She pulled her dagger back around and jabbed at my abdomen. "But it's not good enough."

I stepped back and narrowed my eyes. I took a swing at her, but she blocked it and I took another swing, blocked once again.

I remembered what our training taught me, but I didn't have enough time before Petra sliced through my cloak and into my arm. I hissed from the pain and pulled the string that formed a bow until my cloak came undone, and I tossed it aside.

"Kace better know how to sew clothes, too." My blade clanged against hers as she took more jabs.

Swinging my foot at her leg, I knocked her off her feet. I quickly pushed my foot against her chest. She grabbed my foot and twisted it until I lost balance. She jumped to her feet. "Nobody beats me."

I got back up and aimed at her side but I changed my move and sliced her arm as she blocked me. During the split second that she was shocked, I put my blade against her neck. "I'm not nobody."

She shoved me back and cut across my stomach. "As I said, nobody beats me." She put her dagger back in her belt and left the training area.

I glanced at the drops of blood from my wound. If I could catch Petra off guard, I wondered how well I would do with a training session against Kace.

Kasey gave me my cloak and eyed me suspiciously. "Where did you learn moves like that? I also want to know where you got my cloak and that dagger. Where did you really come from? Don't lie to me. I'll see right through it."

I didn't know what to say. I didn't know how long I'd be trapped in this universe. Even if she was technically Kace as a girl, I wasn't looking to start a relationship. A part of me would feel as if I was cheating on Kace. I needed to find a way back home.

"Well, I guess I can't keep it a secret forever. If I tell you, you have to promise me something."

"Depends on the promise." She rolled her shoulders.

I snickered. "Promise me you won't develop any feelings for me. I'm dating someone else."

"I promise not to fall for you." Her expression hardened, eyes becoming slits.

"Then I'll explain to you everything I know."

29: Murder

Kasey rolled her eyes at me with her arms crossed. "You're lying. I can tell."

"That means you're terrible at catching lies because I'm not. I really do come from another Neverland. Where else did my cloak and dagger come from?" I gestured to them.

She narrowed her eyes. "Yeah. I still don't believe it."

"You're an only child," I said.

"What?"

"You're an only child and your parents couldn't accept you. They tried to force you to fit their mold."

She scoffed. "That's a vague guess. Anyone could guess that correctly."

"Which one was it? Did your parents want you to act more feminine or did they want a son instead?" I asked.

She started to shift her weight from one foot to the other. "They didn't think I was girly enough. I liked making mud pies and playing in the dirt. I didn't like dolls. They creeped me out."

"Ah, so that's the same. Kace was born as a male, but his parents wanted a daughter. He wasn't girly enough either."

Kasey didn't say another word.

Instead, I did. "I just want to go back home and see Kace again. Being a guy is weird. Oh shit, I have to pee. This can't be good. I've never seen a penis before, Kasey. And I wouldn't want it to be my own, or...whoever's body I have."

"What? Kace is your boyfriend?"

"He gave me this cloak. He helps me train. He's been a loyal friend, and he's cute so that's a bonus. He's also warm."

I observed her face and wanted to laugh at the look in her eyes. To make things clearer, I said, "I'm a girl." I'd only told her about Neverland and how it was full of boys, and a Peter Pan. I had conveniently left out the fact that I was really a woman.

"Oh...?" She didn't quite understand.

"I'm a girl originally. Trust me. Periods are the worst feeling ever. Along with that feeling I get when Kace's shirt rids up his stomach. The bastard."

"A feeling you get when you see his stomach?" She tried to hold back a laugh.

"Well, yeah. I don't actively stare at men. I'm demi, which means I don't get aroused at all, without an emotional connection." I shrugged a bit, or what I thought was a bit.

Kasey snorted. "Oh come on. You don't get arouse but you get feelings when you see his stomach?"

"What do they mean? It's like I can't look away. He kissed me last week, or what I think is last week. He tried to slip his tongue in, but he stopped. Why did he stop? Why did I want him to kiss me more?"

Her eyes lowered to something, and when I discovered where they'd gone, I widened mine and yanked the blanket over the bulge in my crotch.

"You're aroused," she said.

"Impossible."

"Are you emotionally connected to him?" She lifted her gaze.

I swallowed, forcing myself to look at the wall instead. "I'm in love with him."

"You're ready to take it to the next level," she said in a quieter voice.

I vigorously shook my head. "Wrong. No. I'm not there yet."

"But you are. You don't have to do anything with that information if you don't want to, but that's what it means. You see his bare abs and want to take his shirt off. Feel him up. Go all the way."

I wasn't ready. No. Maybe aroused, but not truly ready. Too much had been at stake for us to take that step.

"I'm trying not to cry. Stupid, but the thought of wanting to sleep with someone is something I've never experienced. It's terrifying." I laughed a bit and took a deep breath. "But I've seen some crap so it's my right to cry about it."

"Having emotions isn't wrong. What you do with those emotions is another story, but it isn't a sin to be human. And if you're in love, it doesn't make you wrong for someday wanting to sleep with this Kace."

A little smile formed. "Sounds like something he would say."

"Kace is me as a boy, right?" she asked.

Nodding, I glanced at her. "Correct. You're the same person but opposite genders." I neared her desk, grabbing her sewing needles and thread. I picked out the brown thread and struggled to loop it through the end of the needle.

Kasey cleared her throat. "Okay, so you're really a girl who's dating the male version of me. That's weird, don't you think?"

"Hey, in my defense, I started dating Kace before I came here. I can't tell you how long because Neverland doesn't have a concept of time, but it's probably been a few months." I missed Kace and his comments. He always knew what to say at the right moment.

I laid the cloak on the desk and tied the thread to the needle. I began to sew up the rip in my cloak until it was strong enough to hold. I tied it off and cut the thread and put her supplies back. I looked at the cuts on my arm and abdomen. "I need to stitch these up, too. Not sure how well that will hold over. Blood makes me queasy."

"I can do it," Kasey said.

"That's okay. Kace showed me how." He didn't but I wasn't comfortable with Kasey getting her hands near my skin. It's be too awkward.

Before I could grab the supplies I needed, Petra burst into the room. "Why is this boy in your room? Are you even a part of this camp?"

Kasey stood up. "We didn't do anything. I'm just helping him sew his cloak and stitch up his cuts. I am the one who supplies the medicine."

I looked between both of them, the tension hanging heavy in the air. It certainly never stuck around for long where Pan and Kace had disagreements.

Petra grabbed me by the collar and dragged me from the cabin. "Trying to seduce my second-in-command calls for punishment."

"Excuse me, I really was just sewing up my cloak!" I showed her the area where a line of thread was holding the fabric together.

She dropped me on the ground.

I stood up and wiped the dirt from my leggings. "Why do you hate me so much? I didn't do anything to you."

"You're a boy. What else is there?" She glared at me as if I'd killed her best friend.

"I should be judged by my character and not my gender," I said.

"Your character is a male so I'm judging that."

I stomped my foot. "I did not try to seduce your best friend for crying out loud! I am not trying to seduce anyone! I don't even have sex on my mind!" Even in this body, the only one on my mind was Kace. I was very much into men, regardless of my gender.

Petra stepped close, harshly grabbing my arm, digging her thumb into my cut. I cried out from the pain and stumbled forward.

She snickered. "You're so weak. I have the power on this island. You can't be trusted." She let go and I fell into the dirt once again. I didn't bother getting up this time.

The poison in her eyes scared me more than Pan himself could have ever. Pan treated me like I was privileged somehow, but she treated me like I was the scum of the earth.

I swallowed my fear and tried to suppress it.

Petra looked over at the cabin. "I'll be right back. Don't move." She vanished and reappeared with Kasey beside her.

"I didn't realize I was going too easy on you. Girls can be such backstabbers. Kasey was trying to get with the boy because she can't keep her pants on."

Kasey looked at Petra and shook her head. "I didn't do anything with him and why would it matter if I did? I make my own choices."

"You're betraying *me* when you sleep with the enemy." She forced her down on her knees. "And I can't keep someone around if I can't trust them." She grabbed Kasey's head and snapped her neck.

I screamed and moved back farther. "You just killed her!"

"I did."

"We didn't do anything!" I yelled. She did that to her own best friend. Pan never did anything remotely like that. Pan threatened me but only if I *hurt* his best friend. She killed her best friend at the mere thought of us betraying her.

I got up and started running. I had to get out of here. If she could kill her best friend, what stood between her killing me, a stranger? *Nothing*.

I stopped when she poofed right in front of me. "Going somewhere?" She lifted her eyebrow, a cunning smile fully threatening.

"I can't control my DNA. Why are you doing this? Why are you hurting innocent people? Who hurt you?" Pan. Lili. Hurt people hurt other people.

She scowled. "You'll never be one of us."

"I don't need to be one of you. I need to get back home. I wouldn't want to stay here with how badly I'm treated. This isn't living. This isn't an escape. This is hell. This is torture. You are purely wicked, and you have no humanity in you. You claim to save humans, but you can't save a species you have no compassion for."

It snapped into place, like a puzzle piece fitting in the only spot left. I understood so much more about Lili than I ever could've before.

"Why does it matter to you? Why do you care about these girls who only have hatred for you?" She gestured to the island.

"Because I don't need to know someone to care about them. They're in trouble. They need to do better, and they can't do better when you are putting them down every chance you get. Two wrongs do not make a right."

She stepped closer but I didn't back up this time. "You make me sick."

I screamed *dangerous* because I was a hero. Hope. The one being as powerful as her. Surely she knew that.

I kept my feet planted where they were. "Kill me, Petra." I would never tell her where I came from. I wouldn't give her any leverage to get into my world. I may have never made it back but at least she wouldn't know it existed.

She grabbed her dagger from her belt and pushed the sharp edge against my throat. "I will very gladly kill you."

"Do it. Make me believe you will." I was taunting her, and she knew it.

She tangled her fist in my shirt and yanked me closer as her blade cut into my neck. Blood began to pool, a stinging pain beginning to grow. "Don't test me, boy. I have the power to make you believe in anything, and I have the power to make you believe in me."

"You only have as much power over me as I allow you to have."

I wanted to spit in her face, but my mouth was too dry for that. I hadn't eaten or drank anything since I arrived, much to her very welcoming committee.

She hissed and plunged the blade into my neck. She let go and I fell to the ground, grabbing my neck as I tried to stop the bleeding.

She watched me as I inched closer to my death. I lay back against the dirt, watching the leaves in the trees dance above me. "Lia!" I heard my name being yelled, but I knew that not a single soul on this island knew my name.

Someone pulled me into the darkness.

30: Back to Reality

Mermaid Lagoon.

Arms loosened their grip. I turned back to see who, and upon seeing Kace, I grabbed his face and kissed him as if my life depended on his existence. I'd never been more grateful for him.

Threading my hands into his dark curls, I pulled him against me and nearly sucked the life from him. Tongue and all. I'd never let him slip through my fingers again.

He chuckled and grasped my hands as we pulled away. "You okay?"

While breathing heavily, I lifted my shirt, checking for cuts. My skin was as smooth as a baby's bottom. The cloak had no sign of a rip either. "She killed me."

"Who are you referring to?"

Confusion settled into the wrinkles on my forehead. "I… I don't know how to explain it. I understand why Lili ended up the way she has. I know why she desperately wanted to leave this island and why she felt betrayed when I didn't help her. I know why she felt so angry when I was accepted and she wasn't." I looked at our hands. "It's like I was Lili. I think my deepest secret was a part of me that wanted to understand her so I didn't feel like I'd lost my sister."

"I'm so confused."

"I know why she chose Pan. Why she was attracted to him. Why she now wants him dead. I know enough about Lili to finally save her. Kace, I was in *her* shoes," I explained.

He still didn't understand.

I pulled him into camp. "We have to meet with Pan. I have to tell you everything I saw."

I could practically hear the questions running around inside Kace's head, but I didn't answer a single one.

When Pan spotted us, his eyes darted to Kace behind me. "I told you she was fine. You didn't believe me."

Kace rolled his eyes and mumbled something incoherent. He cleared his throat. "She has to talk to us about where she just was."

Pan eyed me suspiciously as if I did something wrong. Technically, I did. Pan warned me not to go to Mermaid Lagoon when I first arrived, and I had just refused to listen.

The three of us walked into Pan's cabin and he closed the curtains. He turned to look at me. "Where did you go?"

I pushed some hair behind my ear, goosebumps forming up my arms. I wasn't sure how he would react, but it couldn't be as bad as what Petra did to me. Pan was secretly on my side. Petra treated me like I was worthless.

"I went to Mermaid Lagoon."

Pan didn't say a word. Was that a good sign?

I continued, "Mermaid Lagoon has the ability to expose your deepest secrets. My deepest secret involves me wanting to understand Lili so I can help her. I wanted to know what it felt like to be her. I went to Neverland, but it was different. Everyone was the opposite sex."

Kace's eyebrows shot up in amusement. "Really? So I was a girl? What was that like?"

Pan looked at him as if Kace had grown a second head.

I loved them so damn much, in different ways of course. But the experience had me appreciating them and their friendship in ways I'd never thought I would.

"You were closed off, but curious. I was a man, and boy am I glad I didn't get to pee before I left. I really did not want my penis to be the first one I saw." I ran my hand down my face. "You were still pretty helpful though. Lucky me."

Kace glanced over at Pan and then back at me. "That sounds accurate."

Pan crossed his arms. "What about me? I was a woman? That's absurd."

"You were far more ruthless. You hated men, including me. When Kasey—the girl version of Kace—invited me to her cabin to let me sew up my cloak, you came in, assuming I was trying to seduce your best friend. You murdered her in front of the entire camp as an example. We were merely spectacles in your game." The cracking of Petra snapping her neck embedded itself deep in my mind.

Pan crossed his arms, tilting his head in question. "I know everything. Why would I have to assume anything? Why would I even care if Kace is with you?"

"She was sleeping with the enemy. Your emotions clouded your better judgment. My sister killed our brother because he didn't help us most of our life." I stared at the floorboards, trying not to notice their faces much. I didn't need the pity, nor the humiliation.

"I was stupid as a woman. That makes sense," Pan said.

I clenched my jaw and looked at him. "Not all women are stupid. I wouldn't kill my best friend over something so petty. Even if she had slept with the enemy."

Pan didn't comment on that, and I hoped it was because I was right.

"You then killed me," I whispered.

Amusement struck his expression. "I did? Why?"

"I just..." I couldn't figure out how to mention that he actually *hated* me. There, he didn't accept me like he had here. I was handed a silver platter when I arrived, but why?

I kept hesitating, opening my mouth to say something, but I closed it every time.

Kace pulled his hood down. "What is it?"

"Spit it out" Pan shot me a bored look.

"Asa told me that Pan treats me differently. Pan accepted me so easily. He handed me everything. I don't understand why you don't hate me at all, yet my sister had to fight for her basic rights with you." I directed that last sentence at Pan.

Pan got lost in his thoughts, reaching for an answer. "I guess it's because I always knew that Lili and I could have something more. The way she could make me want her was dangerous, so I treated her differently to guard myself. I didn't want her to save me from the darkness. Of course, Lili has joined the dark side and I never have to worry about that. She can't tame the demon anymore," he said with a frown.

"It's just weird to me that you're not mad Kace and I are dating, but Petra killed Kasey and I the moment she assumed we'd even be attracted to each other. Why are you and Petra different?" Furrowing my brows, I racked my brain for reasons.

Pan shrugged. "Kace is his own person, and he shouldn't have to come to me for every decision. I have no reason to keep you two apart. Petra...might have been threatened by you. Maybe she was in love with Kasey." Maybe she had been.

"Right."

However, if he'd been right that Petra loved Kasey, why did she kill her so mercilessly? It didn't matter now. It'd all been in my head, and it would stay there forever, questions unanswered.

I rubbed my boot against the floor and pressed my lips into a thin line. "But how did I end up in Neverland where everyone was the opposite gender and why didn't any of my injuries transfer over here?"

"Have you ever heard of psychology?" Pan tilted his head.

"Yes..." I'd studied it, even. One of the classes I enjoyed most.

Kace chuckled to himself, trying not to let us hear him but that failed.

Pan and I both gave him a stern look.

Pan nodded, waving Kace off. "You know that our minds can play tricks on us. Magic can do that, too. Magic can get inside your head and make you hallucinate."

"Ah, like drugs. Magic is a drug. You can get high from it, hallucinate, and apparently come back to life? Well, this makes a lot more sense." I tossed my head a bit. "So, everything I saw was just in my head?" I lifted both eyebrows.

"It was all in your head." Pan exhaled, scanning the room. "If this is it, I have things I have to attend to so you can leave now." He showed us out.

Kace slipped his hand in mine, whispering against my temple, "It was all in your head, cariño."

I pouted. "Kace, that's mean."

He chuckled a little and pressed a kiss to my head.

We got to his cabin and I studied every feature. "I don't think I could've kissed Kasey. Aside from the thought that I'd be cheating on you in a way, I'm just not attracted to you as a girl. Is that weird?"

His eyes moved from mine down to my lips. "You like who I am?"

"I'm attracted to you for being the one guy I can trust around here. You're loyal to Pan, but only in a good way. It's everything about you, Kace. The chocolate in your eyes, the spring in your curls, the flecks in your right eye. Everything about you is just pulling me in. And part of that is your masculinity." I gestured to his muscles, joking.

His face lit up. "That's not weird. You accept me for who I really am, more than my parents ever did. Even better, you love me for who I am. What more could I have asked for?"

I wrapped my arms around his neck. "You make me happy. One of the big reasons I survive everything on this damned island is because of you. I'm afraid to disappoint you."

"You won't let me down. I could never judge you for losing. You can't win every battle and I wouldn't expect you to. You train so you can win the war. The war is what matters the most." The back of his fingers gently brushed over my cheek.

"If I lose the battles, I could lose my life. I don't want to die. I want a happy ending, Kace. I want a happy ending with you." My eyes glossed over.

With a nod, he planted a kiss on my lips. "You will have a happy ending with me."

"But what if you lose your shadow, too?" My heart raced at the thought of losing Kace.

His eyes softened. "It'll be okay. At least we will have failed trying to do the right thing."

31: Losing the Battles

I peered between the bars of the cage, eyes on the very one I once accused of trying to murder me.

His eyes stayed glued to the floor. "What do you want, Lia?"

"You're right. Pan treats me differently from everyone else. However, it never gave you the right to push me away. I feel emotions like you, and a hell of a lot more. I can't control how he treats me. I deserve to be judged based upon my own actions, and I tried to be nice to you. I tried to befriend you. I have never intentionally hurt someone. Do I feel guilty accusing you? Maybe a little. But you were the only suspect and you can't blame me, seeing as I am privileged and you're the only one who had an issue with it." Well, Lili did, too, but I still debated whether or not she'd be able to kill her other half.

Asa gave me the silent treatment for whatever reason.

Pan approached from behind and shooed me out of the way before he opened the cage. "You're free to go."

Asa hesitated for a few moments before scurrying out of the small space. When on his feet, he finally looked me in the eyes. Pan closed the door without a word and disappeared. We both knew Asa never deserved the cage, but Lili had more power than Pan could take from her.

I turned away from Asa.

He started to walk along the path, and I followed him, mostly because Kace and my cabin were this direction. As we neared the middle of camp, near the fire, Asa halted and whipped around to face me. "I push you away. I hate you. And you let Lili punish me for something we both know I didn't do, yet you still want to try to befriend me. Why? Are you sick? Are you that desperate for everyone to like you?" It wasn't the first time I'd been called a people pleaser but it was the first time it stung.

Lowering my eyes, I grabbed the edges of my cloak. "I can't explain it. I guess I just..." My head fell back as my gaze moved to the clouds. I sighed as I tried to gather the words I wanted to say. "I believe in second chances. Of course, this means we have to talk about the situation and how we feel about it, but I just want to fix everyone. And the more I begin to understand them, the better help I can offer." At last, my eyes fell on Asa.

He looked at me like I had just told him I wasn't interested in Kace despite it being so obvious. "I don't believe you."

"I gave up on Lili after I watched her kill innocent people. I watched her kill our brother. I gave up on her because I feared I couldn't help her. I soon found Jaren's letter and chose to keep fighting for his sake because he no longer can, and now I understand how she turned out this way." I pulled the cloak closed to keep my heat inside my body.

"What does this have to do with me?" he asked as he cocked an eyebrow.

"I gave up on my own twin sister because I didn't understand her well enough. Everything she's done can't be justified and I would never demean my brother's worth by trying to say what she did was okay. But she is my other half. She is deeply hurt—messed up and I'm supposed to save her. I have to save her from herself. That's my purpose. If I can understand my own sister even after she killed our brother, I can understand why you're trying to push me away. I'm not saying we have to be best friends. That's not what this is. I just want to mend everything."

"I don't need saving."

I gave him a playful smirk. "You're on Neverland because you come from a broken home. You need saving, Asa."

"What's going on here?" Lili asked, hurrying over to the both of us. "He tried to kill you."

"Why do I still talk to you even if you killed our brother?" When her eyes narrowed, I said, "exactly."

I may have feared what she could do to others, but I wasn't scared of her as a person. Actions could be separated from a person if one tried hard enough.

Asa studied us. "You guys really don't like each other."

"I'd say it's a little less than dislike," I said with a small smile.

But Lili's words were far from comforting. "She wasn't there to save me from Pan."

It hit my heart hard, like being tackled in a football game while the other team stole the ball. I knew she still blamed me for the way she ended up. I used to say it was her fault, but I knew better. It really *was* my fault. I was supposed to save her. My entire job was to play the hero, but I'd failed her. Neverland was falling apart before our very eyes, and I could only blame myself.

Neither of them said a word. I wanted to say something, but I wasn't sure what I could really say. If only I had just been there for her then all of this would've never happened.

I coughed a bit more which broke the silence. "I'm sorry." I coughed more, rubbing my throat. It was as if dust had lined my throat, but it wasn't coming out.

Lili's glare didn't falter.

Asa's demeanor shifted, and he grabbed hold of my arms. "Are you okay?"

I nodded. "I'm fine. A cough never killed anyone."

Asa shrugged. "It has actually."

"I can still breathe. I'll be fine. You can't get rid of me that easily." I shot him a small smile.

My eyelids began to droop. If worse came to worst, I was probably just getting sick. Which wouldn't be unheard of in this kind of weather. It'd been a miracle I wasn't sick already.

Asa brought me to my cabin and helped me lie down. "Let me ask for some extra soup. I'm sure Pan will give it to me if it's for his special lost girl."

"Don't do that. Don't." I rubbed my eyes as my sockets began to ache. "Get me my damn soup and don't poison me, please."

He scoffed and left the cabin without arguing. I curled up to keep the warmth in my general vicinity. Even with socks and boots on, my toes were freezing.

Kace came in and glanced back at the door. "Why is Asa here? He hates you."

"He's just helping me. I think I'm getting sick."

"Sick? No. You can't do that." Was he trying to argue with the virus invading my body?

"My body is going to fight because I'm a fighter, but Asa is just trying to be helpful, too. He went to get me soup." I coughed.

Kace kneeled beside the bed. "What if he doesn't come back?"

"Then I get sick and eventually someone gets me soup." With a grin, I poked his nose lightly. "Don't worry too much. You'll get wrinkles on your forehead. I'll be fine. I always am. I've survived everything at this point." I let out a small laugh.

Asa returned, stopping at the sight of Kace. Kace looked at him. Quiet may have enveloped us, but arrogance stole the show.

I cleared my throat, only to end up coughing again. "Excuse me, put the egos away and give me my soup." I put my hand out.

Asa brought me my bowl.

I sat up to eat. It heated my insides just right. Unfortunately, it didn't feel good against my dusty throat.

Asa sat beside me on the bed. Kace stayed in the corner, watching Asa intently to make sure he wasn't going to pull anything.

After a few more coughs, I finally finished my food. "You guys honestly remind me of creeps right now." My eyes darted between them. "My boyfriend keeping an eye on my cousin."

"He hates you," Kace argued.

"I told you my family was messed up. You better get used to it. I'm the only sane Stone left, my dear Kace."

Asa's gaze raked over me. "I'm not sane?"

"Not in the slightest."

"And you are?" He tilted his head down a bit.

"I haven't tried to kill anybody yet. I think that earns me the right to call myself sane."

Kace pushed himself from the wall he was leaning on. "I haven't killed anyone either. I work for Pan, but I haven't taken a single soul."

I peered at him. "That's why we work so well together. We're both sane. I don't have to worry about saving you. Together, we can rescue everyone else."

Kace took a few steps closer. "Did you worry we wouldn't be a team?"

Asa interrupted, "Wait, what is this about saving Neverland?"

Glancing at Asa, another cough forced its way out. "We are planning to bring Lili and Pan to the light side again."

"And you think they don't know about your plan?" he asked.

I shook my head. "No. They know. But that won't stop us from trying. Kace and I have a history with them, and we can't give up just because things get tough."

Kace sat on the other side of me and slid his hand in mine, intertwining our fingers. "I knew Pan long before he turned dark. He's got good in him."

Asa nodded with knitted brows. "Why don't you count me in?"

I choked on my own air. "Whoa, what did you just say?"

"I'm tired of being in this slump. I want to see a Neverland that could offer more than what I had with my family."

I didn't know what had caused Asa to change his mind, but I was happy nonetheless. "Consider yourself counted. The more, the merrier. You won't regret it." I gave them a thumbs up with the hand my boyfriend wasn't holding. As I inhaled, another cough came up. "The three amigos. I think three is supposed to be lucky or something? Lili tried to save Pan once and failed. I tried and gave up. Now, we are trying again. Third time's a charm. Things tend to come in threes."

Kace squeezed my hand. "Let's hope we win."

Another cough. The insides of my abdomen were starting to feel funny. Could we do this—finally save the island? Would we finally win the war after we lost the battles?

32: Virus

I looked out my window, eyes turned up at the snowfall. It wouldn't stop until we saved Lili from the darkness. Pan loved her relentlessly, more than she could ever fathom. She felt nothing but hostility.

I coughed, turning a thick accent asked, "What's with all the coughing? Are you sick?"

Pan always asked stupid questions. People had that kind of information back then, didn't they?

Nodding, I said, "Of course I got sick. I've spent so much time in the coldest winter." I coughed some more.

He stepped closer. "Let me heal you."

While reaching his hand out, I stumbled back, my back hitting my window. "No, Pan. You can't always do that. I'm sick. Let me fight this naturally. I can survive this just fine." I slid out from in front of him and walked towards my bed. "You have to stop trying to heal me every time. Why are you interested in fixing me? You didn't even want to heal me the first time you cut me." That crush of his was starting to look pretty damning by now.

He couldn't ultimately control if he liked me. Most people did. But he could certainly help his actions, and giving into the temptation was far more destructive. I'd never do that to my own sister.

"I don't tell people this, but I have to tell you, don't I?" He paused. "When I use my magic to heal people, it doesn't just give them a high. It gives me a little high as well. I guess I've been in the dark for so long that I wonder what it's like to truly be happy. Besides, you have blue magic, so I don't have to worry about that anymore."

"You're with Lili. She should make you happy, even to some degree if not all."

Pan smiled—raw and full of wishes. "She's my flower that *blooms* even in the most frigid of the season. But she never wants much to do with me. When I get high, nothing can bring me down. Not the lost boys who disobey me. Not Asa who acts like I'm wrong for bringing him here when he asked. Not even Lili who will beg me to kill an innocent person. It isn't a walk in the park trying to rule an entire island and keep little boys in check. Kings need to relax, too."

I hoped my next words didn't come off as harsh. "You're not going to get high off of healing my sickness." It came out wrong. Most definitely.

Either way, I meant it. I wasn't Wendy, and I wouldn't take the opportunity to be. It would hurt everyone I knew, including myself. We'd all be affected by my choice, and I refused to carry such a heavy shame on my shoulders. I had enough burdens bear.

Our eyes snapped to the door when Kace walked in.

Kace eyed us. "What's going on?"

"Pan wants to heal my illness so he can get high." I wasn't going to keep it a secret from him. Kace and I told each other everything and I trusted him enough to know. I just hadn't trusted him about the shadow Pan created to secretly team up with me. I also wouldn't tell him I was as powerful as Pan—at least not yet. That was my secret to revel in.

Kace met Pan's gaze. "Is this true?"

My eyebrows shot up high as he asked this question. "You don't believe I'm telling the truth? Why would I lie?"

Shaking his head, he hurriedly said, "No, I didn't mean it like that."

"Then how did you mean it? You had to ask him to confirm if I'm telling the truth. You don't trust me. You don't *believe* me. Why would I lie? Do I have a reason to? Have I ever lied to you?" I began to rack my aching brain for any memories of me lying to Kace. I couldn't ever recall a single one. "Except...Asa. I really thought he had been the one who tried to kill me, but I was just crazy."

I'd let Kace believe I was just crazy. For now, he would believe it so Pan's secret could stay between us. That's what this entire thing was about, right? Eventually he'd know. Today just wasn't that day.

Kace started, "Lia, I swear I did not mean it like that."

Pan stepped between the two of us. "It's true, Kace. I want to get high off my magic when I heal her."

My boyfriend fell silent, his eyes moving between us before settling on his best friend. Well, his first best friend. Crossing his arms, he spat, "You're telling me that you actually want to get high with *my* girlfriend?" The way *girlfriend* slipped his tongue put me into a chokehold. He definitely needed to use that word more often with me.

"Technically, being sick is like the opposite of a high... I'm in hell. So I'm low." I didn't know why I'd said that. I was going somewhere with it but then when the words came out, I lost my train of thought and I spit out whatever bullshit I could manage.

Pan shifted his body to face Kace, tilting his head. "Yes, I just said that."

They both stood at the same height so it wasn't as if Pan could intimidate his own best friend. I understood why he allowed Kace to question his authority. He'd never intentionally hurt him.

"Why are you always so concerned with Lia? You have Lili. Go pamper her. Lia is not interested in you. She's not your girlfriend. You need to leave her alone, Pan."

"It's like I told Lia, she's of no threat to me. Lili was always the one who could change me and thus, I was rude to her to push her away. I don't need to be that way with Lia. You remember what I told her. You were there."

Kace shot me an apologetic look, then formed a fist and reeled his arm before it hit Pan's face who didn't bother to dodge.

When Kace dropped his arm, Pan wiped some blood from his lip. Eyes meeting Kace's, he asked, "Do you feel better now?"

With a nod, Kace sidled up to me. "You need to remember that it's not your job to make Lia feel better. It's mine." Was that it? He punched Pan because he wanted to use me to get high?

I put my hand up to stop him. "Wait, you punched Pan and now you guys are cool? Am I hallucinating? In what world does Pan accept a blow to the lip?"

They both shrugged, but Kace answered, "This is how we solve our issues. We just punch each other and go about our days. It's the way of the lost boys." As if he hadn't just destroyed his friend's face.

Pan straightened his back, crossed his arms, and moved his gaze down our bodies. "What did you two do that led to your relationship anyway?" he asked us.

Despite that he'd proven he was the good guy now, some parts of me still had doubts from the past. I'd witnessed things before. Pan wasn't the good guy when I arrived in Neverland. He used me to hurt Lili, but maybe he was trying to learn what healthy looked like. Maybe he wanted that. He definitely feared he didn't really have it.

Kace and I both looked at each other as a smile graced me. "He's loyal, trustworthy, and honest. I know I wouldn't be able to find anyone better than that. He fits me so well, and never have I felt pressured to do anything I didn't want that would hurt me."

Nodding, Kace added, "Lia is strong. She's a sensitive person, which is beneficial when you need compassion. Every time she thinks of a happy thought, her eyes light up. She does little happy dances about things that excite her. She presents this soft persona but deep down she's really just a tough cookie. The kind you can enjoy fresh from the oven or the next day. Her chocolate chips are always as sweet, her middle always the best part about her. And there's always this one curl that falls away from the rest and I'm always tempted to play around with it, just to experience the serenity she does when I'm near. She's a *fire* yet to be ignited. Contagious. Resilient."

A fluttering feeling filled my stomach and my cheeks reddened. I had no idea he'd looked at me that way, and now I could never doubt Kace again.

Pan lifted his eyebrow. "I never pictured either of you together."

"I'm in love with him, and it just happened," I said in a quieter voice.

Their immediate looks made me feel small.

Kace was quick to dampen my humiliation. "She loves me, so at least I have that to hold onto." He jabbed his thumb at himself.

I nodded a little, looking down at the floor. He wasn't ready. He didn't love me yet, and it was nothing I needed to fear, nor should he feel ashamed of. I'd be here when that moment came.

Once Pan finally left, Kace helped me to the bed, and I curled up to keep myself warm.

My nose was stuffed up and my throat felt dry—dusty. Chills racked my body and not just because of the wintry storm. It was a constant battle with my body.

I rubbed my aching head. "Can you please make the pain go away?"

He bent down to my level. "What is it that hurts?"

"My head. I just need to get to sleep. Please," I begged.

Kace looked around the room, but my room had hardly any remedies. He climbed into bed, wrapping his arms around me and pulling me against his body.

"No, I don't want to get you sick," I whispered. I kept my eyes closed as I tried to make myself sleepy, but it wasn't working.

"Nonsense. If it doesn't worry you, it doesn't worry me."

So, he didn't move. It was starting to help as I felt a tinge of sleepiness settle into my eyelids.

Part of me worried about the boy whom I'd met on the beach *that* night.

Was he alive? Had Pan and Lili found him and killed him? I hoped he didn't hate me for leaving him behind, but I feared he did.

Someone started to sing a soft tune. Was Kace trying to sing me to sleep? I'd never pictured him as a musical person at all. He didn't join in when the boys used to dance around the fire. However, I let his deep voice soothe me into a slumber, leaving me with only his promises in my dreams.

33: Cannibal Cove

THE NIGHT BEFORE LILI DETACHED FROM HER SHADOW

Walking along the paths, I marked the trees so I could find my way back. While Lili searched for a way home, I was exploring mine.

I used my dagger to carve an X into the tree and I kept walking forward. I stopped when I saw a beach that looked empty radiated with negative energy.

Danger. Turn back now.

I observed the beach for any sign of death. When I concluded there was none, I took small steps towards the sand. I studied every inch of this place, the grass leading up a cliff to my right.

This beach was bigger than the one we went to when we'd swim. It stretched for miles along the ocean. That must have been why the pirates would dock here. Cannibal Cover, as they called it.

As I counted my footsteps along the sand, I halted when something flashed in my peripheral vision. I turned my head and ripped my dagger from my belt. I didn't know how to use it, but I could at least try.

I whipped around as someone stumbled into the sand, falling to their knees. "Don't kill me!"

Pausing to focus my eyes through the darkness, I lowered my dagger. "Who are you?"

He fixed his posture, but he still appeared terrified. Amazing that I could ever spark that in anyone. "Dixon. I'm not here to hurt anyone." I could tell just by looking at him that he didn't have the strength to do so.

His clothes were made of rags, but not the rags the lost boys wore. No, he came from a pirate ship. He must have been part of Hook's crew. But she'd been dead for so long now. How did he survive? Why didn't he ever come with her?

"How long have you been out here?" I scanned the beach.

Dixon shrugged. "I'm not sure. I came with Captain Hook, and then she never came back to the ship. I came to find her, but I can't get close to Peter Pan. He'll kill me." He frowned.

He had no idea that Hook was dead and gone. She'd been dead for some time now. Did anyone even suspect that she never came alone? I doubted it.

I had to be the bearer of bad news. "Hook is dead." I swallowed. Did I mention that my sister killed her, or that Pan did? Which option was better? "Pan killed her." I wasn't about to tell a pirate that his captain was killed by my own twin. I was out here—alone. Everyone else was asleep and I had hardly any skills. I couldn't win if this boy was pulling my leg. I suspected that he was. I couldn't trust anyone on this island anymore.

Dixon slumped over. "I feared that much. I just can't believe Pan did it, after everything that transpired." I wanted to ask him more about what he meant but I couldn't get myself to say the words.

"I should go. Everyone is wondering where I'm at." A fib. I wanted to leave before something happened to me. If I told him people were looking for me, he was less likely to hurt me. If he was truly afraid of Pan, he wouldn't bother.

He grabbed something from the sand. "Seashells here are magical."

"I suspect they are."

"You can communicate through them, but only with the person who has the identical seashell." He nodded.

"Well, then I suppose I should collect them all. Does it work with the mainland, too?" I picked up a seashell and smoothed it with my fingers.

Dixon nodded. "It's how Hook would communicate with Pan when she would sail away. Before...everything happened."

I stepped back, studying the shore. "Her ship's gone so where have you been hiding?"

He pointed in the direction of the trees. "I never go far. I stay out of sight in case Pan comes near this area. He comes here *a lot*."

When I pictured Pan coming to Cannibal Cove, I saw a vulnerable boy who squatted by the waves, remembering the love he once had for a certain captain. That kind of pain would follow him around for the rest of his days. Lili needed to avoid him at all costs. Pan was dangerous, truly.

I glanced at the trees over my shoulder. "Well, Dixon, Pan isn't coming down here anytime soon. Everyone is asleep. You're safe with me."

"And what about you? Are you safe?"

Facing him, I straightened my posture. "I'm always safe."

Throughout the night, Dixon and I had conversations about anything and everything. He told me about the pirate life, while I told him about mine.

At one point, we played with the seashells and tried to communicate but nobody ever responded to us. It was like leaving a voicemail without a callback number.

I twirled with my cloak. "I'm sorry." I stopped, eyes on Dixon, shaking my head. "I miss the sound of music."

He tilted his head. "Music? Does Pan not have any music?"

"He has a flute, but I can't hear it. It's not the same as the music in my world. Music in my world has so many more instruments. The sky is the only limit, the world our oyster." I placed my balled fist against my chest. "It reminds you that there are people in this world who share your pain. Music keeps me sane."

Dixon scanned the area, grabbed some sticks he found near the trees. He came back and handed them to me. "Make your own music."

"I'm no good."

"Everyone has the potential to be good. You just have to try."

I stared at him for a moment, then took the sticks and walked over to a rock. "Don't laugh."

"I won't." He smiled.

With the sticks in my hands, I started drumming on the rocks. It started as just a beat with no real tune. It sounded wrong. I swallowed my fear and opened my mouth, creating a tune with my vocal cords. It lasted a minute, before my soul was sucked into the music itself and I lost my way back.

After I gained the courage to look at Dixon, all my fear shed off my body. He danced to the music I was creating. I hadn't had this much fun in a while. The lost boys had been wonderful, but none of them understood my world. Dixon understood enough to help me bring a bit of home to the island.

My beat came to an end, and I laughed. "Your moves are wonderful."

He approached me. "Your music is better. You're great at it. Have you ever considered being in the music business?"

I shrugged. "I've thought about it but it just...never really hit me. Overall, music makes me happy but I'm in Neverland now. I don't want to go back home. My sister wants to go, but I told her I'm staying here."

He gave a small nod and shoved his hands into his pockets. "She's homesick. As awful as home may be, she wants to return to familiarity. This will never be home to her, but I can see it is to you."

"It's the only place in this world where I feel like I belong. Back home, everyone expects one thing of me." I frowned. "I'm Lia. I'm supposed to be the girly girl who finds a nice man and has children. That's what everyone expects me to be, but that's not who I want to be. I don't want children. I just want to have the opportunity to dress in a dress and wield a dagger in it, too. Lili is the rebellious one. She acts nothing like a *lady* should, and that angers our parents. That's why they've always been harder on her. I acted the part so they assumed I was doing as a woman should and accepting my role in society.

"That's not me. That's not who I want to be. I want to be able to defend myself and fight my battles. Maybe I do love pink. Maybe I love dresses, but that doesn't mean I can't have the best of both worlds. I can wear a dress and defend myself. I'm not tethered to being solely feminine or solely masculine. I'm me. I'm Lia."

A smile settled on his lips. "That's what makes everyone different. Hook thought the same thing. She wanted her own destiny not the one her father set for her." Sorrow dripped from his words.

I stepped forward, placing a hand on his shoulder. "And every woman should have that right. Every person should have a right to choose their own destiny. Parents can help guide us, but they don't get to choose for us. It's not their life they're living. It's ours."

"It is."

I returned a smile. Something small fluttered inside my stomach, but I backed up to make it go away. I wasn't going to let anything grow from that. Dixon was from a different world. We could be great friends, and that was it.

He peered up at the sky as it transformed from a dark blue to a more colorful shade. The sun was beginning to rise now. Everyone would be up soon.

"I should go before they wonder where I am." I cleared my throat. "I don't want you to get caught."

"Meet you back here tomorrow night?"

"Tomorrow night."

As I looked around the beach, I started to collect some seashells to keep myself busy, and to come up with an excuse in case Pan asked me why I was here. If he found out about Dixon, he'd kill him on the spot. I turned on my heel and ran up the beach, towards the camp. I glanced back at Dixon and smiled one last time before disappearing beyond the trees.

It was difficult but I had the strength to ignore my own wants. I wanted to go back and hang out with Dixon some more. I wanted to let this feeling inside me grow. I wanted to be truly happy with everything I could ever want in life, but that wasn't what life entailed. I had to make sacrifices, and that included ignoring my wants.

I skipped along the trail, humming to myself. We had bonded over music which was one of my favorite things. Dixon was a pirate, but he was harmless. He was just like the rest of us here. He wanted friends, too.

What was so wrong about wanting friends?

Friends kept us sane and reminded us that we mattered. Friends told us that even if our family hated us, they never would. They *chose* us.

I stashed most of my seashells outside the cabin to keep them to myself. When I got to our room, Lili gave me the sharpest glare as if I killed the cat. Had I?

I put my dagger on the dresser and held the other shells under my cloak, out of her sight. She sat in the corner of the bed, wide awake. Had she not slept all night? I took my adventures during the night because that was when I could explore. Nobody would be wondering where I was, yet my sister seemed to prove me wrong.

She finally asked, "Where were you?" Something had gone utterly wrong, and I could sense it. Lili wanted to murder me. I just couldn't quite place why, and I feared she'd end up just like her father.

No. Please.

But alas, the monster couldn't be hidden away forever. Eventually, she'd crack. I'd be the one in the path of fire. Eventually, she'd succumb.

34: Red Cloak

Hot air warmed my earlobe. "I love every last chocolate chip of yours, including the whole cookie," someone whispered into my ear.

I opened my eyes a bit. "Hm?" I turned my face towards him.

Those beautiful brown eyes I adored of Kace's studied every detail of mine, then he smiled. "Exactly what you heard."

I smiled in return while my eyes closed again. "I love you, too." I fell back asleep as the dreams raided my mind once more.

I woke up with a stabbing pain in the area below my stomach. I curled up, whimpering as the pain grew.

"What's happening?" Kace asked.

I groaned. "My period is coming."

He sat up. "It feels like it's never gone."

"They come every month and I've told you this." I felt another wave of pain hit. "Kace, we need to boil water."

He got out of bed and rushed out of the cabin. I proceeded to put pressure on it. I even tried to massage the area.

Kace came back with a soaked cloth. “I left the water boiling, so that when this cloth cools, I can wet it again.”

“Thank you so much.” I grabbed it from him and lifted my shirt a little as I laid the hot cloth across my lower area. I sighed in relief as the pain eased up. “You know, it might be helpful to also get tampons.” I laughed. “There are some in my drawer if you’d mind getting me one.”

Kace grabbed one from the drawer. “What were you dreaming about?” He brought it to me.

“That’s a… I can answer that soon. First, I’d like to put this tampon in.” I gave him a look.

“Of course.” A blush rose to his cheeks as he slipped out. When I’d finished, I called him back.

I lay back on the bed and covered myself with the cloak, trapping as much heat as I could. “You want to know what I was dreaming about.”

“Well, I could guess but I doubt it was about me.” He shrugged, chuckling by my window.

“Lili blames me for everything. She blames me for allowing her to sleep with Pan that night, which ultimately led to her losing the battle. I, too, blame myself. I was messing around. I was…with Dixon.”

“Who?”

“Dixon is—or was—a pirate. I became friends with him. That night that Lili slept with Pan, I was at Cannibal Cove.” I slowly sat forward. “Dixon was my friend. We talked and made music together. We had so much fun, and I promised him I would come back again the next night. I never did…” My eyes watered. “Lili turned to the demon, and I never went back to Cannibal Cove. I never told him why, but I couldn’t risk her or Pan finding out. They would kill him. She would blame him for why I was out that night, fooling around. I was having fun while she was…making a big mistake.”

Kace nodded a bit. “Is Dixon still around?”

“I don’t think so. He probably hates me. I was…dreaming about that night." I released a sigh. "He was my first real crush when I arrived here. I didn't want to admit it at the time, but I was beginning to like him." I refused to look Kace in the eye. "You will need to resoak." I handed him the cloth, keeping my gaze glued to my feet.

After a few trips to the boiling pot of water, the hot cloth finally worked its magic and the cramps left me alone.

"I want to go on a date again," I said.

He looked at me. "Sure. What do you want to talk about?"

I shook my head and stood. "I mean a real date. I want us to go out and dance. I want to feel as if… I want to feel like a woman who's really on a date."

Ideas churned in his eyes. "Wait here." He left the cabin.

I waited for what felt like forever before he came back with a big pile of fabrics. "What's this?" I gestured to the pile.

He laid each piece on the bed and pulled the white fabric up. A dress. "This is something for you to wear. It used to be Wendy's when she was still here. Pan said you could have it. Lili doesn't like dresses anyway."

I grabbed the dress and eyed it. It wasn't anything fancy. It was a plain dress that fell to the ankles, and the skirt had an extra layer or two to make it a bit fluffier. The sleeves covered all the way to the wrist. The bodice had been fitted with a thin layer of lace. Wherever this dress came from, someone had poured their blood, sweat, and tears into it. A gown like this had been handmade.

"And what's that?" I pointed to the red fabric.

Kace pulled it up from the bed as it unfolded into cloak. "This is your new cloak. I thought it was fair that you got your own, and the fabric is much warmer than the one you've been wearing."

"I'm a girl who goes to her grandma's house with a big, bad wolf on the loose?" I cracked a small smile at him.

"Don't tempt me, cariño. You'd make a wonderful addiction to that fairytale."

"Wait, you know about it?"

"Sure I do. It dates back to the seventeenth century, from France. In case you forgot, Spain is right beside France."

I stuck my tongue out at him, to which he just grinned.

Kace stepped out while I changed into the dress and put on the thicker, crimson cloak. Once my brown boots were on, I opened the door for him to come back in and fasten the ties on the back of the gown for me.

Spinning around, his eyes sparkled as they took in every detail. A smile jumped onto his face. "Qué fuerte, cariño," he purred. "You've never looked more like yourself."

"You think?"

"You said you wanted to be different from Lili, right? I see Lia in this look, and solely you. You make the white pop and the red humble itself."

As I asked for his help, He pushed the cloak aside to make little bows with the ties, closing up the back. Then he stepped back.

I looked down at my clothes and smoothed out the dress. "Where are we going to go for this little date of ours?"

"We are going to go to the campfire where it's warm and the lighting would be just right. Oh, and Pan will be playing his flute tonight." He fixed his cloak.

I coughed a bit. "I can't hear his flute."

He frowned, having forgotten that I wasn't the lost girl everyone thought I was. "Then I'll sing to you to the tune of the flute."

"You're amazing, you know that?" I grabbed his hand when he lent it to me.

He centered his cloak, grinning. "I know."

We arrived at the campfire, and I didn't see the lost boys around. "No celebration?"

"They're all training right now. I wanted it to be just you and I."

"Pan is going to play his flute for *us*? As in just us? As in you and I? 'Cause he is not us." I looked at Pan who stood by the blazing fire. "He wouldn't take the time out of his day to play his flute for two people." I knew Pan was on our team, but I could never picture him trying to set the romantic mood.

Except maybe he would for his best friend and his lover's sister.

Pan shrugged. "Playing my flute is like therapy. Whether it be lost boys or my best friend and my girlfriend's sister, I'll take the chance to play my music for anyone. I'm not against those who ask."

I twisted my head towards Kace who nodded. Fingers around my wrist, he tugged me against him. "Whatever it is, I'll do it for you." He placed my arms around his neck and then wrapped his arms around my waist. He swayed gently as I glanced over at Pan who whistled into the flute as he sat on the log. I couldn't hear a single note.

A gravel voice began to sing and I looked back at Kace. I put my head against his shoulder while my eyes fluttered shut. I forgot about all the evil that lived here and threatened my life. I forgot all my worries, and at that moment, I felt *free*.

No more dead brother. No more monstrous sister. No more abusive family, or the pathetic need to be loved by everyone. Not even the emotional side of Lia could surface.

I wasn't held down by the burden of saving everyone and the island. I wasn't reminded of what all I had lost.

I was taught that despite the bad, there was better. So much worth living for. A reason to fight the wickedness. Kace was teaching me what it meant to love and to be loved.

Kace continued to sing, and we swayed as the fire heated just enough of us to battle the icy air.

There was a future for us.

I asked, "What's your last name?"

"Pérez. Kace Pérez."

"Celia Stone and Kace Pérez. Celia Pérez. Mr. and Mrs. Pérez. I think it has a nice ring to it, don't you?" I tilted my head slightly.

"Are you talking about marriage?" He chuckled.

"Is that wrong? I mean, I just assumed that maybe the whole purpose of dating was for marriage, because that's what I eventually want with you. But if you think it's too much and too fast, I can retract it."

His lips moved up one side of his face into a crooked smile. "When I do propose, I will definitely do it at a time you least expect it."

My grin grew so big that even death himself couldn't squander it. "Deal—and I promise I will say yes."

We continued to dance to the crackling flames. I didn't mind that there wasn't any music because this moment was perfect to me. It was our moment that we shared, and nobody else could take that from us.

"What are you two doing?" Asa asked.

Kace and I stopped, facing him. Kace lifted his eyebrows and gestured towards me. "What does it look like? I'm on a date with your cousin. Do you mind?"

Asa nodded. "I do actually. You know we have other important priorities to focus on."

With a groan, Kace rubbed the bridge of his nose. "Wanting to relax from the worst parts of life is a sin now? Who died and made you God?"

Asa's eye twitched. "We only have so much time. If you spend all of it doing silly things like this, we will never be able to accomplish what we are trying to do."

Growling, Kace stepped forward. "Watch it. This is not silly to me, nor is it to Lia. She deserves a little bit of something that makes her happy."

My cousin stepped right into my boyfriend's face.

Before shit could hit the fan, I squeezed between them. "Whoa, whoa. Asa, it's okay. I needed this. Kace and I are in love, and we want to express that."

"You have the rest of eternity to express your love for Kace *after* we do our jobs," he spat.

"If I don't get to be happy once in a while, why am I fighting? Silly things like this are what give me the motivation, courage, and reason to keep going. It helps me. If I'm worried about all the bad things all the time, it increases my stress and weakens my health. It doesn't help me in any way to constantly be down in the dumps."

Asa kept his mouth shut this time, and it was good he did. The fury coming from Kace burned with a temperature so hot even I'd never be able to put it out. Who knew what he could've done had Asa kept raining on our parade. I hadn't truly seen that side of Kace, and I worried that if I saw what he was like, I'd never be able to see him in the same light again.

35: Gold Magic

Staring at the bottle in my hands, the magic inside shimmered despite there being no sunlight. I had told Anna once I wouldn't drink it, but now I wasn't sure I'd follow my own advice.

Pan was on our side, but if I became more powerful than him, I could secretly train to take his place. He'd proven to be a villainous leader. He has killed and made a killer out of my own sister. The more I thought about it and questioned what I wanted, the more I realized I *craved* to be in charge.

I set out on foot towards Zeeslang Waters, where the sea serpent was living. It had saved my life, so what better place to test out gold magic than where I knew I had a chance?

When I approached the cliff after a few hours, I came to a stop and looked out over the ocean. The sea serpent was nowhere in sight, but I knew he'd come and save me if I couldn't swim.

My grip tightened around the bottle as I took a deep breath. It was now or never. I was going to have more magic than Pan. I'd be more powerful. Once I achieved gold alongside blue, I could practice both until I mastered it all. Eventually, Lili would have yellow magic. With Anna's green magic, the three of us could take down Pan together if it came to it.

Red magic still intrigued me, but I didn't need it to defeat Pan. It'd be more like a happy little accident.

I placed the edge of the glass to my lips, tilting my head back. I chugged down the whole bottle and dropped it into the ocean, never to be seen again.

The nerves in my entire body tingled. The molecules inside me rearranged themselves to allow room for a new ability. Every inch of my body fused with gold to create a new Lia—one who could fly and transport anywhere around the island. I'd become one with the air.

The tingling sensation faded away, and my body felt lighter. I stepped forward and let my toes hang off of the cliff. I'd master flying before I could master transporting myself. Flying was easier, right? At least if I transported myself somewhere way off Neverland, I could fly back if I had flying down.

I spread my arms out on either side of me and fell forward. I moved my body, trying to get my powers to kick in, but nothing did. I hit the water, going under. My entire world darkened, but I made it back to the surface before my lungs ran out. I looked around for the sea serpent. Only this time he wasn't anywhere to be seen. I had to do this myself.

I swam towards the rocks and grabbed onto one. My hand landed near a brown boot, and my chin tilted back quickly. Pan was squatting on the rock like I was the biggest idiot in the world. I didn't need this judgment from him.

He reached his hand out. "Grab on."

Doing as he said, I grabbed his hand and he pulled me out of the water. In fact, he pulled me out of the ocean, and we landed back up on the cliff. Was yellow magic like light? Was it warm? I'd kill for yellow magic right now, but I wasn't about to sleep with Pan to get it. I wasn't sure touching myself would do a damn thing, either.

Thinking of an excuse, I said, "I wanted to prove that the sea serpent saved my life, but I guess it was a one-time thing."

Pan laughed, and it sounded so foreign coming from him. Had I ever heard him laugh before? "The trick to flying is joy. It doesn't have to be pure joy, but any joy will help." He pointed to the water. "My joy comes from when I wasn't separated from my shadow. I was still considered the hero in this land. Kace and I would go on adventures to different locations, testing different theories. We were like detectives—scientists. They were such pure memories."

He knew I drank the magic, which meant he knew I wanted to take his place. Why wasn't he angry? Had he truly changed?

I walked towards the cliff. "I just need to think of a happy memory."

Pan reached out and yanked me back. "No, I suggest you try it just on the ground before you go jumping off cliffs again."

I turned my head just ninety degrees his way. "You're here if I don't succeed."

"I'm not going to dive in after you every time. I'm not your savior. I'm your sister's. If you need me to rescue you, how can you expect to save your own sister? You need to start small and work your way up."

I let out a sigh. "All right, you make a good point." I stepped back and shivered. "But I can't think when my clothes are freezing to my body."

He grabbed my hand. "Then we learn about transportation." Zeeslang Waters disappeared and in its place appeared camp. Pan dragged me to the fire to warm me. The blazing flames felt amazing against my clammy skin. It felt amazing for just a few seconds, until my body began to thaw, and my skin ached from the mixture of extreme heat and cold. It was the same feeling after you pulled a goat-head from your foot.

"It hurts so bad, but I know it's a good sign that I still have feeling." I stepped closer.

Pan stood behind me, nodding. "The human body can withstand a lot."

That much was true.

I closed my eyes, picturing the one thing that brought me joy. Lili and I were hanging out and climbing the mountain together. We had a real heart-to-heart. She knew about who I was, and I knew who she was deep down. The sisterly bonding I always wanted.

Seconds later, I couldn't feel the ground beneath my feet, and when I opened my eyes, I hovered. I was *flying*.

"I can't believe I'm actually doing it," I squealed. I landed on the ground and stumbled before fixing my balance. "I was flying!"

"You were. What was your happy memory?"

I smiled a bit. "Lili and I were having a competition about who could climb the mountain the fastest."

I appreciated Pan's help, but I decided to do the rest on my own this time, and he let me. I ventured down to Cannibal Cove to avoid the cliffs this time and instead focus on just flying above the sand.

Most of my happy memories consisted of Lili and I, and a few of Jaren and I before he died. These memories fueled the magic and lifted me off the ground a few times. The feeling inside my body was magical, too, and not just in a literal sense. Everything tingled, yet I felt as light as a feather when I was in the air.

I lost all my focus when a familiar voice called to me, "Lia?"

I dropped into the sand and wiped it from my dress. I stood and faced the boy I once became friends with before I never came back. Guilt washed over me, and I expected a slap. I expected threats or shouts of anger.

"It's been a while. I haven't... You never came back," Dixon said.

Those feelings that once used to flutter no longer did. Those were reserved for just Kace now. I was thankful I had fallen for Kace and not Dixon. It wasn't meant as an offense to Dixon, but it would never have worked.

"I'm sorry. My sister...turned into the demon. I've been a little preoccupied." I knew there were no excuses, but she had to come first.

He nodded before clearing his throat. "I see you cut your hair."

"I was tired of the long hair."

"It looks good."

"Thank you."

"And you have magic?"

"I do." I stepped forward. Why did I feel this need to tell him the truth?

I couldn't even do that to Kace. "I'm more powerful than Pan now. I'm going to take his place as leader, but he can't know that." I narrowed my eyes at Dixon. "Or are you Pan's creation, too? He created Kace's shadow."

Dixon shook his head. "I'm not anyone's creation. I'm just a pirate stranded on this island since my captain is dead."

Of course. Captain Hook.

"Pan created this island. Honestly, I question what is and isn't real anymore. Is Kace even real?" I furrowed my brows.

"Kace, is he the boy with the cloak?" Dixon asked.

I nodded.

He was mine to irrevocably love. We shared so many memories and secrets with each other. No, Pan couldn't have created everyone here. I existed before here, and certainly everyone here did, too? Not just for Lili and I?

Dixon sat on one of the bigger rocks. "I've been building fires every night just to stay alive. I didn't know winter was possible in Neverland."

"Ever since my sister lost her shadow, Pan's emotions became more powerful than before. This is how he feels right now. Chilly. Paralyzing." I pulled my cloak closed.

His eyes lowered. "That's how I felt after you told me Hook was dead." His Adam's apple bobbed. "It angers me that whatever went down between her and Pan, it got her killed. Now I'm the one who suffers for it, but has their hurt changed? No. She's dead and nothing has changed for Pan. I'm the one who has to suffer because of his choice."

"Dixon, there's something you should know." I stepped closer.

His head shot up. "What?"

"Pan didn't kill her." I closed my eyes for a second. "My sister did."

There was a moment of silence, and after the way he reacted when I returned, I thought maybe he was a forgiving person. I'd been so wrong.

He jumped up from his rock and stomped towards me. "Your sister took away the one woman I loved?" Everything inside me contorted from the sound of his words. Of course he loved her. How had I not expected this?

"I don't get to control what she does, Dixon. You know that. I'm trying to save her from this darkness." I stepped back.

Before I had time to react, he pulled my dagger from my belt and held it against my throat. "No, but you are her enabler. If you save her, you're teaching everyone else it's okay to kill if you change. I won't stand for justification."

Any amount of movement could end my life. One nick, one slice, one stab—and it would all be over in the blink of an eye.

Dixon grabbed my wrist and smashed it against the tree behind me. I cried out, afraid of what monster had been created. We had once become friends in a short night and now I was face to face with a boy who blamed me for the death of his captain.

I wanted to fight. I had trained so many times before. I was supposed to defeat the pirates, to never trust them. I made a mistake by trusting Dixon and I was the one paying for it.

He pulled the blade back and for a moment, I feared he would stab it into my abdomen. No, instead his other fist connected with my jaw, and I flew down into the sand.

When I attempted to get up, he kicked me in the side until I rolled on my back. I took deep breaths, finding it harder and harder to breathe.

Dixon swung his leg over until he stood over me. He sat down on my abdomen, holding my face with just his free hand. "Don't you know villains can't be saved?" He swung his fist at the side of my head, sending my head to my right. A metallic taste filled my tongue and traveled down my throat, choking me. He leaned forward and lifted the blade. This was my end. At the hands of a pirate wielding my own weapon against me.

He brought it down, stabbing it down into the sand next to my head. With my face in his hands, he brushed the hair away. His weight was crushing every bruised rib in my chest, and I wanted to scream but I couldn't seem to get a sound out.

He lifted his hand, curling his fingers into a fist. “Goodnight,” he whispered against my cheek before connecting his fist with my face. My nose cracked at the blow, and milliseconds later, my hopes and dreams crumbled to dust. The darkness swept me like a wave.

Ropes kept my wrists restrained as Dixon started a fire. “You’re awake.”

“What are you doing?” I swallowed. Was he just a creation of Pan? Did Pan want to murder me? Maybe. I couldn’t trust anyone here. Not anymore. I’d been too gullible for my own good. “What game are you playing?”

He glanced back. “I’m playing *you*. I make you believe one thing and crush your spirit. It’s my favorite one.” He faced the fire again.

"Someone's gonna come looking." Kace. Possibly Pan. Definitely not Lili.

But someone.

"Let them. Revenge is mine for the taking." He approached me, hooking his fingers under the rope that connected my wrists, yanking me to my feet.

I cried out from the pain, stumbling forward.

Dixon pulled me from the fire, over to the waves. He forced me to my knees. "See that?"

I glanced at him, but he shoved my head forward, tangling his grubby hands in my hair and holding my head up. "I don't see anything,” I said, trembling.

"Exactly." He squatted to me height. "Empty. My captain's ship just gone. She's dead. And you're to blame. Someone has to pay, don't they? Shame it had to be you. I did like you at first, Lia." He stood, stretching his legs.

When his back was turned, I felt for my dagger.

"Looking for this?" When I lifted my gaze to my blade, Dixon held it just out of my reach.

He pushed my head into the salty water, holding me under as I flailed.

My lungs began to burn. I feared for my life. My sister. Kace. Everyone who'd ever counted on me. And I feared for the restriction of my lungs.

Ripping my head back, he cackled. I gasped for air with my eyes shooting to the sky.

"I like you like this, Lia," he hummed. Before I could respond, he shoved my head back under.

I choked, coughing into the water and creating little air pockets that filled up almost immediately. Fire in my chest. What I needed was oxygen to douse that fire, and instead it'd be fueled. I inhaled, water dribbling up my nose, running down my throat. But when it entered my lungs, the burning soothed—the flame put out. Except it didn't fill my lungs to drown me. It became the air I needed. I exhaled, then inhaled.

Dixon lifted my head. "Why aren't you dead yet?"

I smirked just a bit as someone called out my name.

The pirate dragged me to a rock, shuffling us behind it and scraping my cheek on the rough surface. He ripped a piece of his dirty rags and gagged me. "Say a word and I slit your throat." To prove his point, my own dagger dug into the skin under my jaw.

"Lia!" he yelled. "Cariño!"

Kace.

My eyes glossed over, tears threatening to spill. I pleaded, hoping for him to keep searching. To find me.

But instead of looking harder, his calls faded in the distance until he no longer lingered.

Dixon brushed his filthy lips across my ear. "Your boy toy couldn't even find you. What a joke."

I glanced back at him, eyes growing wide, words absorbed by the cloth in my mouth. Rock in hand, he smashed it into my temple.

"CARIÑO," THEY BEGGED. "PLEASE, wake up."

Opening my eyes, the most beautiful chocolate iris' graced my view. Those light brown specks in his right eye, where he'd left them.

He lifted his gaze to someone else. "She's awake."

Lili dropped into my sight as Kace moved back. "Fuck, don't scare us like that again."

Kace scowled. "Don't blame her." He grabbed me by the shoulders and dragged me into his lap, tightening his embrace around me. "You're okay. You're safe. He's dead."

Eyes shifting to my right, Dixon laid in a pool of his own blood soaked up by the sand, his lifeless gaze fixed on the trees. Kicking my feet to scoot further away, I cried out.

"Lia!" Lili reached for me but Kace's hug became warmer as he whispered into my ear that I'd be okay.

He asked me not to speak. To rest. To allow them to take care of the body.

Lili was the one who explained that Kace had found the fire and he knew something was up. He went to my sister for help, and sure enough, she gladly succeeded in her task of taking out the threat.

"You're okay, *cariño*," he mumbled. "I'll take good care of you."

I didn't doubt he would. But every injury I sustained became another scar—a blemish. And how long would he stick around for that? How long before he abandoned me because I was nothing but a shattered soul?

How long before Kace realized he wasn't equipped to save the damsel from herself?

36: Bruises

I kicked the snow and then flattened it with the toe of my boot. A black boot stepped on the path in front of me. I looked up to find Pan. "What are you doing here?"

"What are you doing?"

"I asked you first." I crossed my arms.

He shrugged. "I'm here wondering what you're doing."

I glanced down at the snow. "I'm trying to clear a path. It keeps snowing so much and I don't want to get locked in my cabin, so I'm clearing the snow from my door."

He glanced at the path I was progressing on. He grabbed my hand and used it to wave over the snow before us, and I watched the path form from my door to the camp. "There, it's done. You should learn to use your magic if you're going to have it."

I stood there and blinked a few times too fast.

"What?" His forehead crinkled.

"Why do you always try to make my life easier? I'm with Kace, Pan." I pointed my finger at him.

He lifted his hands in defense. "I just wanted to be helpful. You know why I'm really here."

"Why? You're Pan—not Peter. You are a bad guy. You like to murder people. You even taught my sister to enjoy the same thing when you ripped away her shadow. You don't want to be helpful. Don't lie to me. What is your sick game?" After the incident with Dixon, I trusted nobody but Kace. I feared everyone was using me now.

Pan's eyes seemed to lower, and I followed his gaze and saw he was staring at the bruises that lined my skin. I pulled the cloak together to block them off. "I don't need my bruises giving you ideas. I'm not looking to get high."

He ignored my comment. "Kace is lucky."

My mouth opened a little, but I didn't know what to say. This was far beyond anything I could see Pan saying towards *me*. He was supposed to be with my sister.

With a sly smile, he asked, "Did I do something wrong?"

"You always do something wrong," I mumbled. I looked away from him. "I'm going to go." I started to walk towards the cabin where the royalty slept.

A hand grasped my arm, holding me back. "Where are you going?"

I glanced at him. "I'm going to see my sister." I ripped my arm from his grip and rubbed the area where his fingers had been. A bruise would form there, too.

Pan came closer and the playful spirit left his eyes, monstrous side taking over. His eyes darkened enough that you'd question his sanity, but not the demon title he held.

He moved my arms, throwing my cloak open. "These bruises don't appear out of nowhere, and I can see right through your lies." He grabbed hold of my chin, forcing me to look into his black iris'. Everyone thought I was lying about the nature of these bruises.

I'd worried about Dixon and what Pan would do, but what choice did I have now? Why was I protecting the boy who'd nearly beat me to death? "A pirate who's been camping at Cannibal Cove, named Dixon. He came from Hook's ship and when I told him that Lili killed his captain, he lost it. He was supposed to be my friend."

"Pirates are never your friend, Lia. They fool you. They *always* trick you." He let go of me, stepping back. "You can heal yourself now."

"How?"

"Just picture what your skin looked like, and what your body felt like. When you were healthy. Not battered and blue."

I placed my hand over my bruises, but instead of picturing what he suggested, I faced what happened the moment I woke up.

Ropes kept my wrists restrained as Dixon started a fire. "You're awake."

"What are you doing?" I swallowed. Was he just a creation of Pan? Did Pan want to murder me? Maybe. I couldn't trust anyone here. Not anymore. I'd been too gullible for my own good. "What game are you playing?"

He glanced back. "I'm playing you. I make you believe one thing and crush your spirit. It's my favorite one." He faced the fire again.

The memory disappeared and I caught my breath. Tears started to form, slipping free and leaving damage along my cheeks. "I hate him so much."

Pan stood there, not sure what to do. I didn't want to make this anymore awkward for us. I didn't want to appear weak any longer. *Never show your enemy your weakness.*

I wiped my tears. "It's nothing to worry about now." I went to their cabin and started banging on the door. "Lili, open the door!"

She opened it with narrowed eyes. "What the hell do you want?"

"I..." Did I want to tell her to kill someone for me? No. No, I couldn't stoop to that level. "Did you have sex with Pan?"

"Excuse me?" She crossed her arms.

"I want to know if you got magic yet. Has it happened?" I gestured to her.

Lili rubbed her face. "I'm trying, but it's been hard."

"Try harder. He can't hold out forever." I got closer.

Lili scoffed. "Easy for you to say. Your cleavage is showing." What the hell kind of insult was that? Was she implying things about me? I was the one still a virgin between the two of us, if she really wanted to go that far.

"I don't want to have sleep with Pan and trust me when I say he'd probably give in if I tried." His feelings sure did conflict him. "You just have to do the same." He was easier than she thought. He was just being difficult. Why wouldn't he give in? He knew she wanted the magic and he wanted her to have it, too. Was he afraid? "I mean, he did kiss me once. He'll do anything."

Lili grabbed onto the door frame as she lost her balance. "Don't you dare talk about that."

"I'm not trying to make you angry. I'm trying to remind you that Pan wants to be with you. He's just stubborn at times. If I could get him into bed with me, why can't you?"

I saw a flicker of heartbreak in her eyes, but it was gone within a millisecond. She regained her balance. "Get out of my face before I kill you." She slammed the door and I stood there, not knowing where I was supposed to go now.

"So that's how you want to play?" a thick-laced accent asked behind me.

I whipped around to face Pan. "What do you mean?"

"You're making me into a sex doll, Lia. You said I'm just stubborn at times, and is that not unwanted affection?" He tilted his head.

"You stopped having sex the moment I told her to poke holes in your condoms. That's on you, not me." I started walking past him, back to my cabin.

I heard fingers snap and I froze. I lost control of every muscle. The attachment from my brain to every limb had been severed, and I had become trapped in my own body.

Pan circled me until our eyes met. "I don't think so. You're suggesting Lili do whatever she needs to get magic from me. No mention of seduction. Just *try harder*. Try what harder, Lia? Try to force me to do something I don't want?" He closed the remaining gap, his glacial breath fanning my wide eyes. "I can't do that. This side of Lili is ugly. I'm not as sexually attracted to her as I thought I was." He leaned in so close I could hear his heartbeat. "And I can't force myself to be, either."

I knew where this was going.

"Don't condone assault." He snapped his fingers and my balance faltered but I caught myself as he stepped away before I crashed into him. "If I don't punish you, Lili will suspect something is up." Grabbing me by the arm, he dragged me towards the cage. No. I'd never been punished before. Not me. Not now. Not the *cage.*

"Pan, please, don't do this. I'm your girlfriend's sister," I pleaded.

Ignoring me, he opened the door and threw me inside. He locked it before peering at me. "I'll see you tomorrow." Then he was gone.

I grabbed the bars. I was one offense away from being murdered according to Lili's rules. I swallowed. "Kace... Where are you?" I whispered.

I sat back towards the other end of the cage, opposite of the door. I tightened my cloak around my body to keep myself warm. I didn't need to see my own breath to know I needed heat, but it was confirmation. And this was what the cage felt like. This is what cousin and sister went through.

After trying to close my eyes, I failed to sleep. The cold kept me awake. What had I done wrong? Pan was the one who went back on our plan. I just exposed the truth to him. I'd never ask Lili to force herself on him and they both knew that. I only asked them to get in the mood.

They blamed me, and for what? It wasn't my fault they sucked at getting themselves aroused.

I wanted nothing more than music to distract me. The music that did exist, I couldn't hear it. Why was that? Why couldn't I hear the flute when Lili could?

I survived a night in the woods by myself against other wild animals. I belonged here even moreso. I had real magic. I *belonged* here. I was a lost girl and I had earned my title from everything I survived at this point. I still couldn't hear the flute. There had to be some sort of explanation.

Hell, I was as powerful as Pan even before I got gold magic.

But Lili could always hear his flute. I never could. We were twins.

Weren't we supposed to hear the same things?

I laid my head against the bars as the waterworks started, only subtly.

My silent cries soon became sobs. I pulled my hood on to hide my face. I wanted to save everyone, but I couldn't. *Save everyone...*

I began to question if that's what Lili was doing. She tried to save Pan in the only way she knew how. Was that why she could hear the flute? Was she the only one who could save Pan?

She was supposed to be his second chance. She was supposed to be his savior, to help him find himself again.

"Lili... Why would you do this to yourself?" I gazed up at the murky sky.

Pan had mentioned Lili being the only threat to him. She seemed to be the one person who could save him. I just needed to help her first, so she could rescue him. She could hear the flute because she was the one person who could bring back Peter Pan. It'd been foolish to believe anyone else could've done it. Then, when she played the role of hero, I would take his place as queen.

Her shadow was ripped away. Magic was the immune system to Neverland. If the immune system was infected, maybe the host would be, too. Pan and Lili were the hosts, the rest of us were the white blood cells trying to fight off the virus.

I had to find the source of the virus and kill it.

A place that Pan forbade everyone to go was Skull Rock. But she had been there. Is that where the shadows were?

I needed to get there. The question was—how?

I couldn't exactly swim there in freezing water. I'd be dead after five minutes. I would need to fly. I needed to *learn* how to fly.

And I couldn't let Pan or Lili even know I was going. How would I be able to fly without their knowledge?

I needed to practice controlling my magic. I could try Hangman's Tree for more tips and tricks.

Pan's little hideout.

Was there a secret to the magic in Neverland inside that tree? It wouldn't surprise me if there was. Aside from the books I stole, of course.

Clouds cleared, and I watched the stars in the sky, some shimmering more than others. Maybe we were like stars, some brighter than others. Some had magic, some didn't. If Pan wouldn't help Lili get magic anymore, I had to find a new way to get it to her. I had gold magic, so I needed to give it to her in a way that she would never suspect. She had no idea that I had any, and I was keeping it that way. But the key to saving Neverland was in one small promise—giving Lili access to yellow magic.

37: Tips and Tricks

Kace led me down the path and we ended up at Hangman's Tree. "Be quick. Once Pan knows you've been here, we'll both be killed."

I nodded, studying every groove in the bark. "I'll tell you what I find when I return."

Kace eyed the area to make sure they weren't coming. "Be careful." He snuffed out the distance between us and planted a sweet kiss on me. "I better be able to do that again." He gave me a coy smile.

"You will. I won't break my promise."

Kace helped me get inside. Last time I was here, I'd pissed off Kace. Everyone called me crazy then, and maybe I had been.

I descended into the room and the door closed behind me. I scanned the shelves. "Where do I need to look for some magic tips?" I roamed through some books, deciding they wouldn't be informational enough.

Attempting to speed up my process, I searched everything I could, but I wasn't finding any tips about magic I could use. Happy thoughts to fly, but what else? The book on gold magic didn't give out that kind of information?

I needed a way to get to Skull Rock and flying was the only logical transportation, ironically enough. I glanced over at the skull on the shelf and walked over. "I wonder which head you were from." I picked it up. A little note fell out. I opened it up to find out how each type worked.

Shoving it in my cloak, I put the skull back in its place. I smiled at my little triumph. "Magic." I left the tree now that my duty was fulfilled.

Kace looked at me. "Is it done?"

I showed him the note and smirked. "It's time to fly."

"Be careful. Don't use too much. Just a little goes a long way."

"Aw, you're worried. I think I can handle some magic. I only got high from it twice." I laughed.

"You also hallucinated; don't you forget." Kace smiled as if I was some drug addict. I started to wonder if I was.

Kace walked with me through the forest, neither of us ever straying from the path.

Now seemed as good as a time than ever. "Have you ever been intimate with a girl? I know it's probably none of my business."

Kace smiled a bit. "Well, I mean, technically no. Hook tried to do that, but I guess I just didn't feel up to it. I don't know what life is like where you come from, but in my days, it was very..." He gestured to find the right word. "Many people I knew were raised catholic."

I offered some words, "Taboo? Shameful?"

"Yes. Plus my parents were too busy trying to turn me into their daughter that I didn't really have a chance to meet any girls."

"Do you ever think it's tragic that we connect through our broken families? Shared trauma?"

Sliding his palm in mine, he interlocked our fingers. "All the time."

We stayed silent for a few more minutes on our walk. I looked at Kace again with a small smile. "So, you're a virgin? You don't meet a lot of guys in my world who wouldn't sleep with a girl the first chance they got. I like to think relationships are much more than that. I want us to connect on other levels before we get to that physical aspect." And no matter what my body said, I wasn't ready.

He choked on a laugh. "I think being alive for so long, I've mastered the skill of self-control."

"I love a man with self-control."

"I'm glad to hear that."

We approached a cliff and in the misty fog over the ocean, we spotted a skull-shaped rock. Kace pulled his hand from mine and the cold rushed back to envelope me.

"This is where I stay behind," he said.

I focused on breathing exercises. In and out. In through the nose and out through the mouth. In—hold for a few seconds. Out. I opened the note. "Don't worry about me. I survive everything."

With some happy memories in my mind, weightless I became. "I'm flying!"

"Be careful!" He yelled, hands cupped around his mouth.

I used my arms to swim through the air, towards Skull Rock. As badly as I wanted to fly, I had one goal in mind.

Getting closer to the rock, I immediately thought of the saddest thing I could.

My lifeless brother in my arms, knowing my sister had caused that pain. His life drained, and I had no power to stop it then. And due to my ageless body, I'd never get a chance to see him again.

I landed on the edge of the opening. I wiped some loose tears from my cheeks before I walked into the cave, taking in my surroundings. It was dimly lit by a ball of light that appeared to be protected by jagged rocks. I noticed the hook on the wall as if it was some sort of trophy to be displayed.

I heard voices, and immediately I ran to a tall rock in the dark corner, hiding behind it. The voices grew louder. Lili and Pan were inside the cave with me. Was this part of the plan? No, I was way off course.

The agitation could be sliced with our daggers, but not with ease.

"That is what she wants. She wants to drive us apart. You're going to let her do that?" Pan asked in a mocking tone.

Lili shrugged. "I think it's none of your business as to whether or not I let Lia drive us apart. We are talking about what you've been doing. Quit trying to redirect blame. You're trying to brush off your asshole actions by telling me that she wants this. You are no longer attracted to me. Admit it."

Rubbing his thumb and forefinger over his eyes, he released a sigh. "Don't do this. Don't do this, Love. I do appreciate you."

"You appreciate me, but you treat my sister better. Don't even give me the bullshit excuse you already gave me. Being a threat does not make it okay to treat me like I'm lesser than a human being."

"What do you want from me? I treated you differently because you actually scared me."

"You haven't apologized! You haven't even changed. You still treat her better. You talk to her more than you do me. You're the one who's the problem. You heal her and save her life all the time..." Lili fell silent.

I never knew that she felt this way. I'd only seen the demon side—the side that wanted to kill Pan.

Pan stepped closer but Lili stepped away from him. "Don't come near me. You don't care. We're broken, and you know what it feels like to have someone come by and make it worse. Why would you do that to me? I needed your love."

He mumbled something, but she hadn't quite heard it. Pan was studying her and trying to figure out the right words to say. He wasn't finding anything that could help his case or mend their broken hearts together.

"You don't have a shadow. How could you..." Pan didn't finish his question.

"How could I be hurt? Because I'm still human. I don't need my shadow to feel pain."

He was treading in dangerous waters with the words he chose to say. He wasn't supposed to invalidate her feelings. He loved her too much. More than she could ever love him. That in itself was wicked.

"You tell Lia that I get boring, don't you? Is that why you confide in her so often? Is she the interesting one, now that she's the one you can't have?

Is this why you won't have sex with me anymore?"

Pan didn't answer the question.

"Go on, answer her, you douchebag," a shadow of a female said while stepping from the darkness.

Pan scowled at the shadow, his attention returning to my sister. "You've taken it too far with this dark side."

The female shadow inched closer to Pan and grabbed his shoulder. "You wouldn't merge us, would you? You know that's the wrong move."

He looked at the shadow nearly his own height. "I want my Little Flower back. I don't think her dark side's interesting enough, strictly because she is *one-sided*."

My sister tilted her head. "Why? You made me this way."

"I miss the banter and arguments." He rubbed the bridge of his nose. "Everything we had before. It'd been playful, much more innocent. Now? Now you look at me as if I let Jaren die. As if I'm the most venomous demon you conjured up, and not in the good way. You despise me, Little Flower. You want to rip my heart out and watch me bleed."

I knew they were without shadows, but I never suspected their shadows could walk or talk like we could. Kace's shadow was based off a real shadow, and now I knew that.

The female silhouette sighed, approaching its owner. "Ignore him."

A taller, male shadow appeared from the dark wall. "What's going on?"

The female shadow turned her head towards him. "Your buddy here is going soft." Those words emitted betrayal.

Pan argued for himself, "I am not going soft. I am perfectly dark. I just want Lili to become the same person I was intrigued by the day she arrived. She has been stubborn and disobedient, but she was also..." He didn't finish his sentence.

"Weak," the female finished for him. "You're going soft again."

Lili decided to throw her two cents in. "That's exactly how I felt before you ripped my shadow from me. I wanted to see who you were with a full range of emotions. You refused. You did this to me. You don't get to want me back as myself when you realize you lost control completely. This is who I am now. Fuck you for suggesting otherwise."

The female leaned on her counterpart. "I like her. I say we should keep her the way she is."

The male silhouette walked closer to the three of them, nodding. "Keep her the way she is."

Pan seethed. "Neverland is falling apart. If I don't fix her, we will meet our end—crashing and burning."

Lili scoffed at his suggestion. "If we fix me, we must fix you, too. Fair?"

With the shake of his head, he shot her an incredulous look. "Are you serious? Am I the only person who cares about our home?"

I moved my foot slightly, gravel rubbing against my boot. It echoed throughout the cave, and I froze when the male shadow stepped in my direction. "Someone else is here."

38: Truth vs. Lie

I stumbled but caught myself as my feet landed back on the ground of the cliff that overlooked the ocean. I sprinted down the trail that we made with our footprints on the way up, trying to push my speed faster than it could go. When I arrived at the camp, I busted through the door of Kace's cabin.

He jumped back. "Lia, what's wrong?" His eyebrows furrowed in worry.

"They caught me. All four of them caught me and I'm probably going to be dead soon. I have so much to tell you but not enough time. They could be here at any moment," the words spilled from my mouth like a river going downstream.

"Who? Who are these four?" Kace grabbed my arms to rub them and calm me down. It didn't work.

"Pan, Lili, and their *shadows.*" I inhaled sharply, not sure where to start.

Before I could say another word or Kace could ask more questions, Pan entered in a timely fashion, and a casual manner. "I think we should talk."

"I know."

The words we'd kept so secret from Kace slipped his tongue, "Help me merge Lili and her shadow." His bright eyes studied our surprise. "When I started to get to know this version of her, I began to realize the monster I created." His brows knitted together, gaze raking over the bed. "My first thought was, 'wait a bloody minute, this tosser is losing it.' That was when I questioned my own decisions. I can see how nobody wants me to act this way. I certainly don't like Lili like that. It's not *her*."

Kace nearly choked on his own saliva. "Whoa, and what do we get out of this?"

Pan crossed his arms. "I...might let you merge me and my shadow." *Might* was a strong word.

I shot Kace a look. "This is a good bargain. I think we should do it." Of course, I knew Pan was already on our side. Kace didn't. But I'd play into it like I had no idea.

Kace narrowed his eyes at Pan, taking a step forward. "What's the catch? You can't possibly want to help us make your girlfriend good, or even let us make you good."

Shaking his head, Pan locked eyes with us. "There's no catch. I swear. You'll need my help. I am more powerful than you. After all, it was I who ripped her shadow from her in the first place."

Of course, I wanted to accept the offer. However, this wasn't going to be easy—convincing Kace. "There has to be a catch."

"You cannot merge me with my shadow until after Lili is merged with hers. I work best when my darkness has reign."

"When we merge Lili, you'll start to put up a fight, but we will have Lili to help us at that point. I think it's still a deal we should take." I glanced at my boyfriend who hadn't said a word for a few minutes.

Finally, he sighed. "Who's to say if we do accept this offer, you won't pull any surprises on us? Lia and I are to stick strictly to the plan. We must save Lili first, then you. That is the deal you want to propose."

Pan put his hand out for Kace to shake. "Deal." Kace refused to shake on it, denying any deals. Never thought I'd see the day when he rejected the ideas his best friend—and leader—brought to the table.

"I see you're a skeptic, and I understand that. However, Lia has seemed to accept my offer." Pan tapped his stubbled chin. "Why not you?"

"I think the answer is obvious," Kace answered.

I shook my head. "It's okay. I can handle anything he throws my way. What do you have in mind, Pan?"

"Mooie duisternis."

Kace stepped forward. "No. Pan, don't you dare."

I forced my chin higher. "Mooie duisternis is just a venomous plant. I can handle this. Pan won't hurt me, and I'm willing to prove it to you. Anyway I have to prove to you he's on our side, I will."

Kace pulled me closer to him and rubbed his thumb over my cheek. "No, you don't understand. mooie duisternis is the worst. You saw what happened to Wendy."

"My sister was hung over mooie duisternis and she came back alive. She wasn't too subtle with bragging about her accomplishment. If she can do it, so can I."

He let out a sigh. "I can't stop you, can I?"

"Nothing can kill me." I turned to Pan and pulled my hood on. "I'm ready to prove that you are our ally, and to prove to Lili that you are not on our side. That you treat me worse than her now."

I followed Pan into the woods, and we ventured the opposite direction of the beaches, and the cliff where I had seen Skull Rock. We came upon the patch of mooie duisternis Pan warned me about when I first arrived.

Stopping, he turned to face me. "I can't do what I did to Lili. It'll be like I expect you to survive. I have to make it harder for you."

"What do you have to do?" I gripped the edges of the cloak in front of my torso. It gave me some sort of comfort.

He waved his hand over the large bush and created an opening. "I have to trap you inside and make you get out on your own."

"Pan, that's *suicide*."

"Exactly. I must make it look like I'm intending for you to die. If I expect you to die, if I send you to your demise... She will have to see that I don't care about you."

"So how the hell am I supposed to escape?" I gestured to the bush.

"I can't help you. You survived a lot, so this will be like a walk along the beach. Now go in." He gestured to the tunnel.

I dropped to my knees. "This better not be a trick. I can't survive the venom and you won't be able to save me this time." I began to crawl through. My cloak snagged on the thorns, but I kept going, the tunnel closing behind me. I got to the middle and rolled onto my butt, wiping the dirt from my white dress.

"Good luck!" Pan shouted. After that, stillness.

Studying the vines, my breathing became shallow as claustrophobia began to set in. If I died, it was my fault. If I survived, it was my win.

If Pan believed in me, could I believe in myself?

The number one thing I had to focus on was not getting stabbed by a single thorn. Like that was so easy.

I searched the dirt for any thick branches or sticks, but I didn't find any.

Looking at the red cloak, I rubbed the fabric between my fingers. Was it thick enough to shield me from the thorns?

As I looked at my hands, I knew I'd have to shove my hands inside my cloak and use my head to push through the thorns.

I yelled out for anyone. Even a wild beast. Nobody came.

The vines had been so thick that not an ounce of light entered. Too many layers. I was the prey.

Gasping, I glanced at my sheath. How could I forget about my own weapon?

So I pulled out my dagger. "Surely this has to work." I sliced through a vine, and it squealed as it shriveled up into the dirt. "You sure hate that." I cut some more, extra cautious about the distance I cut from. I used the blade to shove them out of my path.

I stopped for a moment to take a break. "This is taking forever. I've barely made a tunnel!" I looked back at the stomach of the bush only two inches away. My arms were growing tired, and at this rate, it'd take the entire night.

As I crawled back into the center, something pressed against my side. *The note*. "Damnit, Lia, you're a moron." I slipped it from under the leather of my belt. "You have magic now!" I crawled back towards the small tunnel I'd started.

I read the tip about controlling the wind, and I blew at the vines, and they began to curl away, forming a tunnel. How had Pan never used this?

"Magic makes you bend at *my* will." I scurried through. Upon exiting the bush, I leaped to my feet. "I did it!" I threw my arms up in victory. I had survived the venomous plant they called mooie duisternis. Of course, I cheated, but Pan never said I couldn't.

I walked back to the camp, the light glimmering in Kace's eyes as he saw me return in one piece. He rushed over and wrapped his arms around my waist, lifting me and spinning. I clung to his neck.

Kace put me down and grabbed my face, pulling me in for a deep kiss.

For the first time, I was the one to slide my tongue, and he happily accepted. Every kiss had been desperate. Grateful. But when we began to makeout, I fisted his shirt and let out a low moan only seconds after him.

"I knew you could do it," Pan said in a whisper beside us.

Heat creeping up into my cheeks, we pulled away and I wiped my lips. Kace, however, licked his. "I worried."

"Come on, by now you must know I can defeat anything," I joked.

"So you defeated mooie duisternis I hear," we all heard her say from behind.

We turned to face Lili. Amusement danced in her eyes, along with disappointment.

As quickly as it came, it had been replaced by envy. "You're always better than me, aren't you? You're still the perfect twin even if my own boyfriend punishing you."

"Lili, don't do this." I hated it when she pulled that card. She always saw me as the better version of herself—the version she could never achieve.

"No, I think I will do this. First Pan, then the lost boys. Kace can't keep his tongue to himself. Nice boner, by the way," she directed the last part to Kace. "You can defeat *everything* that comes your way. Even Asa is now taking a liking to you. Somehow, you win everyone over. You can do no wrong."

"I cannot control how people feel about me. If someone doesn't like you for who you are, forget about them. You are the one who has always withstood everything. You are much stronger than I am. Don't you see that yet?"

Lili shook her head. Heartbreak laced her tone, "I guess I was just dreaming when I thought I could come close to having it as good as you do."

I TOSSED THE BOOK across the room, screaming in a fit of rage. Why had it been so damn hard to research red magic? All I needed were answers. Answers so I could deal with my own sister and her endless supply of loathing.

But yet again, I came up empty. No word about where it came from. How to get it. What kind of abilities it pertained to. Just that red magic was tired to the fire element, and that was as much as Pan knew.

If I could just figure it out, I'd finally be more powerful. I'd be the one able to defeat him without any question. I'd be able to make promises to Lili, to mend all my mistakes from the past. But how did I find it?

Jumping off the bed, I left the cabin, slamming the door on my way out. I ventured off into the woods, towards the lagoon we once swam in, before the mess became a desolate wasteland.

Nothing but a skating rink. No waterfall.

Not even a sliver of hope.

39: Red Magic

I attempted. With my boots, I attempted to skate across the ice. I never fell through because I did make it to the other side where the waterfall once had been. A stunning accomplishment.

A hollowed out cave the size of a small window stood out in the rock, and as I got down on my knees to look inside, I caught sight of something.

Something *red*.

Flattening onto my stomach, I stuck my arm and head in the opening, reaching out and plucking the flower. After pulling myself out, I leaned back with my legs folded underneath me. A tickle in the nose. Then I sneezed.

The vibrant red muted before its petals began to droop. I brushed my fingers over them, frowning. "Such a pretty little flower in the dead of winter, and I've already killed you. I'm so sorry."

Lowering my head, I peeked into the cave. No other buds. No leaves. Nothing. Just one flower. Much like an agave americana.

Regardless, I felt bad. Maybe I'd show it to Kace and Pan, asking them about where it came from.

So I took it with me as I skated back across.

This winter had been far too cold, so I had to keep Diego locked up in my drawer all the time. He was warm in there. And I didn't want Lili to know about him. At the time, I hadn't wanted Pan to, either, but now that wasn't such a big deal.

I trudged through the trees, pulling my hood up. Halting, I furrowed my brows and glanced at the trees behind me. I pushed my hood down, rubbing along my neck. "Don't tell me..."

I thought maybe I'd just had my period, but time passed so sneakily. How the hell could I keep track anymore?

My neck burned, and so I tried to put snow on it to cool it. It worked for a minute or two, but the heat spread. Quickly. And I was blazing, even in the dead of winter.

Untying my cloak, I dropped it to the ground with the flower. "Damnit." I fanned myself first, but it did nothing. Then I dropped into the snow and allowed it to sink into my dress. I rubbed it along my face. My neck. My hands. My collarbone. Nothing.

"Is this really what they feel like?" I gasped, jumping to my feet.

Hot flashes were this brutal. I wasn't supposed to get them until I hit menopause—which I'd never do now—but I had also heard about them becoming period symptoms. I just so happened to be the lucky winner today.

I struggled with the back of the dress, but after contorting my body, I got the ties and slipped out of the dress, throwing it on top of my cloak. I hurried to get my boots and socks off, kneeling into the powder to take in the cold. It was a massive relief against the heat.

Yeah, I'd wished for warmth for a long time now. I hated winter. But hot flashes? They were torture. Every inch of my flesh blazed like the flames in the center of camp.

I reached behind my back to remove the clip of my bra, freezing at the sound of Pan's voice, "What in the actual bloody hell are you doing?"

Lifting my gaze, he stood a few feet away. His brows had shot up, but his eyes weren't prying, surprisingly. They'd been far more curious about why I'd stripped myself nearly naked in the woods.

Kace skidded just behind him, eyes wide as his mouth dropped. "Cariño?"

With a pink face, swallowing, I lowered my gaze. "It just came out of nowhere."

He shoved Pan aside and grabbed my dress, using it to cover my body. "What are you doing? You're gonna get frostbite or hypothermia."

"Hardly. I'm burning up."

He pressed the back of his hand to my forehead. "Why?"

I held the dress against my front. "I think my period is starting soon. And...it's less common, but not impossible to get hot flashes. Normally they come after periods, when I'm fifty and hitting menopause. But I guess it came now."

"Hot flash?"

A small laugh slipped my throat. "I'm sorry. It's like what it sounds, but yes. Hot flash. It's a flash of hot. It hits suddenly. It can last a little bit. And your body is on fire. I just wanted to cool down. I'm sweating so bad."

Pan seethed, "Sweating? Kace, get her home. Now. Before she gets herself killed."

"What's so wrong?" I got to my feet with my boyfriend's help.

Stepping forward, Pan shot a look at Kace who had put his arm out to tell him it was close enough. "Sweat in the cold evaporates at rapid rates. It leads to freezing to death much quicker."

Kace grasped for my cloak, but I shook my head and grabbed it, slipping the flower into the band of my underwear before pulling the cloak around myself. I was gonna show the flower later. For now, I'd let them do their thing.

"Is it wrong that I don't feel all that embarrassed by my body?" I glanced at the man I loved.

He kept his eyes forward, clearing his throat. "No, what's to be ashamed of? Wait, I didn't mean like that. I was hardly looking." A blush rose to his cheeks as he stumbled over his words.

I let out a giggle. "It's okay. I'm not all that upset if you saw something. I *am* half-naked in the middle of the woods." I reached for his hand but he grabbed my boots instead, and when he turned to look at me, I snapped forward and hid the reddened expression of humiliation.

We began walking, but I yelped when Kace scooped me into his arms from behind. I wrapped mine around his neck, questioning him with my eyes.

"You might be hot, but it's best we keep you out of the cold." He choked. "Hot as in temperature wise."

I lowered an arm, brushing my thumb over his rosy cheeks. "You're so adorable when you're flustered. You don't have to be embarrassed about calling me hot. You know that, right?"

"Noted." His Adam's apple bobbed.

Pan disappeared from sight as soon as he ensured we headed back to the comfort of my cabin.

When we entered, Kace set me down on my feet. "I'll let you get dressed."

As he started to turn, I tangled my fingers in the edge of his cloak, yanking him against me. I took his lips with my own, an ever-growing warmth in the pit of my abdomen.

His hands slid to my bare waist as I dropped the dress, but when he pulled away for a moment to catch himself, he mumbled, "We don't have to do anything."

"We aren't doing anything," I breathed. "Just making out." Stealing his next exhale from him, I slid my tongue in. Where the surge of confidence came from, I couldn't say.

He groaned a bit, pulling back. "Lia, you should really put some clothes on."

I glanced at my bra, then caught sight of his bulge. "Oh. Damn, Kace. I'm so sorry." The heat swiftly drained my body, shivers running up my spine as the chill settled in.

I snatched my dress and stepped into it, slipping my arms in before letting him close the back. "I'm sorry, truly. I didn't mean to put you in a tight spot."

His knuckles grazed the skin peeking through the ties. "It's just not always my decision to control it. The smallest things get me going, and I'd never want to pressure you. Of course, people would tell me I'm wrong and that I need to confess my sins. Maybe they have a point. But Pan has informed me that you really can't control it. It happens. The best you can do is take yourself from the situation and let it naturally go down. So, in that case, what do I have to confess? I've never done anything wrong. Never forced myself onto a girl. I've removed myself from the incident."

Opening my mouth, the words lingered on my tongue. I could tell him he didn't have to hide with me. But if I did, he'd suffer from the temptation and that didn't seem at all fair to either of us. So I kept quiet.

Because ultimately, removing himself from the situation was a smart move. The way I'd need to.

"You should probably go. You know, so I don't make it worse on your part. Allow the heat to calm."

He grabbed my shoulder and turned me to face him. "Will you be okay here? Is it still too hot?"

I forced a smile. "I'll be fine. And the heat is gone. I'm actually cold now. I'm gonna grab some candles and stay in, and I promise I won't do that again." Well, mostly a promise. Hot flashes were pure torture. And in winter?

He went to leave a kiss but decided against it. He ripped his cloak closed and exited the cabin swiftly.

Searching the drawers, I pulled out the white candles, most of their wax dripping down the sides. I set them up after trimming the wicks and stepped back in awe as a flame ignited amongst each—one by one.

"What in the hell?" I reached forward, running my fingers over the fire. It'd been warm, but it didn't burn. I held my fingertips there for minutes, and when I pulled back, the skin had been as smooth as ever, the ridges if my fingerprints still identifying.

It was impossible right? Or was it? Had blue magic done this? No, I hadn't been using it. Gold? Had Pan ever tested his retardant skin with the roaring flames of the campfire? Likely.

But gold magic didn't light candles from inches away.

Gold magic was wind.

Blue magic had been water.

But...red.

Red magic was *fire*.

With a gasp, my eyes grew big as I bunched my skirt up and pulled the dried flower from the line of my underwear. I laid it on the dresser and blew out the candle. Waving my palm in front of it, it sparked, then lit.

"Holy shit," I whispered. "I have red magic."

40: Treehouse

Laying the book down on the table, I found a pen in Pan's jars at Hangman's Tree. I leaned over, scribbling down my findings.

"Red magic comes from a flower. Flower wilted upon plucking. Not yet confirmed if the pollen or the petals release the magic. Red magic is sudden. A hot flash. It's fire. Lights candles without a thought." Tapping the pen against my lip, I started again, "red magic is found in the cave behind the waterfall at lagoon. Not yet confirmed if it grows any time of year or only during winter, but given it's not harmed by the subzero temperatures, I'm banking on it being strictly a winter flower."

And that was why nobody had ever known about it before. Winter never existed in Neverland before Lili lost to the demon.

Taking the book with me to my cabin, Lili stopped me along the way. "What are you doing? What's that?"

"What I'm doing is going to my cabin. Do you mind? This is yellow magic." Well, sort of. I wasn't about to reveal to a single soul yet my findings. I needed the time to let the taste settle. Savor the power. Understand the pros and cons of letting others in on my newfound secret. Kace knew about my blue magic. Pan was aware of my gold magic, possibly my blue. Lili knew about the yellow magic and how I was fighting for her to attain it.

But this? Red would stay my little secret.

"Show me." Detestation filled her gaze. If I didn't know better, her fiery emotions would have me believe she had red magic.

"Oh, shit, there's Pan," I pointed.

She whipped around. "Where?"

But before she could ask questions, I pictured puppies, flowers, and Kace frolicking through a field with me. Seconds later, I was up, flying over the trees. Gone before she could catch me.

Her scream shook snow from branches, sending the crows scattering, flapping their wings right in my face. I squeaked, hitting a blanket of snow, thankful it cushioned my fall.

Rolling onto my back, a grin broke out onto my lips. "I'm more powerful than Peter Pan himself."

THROWING MY ARMS OUT, I yelled, “Stop!” The snowfall did exactly as I’d commanded. I placed my palms against the frosted window of my cabin, the world before my eyes falling apart. She blamed me for everything wrong in her life. Not Pan. Not our parents. *Me.*

Pan and I thought this plan would work. We thought the mooie duisternis plan would work and Lili wouldn’t suspect we were up to something. We were so wrong.

Lili suspected something more than ever. She thought Pan was treating me differently, and he was, but not in the way she thought. If she tried to spy on us, she would find out the truth.

I wanted to go out there. I needed to. Despite the fact that she was there, I couldn’t stay holed up forever. Pan knew we couldn’t talk about the plan for a few days. We had to throw Lili’s suspicions off track, and in the meantime, I was going to research more about both of them. They couldn't stop me, nor would they know if they were busy keeping an eye on each other for business purposes.

There was one location I hadn't visited in at least a year, and it was one location I could access easily with my new abilities. Fee Abyss.

Sure, there was a ladder. But who wanted to climb down that far? When I could fly?

I left my cabin and walked straight through camp. Some gave me looks, but most people didn't care too much about what I was up to. They had their own day to worry about.

Passing through the mooie duisternis patch, I slowed my pace. I wasn't about to miss a loose vine and get myself killed by tripping over it.

As soon as I exited the poison, I came to an abrupt stop at the edge of a cliff. When I peeked down below, the only thing I could see through all the mist were a few faint balls of light along the edge of the river. Fee Abyss was the very location Pan took me to himself, but we never went below the mist, not until his little party. Now, I could try it for myself. I could explore something.

"What are you doing?" Kace asked.

I looked at him. "I'm going to prove to you that Pan is the good guy. Lili thinks she shares something special with him, but she has no idea what she's in for. She's broken and she needs to see the truth."

He stepped closer. "You can't go down there, Lia. Fee Abyss is not your normal river." He grabbed my hand, pulling me closer to him. "It's backwards. It's endless. You get lost in it. You'll never find the surface once you're under."

I patted his hand that was holding onto my other one. "I suppose I just have to avoid the water then."

"It's not a joke. You're not invincible."

Pulling my hand from his, I lifted my chin. "I'm not joking, Kace. There are things you don't know about me. I'll be okay. I promise." I stepped back towards the edge, my heels barely hanging off. "Have I lied to you yet?" I leaned back, falling into the mist.

The sound of Kace yelling my name echoed, but eventually it became muffled—incoherent. A ghost.

With happy thoughts in my head, gravity could no longer hold me down. I flew above the water with my arms at my side, and I loved every second of it.

I screamed when I smashed into the side of a treehouse. I had almost fallen into the soothing waves, but I caught myself and grabbed hold of the window, climbing inside. "Whoa." This treehouse was bigger on the inside than it looked from the outside. It appeared much different than the one Pan hosted his ball in.

A bed stood against one wall, and a dresser on the other. I walked over to the dresser and opened the drawers. I almost choked at the sight. Lingerie. Why would this be in a treehouse?

When I pulled some of it out, I noticed the size. When the name of who these belonged to flashed in my mind, I yelped and jumped back, dropping it. Captain Hook. Pan and Hook came here. That explained the bed and fancy lighting.

"This is absolutely disgusting," I mumbled to myself. I turned on my heel to leave, knowing nothing here would help me. Something stuck in the crack where the wall met the floor caught my eye. I reached down and grabbed it, swallowing as I unfolded the note.

"No," I gasped. "Kace..." I glanced at the lingerie I had dropped. I rushed over and picked it up, searching the treehouse for anything else.

Kace had written a letter to Hook, telling her that he couldn't be with her because he would never hurt Pan that way. Pan was his best friend, and loyalty couldn't be bought.

What did she do to him?

I found another note wedged between the crack of an adjacent wall meeting the ceiling. I climbed onto the dresser and stood, pulling it free. I opened it up, reading. "No." I jumped down to the floor. I refused to believe what was written on the note.

I loved Kace, and as much as I wanted to jump to conclusions and pester him with questions, that wasn't the right thing to do. I had to ask him the truth, and I had to ask him in the least judgmental way possible.

Pan was on our side, and I intended to keep it that way. He wouldn't learn the truth about Hook and Kace. If he knew, he'd never help us save Lili.

I jumped out of the doorway with the notes in my cloak and shot straight up through the mist. However, the cliff I landed on was far from where I had come up. Was the mist just like the water—endless and impossible to steer through?

I walked along, closer to where I'd left my boyfriend.

Kace was waiting at the edge. When he saw me, he embraced me in a hug, but I knew soon he would question how I had gotten back up. Lili's ladder was still here, so I could use that as my excuse, but that didn't explain how I survived falling into the river. Well, I *hadn't* fallen in, and that's what I'd have to explain.

He pulled back from me, searching my face. "What happened?"

"I found Pan and Hook's treehouse." I pressed my lips together. "Sex room, I should say." I swallowed.

Something—maybe jealousy—flashed in his eyes. But he shook his head and dismissed it, kissing me. Even with a kiss, I still couldn't focus on us. The note was poking my side.

"Kace," I whispered as we pulled away. "We should talk about what I found."

"I don't want to talk about that." He cleared his throat. "It's between Pan and Hook."

"I don't think it is..." I pulled out the notes. "I think it's between you and Hook."

He eyed the pieces of folded papers, stepping back. "Where did you find those?"

Taking a deep breath, I dropped the notes into his hand. "In the treehouse. They belong to you. They don't belong to Pan, and Hook is...dead." I held onto his hand. "But I want to ask one thing. Is it true?"

Kace stared at the notes. "If I admit to it, everything Pan believes becomes a lie."

"It already is," I whispered.

He looked at me, nodding a bit. "It's true."

I glanced at my fingers, blinking a little too fast a few times. "You wanted to get married. That's not a decision you make with the villain." I shook my head, pulling my fingers from his.

Kace pulled his hood down, scanning the snow around us. "She wasn't the villain, Lia. She never was. Kristin and I were...in love. We were together before Pan ever dated her. We hadn't had sex, but that's beside the point. When Pan found her, I had to pretend I never knew her. He always hated outsiders, and that's what she was." He lifted his glossy eyes to meet mine. "She had to date Pan to hide the truth, but things went south. She took it too far with him. She tried to play it off as if she was using him, to make him break up with her. But that didn't go as planned. He found out about us, and before I could tell him the truth, he assumed she was cheating on us both. He blamed *her* for everything."

I stepped back. "That's why Lili and Pan believe she's responsible for everything. She kept up the lie to protect you, didn't she?"

A tear escaped. "She wasn't the bad guy everyone turned her into."

I dropped my arms to my sides. "And my sister is the one who took her life." What Dixon did to me was warranted. Hook was never the bad guy. My sister killed an innocent woman, and I then swooped in and picked Kace up when he was hurt. I'd been part of the problem all this time.

"Lili killed her, yes. She didn't know the truth. She was thinking about Pan and how he felt. She wanted Pan to be happy."

"She killed an innocent woman. She killed the woman you were going to marry. She just believed Pan's story, even though he was already the demon. Demons tell lies. They see only the side they want to see, to justify their actions." I let out a sigh. "She told Wendy and I the truth, and we never once questioned her decision. We never thought maybe she had killed someone who didn't at all deserve it." I knew I never supported Lili's kills, but I never defended Hook. I tried to tell myself that Hook deserved it just to feel better about what Lili did.

Kace rubbed his face. "You can't possibly blame yourself for what Lili did. You aren't her, remember?"

I took a deep breath, a sore pain making itself known in my chest. Right where Dixon punched me. "Everyone else compares us. They hold me responsible for her actions." Shaking my head, I locked his gaze. "I never understood why Dixon beat me. He got so angry when I told him my sister killed Hook. Now, I know why. Lili killed an innocent woman for personal gain. It's wrong. It's sickening. I'm disgusted with myself for even trying to justify her actions."

"You can't be saying that what Dixon did is okay."

"Kace, what I'm saying is I understand *why* he did it. My sister killed the woman you love, then I ended up taking Hook's place in your life. Does that not seem wicked to you? It doesn't sit right with me. She killed the woman you love so I could have my happy ending. It's not right."

He stepped forward. "Cariño, you're not at fault."

Yet, I still felt pure shame as if I had stabbed her myself. "You wanted to marry her. It's been maybe a year since her death, and now you say you love me. I'm afraid, Kace, that maybe you just want to be in love again and I was your best option." I turned on my heel and headed to my cabin before he could stop me.

I locked the door, leaning against it. There was no way Kace could get over Hook that quickly after her death. He loved her, and they planned to get married. I tried hard not to believe that maybe our relationship was based on what he wanted with Hook, but part of me believed that I was the replacement. Part of me believed Kace didn't love Lia.

He still loved Hook.

41: Queen

As hard as I searched, I couldn't find anyone else on this island who spoke Spanish well enough to teach me. Hook spoke had and Kace had loved that. I, however, could only speak English. It was catching up to me now, reminding me how limited I was.

I knew the basics that everyone else did, but it was never enough.

Someone grabbed my shoulders, pulling me against them. Kace pulled my hood from my head and wrapped his arms around my stomach. "I've been looking for you everywhere."

"I've been here the whole time." I didn't attempt to push him away. Not yet.

He pressed his lips to the side of my head. "You are not her, and I know that. What happened was tragic, but I fell in love with Celia." He lowered his lips to my ear. "I fell in love with you and only you."

Shivers ran down my spine. "I didn't mean to overreact. I know you were telling me the truth. I jumped to conclusions. I'm sorry for turning a confession about Hook into my own problem." I threw my eyes over my shoulder, at him.

He turned me in his arms until our chests touched. He rested his forehead against mine, speaking low, "I don't like being away from you, worrying about if our relationship is okay."

"I know," I whispered. I placed my hands against his collarbone, staring at his lips. "I don't like it, either." I slid my right hand up and grabbed his neck, bringing him closer. Our lips connected, and every emotion we ever felt in the past twenty-four hours was exposed. Shame, regret, love, sorrow, and hatred. I hated myself for accusing him of lying about loving me, but he'd never let that last for long.

We kissed each other with so much passion that we forgot why we were even worried to begin with. Maybe I couldn't speak his language, but that didn't mean he couldn't teach me how.

Kace's hand slipped down to the lower part of my back, keeping me as close to him as I could be. Unfortunately, we had to pull away for air.

Air. Gold magic. It was time to tell him the truth.

I stepped away and grabbed his hand, pulling him towards his cabin. I closed the door behind us. "We should talk." I glanced at him.

"About what?"

"About me." I opened his curtains, showing the snowflakes as I held my hands up, freezing them. "About my magic."

His eyes widened. "You have magic?"

"You saw me drink the bottle of blue magic, Kace. You knew this. But what you don't know about is the other bottle I drank." I faced him. "Gold magic. I have more magic than Pan." I shook my head. "But that's not the biggest news." I peeked over at Pan's cabin. "I'm as powerful as Pan."

"That's impossible. Nobody is as powerful as him."

Glancing at my boyfriend, I said, "He told me himself that I am. He wouldn't lie about that. He's scared because he knows someone on this island is as desperate as he was. I can fix Neverland. I'm the key to everything." I closed the gap between us. "I'm going to defeat Pan. I'm going to take his place."

He shook his head, browns knitted together. "That's dangerous. Why would you do this?"

"Because Pan has proven he isn't fit to be a leader anymore. It's okay for him to step down and focus on himself without all eyes and responsibilities on him. I'm ready, Kace. I'm ready for all of this. I've built up a version that can handle this task and I'm going through with it, whether you're on my side or not."

Approaching his dresser, he put the notes inside it. "He won't accept this."

"That's why I'm practicing my magic."

He paused, grunting. "You have blue and gold magic?"

Looking out the window, I pointed to the sky. "See all these snowflakes? I froze them. Pan told me I shouldn't have been able to freeze an entire sky of snowflakes on my first try, but I did. And I can fly. I have yet to master transportation, but I'm going to learn. I'm taking slow steps not to burn myself out."

"And what about Pan?"

I leaned against the windowsill. "He's not going to have a clue. Well, he might already know but I'm not going to give up." I whipped around. "But we have to team up with him. Lili is my priority, and you may not believe me when I say this...but he has been on my team for weeks."

He choked on a laugh. "No, I don't believe it."

I hurried over and grabbed his arm, making him face me. "When I told you that a shadow was in my room, it was Pan. He came to me as *your* shadow. He tried to kill me that night, and I thought it was Asa. He has been trying to toughen me up and make me a fighter for the war. He wants to save Lili and he needs our help to do it. He means what he says."

"And what if we are the one's screwed over?"

I suspected this would happen. I closed my eyes, thinking of a happy thought. In my mind, Kace was singing to me. And in seconds, I was hovering above the ground, our heads level. "He taught me how to fly. We are not the ones being screwed over." I grabbed his face. "I don't expect him to let me take the throne from him, but I know he wants to save Lili and himself. He taught me how to be a fighter. He's been helping me for weeks, and even if you don't team up with him, I already have." I dropped.

He grabbed my wrists and lowered my arms to my side. "My opinion doesn't matter. You've made up your mind."

"Yes, I have. Heaven forbid I have my own thoughts." I rolled my eyes. "I just want you to team up with us. I'm trying to tell you that if you want to save your best friend, this is your best option. He already knows if you're going to turn your back on him, so there's no use in trying, and no use in continuing to fight him. The best way to win a war is to team up with the enemy. The enemy of a friend is a friend." I furrowed my brows. Was that the saying? No, it wasn't. "The enemy of my enemy is my friend."

He released a sigh. "Are you certain that this is the right side?"

"I'm positive. We tried everything else and got nowhere. The one thing we haven't tried is teaming up with Pan. He offered his help, and we should take it. I've made more progress since teaming up with him than I have on my own. He's been teaching me tips and tricks. He helped me admit I love you," I said.

Kace walked towards the window and glanced at me. Something was bothering him, but he wouldn't say what it was. Instead, he cleared his throat and opened the door. "I accept this deal then."

I walked over and placed my hands on either side of his face, pulling him towards me. I placed a kiss on his lips, whispering, "Thank you."

He nodded, smiling a bit. "I trust you to take the lead on this."

I wanted Kace to tell Pan the truth about Hook, but I feared the repercussions. The best decision was to get Pan to merge with his shadow before telling him anything. Pan loved Hook, too, but her feelings were solely for Kace. Regardless, Pan deserved to know the truth.

As for Lili, I couldn't be sure. Eventually she would find out the truth if Kace told Pan who Hook was to him, but I worried about how it would affect Lili. She killed an innocent woman, and she had no idea. If I told her the truth, she may lose all her sanity. It was a risk, but it was one we had to take. The truth could never stay hidden for long.

"I have a few things to do. I'll see you later." I gave him my best grin before exiting his cabin. I ventured through the snow, down to the beach. I closed my eyes and pictured a wave rising from the ocean, creating a wall between me and the rest of the water. I lifted my hands, opening my eyes to see my progress. It was wrong. I'd lifted the smallest wall, but nothing that was as big as what I'd imagined.

I tried again, picturing and focusing harder this time, but nothing.

I shook my head, pulling the note from my cloak and reading it. "Blue magic doesn't work the same way. Controlling snow is different from water. Of course, one is solid, one is liquid. I should have suspected there was something wrong."

I put the paper away and faced the ocean. "You got this Lia." I locked my posture, holding my hands down below my waist. I stared at the ocean, lifting my hands and imagining a heavy weight in my hands. The higher I lifted the heaviness, the higher the wave started to rise. A wall was forming before my eyes, but it dropped within seconds.

A wave had to be thousands of pounds. I had to recreate *that* in my hands.

Rubbing my hands together, I positioned myself and started raising my palms again, adding more weight as I pulled them upward. The wave rose from the ocean, and I stopped, picturing tons in my own hands. A wall stood before me, and a few fish passed through.

I lowered my hands, the wave falling with it. "Back to gold magic."

If I had to think happy thoughts by flying, I had to do the same to transport somewhere.

I closed my eyes, picturing the happiest memory I had on this island, and when I opened them, I was flying. "No, that's not right." I forced my feet back into the sand, looking around. Shaking the tension from my muscles, I pictured the happiest place. I pictured the place and focused on the feeling it brought me, and not the scene of the memory that caused it.

A scream erupted as I lost my balance at the top of the mountain, falling down the side.

After playing with the memory in my mind, I was no longer falling with air rushing against me. Now I was flying, and I flew around the mountain.

I laughed, shouting, "Wooooo!" I landed at the base of the mountain. I was going to need more practice, but I knew that I could at least access more abilities. Transportation, control of water, control of snow, and flying.

I called that progress.

The thought of being the Queen of Neverland was exhilarating. I had never imagined running an island or overseeing everything here, but now that I could unleash all this magic inside, I never wanted anything more.

I wanted to experience being the leader and making the decisions. I no longer wanted to take orders from anyone. I wanted to *give* orders. I wanted to create the solutions we needed.

Pan would hate this idea, but it was time for him to accept fate. He wasn't going to be the one connected to Neverland anymore. I'd get his dagger, his tree, *and* his power. I'd get to be in his position as the ultimate leader, and the thought excited me and scared me all at once. I'd be the sole keyholder—the one who decided who got to come and go from this island. Nobody would get to say I didn't belong here ever again.

42: Revenge

Had I known about gold magic in a bottle sooner, I could have taken Jaren home. It was far too late, and now I stood in front of our home, watching life move on without us.

Jaren was dead.

Lili was a monster.

I was on my way to ruling Neverland.

All who were left were our parents and brother, Austin. He probably feared he was next. The rest of us were gone, never to return. He took the full force of everything our parents once spread between the four of us.

I stepped forward, ready to walk inside the house. I wanted to save him. I wanted to save him from them, but it wasn't a good idea. Was it? Maybe it was. Our parents deserved to hate themselves. If all their kids were gone, surely the police would investigate and lock them up. There was something highly suspicious about four missing kids in one household. Our parents couldn't hold up their act forever.

I watched as the woman I once called Mom walked out the front door and drove off. Wherever she went was none of my business.

Our father was next, disappearing around the corner. Everyone has always questioned how our parents got away with such abuse, but the answer was always simple. *Money.*

Money could buy the best lawyers around. Our parents were rich, and that was exactly why we all got our own rooms with nobody to question what happened behind closed doors.

Because with our own space, we never talked to each other. We never teamed up.

I walked into the house, quietly closing the door behind me. I made it to my old room, to pack up things I wanted to keep. I was tired of having nothing in Neverland. I was tired of washing the same few pairs of underwear every few days.

I grabbed a duffel bag from the closet and set it down on the bed, stuffing clothes inside. I tapped my chin while scanning the items in my room. Was there anything else I wanted? I wanted another pair of shoes, and maybe a few activities. I could bring my books, but I'd be done with those quickly and have nothing else to read.

"Lia?" I heard a voice from the doorway.

Turning around, I faced Austin and sighed. "I'm not here to stay."

"Where did you all go?"

There was no use in lying to him. He wasn't the same unruly boy we'd left behind. He was nearly ten now, and he knew better. "Lili and I went to Neverland with Peter Pan. Jaren...died." I twisted my head, hiding the tears.

He looked at the ground. "He's dead?"

"He came to find us and take us home, but he never got a chance to leave." I felt responsible for everything. If I had gotten him home, we wouldn't be here mourning over the brother who wanted to be better for *us*.

Austin looked at me with pure sorrow in his eyes. I couldn't leave him here alone. I couldn't just let him live in this household, under our parents' authority. I was going to take him back with me. Austin was always farther apart in age from the rest of us, so he never formed a real bond. Maybe now we could.

"Pack some things, and hurry before our parents come home. We're going to Neverland and I'm going to take you away from here for good." Austin had grown up solely in the world of technology. He didn't play outdoors and meet friends by going around the neighborhood for kids his age. I wasn't sure how well he could adapt to Neverland—a land where technology didn't exist. Either way, it was better than this.

Austin nodded his head and went back to his room while I continued to pack the best I could. I heard a car pull up in the driveway and I quickly grabbed my bag and ran to Austin's room.

"Why aren't you packed? They're home." I grabbed his bag.

"I'm not going."

I whipped around and faced him. "What? You can't possibly believe you should stay here with *them*. They are pure evil, Austin. They're going to hurt you."

He wrapped his arms around my waist, sighing. "I can't go. I don't want to live in that world, Lia. I only have eight more years, and maybe I could get emancipated before then. I have dreams rooted in this world."

I wrapped my arms around him, letting some tears fall. "I understand. But you must know this means we can never see you again. You'll never be able to visit us, and we may not be able to find you."

He pulled away with a dangling smile. "I know. But I'll remember what you did for me." He patted his chest. "I have you in here."

For a kid who was barely ten, he had matured so much. Without the rest of us around, he had no choice. Our parents forced him to grow up, while the rest of us never would.

I grabbed my duffel and backed away from him. "I love you." Tears stained my cheeks, and I couldn't get them to stop. No matter how hard I tried, I bawled.

"I love you, too."

I closed my eyes and embraced the feeling of being with Kace. Within seconds, I was standing in his cabin, sobbing.

He jumped from his bed and rushed over. "Lia, what happened?"

I wrapped my arms around his chest, under his arms, burying my face in his shoulder. I screamed into the fabric to release all the pain I'd been holding inside of me. Everything was falling apart despite how hard I tried to fix it.

The only family I had was Lili, and she couldn't stand my existence.

For hours, I cried while Kace cradled me. Eventually we sat on his bed, and the tears ran out. I had nothing left to give. Not a damn thing.

Kace stroked my hair as I placed my head in his lap. "Do you want to talk about it?"

"He didn't come with me. He didn't want to come," I said in a quiet voice. I was exhausted. Even talking was tiring.

"Who?"

"My brother..." I took a deep breath.

"Jaren?"

"Austin." I closed my eyes. Swollen, mixed with a burning and stinging sensation.

Kace ran his knuckles down my cheek. "I'm sorry." He reached over and grabbed my hand, intertwining our fingers.

After a few minutes of pity, I sat up and looked at Kace. Something inside me hit, and at first, I had no idea what it was. I'd never experienced such a feeling before. Then I knew what it was—what I wanted.

I wanted Kace. Truly craved him.

I stood from the bed and faced him. I grabbed his face and pulled his lips against mine, kissing him with every bit of my soul. Leaning my body forward, I folded my legs on either side of him, sitting myself in his lap.

Kace didn't think twice before grabbing my waist, but before he had a chance to kiss back, I lay him back on the mattress. He slid his hands down to my thighs and flipped us until I was underneath. He grabbed my wrists, pinning them above my head. I expected him to undress me or kiss me again. I expected more from him, but I didn't get any of that.

"Lia, we shouldn't do this. Not now. You're vulnerable and hurt, and I don't want you to regret this by any means. I don't want our first time to be because you were feeling down. I refuse to take advantage of you like that." He leaned down and kissed me, but it wasn't the type of kiss given by someone who was ready to rip your clothes off. It was given by someone who was willing to protect you at any cost.

He slipped his hands up my wrists, locking our fingers together. I'd been ready to go all out with our relationship, but he wasn't feeling the same way.

As I closed my eyes, I held onto the feeling of when Lili and I had fun in our own cabin. We talked about things and enjoyed ourselves then. I missed that so desperately.

When I opened my eyes, I was in my cabin, lying on my bed. I sat up and glanced at the window where the camp could be seen covered in a thick blanket of white snow.

I was angry with Kace for turning me down. I wanted to bond with him on a new level. Now had been a better time than ever with the cold snow around us, and nobody to interrupt. But he didn't want to.

This fueled my rage. My brother stayed behind. My other brother was dead. My own sister hated me. My parents were still there, living their best life. What did I have? Magic? Hardly.

Where were the consequences for my own parents? They had so much money, and they got away with their crimes. It was a *cruel* world, and a cruel world that I would have to fix.

I heard a knock on my door and I opened it, expecting Kace. Maybe he changed his mind. Maybe his boner decided for him.

Instead, Lili stood there and by the faint glow of her skin, I knew she had succeeded with the task I gave her. She had *yellow magic*.

That wasn't what irked me, though. No, what irked me was the fact that Pan wanted to have sex with her, despite disagreeing with all her decisions, but Kace didn't want the same with me even though we were compatible.

She leaned in, holding her hands out until a ball formed in each palm. A ball of light. "I did it, and you were right." She shoved me aside and stepped into our cabin. "I was confused as to why Pan hadn't slept with me for a while, so I formulated a plan." She faced me. "I had to make Pan believe I was truly upset. I was angry that he treated you better than he treated me. I made him feel guilty to the point we'd have sex to make up for the fight. He would prove to me that he still loved me. He was so desperate to make me feel better." She reeled her shoulders back. "My plan worked."

I wanted to shake her and ask if she was crazy, but I didn't have the energy. A plan. A ruse. That's all this had been? The way she made me feel was never about how she felt inside. It was a lie told through another lie. It was a piece of plastic that left her mouth to get what she wanted.

"I can't believe you did it. You have magic." I stared at her. "How does it feel?" Surely it felt different from blue and gold magic. With gold magic, I felt as light as a feather. With blue magic, I felt refreshed when I used it. With red, a cozy feeling poured into me, like reading a good book in front of a fire in the middle of a snowstorm.

With a laugh, she twirled around. "Amazing! I can't believe Pan kept this from me." Her smile faded. "I feel so happy one moment, then the next I feel pure dread. Is that normal?"

I wasn't going to be the one to tell her. "I can't be sure." I shrugged a little. She was battling her inner conflicts. Light and dark..

I, too, was fighting myself. Part of me warned me not to go back home to enact revenge on our parents. I knew it was wrong. The other part of me begged me to go, and I had a good idea about which side was going to win.

"Lili, I have some business to take care of. Tomorrow, we begin mastering your light magic," I said.

Lili eyed me. "Where are you going?"

Was I going to risk letting the darkness win? No. I couldn't. "It no longer concerns you." I opened the door, letting her out. She turned to say something, but I closed it before she could get a word off her tongue. I locked my door, realizing I left my duffel in Kace's cabin. I'd get it later.

Tonight, I was going to serve justice for every last Stone child.

43: Control

Blink once. Twice. Three times. Now my vision has become clear, and my parents stood in front of me. Did I tell them the truth? No, that was absurd. If I did, they'd find a way to follow and they'd, too, die a horrendous death.

Did I want that? Maybe.

Rage swirled around inside my blood, boiling every drop. They did this to us. I blamed them for Jaren's death. It was never my fault, nor Lili's. They were the ones who drove us to the brink of insanity. We begged for help, and we searched everywhere for Lili when she received it. If they had treated us the way kids were supposed to be treated, we never would have gone to Neverland and Jaren would still be alive today.

Lili didn't kill Jaren. She only fulfilled his wish when she let him stay. He never wanted to leave because we were still there. She respected his right to die with honor. She wasn't the monster I thought she was. She was only a product of destruction, but we could reverse that. Deep inside, she *felt* remorse. Our parents never did. She wasn't our parents, and she never would be.

I balled my hands into fists, stepping forward. "You did this to us."

Mom glanced at Dad, shaking her head. "I don't know what you're talking about."

"Liar! You have abused us and treated us like shit from day one. You purposely had kids to *control*. You have made us out to be the bad guys, and now Jaren is dead. Lili has killed people because she feels like she's not good enough otherwise. You raised her to believe that this is the life she wants to lead." I swallowed my anger. I couldn't let them make me into someone I wasn't.

"I think it's time you come home and think about what you've done. You ran away. You had us worried sick," Dad said. His famous words—*worried sick.*

I relaxed my fists, stretching out my fingers and taking a step back. "We're adults now. We aren't obligated to do anything you say, and we will never see you again. You dug your grave, and now you have to lie in it, daddy." I locked eyes with him.

He reached out to grab my arm, but I backed away before running off. I stopped when I made it around the corner, pressing my back against the wall. I looked up at the sky and took a deep breath.

"I'm doing this for you, Lili, and you, Jaren. I'm going to be the bigger person." My shallow breathing became more even and drawn out as I caught up with my lungs.

As much as I wanted to take revenge on our parents, it wasn't the right thing to do. It wouldn't solve anything, and in the end, it would stain my hands. If I left them alone, they'd have no choice but to wallow in their own guilt for the rest of their life. They deserved to live with their decisions. That was the best revenge of all.

It was time to get back home.

I screamed when a hand grabbed my arm, but who was attached threw me in for a loop. I expected my father, or even my mother. Neither of them cared enough to chase me, though.

"Mateo," I breathed. Mateo had been one of my friends in high school. In fact, he was one of the friends who had a crush on me, but I never returned the feelings. He'd been sweet about it, but it never felt less awkward even then. We both knew he still liked me.

"Lia...you've been gone for a while." He cleared his throat. "Nearly two years. I thought I was losing my mind when I saw you. *You couldn't have come back*, but here you are."

"Here I am," I said, shifting my eyes towards the ground. He leaned in, and I stupidly assumed he was trying to kiss me, so I said, "I have a boyfriend."

Mateo pulled back. "Oh?"

"Sorry, I just..." I cleared my throat. "His name is Kace. He's a wonderful guy, and as much as I'd love to stay, I want to get back to him and my sister."

He rubbed the back of his neck, his eyes wandering anywhere but me. "No worries. I'll let you get back, then. It was good seeing you." He turned on his heel, shoving his hands into his pockets.

"How was graduation?" I asked. "What was that like?"

Mateo stopped turning to face me. "It was fine. We all assumed something happened to you guys. We thought you were kidnapped, or worse. There was...a memorial at graduation in honor of you and Lili." He released a sigh. "Turns out you just ran away."

Everyone was going to think we ran away and pin all the blame on us. They wouldn't even see our parents as the problem. That wasn't what I wanted.

"What if we...were kidnapped?" I met Mateo's eyes. "What if Lili and I were promised a better life and we took it?"

"Isn't that running away?"

He was right, in a sense. "Maybe we weren't forced against our will. But once we arrived, we weren't allowed to leave. We were still minors. We can't be held accountable for being promised something better, only to find out it was a trap."

He stepped forward. "So why are you back now?"

"I found a way to leave." I glanced around the corner, searching for my parents. "But despite my freedom, I've discovered that home is not home anymore. No matter what I do, it never will be. I'm leaving for good and on my own terms."

When Mateo leaned in, I didn't pull away. He wrapped his arms around me, placing his head on mine. "I'm glad you're okay."

I returned the hug, relishing the feeling of being missed. Our parents didn't care, but at least a few people did. Lili had never seen the aftermath of her disappearance. She would never know what it was like to be in my shoes, scared your own sister was locked in someone's basement.

For three months, I spent every night awake. I couldn't close my eyes in fear of what I'd see happening to Lili. Everyone kept saying she ran away, and I hoped that was all it was, but no evidence showed that she did. She had left everything behind. If she had run away, she would have packed.

After saying goodbye to Mateo, I returned to Neverland. It was best to leave every trouble behind, including taking revenge on our parents. I had access to home and yet I never wanted to go back. I belonged *here*.

With all my emotions in check, I now saw everything in a new light. I knew what I had to do.

I ventured over to Kace's cabin, knocking on his door. When he opened the door, I threw my arms around his neck and kissed him with every ounce of passion inside me. I pulled away before he had a chance to kiss back. "I'm sorry." I dropped my arms and grabbed his hands, squeezing. "I'm sorry for making you have to make that decision for us both."

"It's okay, cariño."

"It's not okay. I put you in a position where you have to choose between your wants and your needs. I just want to say thank you for making the right choice." I rubbed my thumb over his knuckles.

Kace closed the gap between us, bringing me in for a slow kiss. Without hesitation, I kissed back, ignoring everything I'd just experienced in the past few days. The feeling returned to the lower area of my stomach, and I pulled away, his brows moving inward.

I swallowed. "My body is ready, but my mind isn't."

It took a few seconds for Kace to understand what I was saying, but when he got it, he stepped away. "We won't do anything until you're ready." It was at that moment that I realized he was ready.

However, I wasn't ready to take that step. I wanted to make sure Neverland was back to normal before I went down that road. I wanted to focus on saving Lili and taking Pan's place.

He turned around and grabbed my duffel bag from the floor. "This belongs to you." He handed it to me.

I thanked him and took it back to my cabin, unpacking all the clothes and little goodies. I had packed very few winter clothes, knowing that Neverland would soon return to its summer season. But for now, I'd get to sleep better. My red magic didn't work at all times, and I had little control over it.

I took off the cloak, my belt, then the dress. I pulled on a pair of thick, red leggings. I laced up my boots over them before putting on a white sweatshirt and gray beanie. I didn't have a scarf, but I'd be fine without one. I left my dress and red cloak in the corner, but for now, I would need to get in some training, and I didn't want to get too hot in this material, despite how cold it was outside. I put my belt around my sweatshirt to always keep my dagger with me.

Once I arrived in the training area, I stopped almost immediately. "Pan, haven't seen you in a while."

"I could say the same about you." He approached me.

I swallowed. "I went home. I didn't kill my parents. I never even touched them, I swear it. I just packed up some things and that was it."

He shrugged. "I don't care what you did. I'm just surprised you've been practicing your magic."

"What's the point of having it if I'm not going to use it? It's fun." I shifted my weight to my other foot. "What are you here for?"

Pan circled me and grabbed a bow and arrow. "Kace told me you decided to team up with me. I'm glad." He aimed at the target. "He also told me that you're more powerful than me. He wanted me to tell him it was true."

I turned my head his way. "Did you?"

Pan let the arrow fly, hitting the bullseye. He shifted his eyes my way. "More importantly, why did you?" He lowered the bow. "Don't get me wrong, Lia. I'm grateful we are teaming up to save Lili and return my shadow. Shadow or no shadow, you're not taking my rightful place on the throne."

He knew. Of course he knew. Pan knew everything.

"Why have you let me practice my magic?"

He faced me. "I always liked a good challenge. I want to see how it plays out." A cunning smile tugged at the corners of his lips.

He was going to fight me at the end of this for his spot on the throne. I was intrigued, yet worried. There had to be a catch, right? We were far from equals.

"What happens if I win?" I lifted my chin. "What happens to Neverland if I'm the one in control?"

He put the bow down and decreased the distance between us. "Bold question to ask, don't you think?"

"Answer it."

Chuckling, Pan folded his arms across his chest. "It's simple. Neverland becomes your wish, and your desire. You can change it anyway you like. You'll be taking my dagger, and Hangman's Tree. You'll be taking my cabin, and my magic." He laid his dagger flat in his palms in front of me. "But I warn you, Lia, that every wish is just a front for the consequences. Everything requires a sacrifice."

44: Sunrises and Sunsets

Today, the snow had stopped. We were getting closer to saving Lili, and all hope was returning at full force.

In fact, the sun peeked through. The clouds had cleared for a blue sky, and a sunrise began to display pink and orange hues along the horizon. I hadn't seen one in so long. In fact, when I left my cabin, I started to cry with joy. It was a miracle, and I missed the feel of the sunshine against my skin.

Kace exited his cabin and walked towards me, eyes fixed in the direction of the sun. "Something's wrong."

"How can anything be wrong? The sun is out! The snow is beginning to melt. Kace, life is going back to normal."

I hugged him, but he peeled me off. "The sun is rising in the opposite direction."

"What?" I looked over towards the star, avoiding direct eye contact.

He pointed at it. "That is the west. The sun is supposed to rise in the east."

"Which means it'll set in the east when it's supposed to set in the west." I released a sigh. "And here I thought we could enjoy a day of sunshine."

He looked at me and cleared his throat. "That's a new outfit."

I glanced at my clothes. "I thought I would change it up a bit so I can wash my cloak and dress. Enough about the clothes, though. The sunrise and sunset are backwards. Why?"

Pan appeared right in front of us, nodding towards Lili. "I think she might have something to do with it. Nobody on Neverland has ever had light magic before. Now that someone does, things have changed course. She's fighting the darkness."

Nodding, I added, "That's not a bad thing then. The sun is shining again despite the fact that you feel numb inside. The balance of Neverland is shifting."

It was shifting, and it was abnormal. It further proved to me that I would be the best fit as the new leader. Pan may have known my secret, but I wasn't about to back down now.

"I feel numb?" Pan asked.

"Of course. Why else would it be winter here for so long? We knew you weren't happy with Lili for a while now, before you told us. Your emotions are connected to the island." I tilted my head, staring at the snow. I furrowed my brows, remembering the sudden storm that came over a year ago. Had it been a year? "That storm we had was because of you, wasn't it?"

He didn't say a word, and I got my answer. He *was* connected to the island. Would I be the same when I took his place? There was no doubt in my mind.

Clearing his throat, he pointed to the powder. "It stopped snowing because Lili is able to get some of her good traits back. The demon Lili won't hesitate to seduce me. The—dare I say—angel Lili..." He chuckled. "She's another story. She fights me."

A smile blessed me as I wanted Lili who tested the balls of light in her palms. The sister I knew was slowly coming back. She just needed help from us to nudge her in that direction.

Lili saw us and her eyes lit up as she hurried over. "Have you seen what I can do?"

"I think Pan and I have, but Kace hasn't." I looked at Kace, smirking.

Kace put on a genuine smile. This was the version of her we all missed, so he'd listen to her endless rants if it made her feel better. I'd make him if he refused. "I haven't."

She showed him her balls of light. "This is my magic. I have *real* magic!" She hopped like a child with a new toy.

I spun the other way, hiding my face as tears rolled down my cheeks. I had missed her so much, and she had no idea. A sob escaped me, and I tried coughing to hide it, but everyone heard.

Kace grabbed my arms and spun me back around. "What's wrong?"

"Nothing." I forced a smile. If I told everyone the truth with Lili around, her dark side would hear me. It'd try to grow more powerful. I refused to jeopardize her happiness—her victory to defeat the darkness once and for all.

She dropped her balls and pushed Kace out of the way. "What is *wrong*?" She emphasized in the last word, telling me she wasn't about to take no for an answer.

Make up a lie. Any lie. "I'm just happy because the sun is out again. I haven't seen the sun in so long. I thought I'd never see it again." I wiped my tears.

Lili looked up at the sky, nodding a bit. "Oh, well, I can see how that makes you cry." She stepped back. "You've always been weak."

"What?" I sniffled.

She shook her head, furrowing her brows. "I'm sorry. I didn't mean that." She sighed. "But I did." She stomped her foot, whipping the other way and storming off.

I glanced at Pan and Kace, but Pan was the first to speak up. "That's Lili fighting her dark side. She wants to be nice to you, but she also has trouble doing that. She's the opposite with me." He watched her disappear into the trees. "She's nice to me when she's evil because we're one and the same. When she's mean to me, you know it's the real Little Flower coming through."

Nodding a bit, I looked at Kace. "At least she has a chance. We know what to do, right?"

Pan agreed. "But we have to still lure her to Skull Rock somehow. We can't let her think it's the three of us against her. I'll make her think you guys are against us, so she'll think I'm on her team." It had to work.

He left Kace and I, so as not to spend too much time with us. Kace and I decided to head to the beach to admire the ocean. It was as beautiful as ever, and even more so with the sun sparkling across the soft waves. I never thought I would miss the sun this much, but after this winter storm we've had for nearly a year, I was certain I never wanted to see snow again.

He studied Cannibal Cove, and I knew who he was searching for. Dixon.

I didn't entirely blame Lili for taking his life after beating me, but I had also felt guilty knowing what I knew now. She had killed an innocent woman, and then when a man lost his mind over it, she took his life, too. Hardly fair.

But Dixon had been barely seventeen, clearly younger than Pan or he would've decayed. Hook had been at least forty by the time she came back. Dixon had actually fallen for someone over twice his age, and did anyone question it? But I doubted Hook reciprocated. She probably lingered for Kace. But she died, keeping their secret.

A part of me still bathed in the shame.

When Kace faced me again, he planted a kiss right above my eye, where the edge of the bruise was. It was so faded by now, but it was still there. "As much as I hate the evil that controls this island, I'm glad Dixon is dead," he said.

I smiled at him as I stared into the brown eyes that I adored. Every inch of Kace had been so perfect and I was thankful I never returned to Dixon the night he asked me to. Had I ended up with Dixon, I could have been stuck in yet another abusive relationship. My father taught me I was never worth more than a beating, but I never believed the lies. I knew I was, and

Kace saw it, too. "I'm glad that I get to call you my boyfriend."

Kace chuckled. "That's also a good thing."

The rest of the day went on as one of the best days in a long time. Kace and I watched the waves roll up onto the shore. We watched the sunset, even if it was on the wrong side of the sky. We laughed, and we talked about so many different things. It was the perfect night, until Asa decided to come join us.

I had nothing against Asa, but I was a bit frustrated that he was interrupting what was essentially *our* date night. Kace and I knew the one time the sun was shining was the perfect time for us to go on another date.

Asa had a bad habit of ruining whatever romantic outing we had.

"What are you two lovebirds doing here? Hopefully not fucking, right?" Asa joked.

"That's none of your business." I said.

Asa's smile dropped quick. "It was a joke."

"It wasn't funny."

Kace glanced up at Asa, shrugging. "I wouldn't piss her off. She has magic now. She can return you home." Now that—that was a funny joke.

Asa shot Kace a glare while I smiled.

Clearing my throat, I stated, "We should talk about something."

"What is it?" Kace asked. Asa sat beside me.

"You know I have the power to take Pan's place, right? I plan to, in fact. But the problem is that Pan knows I plan to take his place. He doesn't intend to stop me, but I'm just worried that...this could be the death of me." I exhaled, trying to get rid of all my worries.

Kace gently squeezed my hand. "Don't say that. Pan wouldn't kill you. Would you kill him?"

"No."

"Exactly."

"But what else can he do to stop me besides murder? I know that I can stop him by winning and severing his bond with Neverland. I don't have to kill him to stop him. But what can he do to let me know he's won, without killing me?"

Kace leaned in close. "Pan knows things. He'll know if he's won, and he doesn't need to kill you. Not every war ends in bloodshed."

"But every victory does," I whispered.

Pan told me I would have to sacrifice something to take his place. What had Pan sacrificed to rule Neverland? He had everything, right? It made no sense.

I would never sacrifice Kace, or Lili, or anyone I loved. Not for a position of power. It wasn't worth it. Did I have to sacrifice my magic? No, because Pan had magic. Neverland gave magic to the keyholder of the island. If I gave it up, I'd only get it back.

I feared what I'd have to give up just to run this place the way it was meant to run. Everything in my life was perfect, but it came as no surprise that I'd have to lose something to gain this power. I couldn't have it all, could I?

The sun had now set, and the stars twinkled in the sky. As much as I wanted to return to the cabin and sleep, I couldn't. I hadn't seen the stars in a while, either, and they certainly were stunning on a night like this. No matter what happened, I'd always find a way to be happy and save the ones I loved.

Everyone knew this. I became a fighter.

When I'd first arrived, I was the type of girl who cried. I was the girl who wanted to make Lili happy and *be* happy. Things changed.

I still wanted to save Lili and that would never change, but now I was the girl who wouldn't give up. I'd put others above me. I'd always fight until my last breath, and now I knew I was ready to be a leader.

I'd always been the quiet follower, Lili the leader type. But those who wanted power were the least fit to get it, and those who never strived for power were the best for the job.

Neverland needed a new leader.

And it just so happened to be me.

45: The Last Winter

I took small bites of my salad while Kace watched me with intensity. He finally asked, "What's on your mind?"

Shrugging, I took another bite. So disgusting. I never expected anything to turn out this way and yet life always took me by surprise. "Did Pan know it'd end up like this?"

"I don't think anybody, including Pan, thought it could. Even the Demon King can't predict the future. Demons aren't psychic." He chuckled.

"That is true, I suppose. How do you know demons can't predict the future?" I glanced at him, my head tilted.

He sat up straight. "Religion was a big deal where I came from. If you recall, I was raised catholic."

I nodded a little. "Right, I remember. You were raised that way for seventeen years? And now?"

"We all were. The whole town was. That's why the doctors refused to do any surgery on me. They didn't see a point in removing parts of me that God put there intentionally. It's not like I needed them removed anyway. My parents were just selfish. They let it get to their head, but my parents didn't care. It wasn't their body going through it." His eyes shifted over to the fire and he watched as the embers separated from the flames, floating away into the cloudless sky.

"I'm sorry. I don't want you to think that it's still like that. I mean, it is in a way. We still have bad people and bad parents. Humanity always finds a way to hurt others but...things are different. Nobody supports that. Not sane people anyway. But most people care about abused kids. Most being the key word."

"And you were never abused like Lili?" Kace asked.

My eyes landed back on the ground. "No. I wasn't as rebellious." I took another bite, swallowing a berry. "Pan has barely punished me while she got punished all the time. She probably views it as me being the favorite twin. It's not true. I'm not the favorite. I want to save Pan because I want to see his good side. I want Lili to see it. I need her to see how she's supposed to be treated."

Kace nodded.

Finishing my salad, someone sat on the other side of me. I looked over at Asa. "Yes?"

"What's the plan?"

"The plan is to have Pan help us."

He shook his head. "No. He won't help us. He's the bad guy."

"He already agreed." But the words didn't come from my lips. They'd come from *his*, laced in that thick accent.

We lifted our eyes to meet Pan's, and Asa didn't know what he was supposed to say. Based on the terror in his eyes, he had stepped right into line with their rules.

Pan bent down to his level. "You should never judge a book by its cover. You would be surprised at what you might find inside." He stood, peering at Kace and I. "Skull Rock. That's where the shadow is. If Asa screws this up, I won't hesitate to end his life then and there. Lili comes first."

"But it's not because the balance it off. It's because of Pan's emotions. Kingdoms are run by a king and a queen, so I'm not all that surprised. However, the man-eating animals are because of the wicked nature of our dear leader here." I didn't quite understand the full logistics behind magic, but I would soon. *Soon.*

Pan nodded, adding, "Another side effect was the downfall of Neverland. It's been dying ever since. I kept it a secret because I didn't want to be anything *but* evil. When Lili became dark, and two shadows inhabited Skull Rock, the balance shifted even more. The downfall sped up. Skull Rock is technically supposed to be empty. Visitors are normal but nobody should live there. It makes our world unstable.

"I am also the ruler of this island, so I possess magic. Only I can possess magic, and when my shadow separated, he held some magic as well. Lili was never supposed to have magic. Nobody was but *me*. Not only is Skull Rock a home to shadows when it shouldn't be, but too many people on this island own magic when they shouldn't."

"So as long as we merge you with your shadows, everything returns to normal?" Asa asked.

"Yes. Lili can still rule with me. But Skull Rock is a dangerous place. It has great power which is why I always advise people to stay away. I have never kept you guys from these locations out of selfishness. I was always trying to protect you from the dangerous magic," he explained. "When Wendy attained magic, things shifted, but I managed to control it. Then it got worse from there. When I return to my shadow, I have to take all that magic for myself if Neverland is to survive." His eyes fell on me.

No, I didn't want to lose my magic. I wouldn't. He made it sound like no matter who won, Anna and Lili could keep their magic. Of course he'd lied. That's what he did.

Demons lie.

Ignoring his attempt to threaten me, I said, "That's why you kept us from Mermaid Lagoon and Cannibal Cove."

I never thought any part of Pan could be selfless, but it was true. Mermaid Lagoon was not a safe place to go. When Lili visited Skull Rock, it cost her so much and now she would forever pay the price. She was going find the light and realize all those she'd killed. It all started when she visited Skull Rock the first time. I should've stopped her. I was right *there*.

Kace placed a hand on my shoulder. "You okay?"

I shook my head and wiped the tears that I noticed were falling down my cheeks. "Lili's going to have to face the reality that she's killed innocent people. She's going to realize she killed our brother. She's going to break."

He pulled me into his shoulder. "We will be there to support her when she does. Someone has to hold her up when she falls."

As if volunteering, Pan cleared his throat. "I should go get this plan into gear. I expect you guys to be at Skull Rock by tonight. No later." He vanished using the air.

Kace looked at my cousin. "Meet us at the cliff overlooking Skull Rock. We'll meet there tonight. Lia will fly us over."

Asa nodded. "Flying. I like the sound of this. Got it. Now to go craft myself a weapon." He stood from the log and went to his cabin.

I dropped my head. "What if we don't win?"

"Then we could say we tried. If we don't win, at least we had our time together. If we win, we can say we just had the date as an early celebration." He lifted my chin with his knuckles.

"Shouldn't we make weapons like Asa is?"

"That's assuming I haven't already made some. I've lived here for an exceedingly long time. I have all kinds of weapons prepared. And we have our daggers." Kace gave me a teasing smirk.

My cheeks heated. "Oh."

Getting up, he pulled me with him. "Come on. Let's go enjoy one last date."

"Where are we going?" I asked him as we walked, hand in hand.

He glanced back at me. "It's supposed to be a surprise."

"Oh." I smiled a little. "Let's see how well you know me."

He let out a low chuckle. "I hope it's pretty well."

We arrived at what used to be the waterfall Lili would swim at. The sunset reflected off the rink, an array of warm colors the stunning result.

"What are we doing here?" I tilted my head back.

He sat down on a rock after brushing off the snow. He sat me down on his lap and pointed to the water. "Just admiring the beauty that Neverland still holds even in its darkest days."

"So poetic," I joked.

Kace put his chin on my shoulder and wrapped his arms around my waist. "This is the last we will see of the winter. I want to admire how beautiful it can be despite how cold it is."

I turned over my shoulder to look at him. "Whether we die or succeed tonight, this is the last we will see of winter. I'll be glad to see it gone but at least I can say I knew what it was like. I won't miss it an ounce."

"You'll never have to worry about another winter storm again," Kace whispered.

We both stayed there in silence and watched the sunset until it was the moon's turn to shine. We hopped off the rock and started to head to our meeting spot now that night had fallen. Even with such suspense hanging in the fog, the stars twinkled brightly. I wondered if this was a sign that good was to come after this, or if it was just nature's way of letting us enjoy one last time before we lost everything.

Kace and I walked towards the cliff, and we saw a silhouette of a man waiting for us. Asa turned to greet us. "Glad you two could make it. We need that magic that Lia supposedly has."

I grabbed his hand, along with Kace's. "Ready to fly?"

"I was born ready."

I giggled. "Such a cheesy line."

As happy memories filled my head, we began to lift off the ground. I started towards Skull Rock. Kace was struggling, shaking, but I squeezed his hand to remind him I was there. "What's wrong?"

He laughed nervously, eyeing the sea below us. "Heights terrify me, and falling into the deep depths of the water and never returning *really* freaks me out."

I softened my expression. "It's okay. I won't let anything happen. It's *my* turn to rule."

Landing, Kace stood on one side of me with Asa on the other. We stopped when we found Lili standing by the ball of the light—the source of all magic. "I hear you guys are planning to merge me with my shadow, and Pan with his? I say we should rip your shadows away, too. Wouldn't it be wonderful if we were all this vicious?"

The shadows stood behind Lili.

Pan walked around the room and looked over at her. "You heard right, Love. We can form this island to be exactly what we want. We can bring them to the dark side."

She smirked, eyes darting from Pan to us. "I like the sound of that." She stepped forward. "We'll see how truly wicked I am when I win."

Lifting a palm, Pan studied us. "Nobody defeats me, Little Flower. You know that too well."

Just when the plan was going right, Anna climbed into the cave and stood. "I see everyone made it here without me. Thanks for leaving me behind. Plan is to merge Lili with her shadow, right?" She searched our faces for confirmation.

My sister narrowed her eyes. "Why is she talking about just me?" Her gaze raked over Pan.

He lifted his chin, shoulders back. "This isn't about ripping away all of their shadows. This is about merging you with yours."

She charged at him, and he waved his magic, causing her to freeze mid-sprint.

He walked over, circling. "I still have the upper hand and I always will."

The shadows attacked Pan. Kace grabbed Lili's shadow and pulled her off, but Pan's shadow blasted magic at me, sending me backward.

Kace struggled to grab hold of Lili's shadow to drag her to Lili, but she'd been much stronger.

Pan's shadow waved its black, misty hand at Lili. She came to life and stopped herself from running before she crashed into the wall. She turned and spotted me.

Unfortunately for her, I had magic now. She did, too, but I had more practice with mine. And a secret weapon.

She pulled out her dagger, aiming to stab me in my abdomen. I moved out of her way before she got to me, letting her hit side of the cave. I pulled out my dagger, shaking my head. "I don't want to do this."

She growled. "I have been dying to get revenge on you since you took my place as the best lost girl."

"Are we still going on about that? You're Queen now!" Spitting a lie to protect her, I twirled my dagger between my fingers, "You'll still be one when we save you."

She shoved me into the wall, her blade at my throat. "And yet Pan still treats you better than me."

I jammed my blade into her stomach, hoping I didn't hit a major organ. I just wanted to slow her down.

With wide eyes, she stumbled back, covering her wound. "You stabbed me."

"I defended myself."

Her shadow rushed over to help her sit before coming at me, grabbing my arm. "You bitch." She pulled me from the cave, pushing me out of the mouth.

Kace yelled out for me as I fell back into the shallow water, going under for a moment. Then I surfaced I gripped the rock and gasped for air.

I climbed back up to the entrance. Pan and his shadow fought, careful not to touch each other. Pan didn't mind if they had merged, but it was his *shadow* that was avoiding all contact.

His shadow flew around him to the other side, shooting magic at Pan. Pan fell onto his hands and grumbled. He got up and looked at it, waving his hand and causing him to freeze as Lili had.

His silhouette used its own magic to unfreeze. "Nice try, but I'm at your level."

Pan reeled his arm back a bit and shot his hand forward, aiming up at the rock above his shadow. His magic separated the jagged rock from the ceiling, sending it onto its head. "I'm still Peter Pan. You're just my shadow." Pan walked over to the silhouette before it could get away. He stepped on his feet, and with that Pan collapsed, and everything stilled.

When the smoke had cleared enough, Pan stood from the ground and looked at Lili's shadow. "It looks like you lose."

Her shadow shook its head and backed up into Kace who wrapped his fingers around her biceps, keeping her planted. Pan walked over and helped his best friend drag the silhouette to its rightful owner.

Lili spat blood, glaring up at Pan. "You are going to pay for this. You will lose one day."

"Don't make empty threats, Little Flower. I had already lost the day I ripped your light away from you." He bent down and grabbed its feet, putting them against Lili's.

I took this chance to crawl into the cave, scooting by the wall. Kace and Pan stepped back as the human and shadow became one, sending Lili into a blank state.

We watched in anticipation to ensure the two didn't separate again.

Pan looked over at Kace. "Do you think this wound will be a simple fix or will I need to use my magic?"

My boyfriend bent down and took a quick look at the injury on her stomach while she'd been stunned. "From the looks of it, it went into her stomach. I'm not going to be able to stitch that up so she can eat."

Nodding a bit, Pan laid a hand on her stomach to seal the wound. "Magic it is, then."

He then carried her back to the island while the three of us used me, and Anna used her green magic to lure some vines over. Pan took Lili to his cabin for a while, keeping her away from the public as she got high for the first time. She'd get some blue magic now, but I had to be the one who hurt her in the end. That was *my* sacrifice.

I scanned the island, the temperature gradually rising above zero and towards summer.

The snow began to melt beneath our feet, taking its sweet time to say one last goodbye before it left for eternity. The balance was being restored in Pan's emotions. Too bad I'd have to rip them from him. When I did, at least his emotions wouldn't be tethered to bring about another storm.

But mine might.

Asa watched in awe.

Anna approached with her arms crossed. "I suppose you didn't need Asa and I. You two got it all on your own."

"Three. Pan was on our side, remember?" I asked.

"Three. Right."

Kace reached for my hand. "We've won the hardest battle."

"But not the war."

He planted a kiss on my forehead and took me to my cabin. "I'll see you in the morning." He left for his own, and I sat on the bed, staring at the dresser.

Now that the snow was melting and summer was coming back, I would need to change my wardrobe back to breathable clothing.

Laying back, I drifted off into a peaceful sleep, warm and happy for once in a long time. Everything was going to be different now. I just needed to make sure it stayed that way—with me in charge.

46: Neverland

I awoke to birds chirping and the sun shining through my window. I sat up with a grin. Today was a new day, and the day I would take over.

After getting up, I rummaged through the clothes in my dresser, putting on a white tank top and black shorts. I put my boots and socks on and then tightened my belt around my hips.

I walked outside and breathed in the fresh air. The temperature was blazing, but it meant it was a good day to go to the beach, after I stole Pan's place from under him.

Kace came out of his cabin, wearing something different from his usual attire. Baggy shorts and a tank top. I realized I'd never seen him without his cloak, and it was something exciting to admire.

"How's Kace?" I tilted my head and smirked a bit. "You look different."

"So do you." He paused. "Pan says I need to deliver you to Hangman's Tree for the final battle. Don't lose, okay?" I'd never heard such concern and praise coming from him. He wanted me to be in charge.

He wanted Pan to step down.

We approached Hangman's Tree where Pan waited for me. He shooed Kace, who hesitated at first, but I assured him that this was something I had to do alone.

After Kace exited the area, Pan stepped forward. "You're well aware of the consequences, correct?"

Snow still covered some of the ground, melting away as the sun rays beamed down.

"I think I have a good idea." I pulled my dagger out, feeling the cool metal in my palm. "Let's cut the chit-chat." I ran towards Pan and attempted to cut him with my dagger, but he vanished. After losing my dagger to the tree, I yanked it out.

He appeared behind me, and I whipped around to face him, but he trapped me against the tree, his dagger against my neck. He forgot about my own magic.

I closed my eyes and the nicking disappeared. I showed up behind him and lifted my foot, kicking before he had time to react. He stumbled against the tree but straightened himself again.

He lunged towards me, but before he could catch me, I teleported inside the tree. I grabbed a book before he realized where I was, opening it up. "How do I steal his position?" I skimmed the pages, and the answer practically glowed for me.

I had to take his dagger and make a wish for Neverland to become mine.

When the door opened, I quickly hid behind a bookshelf. Pan came into view, but he wasn't facing my direction. *Perfect.* I tackled him.

With me on top, I had leverage and access to his dagger. He attempted to throw me off, but I pressed my blade into the soft part, pointed up under his chin. "Don't move."

In a blind rage, my red magic surfaced and Pan howled at the burns radiating from my body. "Lia, bloody hell!"

"Forgot to mention I have red magic." I shot a smirk.

I reached for his dagger, but before I got hold of it, he vanished once again. My breath hitched as I fell onto my weapon. I rolled onto my back and touched the handle sticking out of my chest. I didn't dare remove it, or I would bleed out. But it wasn't that serious.

"Lia?" Pan asked as he stood over me.

Carefully, I got off the ground, the blood staining my shirt. "I need to see Kace."

"I can heal it." He reached out towards my dagger.

"So can I!" I hissed, skidding away from his touch.

We left Hangman's Tree and walked towards camp. I stumbled a few times, afraid to look at the dagger again. I'd been hurt many times, and even cut, but this was terrifying to witness. I was afraid to remove the blade myself. I'd faint before I could even heal it. Far too much blood.

I glanced back at Pan as I rounded a corner, pressing my back against a tree. As soon as he passed, I yanked his dagger from him and backed away. His eyes widened, and I took some deep breaths, avoiding eye contact with my wound.

I had it in hand. I just needed to make the wish.

"Lia, don't. That's cheating."

"It's not cheating. I'm just smarter than you take me for." I leaned against a tree, feeling sick to my stomach. I tightened my grip on the handle, closing my eyes. "I wish to take Peter Pan's place as the keyholder of Neverland."

Before I had a chance to see my own victory, lightheadedness hit me, and I collapsed.

KACE HELPED ME UP as he handed my dagger to Pan. "This is yours now."

Pan grumbled before looking at me. "You have one last thing to do if you want to run Neverland the proper way. You know what you have to do."

I knew I had to steal all the magic for myself. Pan expected this, and he had accepted his fate. However, I couldn't say the same for Lili and Anna. I was certain I'd have some damaged bridges to fix when this was over. "How do I do it?"

What he explained to me was heartbreaking. I didn't want to, but he had warned me I'd sacrifice something if I became the ruler.

I called Lili, Pan, and Anna to Skull Rock. It wasn't hard to get them there when they all had their own magic. For now. Getting them back to Neverland would be the tricky part.

"There's some...news. Good and bad news. Which news do you want first?" I asked.

Lili answered quickly, "Bad news."

I hadn't expected that answer, but I couldn't take her suggestion. "All right, good news first." Lili was eyeing me like I stole the last cookie. "Good news is... Pan is no longer your leader."

Lili and Anna whipped around to face, but he didn't say a word.

So I did. "I am."

Everyone froze. Now for the bad news.

"With that comes a responsibility, one that Pan didn't take seriously when he was a monster." I exhaled, mentally preparing myself. "To keep the balance of Neverland intact, I must take all your magic."

Reactions kicked in almost immediately. Lili and Anna refused, but before they had a chance to run away, I placed my hand against the ball of light.

A transparent string shot out of each of them, every single one a color of the magic it represented. The string attached to me before detaching from each of them.

Anna fell to her knees, tears running down her face. "That was all I had left from Wendy."

Pan didn't look as upset as her, but Lili showed some sadness. I'd stolen something from each of them, and that made me the bad guy. Thankfully I had a lifetime on this island to make up for my mistake.

After we all returned to the island, everyone left except for Pan. I'd once been the hero, and now I was the villain in their eyes. He reminded me that they'd come around.

Kace came running and hugged me, making sure he didn't hurt my wound. I could heal that now. He pulled away, cupping my face and peering into my eyes. Once I told him what I'd done, it all became much more real.

He brushed his thumbs over my cheeks to wipe the tears, letting me know it would all be okay. I hoped he was right, because Anna wasn't speaking to me anymore. I feared she never would. Kace led us both to the beach to take my mind off what I'd done.

When we arrived, Pan and Lili were splashing each other in the water. Lili was wearing her shorts and T-shirt, a big smile plastered on her face. "It feels good to be a kid, doesn't it? It's so freeing," she yelled in his direction.

Pan had rolled up his tights and left his boots on the beach. His shirt laid beside his shoes, exposing his chest in front of me for the first time. It wasn't anything special to me. Maybe Lili. It was just strange to see *this* lost boy be so carefree.

I looked at Kace who had already taken off his boots and socks, removing his shirt next. He dropped it in the sand and ran towards the water.

I wiped the single tear falling down my cheek. It was hard to contain the joy I felt, seeing everyone I loved so happy now.

"Come in!" Kace shouted at me.

I unlaced my boots, then removed my socks and shoved them into my shoes, sprinting down the shore. I hit the water and fell, laughing as I pushed my wet hair back.

Kace helped me to get onto my feet and Asa came in to join. The five of us splashed each other like we were kids again because we were. We would be kids for the rest of our immortal lives, and that didn't scare me as much as it used to.

We walked out, soaked, as the sun began to set. Sitting in the sand, we watched the sky dance in tropical hues, waving goodnight. I put my head on Kace's shoulder while he wrapped an arm around my waist.

"Pan and I have decided to be single for a while. It would be best if we both found ourselves before we tried to date as new people. We need a break," Lili stated.

"I did not decide anything, Little Flower," Pan tossed at her. "My love for you has been very real, and that was never the darkness talking."

"You still love me? After everything I did? I killed Hook."

"Yes, but she'd cheated on Kace and I. That's hardly your fault." Little did they know...

"Why do you still want me, Peter?" her voice came out in a whisper.

He leaned closer, his nose brushing hers. "Because, Love, you always brought out the best in me. Even if I didn't want you to."

"But you want to rely on me you keep you sane."

"Or maybe," he started, "I want to cherish the sunshine from my darkest days. Don't you love me in return?"

Her lips formed a frown. "I worried I didn't. When you stole my shadow, all I wanted was to break you into pieces. I craved such a thing. To watch you bleed and beg for mercy. But that had been my father talking. Never me. What I want from you, Peter, is the promise that you'll always be there. That you'll be my rock when I can't fight as hard. Can you guarantee you'll help me when I need a shoulder to lean on?"

A grin appeared. "I can promise that and so much more."

I had seen the raw emotion swirling in her eyes. Begging. Wanting. Pouring from every crevice.

Lili had always been remorseful. Never sociopathic, nor psychopathic. Her guilt had been stored in a box. Her brain compartmentalized her shame to protect her from the trauma, and now that I'd seen it, all was right with the world.

She faced me. "I also understand your decision. Pan explained it to me, and as much as I loved my magic, I hadn't had it for long. I'll get over this quickly. I can't say the same for Tinker, but hopefully she comes around."

I nodded a little. "I didn't want to make that decision but if I didn't win and do it, Pan would have. It was better me than him, because then you know my intentions behind it were pure. I'm only trying to be a good leader, to ensure the future of Neverland."

A smile graced her features. "I always meant to tell you that you guys are really cute together. I never imagined you as a couple but I'm glad you are. I'm also glad you're the leader and not me. That's too much power and I don't really want that."

Pan chuckled from the other side of Lili and shook his head. "You kept that to yourself all this time?"

"Of course. A Demon Queen cannot admit she hates having power. Using the word cute is wrong, too. It's against the handbook."

"There's no handbook," he replied.

My sister lifted an eyebrow, a sly smile replacing the old. "You say that because you told them they were cute together when you were still dark, huh?"

Kace pipped in, "Lia named us."

I wrinkled my nose in confusion. "What do you mean? When?"

"You gave us boat names when you got high off magic the second time. We are named Kala and they're named Pali."

Lili looked at Pan and nodded a bit, amused. "I like it. Kala. I think it suits them. Pali is interesting."

Asa snorted. "That's only because it's your name. From an outsider's perspective, they're not that grand."

Kace shoved him into the sand without looking in his direction.

My cousin grumbled and rubbed his arm, sitting back up. "Fine then, I won't express myself."

My boyfriend nudged him. "We like it when you're quiet."

Asa glared at him, but Kace ignored his weak threat. The rest of us laughed as the stars peeked out from behind the sun rays, night falling over us.

"I have red magic," I blurted.

Every eye turned to me, and to show them, I lit a small flame on the tip of my finger.

"I found it weeks ago, maybe. In a small cave behind the waterfall. A red flower. That's why I stripped naked in the woods, where you found me." My eyes moved between Kace and Pan. "I'd gotten red magic, but I had no idea. It's impossible to attain because it grows only in a flower in a frigid place. Heat that blooms in the dead of winter. So now all I really have left to attain is practice. Green, yellow, blue, red, and gold magic. I'm far more powerful than Pan ever was."

He gave me the same fake smile a teenage mean girl would.

"Love that for me," I said with the widest grin. "And if it helps at all, I'll find a way to return the magic to its owners. There must be a way. Pan once mentioned that when I took over, the wish of Neverland became mine to change. I'll make tweaks. Eventually, Anna will get her magic. She may have lost her love, but not *all* of her. I'm not a monster. Never vicious."

Silence ensued. Crickets chirped.

And lost girls would be welcomed with open arms as much as boys. Meaning if Anna ever had a second chance, somewhere roaming out in the world, I'd let the opportunity become hers. I believed in happy endings. Far more than the ex-leader of this island.

I laid my hand over Kace's, intertwining our fingers. "I wanted to quit so many times, but we made it here. It was worth everything. I'll make it up to everyone for the way things have been—that I can promise. We lost so many good people," I said, directing that at Kace about his ex. "But at least we know we never have to say goodbye to each other. Nor do we have to forget those we love."

And we certainly never would.

Also by

Monica Shantel

THE FEATHERS AND FLAMES TRILOGY

Beauty of a Crimson Soul

Beauty of a Burning Flame

Beauty of a Permanent Love

Acknowledgements

Thanks to my mom for always supporting my writing, even as a valid career. Thanks to my brother who's asked questions and made me think about my plots, and to the other family members who have picked up my books just to say they were proud of me.

To Ashly for always supporting me.

And thank you to my beta readers for pointing out the rights and wrongs of this book to help me make it the best it would be. This book needed all your help.

About the Author

Monica Shantel has always had an interest in artistic and creative hobbies of sorts, including but not limited to: drawing, crafting, graphic design, and painting. Although all she has is a high school diploma under her belt, she is not new to the writing community. At the age of twelve, she began building stories to escape reality and find hope in life once again. Her debut novel is Beauty of a Crimson Soul. Along the same genre, she writes dark tales of mythical romance which only add more to the growing fantasy worlds inside her head.

www.ingramcontent.com/pod-product-compliance
Lightning Source LLC
Chambersburg PA
CBHW020339310726
48979CB00015B/2428/J

* 9 7 8 1 9 6 0 6 9 6 0 7 6 *